CW00794579

By the same author

Cornish Fiction

The Magical Isles Trilogy (Compendium Edition)
Where Seagulls Fly
White Sands (The Magical Isles Trilogy Book One)
The Butterfly Riders (The Magical Isles Trilogy Book Two)
Holy Vale (The Magical Isles Trilogy Book Three)

Other Fiction

The Black Rose
The Darkness Inside
Distance
The Dream Factory (under Ed Page)
Fey
For Love or Money
Greetings from the Edge of Nowhere
Heart's Desire
Into the Depths
The Liquid Room
Love & Other Oddities
Lukewarm Bathwater or Apocalypse? (under Ed Page)
Minos
My Life as an Alien
Orc: It's Not Easy Being Green (under Ed Page)
Quiddity
The Red Brick Road
The Sausage of Doom (under Ed Page)
Spontaneous Combustion
Sub-Zero
Synergy

Non-Fiction

Enlightenment: One Man's Search for the Truth of Existence
Everyday Magic
Handbook for the Living Dead (under the name R.I.Peace)
Intuition: A User's Guide
There is Only Now

Song of the Sea

By Edwin Page

First published to Kindle & paperback
by Curved Brick, 2015

Copyright © Edwin Page 2014

All rights reserved

Dedicated to my mother, Ellen

Without whose support this book & all those before it would not exist

With special thanks to Rhona & Sue

Author's Note

The small village of Zennor, around which this story is predominantly set, rests slightly back from the rugged north coast of Cornwall on the last stretch of south-west England. This small nub of land reaching into the Atlantic is dotted with burial chambers, stone circles, standing stones and sacred wells. It is a place of sea mist and magic, folklore and legend. One such legend is that of the Mermaid of Zennor, which was the inspiration for this story. If you visit St Senara's Church in Zennor you will discover a carving of the mermaid at the end of one of the pews. Though that story and the one within this book are completely different, they both contain the beauty and mystery of that region, one that remains an inspiration not only to writers, but also to many others who visit the far west of Cornwall and become enthralled by its enchantment.

There was dancing, singing and the clapping of hands. The meadow beside the church was busy with noise and activity. Bright pennants fluttered from poles erected in each corner and Zennor Hill rose beyond the rear wall to the east.

The entire village had gathered for the feast of Guldize, which marked the end of harvest. More than forty were present, even those from outlying farms having made the journey. Those not dancing were seated upon stools around crude benches set along the near side and only used for such celebrations, which were held in Old Jacob Trewey's barn in inclement weather. Each was adorned with a straw doll around which were scattered boards of bread and cheese, bowls of soft fruits, cuts of meat and jugs of mead.

The sun was shining and Jory Meryn was playing a jig on his rote, seated on the stump of a tree at the upper end of the gently sloping meadow, his bow moving hastily across the strings. A knot of dancers were before him, linking arms and circling, breaking into lines and then weaving between each other with skips and bounds, the women wearing crowns woven of golden corn upon the veils that covered their hair.

Some of the more inebriated men at the tables were singing the song of Gallon the Gannet, clapping out their own rhythm without heed of the tune being played in the upper portion of the field. The ditty came to a raucous end and they downed what remained of the mead in their wooden cups, banging them down while wiping their glistening lips, the heat of the alcohol warming the backs of their throats. They burst into laughter, cheeks reddened by consumption and the sleeves of their woollen shirts rolled up in the warmth of the sun.

Jory's playing came to an end. The dancers dispersed, making their way back to the tables and taking their seats, the women wearing tunics over their simple dresses of greens and greys.

'Lend us your voice and sing us a song, Breaca,' called one of the drunkards.

'Aye, sing us a song, Breaca,' concurred another.

There was a chorus of agreement from the folk of Zennor.

A young woman in her teenage years rose from her stool at the last table, which was tucked into the corner of the small field. She held her son to her breast, one of the babe's hands reaching from the swaddling as he yawned. Breaca rocked him as she began to sing.

'Oh western lands of heaving seas, of hills and sacred stones, you are the land that I call home, that I call home.'

The babe gurgled and she glanced down briefly before continuing.

'Oh western lands of weaving mists, of trees and blessed vales, you are the land where I belong, where I belong.'

She paused and Mathey Trewella, who was acknowledged as the best male voice in the village, prepared to harmonise with her.

'Oh western lands where I belong,' they sung together, 'I shall always come home to thee. Oh western lands where I belong, bounded by the mighty sea.'

Mathey smiled and Breaca continued with the next verse.

'Oh western lands of horizons far, of tides and sinking suns, you are the land...' Her melodious words faded as she stared at the figure approaching along the track that wove through the village, her expression tightening.

Everyone turned to follow her gaze. There were a few audible gasps from some of the women present and the looks on most of the men's faces became distinctly unfriendly, though Marrek Trelawny found that he could not focus on whoever was walking up the lane due to the amount of mead that had been drained from his cup.

Father Blyth rose from his stool, his position central to the festivities. He nodded at Golvan Trewey, younger brother of Jacob. The black haired farmer got to his feet, large nose reddened by his slight drunkenness. The two men then hurried to the gate in the north-west corner of the dry stone wall that bordered the meadow in order to stop the interloper's unwanted entry.

Golvan quickly closed it and secured the fastening rope. He crossed his arms over his large chest and adopted a steadfast pose, jaw flexing in anticipation of the confrontation to come.

Father Blyth stood by his side in his black vestments, a rakish man with the merest hint of grey amidst the brown hair at the sides of his shaven scalp, thin nose glistening with grease. 'Ye are not welcome here, Thomas Carrow,' he called as the man drew near.

'Leave him be,' said Gerens loudly from the table nearest the gateway, the blacksmith receiving a few unkind glances from those about him.

'Aye, let him join us,' concurred Marrek's long-suffering wife, Nonna, her mane of sandy hair bearing a crown of corn, but without a covering veil.

Father Blyth briefly glanced at the tables to his left with an expression of disapproval, both he and Golvan mindful of those who had voiced their support for Carrow. The priest was especially aware of the blacksmith's intervention. Gerens was the only member of the community not to attend Mass. Thanks to his highly respected position as smith, he could not easily be challenged, but Blyth waited for the day when an opportunity presented itself by which to rid himself of the heathen cur.

'You have no part in this feast,' stated the priest, focussing his attention on the man in his early thirties who was drawing up before the gate, his dark brown hair unkempt and face darkened by stubble.

'This village is my home,' replied Thomas, 'as it was my father's and his father's before him.'

Golvan shook his head. 'You are not of Zennor.'

'I was born in the house upon the hill,' he said, glancing over his shoulder at Trewey Hill rising to the south-west before looking to his small hound as she padded over after scenting the nearby wall. 'I grew up here and played in these

3

fields and upon the moor. I am as much one of the folk as anyone else who attends.'

Thomas reached for the gate. Golvan took hold of the crossbar to hold it in place, a look of determination upon his bearded face.

'You shall not pass,' stated the farmer coldly.

'There is naught of the boy who once roamed these lands left in you,' said Father Blyth. 'You are...' He sought the right word. '...*Unnatural* and unwelcome among us. Your time up-country has changed you beyond the likeness of the lad who left these lands.'

'It is not I who has changed, but the folk. Coldness there is where once there was warmth.' His arms fell to his sides and he glanced at the graveyard visible over the nearby wall to his left.

'My mother is buried in that yard,' he said sadly, 'and beside her rests the memorial stone bearing the names of my father and grandfather.'

'Your past is buried with her,' stated Golvan with a hard tone. 'You are no more a son of Zennor.'

'He is more a son of Zennor than you, Golvan,' called Nonna. 'Your father was of Pendeen.'

Golvan glanced over with narrowed eyes.

'Hush woman!' scolded Marrek, concerned that they would suffer the consequences of his wife's loose tongue.

Nonna glared at him, but spoke no more in defence of Thomas.

'Be gone, for we will not tolerate thy presence here.' Father Blyth held Thomas' gaze, grey eyes laced with ice.

Thomas paused before the gate and then turned away, his head bowed and shoulders sagging.

'You are not welcome among us,' called Jago the rat catcher from one of the tables, the scrawny man finding his courage now that the intrusion was coming to an end.

'If you know what is good for you, you will stay out of Zennor,' stated Golvan, grinding the axe he bore. Carrow had witnessed his poaching activities on a number of occasions and the farmer worried that he would inform the authorities,

4

the thought of losing his hand as punishment filling him with dread.

Thomas walked away with his hound at his side, feeling the cold stares upon his back, which was bent under the weight of his misery. He had hoped to find acceptance after having returned five years previous, but the suspicions and rejection remained.

Boots sinking into the mud, he passed off the main track and headed west towards the slopes of Trewey Hill. He trudged between the stone walls of the fields, their coldness as naught compared to that of the folk at his back, and made his way to the haunted vacancy of his home.

Thomas walked along the cliffs in the early morning light. Sea mist had drawn in during the hours of darkness and masked the waking world.

He looked down into the well of paleness to his right, the shoreline hidden from view. The soft repetition of waves washing against rocks was diffused by the moisture in the air which caressed his face with refreshing coolness.

He savoured the isolation that the mist afforded him. It had been weeks since his harsh treatment at the Guldize celebrations, but its sting still throbbed in the back of his mind.

A tangled patch of undergrowth scraped against the long leather coat which had been made for him by his uncle and aunt in Truro, the hide stained dark brown. He wore a jerkin beneath and a woollen shirt dyed a deep nettle green. Hide leggings protected his legs from gorse thorns and his large boots made barely a sound as he followed the coastal path. The heavy scent of the ocean, of seaweed and salt water, invigorated him as the dawn light steadily grew brighter.

Thomas' heart leapt as Shenty materialised through the mist and came bounding along the path. He shook his head as his pulse settled, the faintest touch of a smile arising in response to the small hound's enthusiasm and confidence so close to the cliff's edge.

Bending as she drew near, he lifted her into his arms, short brown fur glistening and damp to the touch. He cradled and fussed her, Shenty affectionately licking his chin.

'Aye, and the same to you,' he said to his companion, whose company alleviated a little of the loneliness that clouded about him much like the mist, but that the sun could not burn away nor the wind usher onward.

Setting her down, he continued on his daily trek to Treen Cove in order to cast his net. Only once in the past year had they not taken the path along the cliffs. That had been a stormy day in February, the wind grasping and fierce, sea boiling with froth and causing the cliffs to tremble as waves beat against them, the crash and clatter of displaced rocks audible even within the shelter of his cottage.

Thomas took a deep breath, the fall of his steps emphasising his isolation as the hound once more vanished from sight. The sharp sound of barking soon cut through the hush. He cocked his head to one side and listened, trying to discern her whereabouts and noting the calls were of excitement rather than threat.

'Probably a rabbit or the like,' he mumbled to himself, walking onward.

A gull called out in the shroud above and Thomas glanced upwards. His left foot slipped on a rock jutting into the path and he inhaled sharply as pain erupted in his twisted ankle.

With teeth gritted, he sat on the short grass and thrift beside the path. He glanced at the rock and shook his head. It was familiar to him, as were all the characteristics of the path he and Shenty so often trod. He should have known, should have seen it and stepped over as he usually did.

Shenty came trotting along the path, looking at him curiously, aware that something was wrong. The expression on her master's face was tight and pale, and he ne'er rested until they reached the beach.

She nuzzled his hands. Thomas scratched her behind the ears as he winced in pain.

'All will be well,' he said with a strained tone as she licked his fingers.

Testing his weight, Thomas stood and glanced around, the view restricted in every direction as Shenty waited on the path and looked up at him expectantly. He wished for something to serve as a walking stick, but finding such on the sparse cliff-top was unlikely.

Thomas wiped a thin layer of perspiration from his forehead with the back of his hand while staring regretfully into the mist ahead. Turning to Shenty, he carefully crouched before her.

'We shall not be visiting the cove today, my friend,' he stated, rubbing the length of her back as she wagged her tail.

He continued to give her attention for a few moments, feeling a touch of guilt in regards his inability to take her down to the beach in Treen Cove as usual. The thin path that clung to the cliff was precarious even in full health. With his ankle weakened and painful, the descent would be dangerous, even with the aid of the thick rope that was attached to the rock-face as a handhold.

Shenty licked at his hands and he smiled at her.

'Do not worry, we will visit the beach again soon,' he said. 'Today there is a new adventure ahead of us. We shall visit with Bersaba.' He rubbed her beneath the chin and then stood, expression tight and forehead creased by the pain in his ankle.

Thomas began in the direction they had come as his thoughts turned to the traps he needed to check. He hoped the wizened healer would be able to bring him some relief. The longer he left the snares unattended the greater the chance that carrion crows would take any creatures that had been caught during the night. The sacked vegetables in his cottage were plentiful, but meat was the sustenance that gave both Shenty and himself the strength to continue through the late autumn and winter.

With jaw clenched, he limped back with Shenty trotting a few yards ahead. He would pass inland to the southern foot of Trewey Hill, there to visit with Bersaba at her hut. The old crone was one of only two locals who would deign to venture close or speak with him.

Shenty suddenly bounded off through the tight heather on the right, ears up in alertness.

'Another rabbit,' Thomas mumbled to himself as he limped on and felt his isolation weighing heavily upon him.

The hillside track curved to the west and began its misted descent down the southern slope of Trewey Hill. Thomas hobbled along it with Shenty a short distance ahead, feeling the looming presence of the rocky moor rising to his right. On the other side of the path the land fell away to rolling hills covered in a patchwork of fields that were hidden in the pale robe adorning the landscape.

Bersaba's hut came into view a few minutes later, the mist thinning and drawing back to reveal the dwelling fifty yards away as the path levelled out and moved into a small fold of land. It rested amidst a copse of twisted yews that partially concealed it from sight, ragged tendrils of paleness winding about their trunks. The thatch of its low roof was marked with patches of rot and moss, the stones of its circular wall darkened by moisture.

The track passed between tall grasses that had been flattened by recent rains. Shenty slowed her pace until Thomas was nearly clipping her back legs with his boots, the short-haired hound glancing over her shoulder, apprehension evident in her brown eyes.

'Do not fret, Shenty, I am sure the rumours are not true,' he said in a soothing voice, recalling the stories of local animals going missing that his father had told him as a boy, the villagers convinced that Bersaba was snatching them for use in her rituals.

As Thomas neared the modest dwelling he noted smoke curling from the hole in the centre of the thatch. The thought of the fire within and his close proximity to the crone's abode brought forth the recollection of a young witch who he had witnessed being burnt at the stake in Truro.

He shivered and pushed the images from his mind as he tried to settle himself in readiness. Shenty pulled to the side and looked up at him worriedly.

Thomas drew up beside her and crouched, wincing as he did so. 'You can wait here, if that is your wish. I shall not be long,' he reassured while rubbing her head.

Straightening, he limped the final twenty yards to the hut, passing between two of the watching yews, their leaves whispering despite the stillness, as if harbouring a life of their own. He glanced back at Shenty, who remained seated upon the grass, alert and staring after him.

His pulse elevated and hands trembling, he came to a stop before the door. Thomas took a steadying breath and raised his hand to knock.

The door opened before his knuckles touched the wood and gave him a start. Bersaba looked up at him as she stood on the threshold, milky eyes perpetually narrowed as her sight waned. Her face was weathered and deeply lined, neck sagging beneath, white hair long and thin, like spider's silk framing her long features.

'Young Thomas Carrow, is it not?' she croaked, her figure thin and hunched within layers of rough furs.

He nodded. 'I have come in the hope you can…'

'It is thy left ankle,' interrupted Bersaba, turning and shuffling into the shadows of her home, her feet bare and heavily veined. She came to a stop with her back to him as she stared down at the fire pit in the centre of the room, the flames leaping and dancing as they devoured the kindling she had piled upon them.

He looked at her in surprise. 'How did you…?'

'Do not fret, Young Thomas. I simply note the way in which thee stand at my door. Thou art lopsided, avoiding putting weight on thy injured leg. I also know thee to walk the cliffs every morning. I simply put these things together in order to divine what ails thee.' She looked at him over her shoulder.

'Now come and sit by the fire. I will see to thy injury.' She waved him in and then turned her attention back to the fire.

10

After a brief hesitation, Thomas bowed his head in order to enter the abode. Shutting the door with a last glance at Shenty, he turned to the old woman.

'Sit,' she instructed, pointing a withered and bony finger at the ground to the left of the fire as her back remained to him.

He stepped over, keeping his head low despite there being room enough to stand, the roof close and oppressive. The golden glow of the hut's interior was in contrast to the misted paleness outside, the firelight captured in a thin haze of smoke filling the air.

Thomas seated himself slowly, tucking his leather coat beneath. A jolt of pain shot up his leg, causing him to inhale sharply.

Bersaba looked down at him and then padded over to a rickety table on the far side of the room from his position. The only other item of furniture was a small cot at the rear of the hut with furs resting untidily upon it. The musty smell of thatch mingled with that of smoke and the earthen floor. The scent of various roots and dried herbs hanging from the eaves was also woven into the still air, Thomas noticing one particular root that had the semblance of a bulbous and pale man with spidery fingers.

'That be mandrake,' commented Bersaba, apparently knowing the direction of his gaze without needing to turn to him.

He stared over at the crone as she looked through a selection of wooden bowls gathered upon the table, most covered with cloth that was secured in place with twine. The old woman began to lift them one at a time, sniffing their coverings, long nose close to the linen as her nostrils flared and eyes closed with each assessment of what was contained within.

'Ah, here it be,' she said after a couple of minutes, turning back to him with a toothless smile and a bowl cradled in her left hand, a small and flat wooden implement in the right.

She moved across the room and passed around the fire, crouching beside him. 'This will soothe the pain and heal thy ankle,' she stated while pulling the knot in the twine that held

11

the covering in place. Bersaba removed the cloth and placed it on her lap, a thick honey-coloured paste revealed within the bowl.

'Take off thy boot,' instructed the crone as she slowly folded the contents over and over with the length of wood so as to even its consistency.

Thomas did as instructed, sliding off the leather boot to reveal his dirty foot, grime ingrained between his toes and a mouldy scent rising into the air as the fire before him crackled. He lifted the bottom of his leggings to reveal the swollen ankle, Bersaba taking some of the salve on the end of the spatula and preparing to apply it.

'This will be cold,' she warned.

He braced himself, but was still shocked by the chill touch of the paste. It was ice cold and he gritted his teeth as the old woman spread it over the bulging ankle.

She set the spatula in the bowl and turned his foot so she could administer some of the balm to the other side. Thomas once again readied himself for the cool smear of the paste, Bersaba covering the red skin with the concoction.

'What be in this curative?' he asked as she continued to apply the mixture.

'A healer does not pass on their knowledge easily, Young Thomas,' croaked Bersaba. She withdrew the spatula and sat back, re-covering the bowl and placing the length of twine atop it before rising to her feet. 'Thou only needs know that when the morrow dawns ye will find little evidence of the injury.'

'And what of today? I have traps in need of checking,' he enquired, looking up at her, already feeling the painful throbbing beginning to lessen, numbed by the chill of the salve.

'Find a strong bough to aid thy passage and do not place too much weight on thy ankle,' replied Bersaba as she moved to the table and rested the bowl on its battered surface. Taking up another, she shuffled back to the fire pit and settled opposite Thomas with surprising ease considering her age and infirmity. The light of the dwindling flames lit her face, casting deep shadows in her sunken sockets, the merest glimmer hinting as to the existence of her eyes as she placed the bowl of seawater she had been carrying on her lap.

Bersaba took up a handful of seaweed which had been draped in the bowl. Her expression became thoughtful as she held her hand out before her and the skeletal fingers squeezed the glistening plant stems, water dripping to the fire in sizzling demise and running down her forearm.

'As I suspected,' she stated with a vague nod, carefully placing the seaweed back over the bowl so that it sagged into the darkness of the water therein.

'What do you suspect?' asked Thomas after she had remained silent for a few moments, the volume of his voice lowered in the hush.

She stared into the fire for a while, the milky paleness of her eyes apparent until she lifted her gaze to his and they were once more lost in shadow. 'There is a storm coming, Young Thomas Carrow, and 'tis a storm which will change thy life forever,' she said with utmost certainty.

'A storm?' he whispered, a shiver passing the length of his spine and causing his shoulders to tremble in the last.

'More I know, but more I shall not tell. 'Tis not good to know too much of one's future for 'tis in the present that life dwells and no other place,' she replied, looking at the flames between them and then glancing beyond his shoulder at the woodpile against the wall behind him. 'Wouldst thou be so kind as to stoke the fire?' she asked.

Thomas stared across the fire at her lined face and considered reiterating his question, his curiosity burning and demanding to know more. He fought the urge to ask once again and instead struggled to his feet, mildly surprised to find the pain much diminished.

He looked down at his bare foot and tested his weight on it.

'Do not be fooled, the injury is still present,' croaked Bersaba as the fire cracked and a scattering of sparks were spat onto the ground by his feet.

As soon as she fell silent a jolt of pain shot up his leg. Thomas inhaled between his teeth, brow creasing. He glanced at Bersaba and saw the faint smile upon her thin and pale lips.

Carefully limping to the wood pile, he selected a small armful of logs and carried them to the pit. Crouching, one slipped from the crook of his arm and thumped softly upon the earth. He placed the others onto the flames, a few glowing embers lifting on the heat. They rose towards the hole in the roof, their light fading and dying until they were mere specks of soot amidst the escaping smoke.

'Will you not tell me any more of what you see in my future?' he asked as he reached for the stray log.

Her smile grew, but she did not answer.

Thomas kept his gaze averted, stared at the fire as he placed the last log onto it. 'What change is coming?'

'Does thy uncle Rumon remain a tanner?' she asked, ignoring his questions.

He frowned and sighed, moving back to his position opposite her. 'He was when last I saw him, which was nigh on five years previous,' he replied with a nod. 'He still worked the leather for Gwennol, who cut and stitched it into garments for the folk of Truro.'

'I knew theirs would be a lasting partnership.' She looked across at him, her smile fading. 'I also knew their loins would not bear the fruit of offspring.'

'How did you know?' asked Thomas, hoping that through this line of enquiry he would be able to return to the subject of her knowledge of his own future.

She shook her head. 'No more of this now, Young Thomas. I will not reveal my secrets nor the secrets of what shall come to pass.'

'Will you not at least tell me whether this change be good or bad?' he asked.

The fire spat again, embers landing on the furs of Bersaba's lap. She casually brushed them away, seemingly unconcerned. ''Tis neither and yet both,' she replied cryptically.

14

She chuckled to herself, misted eyes alight as she regarded the disheartened expression upon her guest's face. 'Trust me, Young Thomas, when I say that not knowing is a blessing that knowing seeks to undo. We all have a path to follow, one from which it is impossible to stray, and knowing what is to come does naught to improve the journey. It is the journey that is of import, not the destination.'

He stared at her across the flames, which were reaching higher as they fed upon the new wood. No more would be revealed by the old crone, of that he was sure.

'Put on thy boot and go check thy traps,' she instructed. 'Think on what I have said no more, but live now, for there is no other time in truth.'

Thomas nodded despite knowing that her mention of change would haunt him. His mind would fail to find rest but would pick at what she had said like crows picking at the rabbits in his traps, unable to resist temptation and attempting to be satisfied. He would invent scenarios and create stories of what would come to pass as he guessed at the future.

The fire crackled and Shenty began to bark as she waited outside by the path.

'Ah,' said Bersaba as she rose to her feet, no trace of her age in her movements. 'It would seem that I have another visitor?'

'Visitor?' asked Thomas as he looked to his right and stared at the door, Shenty continuing to bark beyond its concealment.

'Aye. Elowen is her name as she comes by most days.'

'Elowen?' He turned to find that the herbalist had gone back to her table and selected a bowl containing red berries.

Bersaba nodded as she padded to the door. 'She is bewitched and not herself. There is no telling when the enchantment may end,' she replied. 'Come, put on thy boot and meet her.'

Thomas hesitated and then took up his boot, putting it on as Bersaba opened the door. Shenty immediately fell silent as she stood twenty yards away in the misted vale, the yew trees greeting the old woman's appearance with gentle whispering.

'Good day to thee, Elowen,' croaked the herbalist as she passed to the left and out of sight.

Thomas got to his feet with care and made sure not to place too much weight on his ankle as he hobbled to the door. 'My childhood friend went by that name,' he commented as he went. 'She was a deer and I a hound. We would go racing across the fields and chase each other upon the moors. We were...' His words failed as he reached the doorway and caught sight of the healer and her companion.

'Do not worry, he is a welcome guest,' stated Bersaba as she crouched before a small roe deer. It had rust coloured fur and short single-pronged antlers, dark nose glistening as it sniffed the air upon his arrival, seeking his scent.

Their eyes met and Thomas' spine tingled. He saw the light of a keen intelligence shining. She was studying him and thinking, taking in his presence. There was a depth to her gaze that was unnatural for such a creature, a depth that he recognised from his youth.

The deer snorted softly and nodded in greeting before turning her attention to the bowl of berries that was being held out to her. Thomas watched as she began to tuck into the simple meal.

'She bades thee good morning,' said Bersaba over her shoulder.

'And I her,' he responded with a nod. 'Now I must take my leave so as to check the traps before they are emptied by crows,' he stated, looking down at the healer as she remained crouched before the deer. 'What do you wish as payment for the treatment of my ankle?'

'A rabbit will suffice,' she croaked, looking up at him with a kindly smile. 'Just leave it before my door next time ye pass this way.'

He nodded. 'I will bring it before the week is out,' he replied before limping to the path that led away from the rough patch of soil and patchy grass about the front door.

'Take good care, Young Thomas Carrow,' she said to his back as Elowen finished the last of the berries. 'May Dor Dama bless thee with her bounty.'

16

'And you, Bersaba,' he replied over his shoulder before turning to Shenty, who still would not come any closer, as if some invisible barrier held her at bay.

As he drew up to the small hound she leapt, feet upon his upper thighs and eager for his reassuring attention. Thomas crouched before her and rubbed her cheeks, Shenty eagerly licking at his hands. He briefly looked into her eyes, seeing none of the glimmer that had been evident in regards the roe deer's gaze.

With a thoughtful frown, he began to limp away from the hut and its gathering of whispering trees, the mist taking them into its pale concealment at his back. Shenty took the lead, clearly happy to be vacating the area as she trotted ahead without a backward glance.

4

Thomas sat on a rock in the lea of a small bluff, the branch he was using as a walking stick leaning to his right. He looked to the north-east, the view down to Zennor taken in the pale of the mist, which had thickened to fog upon the moor, its dampness clinging to his simple clothes.

He had checked only three of his traps, the going slow thanks to his injury, over which he had chided himself numerous times. The first two had been empty and at the third he had found the tail of a large rat along with a bloody smear of entrails, the crows having feasted despite his hope that the mist would have concealed any creatures that had been ensnared.

He shook his head and brushed back the damp hair of his long fringe. Glancing down at Shenty as she lay on the shingle, his frown deepened. He had found a few mushrooms while upon the hill, but they had no meat by which to sustain themselves and he would not be able to attend the beach in order to catch fish for at least a few days due to his condition.

Thomas stared at the bread in his hand as he raised it to his mouth. There was still some left at the cottage, but he would need to visit Trewey Farm in order to barter for more in the near future.

Having no appetite, he held the rest out to the dog, who sniffed it with little interest. 'There is naught else but vegetables, my friend,' he said, reaching out and rubbing her head.

Thomas wrapped the cloth laying over his knees about the bread and tucked the parcel back into the left pocket of his long coat. Taking up the walking stick, he stood and braced himself for the journey to the next trap.

Limping through the fog, he regularly brushed hair from his eyes, the additional weight of moisture causing it to fall again in time. While Shenty explored the rocks and clumps of yellowing grasses, Thomas explored possibilities within the corridors of his mind, searching for answers. What great change could be coming? What did the future hold in store?

Bersaba had instructed him not to dwell on what had been said, but his mind kept returning to her words. His life was one of lonely routine and he kept company only with animals. He could see no avenue by which such change could arrive.

The next trap marker came into view; a rock baring the face of an old man with a large nose and deep frown, heavy brow casting a shadow that formed the eyes. As he drew near, Thomas heard the sounds of faint scrabbling.

At the base of the Old Man of the Moor, below its prominent nose and largely hidden from sight by grasses, a rabbit came into view. It spied his approach, Shenty moving in from the right and staring expectantly at the beast as its back legs scrabbled in weak desperation. The cord about its neck tightened further, tethering it to the peg securely fastened in the ground.

Thomas came to a stop and the rabbit stared up with bulging eyes. Despite having seen its like in traps many times before, sorrow arose due to the suffering caused to the beast.

He crouched and took its head and shoulders in his hands, twisting sharply. Its back legs twitched a few times in fits and starts, as if it still tried in vain to gain its liberty. Its sorry form then fell still, fur damp and tongue lolling from its mouth.

Thomas released the snare from about the rabbit's neck. He took his three inch blade from the small scabbard at his left hip and sliced between the bones of one its back legs. Passing the other through the gap, he tied the beast to his waist with the lengths of leather cord that hung beside the knife's sheath.

Shenty licked at his hand after the blade had been wiped on the stained hide of his leggings and returned to its resting place.

Thomas looked at his companion and nodded. 'Aye, we shall both have meat for supper tonight,' he said, scratching her chin.

Thomas grasped the walking stick in his hand, a twist to the top like a coiled snake. He tested his weight, the pain of his injury having become only a dull ache, and then set off through the fog hugging the rugged moor.

5

The cottage appeared out of the paleness, at first a mere shadow, but gaining definition as Thomas and Shenty drew closer along the hillside. Its uneven thatch was darkened by moisture as it sat low in the mist. It rested upon a small artificial tableland on the north-eastern slopes of Trewey Hill and was set amidst grassland. A patchwork of walled fields lay below its position, descending into the shallow vale to the east and bordering Zennor Churchtown. The hill had been cut away to the west of the building and was shored up with buttressed timbers in sore need of replacement as they succumbed to rot. The seven foot embankment which has been created rose a few yards to the left of the abode, offering protection from westerly winds.

They moved to the gate and passed into the stone-walled garden before the southern side of the house. The hound trotted up the path between the overgrown grasses and waited before the door, watching her master's steady progress. Thomas glanced to the right and saw the spectre of the tree his mother had planted in memory of his father. It was barely ten feet tall and had been sculpted by the wind, seeming like a cresting wave about to tumble onto the wall.

Reaching the door, he ran his fingers over the sign attached to the granite beside it. Their tips ran over the ridges of the words which had been carved into the piece of driftwood by his father many, many years before.

'Ocean Mist,' he whispered with a sigh, recalling his mother telling him that it was her wish to bless the house with a name, to give it an identity.

Thomas entered and was faced with the gloomy emptiness of the interior. The constant feeling of loneliness that dwelt at the back of his mind was brought to the fore and echoed within his heart. He ached to find someone with which to share his life, to bring light to his existence. He longed to be saved from himself and the isolation he felt, one intensified by the folk whom he had known as a boy but who now turned their backs on him as a man.

Shutting the door, he walked past the cot positioned against the wall to his left, its furs in a state of mild disarray. Moving beyond the fire pit in the centre of the floor, he went into the Old Pen, which was a separate room in the left rear corner of the dwelling. It had been constructed by his grandfather as a place for his goats to over winter. He had gathered rough stones from the hillside and built walls of over five feet in height, the gap above to the eaves laced with dusty cobwebs.

Thomas ignored the bench cluttered with oddments resting along the left-hand wall and went to an old table in the middle of the small room, its top scarred by years of use and a pair of backed stools resting beside it. Once there had been four, but on his return from Truro he had found the others too rotten to warrant repair and so they had been used to stoke the fire.

Setting the rabbit upon the tabletop, he ushered one of the two chickens that resided in the cottage from the back of the nearest chair, the creature clucking and fluttering to the ground. He took off his long coat and draped it over the seat, a childhood image of his parents sitting opposite each other coming to mind.

He stepped over to a counter set to the left of the seaward door, a dinted tin bowl resting atop filled with water. Staring out of the window above, he saw naught but whiteness, the vast emptiness of the ocean hidden from sight.

After a few contemplative moments, Thomas turned and found Shenty sitting on the earth by the table, her expression expectant as she looked up at him. Rubbing her head briefly, he then moved to the doorway leading into the main living area. He stared across at the bench covered in pieces of driftwood found during his trips to the cove, the straw upon which the chickens nested lying beneath. His gaze lifted to a pair of shelves where his carvings were gathered above. Seahorses, fish, shells and dolphins were crowded together as if seeking each other's company, a moon-gazing hare at the centre of the lower shelf.

He stepped around the old chair which was placed before the second seaward window of the cottage and went to the bench. Noting a piece of driftwood that looked like the peak of a hill, he picked it up. Turning it in his hands, he sensed its past, but could not know its journey. His thumb rubbed its smoothness as he waited to see if it would whisper its desire for change into the stillness of his mind.

Finding that naught presented itself, he carefully placed it back with the wide selection before him. His gaze settled on a knot of wood shaped like a rugged heart. It was resting towards the rear on a few lengths of timber that looked as if they had once belonged to the hull of a boat.

He reached for it without hesitation, ignoring thoughts of a fishing boat floundering in stormy seas. His hands caressed the piece as if it were fragile. It spoke softly, told him what form it wished to take.

Thomas went to the chair, seating himself and glancing out of the open shutters, seeing only misted paleness beyond. Withdrawing his knife, he began to carve. His movements were measured as wood chippings fell to his lap, some tumbling from his knees to the earthen floor. In the quiet stillness, he gave the wood its wish, created the form which waited to be revealed.

6

He took the cooking frame from where it rested behind the fire pit. His tinder box rested on the ground nearby and a large woodpile was gathered in the corner, spilling towards the south-facing door. Thomas placed the frame's feet to either side of the flames before attaching a pot containing rabbit stew, fastening it to the horizontal bar that passed over the fire using a length of chain.

Satisfied that it was secure, he made his way back over to the seat, glancing at the carving he had begun earlier as it rested on the bench with the rest of the driftwood. Deciding not to continue for the time being, he sat in the chair, Shenty padding over and leaping onto his lap, as was her habit. She nuzzled his neck and chin before circling a few times and finally curling up after nipping at her flank. Thomas sat in silence as his thoughts turned to his father and grandfather before him, both men having found rest upon the seat.

Glancing at the arms of the chair, Thomas could see the stains of all their yesterdays, the wood darkened by their touch. He caressed them with his fingertips, sensing the life of each man still within the grain. His grandfather had made the seat, giving it a back like the stools in the Old Pen. Thomas had been told of how he had sought out oak branches, whittling and then smoothing them with sand from Treen Cove in order to make rests for his weary arms.

He lifted his gaze and looked out of the window. A wind had risen in the east and ushered away the mist, the shutters bumping lightly against the granite. Thomas stared at the ocean in the distance, its waters stretching to the far horizon. It had claimed both men one stormy day and taken them down into the cold silence. It was a day he remembered. It was a day he could not forget.

His mother had been busying herself in the Old Pen, glancing from the rear window at the swollen rollers as the wind ripped spray from their peaks. The men were late home.

Thomas had been only nine years of age, sitting on the edge of the table while swinging his legs over the side of the old oak top. He had listened to the howl of gusts churning around the house, banging the shutters and rattling the doors as they headed inland. He had been singing a little ditty about a seal, his child's high voice like a faint melody of hope amidst the maelstrom, but what faint hope there was had soon been dashed when a loud knocking sounded at the south-facing door.

His mother had rushed from the room, her expression tight and filled with worry as she wiped her reddened hands on the water-stained apron tied at her waste. He had hopped down and followed at her heels.

Harold Pendar had been revealed beyond the door and his mother had burst into tears as soon as she set eyes on the old man's weathered face. His expression said all that needed to be said as he struggled to find words, clutching his woollen cap before him in both hands as the wind toyed with his greying hair. That is when the rain had begun to fall, whipping in from the sea in stinging sheets. It did not stop till the day of the funeral, when a solitary stone was laid in Zennor churchyard bearing their names.

Thomas' mother had passed away with six months, from grief many said. She had become shrivelled and withered, the outpouring of her loss having taken with it her vitality, emptied her of the will to live.

He had been by her side at the end. She was a wraith, life all but vacated, skin translucent and sunken over bones. The power of speech was taken from her in the last days and she had feebly reached for his hand as he perched on a stool placed by the cot in which she rasped and waited for deliverance. A soft smile had then graced her bloodless lips before the light in her eyes went out.

Before the ability to speak had been lost in the final stages of her wasting, she had made Thomas promise ne'er to go out to sea. He had remained true to that promise ever since.

His uncle, Rumon, had taken him to live under his roof in Truro. He had not returned to Zennor until fifteen years later, a stranger to those who had known him as a boy, an outsider to be regarded with suspicion and kept at a distance despite being born in that very cottage. Though the suspicion had lessened in time and with it the distance, he was still seen as different.

Thomas continued to stare out of the window as he idly stroked the dog sleeping upon his lap. The sea was calm, vague shapes of gulls wheeling in the sky at the coast in the middle distance as the sun sank into the west and sought out its watery rest. Unlike his father and grandfather, it would rise again.

The chair creaked in the thoughtful silence as he shifted and narrowed his gaze, spying pale sails in the far distance, dark clouds beyond highlighting their presence on the edge of the world. He stared at them and then let his lids fall across the view. The faint touch of the sun's last rays was like the breath of a lover upon his skin and he yearned for companionship, for an end to his solitude.

Opening his eyes a few minutes later, Thomas found the sun departed and in its place a vein of rich gold drawn across the west, painted upon the line of dark clouds to the north and hiding the presence of the vessel beneath. He turned to Shenty as she lay curled upon his legs.

He smiled sadly. 'You are all I have,' he commented quietly.

She let out a brief moaning yawn. Thomas took a deep breath and turned back to the view, his rugged face lit by the failing light. He began to hum a sorrowful tune, one which his mother had taught him while his father was at sea. It was The Lay of Ailla. His mother had told him many a tale of sirens and mermaids, giants and goblins, but the story of Ailla had haunted him. She was a siren who had fallen in love with a sailor whose ship she had called to the rocks. One look and she had lost her heart to him, saving him from the raging sea and taking him safely to shore. But their love could not endure, for every day she spent upon the land her longing for the sea grew. Ailla was torn by her love and her need to return. Eventually taken by madness, she dove from the cliffs at Zennor Head.

The tune came to a melancholy end and the silence that took its place felt oppressive. It closed in, its pressure making Thomas feel claustrophobic.

Shenty suddenly raised her head, ears pricking as she stared out of the window. He looked down at her and then heard the distant sound of music carried on the wind.

Shenty leapt from his lap and stood before him looking up at the window. He got to his feet and limped into the Old Pen, the hound quickly passing him and standing expectantly by the seaward door. Reaching it a few moments later, Thomas opened it and Shenty rushed out and over to the right, stopping ten yards away and looking north-east down the slope of the hillside to where much of Zennor lay hidden within the crease of the land.

He hobbled over to join her, the coming night heralded by a swathe of rich, deep blue arcing across the heavens from the east with darkness on its tail, the first stars beginning to make their presence known. Standing in silence, he listened, the music faint as it rose on the wind and was carried across the landscape.

'The festival of Kalan Gwav,' he stated, Shenty glancing up at him. 'The first day of winter,' Thomas added, able to see the top of the pale church tower rising from the foot of Zennor Hill.

He listened to the music a little longer, knowing that he only need walk a few steps further and the whole of the village would be revealed below, but standing his ground. The night chill began to bite and he felt the keenness of his solitude upon the hill.

Arms wrapped about himself, Thomas made his way back into the cottage. Shenty remained briefly, a curious look upon her face before turning and following her master.

7

Thomas stood before the thirty foot drop to the rocks and sand, the hills at his back. He stared at the steep path descending before him. It was no more than a foot wide and clung to the easterly cliff as it made its way into Treen Cove, which was still in shadow, the sun low in the eastern sky and hidden from sight. There were narrow steps carved into the top third, but the climb then became much more precarious, the lower rocks dark and slick with the wash of the night's high tide.

He tested his weight on his left ankle, finding no trace of pain. The salve Bersaba had applied the previous day had taken effect and there had been little swelling in evidence when he had woken that morning.

Shenty stood patiently by his side, waiting to see if they would make the descent and always preferring her master to take the lead. He glanced down at her and smiled faintly as his long coat stirred in the wind and his unruly hair was messed by its passing.

Taking a few tentative steps down, Thomas took hold of the rope that was threaded through metal hoops and acted as a handhold. His grandfather had been one of the men who had originally hammered the hoops into the rock face, the iron now brown with deep rust and covered in pockmarks of corrosion.

He began to make his away down, looking at the slippery rocks beyond the carved steps and feeling apprehension despite the injury no longer hampering his movements. He took additional care, the grip of his hand tighter than usual, fingers clenched about the rough rope.

Pausing when he reached the last step, he wished that the men that had began chiselling the stairway had finished their labour, but recalled what his grandfather had told him. One of their number had fallen to his death and the work had been brought to a halt indefinitely, the cove earning the reputation of being a place of ill fortune, something that afforded him privacy within its confines as none of the folk ventured near despite the good fishing to be had.

Thomas began to make his way over the rough and glistening rocks. The sound of a stone skittering down the cliff caused him to look over his shoulder.

There, standing at the start of the descent, was a small roe deer.

'Elowen,' he whispered.

His left foot slipped on the rock. Teetering dangerously over the edge of the drop, he quickly grasped the rope in both hands, boots finding little purchase on the path. His body leant out over the emptiness as he clung on, the rope pulled taut and drawn two feet from the cliff before him by his weighty grasp.

Shenty barked as he struggled to regain a foothold. Hand over hand, he pulled himself back to safety, heart pounding desperately. His body trembled with the adrenalin of fright and fear as he leant against the rocks in relief, glancing up at the cliff-top to see that Elowen was no longer in sight.

Thomas took the sea air deep into his lungs. His pulse calmed as he wiped the curtain of hair from his forehead, the coolness of perspiration upon his skin.

'That was too close for my comfort,' he said quietly, reaching down to rub Shenty's head as she stared up at him with a questioning expression.

He looked down at the rocks below that gave way to sand in the middle of the small cove and which would have most likely brought about his end had he fallen. Thomas then glanced up the path, considering a retreat back to the relative safety of the cliff-top.

He shook his head. If he did not make his way down then the fear would be greater the next time he visited. He had to make the descent, to overcome the trepidation that set his mind to thoughts of caution and the reputation of the cove.

Taking a tentative step forward, Thomas began to make his way along the path once again, feeling the coolness of the night still gathered in the shadows of the cliffs that encompassed the cove. He shivered as he made steady progress, Shenty at his back being careful to keep a little distance, watching his feet as if expecting another mishap.

He reached the bottom and stepped onto a patch of sand between boulders rising from its paleness. With a sense of relief, he glanced back up the steep path as Shenty leapt past him and bounded over the rocks to the stretch of sand at the centre of the cove.

Thomas watched her scamper to the surf, disturbing a small flock of oyster catchers that had been wandering along the sands just above the tide line. He turned away with a fleeting smile as the hound began to playfully snap at the gently tumbling waves and made his way to the back of the cove.

Walking to the tumbledown rocks at the base of the cliff, he took every care as he carefully climbed up. At their peak he stretched up with his right hand, taking hold of the weighted net he stowed on a ledge above. It dripped as he dragged it from its place, a few strands of seaweed tangled in its mesh of rope.

A gull called out as it glided over the cove, heading seaward and scanning the surf as it passed over the ocean. Thomas watched and then made his way back to the sands. His boots left shallow impressions in its dampness as he walked to the receding tide-line thirty yards away.

Going to the side, he climbed along rocks that edged the cove, moving out beyond the cliff and the breaking waves, the waters undulating to his left with a calming regularity. The wash and scent of the ocean filled him as he drew up to the raised end of a substantial tidal pool in which he had swum as a boy. The sun would warm the waters to a depth of a few feet, but diving below there had been an invigorating chill which had tightened his chest, the golden rays penetrating but stripped of their heat before they reached the lower reaches. As a man it was the ideal place to cast his net. When the tide was in the sea washed over the worn far side a full twenty-five feet across from his position and fish were often left in its confines as the waters receded.

Untangling the net, he made sure the weights tied along its lower edge were firmly attached and then checked the floats tied at regular intervals along the top. He prepared to cast it out, standing with it held out to his side, swinging it and steadily building the strength of the motion. In his left hand he held the ends of ropes tied to the corners of the net, ones which would be pulled back to him in order to draw the net in and close it about any fish concealed within the waters.

Feeling that the net had gained enough momentum, Thomas released it on a forward swing, the weights taking it sailing out across the waters. They plunged in near the far end of the pool, dragging the net down and out of sight. The floats bobbed on the surface, marking its place of rest, and he felt satisfied that the positioning was good.

He began to draw it across the pool, the ropes attached to its corners slowly pulling it about any fish that may be present. The wind rippled the surface so that the depths were hidden from sight as the net was dragged up and broke the surface.

Thomas stared at its emptiness and sighed, glancing at the waves washing over the far end of the pool. There was still time for fish to enter before the tide receded beyond its seaward side. He would wait and cast the net again in time.

Numerous gulls called out and he looked to Gurnard's Head on the left, the cove sheltered in its lea. A group of the seabirds wheeled and turned over the rugged finger of land that reached into the waves and he wondered what may have disturbed them from their rest upon the waves.

Seeing naught untoward, Thomas moved to his usual seat; a hollow bowl within one of the larger rocks close to the cliff at his back. Tucking his long coat beneath him and sitting within, he stared out to sea. Beyond the shadow of the land, the waters changed from deep grey to a vivid blue beneath the clear autumn sky. A single white cloud drifted along the

31

horizon, its vague and lonely reflection drawn down across the distant waves.

Reclining, he rested his head against the side of the bowl and closed his eyes after checking Shenty's location. The hound was still by the surf, standing ankle-deep and snapping at the tops of the small waves as they tumbled before her. He smiled and relaxed, hoping that the sun would not be long in rising beyond the concealment of the hills so that its warmth could chase away the last of the night's chill.

8

Thomas approached Bersaba's hut, the brace of rabbits hung at his hip bulging beneath his coat. It had been five days since his visit and there was no evidence of the injury to his ankle.

Shenty drew to a stop and moved to the side of the track, her tail falling. She was still unwilling to go any closer to the healer's dwelling and looked up at him apprehensively as he passed.

He stepped up to the front door and raised his hand to knock. His knuckles stopped barely an inch before the wood and he looked to either side, noting the silence of the yews despite the stiff breeze.

Thomas slowly lowered his hand, intuitively knowing that the old crone was not in residence. She had told him to leave a rabbit at the door. Had Bersaba known she would not be home when he called?

He untied one of the rabbits and placed it on the earth before her door, still listening for signs of occupation. Straightening, he stared at the grain of the wood before him, wondering at the true nature of the healer. Many were the rumours he had heard as a child. There were those that said she was a witch whose magic was woven into the salves she used to treat injuries and ailments. Whenever animals went missing there was always at least one finger pointed in her direction. Some folk used to say she practiced ritual sacrifice, others that she was using the entrails to cast dark spells and curses, though Thomas found the latter hard to believe considering her kindly nature.

He shook his head and turned away, glancing at the silent yews to either side. 'Tell her that I have been,' he said quietly, suddenly overwhelmed by the feeling that they watched and listened.

Chills ran the length of his spine. He walked away, stride quickened by the sensations.

Shenty's tail wagged as he approached, happy to be leaving and taking the lead up the gently sloping path as they headed home.

Thomas passed around the bend in the hillside track and Zennor Churchtown came into view to the north-east, the sea rising to meet the horizon in the distance behind. What few trees remained now lingered near the scattering of cottages and barns, as if seeking refuge from the felling axe. Once, so his grandfather had told him, the shallow fold between the moored hillsides had been wooded, but that time had long since faded into memory and would soon pass into forgetfulness.

He looked over to Saint Senara's Church as it rested beneath the far hillside, a few of the settlement's buildings scattered about it. His mother was buried in its small, circular churchyard, but he had only visited her grave once since returning five years before. Overcome with grief, he had found himself hurrying from the village with tears streaming down his face, gut twisted and barely able to breathe.

Thomas averted his gaze from the church, spying a kestrel above the moor rising to his left. He stared at its silhouette and felt an affinity with its solitary presence as it hovered in the vast expanse of the sky.

Drawing in its wings, the hawk suddenly plummeted to the rocks. Thomas thought he heard the brief squeal of fearful death carried on the wind before it rose into view once again and flew west, vanishing over the brow of the hill. With heavy heart, he continued the journey back to his cottage as the sun steadily sank towards the ocean and the chill of coming night gathered in the deepening shadows.

9

Thomas sat in the failing light, Shenty curled upon his lap and a few stray wood shavings upon her short fur. He stared at the carving held in his left hand, elbow upon the oaken arm of the chair. The piece of wood that had looked like a rough heart had been transformed during the long evenings into the likeness of a mermaid.

He followed the curves of her body as it became a tail curling around to the left and over to almost touch the creature's long hair, which cascaded down the sides of her face as she looked towards him, arms to her sides. Each scale had been carefully carved and the waves of her hair had taken many hours. She felt as if she had always been waiting to be freed from the wood, always dwelt within waiting for some kindly soul to bring her liberty.

Thomas' gaze moved to her face. There was something about her visage that triggered a sense of recognition. He had carved it while totally immersed in the task so that he and the procedure of carving became one and the same. The blade had scraped and picked, cut and sliced without need for conscious thought. In those moments he became lost, forgetting himself, becoming united with the mermaid. Whence she had come from he could not say, but he was sure it was from some place beyond him, beyond his conscious mind. She had come to him as if in a dream, an entranced state of creation.

He moved the mermaid closer and blew upon her face, a small flake of wood coming loose from beside her nose and falling to his lap. Shenty glanced up at him and then settled again as he carefully lay the knife on the right arm of the seat, not for an instant taking his gaze from the mermaid's face as he puzzled over his strong feeling of recognition.

Thomas thought of the women he knew in Zennor Churchtown, but the carving resembled none. He cast his mind back to his time in Truro, the image of the castle above the settlement rising into mind, trading with the garrison there bringing increasing prosperity to the inhabitants. There was no face that echoed that of the figure in his hand.

He blinked and shook his head. His familiarity with the carving's face was to remain a curiosity.

'It may be that I will remember on the morrow,' he stated, still looking contemplatively at the figure in his hand, which was no more than five inches high and wide.

Shifting on the seat, he lifted his legs slightly, signalling for Shenty to vacate. Knowing her master's habits well, the small hound leapt to the ground, moving over to the soot-blackened stones surrounding the fire pit and settling beside the low flames.

Thomas took the knife from the arm and placed it back into its scabbard before rising. Stepping over to the bench of wood, he looked at the shelves above, reaching up to move the moon-gazing hare from the centre of the lowest and then placing the mermaid there.

Shaking his head again as if trying to free himself of the spell it had cast upon him, Thomas made his way to the fire, shivering as he noticed the chill for the first time. Taking a few logs from the pile in the far right corner, he placed them on the fire and watched a few sparks rise on the heat towards the hole in the roof through which the smoke was gently pulled.

Seating himself beside Shenty in the golden haze of the interior, he let his mind drift as he stared at the flickering before him. Thomas held his hands towards the flames and felt the heat, allowing it to draw out the chill from his bones as the wind rattled the shutters of the seaward window before the chair.

The fire crackled and he began to stroke his faithful hound. Shenty groaned and yawned as she waited for him to go to his bed, at which point she would leap up and curl at his feet in the warmth of the furs.

Thomas glanced over at the carving of the mermaid resting on the shelf, finding himself drawn to her. He could not see her face clearly, but even from that angle there was something about it that set his mind to wondering.

He sighed and looked to the fire once more. Alone on the earth floor, his hound dozing at his side, Thomas felt the presence of the night beyond the small cottage like a pressure pushing in on him. He felt the intensity of his loneliness and began to sing The Lay of Ailla, the mournful tune rising into the hush of Ocean Mist.

'She sung to the sailors upon the sea,
She sung to the sailors, 'come to me,'
Her siren's song a bewitching call,
To jagged rocks which would claim them all,
Send them to the crushing depths,
Into darkness and their untimely deaths.

Then upon one stormy night
A floundering ship came into sight,
Ailla's melody lifting fair,
Carried on the winter air,
Calling through the murky gloom,
Singing them to their watery doom.

Upon the rocks the ship did crash,
Amidst the waves sailors thrashed,
Ailla's song the final sound
As they weakened and were drowned,
Until one man came into sight,
Until her heart took loving flight.

She pulled him from the crashing sea,
Freed him from her melody,
Saved him from her song's sweet spell,
Amidst the ocean's raging swell,
Took him in her soft embrace
Brushed death's shadow from his face.

She made her peace with the land,
There they dwelt hand in hand,

In his cottage by the shore,
Where the tide breathed evermore,
The song of her lips now of her heart,
Wishing they would never part,

Alas another song was sung,
That of the sea where she belonged,
Its depths singing for her return,
Though her love she could not spurn,
Setting a malady within her soul,
Each gull's cry a mournful toll.

Then one sorry day of mist,
Ailla found she could not resist,
The haunting wash of gentle waves,
The promised embrace for which she craved,
Calling her to be away,
Though with her love she longed to stay.

To Zennor Head she did go,
Dove to the rocks that lurked below,
Falling to her bloody death,
The name of her love in her last breath,
Her body taken by the sea,
Her heart forever his to be.'

10

It had been nearly two weeks since Thomas had heard the sounds of the festival of Kalan Gwav rising from Zennor and now the first of the winter storms gripped the land. He hurried against the push of the wind, which buffeted him with ferocious strength as he held his leather coat closed upon the solitary rabbit that hung at his hip. He had noted the dark clouds coming and had hoped he would reach Ocean Mist before the rains came, but the deluge had begun before he could reach its shelter.

Coming down the slope to the left of the cottage, his feet slipped on the slick grass and he skidded. Losing his balance, he fell onto his backside and slid a few yards forward as the rain stung his cheeks, water dripping into his eyes from the hair plastered to his forehead.

Struggling to his feet, he continued on and moved to the garden wall. Rather than wasting time passing around to the gate, he climbed over, knocking one of the stones from the top in his hastiness, its dull thud lost in the howl of the wind. He hurried to the southern door, where Shenty waited expectantly, her fur soaked through.

Bursting into the house, he quickly shut the door behind them as the hound shook herself, sending a shower of droplets into the air, some landing on the cot to the left. The cottage was filled with the sound of the seaward window shutters banging against their fastenings, as if angry spirits sought entry. The rain pounded against them, seeping in between and beneath, running from the sills to darken the earth at the foot of the wall.

Thomas went into the Old Pen. The seaward door shook and struggled against its containment, a pool of water gathered before it as the wind drove sheets of grey downpour against the seaward side of the cottage.

He took the rabbit and placed it upon the table. Wiping his eyes, Thomas then took off his dripping coat, shivering and feeling the dampness of his woollen shirt against his clammy skin. He hung the coat over the back of the near chair at the table and then returned to the main living area.

Taking up his tinder box and a handful of kindling from a sack beside the woodpile, he moved to crouch beside the fire pit. Thomas placed the twigs and dried grass onto the ashes from the night before. He removed his flints from the wooden box and set about the task of lighting the fire, all the time feeling the chill bite deeper as he remained in the wet clothes.

A spark finally sprung into flames. Thomas protected their fragility from the drafts that circulated the gloomy interior, feeling the faint touch of heat upon his palms.

Satisfied that the fire was truly lit, he moved to the woodpile and selected a few sticks and thin branches, making a mental note that he would soon need to replenish his supplies. He took them in the crook of his left arm and laid the smallest upon the fire, placing the others on the ground in readiness to feed it once it had grown stronger. The flames phutted in the breeze and smoke swirled above, only a little making its way to the hole in the roof.

He coughed and backed away a little, not wishing to move beyond the growing warmth. Stepping around the pit, Thomas moved the cooking frame from beside the granite wall and placed it closer to the fire. Taking off his boots, he placed them beneath. He straightened and slowly took off his clothes, hanging each garment over the crossbar of the frame in order that it should dry.

Soon standing naked, he tried to ignore the cold as he went back to his original position. He crouched and took up the larger branches, placing them on the fire as Shenty walked over and licked his bare knee.

Putting the last branch into the flames, he fussed the small hound briefly while savouring the warmth. The currents of air moving through the cottage and brushing against his back caused him to shudder. The seaward windows and door continued to rattle as the rain cascaded against them, the wind howling across the moors as the storm continued unabated.

'It seems as though this may be a long night,' he mumbled as his isolation weighed heavily upon his bare shoulders.

11

He woke suddenly from a terrible dream, body damp with sweat. He had been standing on an outcrop in the middle of the ocean, waves thrashing and pounding all about him, the air filled with spray and rain. Naked and running with water, lightening had lit the scene as thunder boomed and the sea roared. All was violent noise and movement.

A high scream had pierced the night, heard over the cacophony of nature's fury. Thomas looked into the frothing swell, glimpsing a mermaid floundering, reaching out to him. Her face was the same as that on the carving, one that triggered an intense feeling of recognition.

She screamed again, head vanishing beneath the surface momentarily, a gash on her forehead running with diluted blood.

Thomas had struggled to make his way down to the edge of the rocks. The waves crashed before him, rising up in a wall of water as they hammered against the shoreline.

A third scream arose and he looked to the waters. Only the creature's hand could be seen as she was swallowed by the waves, reaching towards him, begging to be saved. It sank from sight as lightening flashed across the undulating expanse. Thunder rolled through the dark clouds, the very rocks shaking as the tips of the mermaid's fingers vanished beneath the surface.

Thomas lay on his cot and tried to calm the beating of his heart, the residue of the dream still filling him with tension. He raised his head from the worn leather stuffed with straw which served as a pillow. The room was faintly lit by the dawn light coming in through the gaps about the window shutters and south-facing door. Thin trails of smoke rose from the ashes, the air still hazy. His eyes were raw and puffy after finding only a little sleep despite the storm blowing itself out in the early hours.

The mermaid rested still and silent in the centre of the lower shelf above the bench. It was her face that he had seen amidst the waves of his dream. It was her hand that had reached pleadingly towards him as she sank from sight.

Thomas rested his head as Shenty stirred, the hound curled by his feet as they lay hidden beneath the patchwork fur cover. He took a breath in readiness and then slipped out from beneath, the chill immediately embracing his nakedness.

Moving quickly to the fireside, he took up the end of a branch that rested on the blackened stones at the edge as one of the chickens beneath the bench of driftwood gave a gentle squawk. Poking the ashes with the smouldering tip, he uncovered the warmth beneath, cracks of orange glowing between the gathering darkness of soot.

Thomas went to the sack of kindling and placed a handful on the embers. He blew softly until new flames took hold and began to eagerly devour the dry grass. Placing the remains of a few logs and branches scattered at the outskirts of the fire pit onto the centre, he watched as the heat pushed back the cold that lingered after night's departure.

He stood and stepped around to the far side, checking the clothes that hung on the cooking frame. All were dry.

Dressing, Thomas smelt the heavy scent of smoke clinging to his garb. The fire crackled as he scratched the thick stubble on his chin and stepped to the seaward window. He opened the shutters and stared out. The clouds beyond were low and dark. Below them, a bank of mist hid the horizon as it hugged the Atlantic and steadily made its way towards the coast.

He padded bare foot into the Old Pen and took some bread taken from a lidded wooden box on the bench to the left. He tore off a large piece and returned the loaf to its containment.

Shenty trotted into the room and went over to her wooden bowl resting near the seaward door, the earth all about darkened by water which had seeped in during the storm. Seeing it empty, she looked over her shoulder at her master.

43

'Food is coming,' stated Thomas through a mouthful of bread as he picked up the cooking pot resting to the rear of the table.

He crouched beside the hound, who sniffed at the pot as it was tipped and then licked his hand. Thomas smiled as he poured some of the remaining stew into her bowl and she began to lap at the offering.

Straightening, he put the pot back on the table and pulled out the chair over which his coat hung. Sitting, he sighed and rubbed his hands on his face as he yawned. There was no energy in his body, only the wish to climb back into the cot and find sleep once again.

The sounds of lapping abated and Thomas looked down to find the bowl licked clean and Shenty sniffing the ground in the hope of discovering spilt morsels. He patted his knees and she turned to him. Glancing at the ground one last time, she then trotted over and leapt onto his legs, licking at his chin as he rubbed her cheeks and head, her breath carrying the scent of the stew into his face.

He sat fussing her, scratching the dog's back and letting her sit as she cleaned her coat. Turning to the window, Thomas saw that the mist was close and would soon subdue the land within its veiling presence.

Waiting until Shenty had finished her grooming, watching fondly as she nipped along her right flank, he then gently pushed her from his lap. 'Time for our walk, my friend,' he stated as she looked up at him.

Making his way into the living area, he went to stand by the fire, the flames still flickering. Taking up his boots from beneath the cooking frame, he put them on and went back through the Old Pen to the seaward door with Shenty at his heels, tail wagging as she anticipated their exit and the freedom of the rolling hills.

44

12

Thomas drew up to the cliffs of Treen Cove with Shenty by his side, the steep path descending before him and swallowed by the mist within ten feet. The gentle wash of the waves rose to greet him as he passed down it, moving from the steps and onto the uneven rocks, right hand firmly holding the rope strung along the cliff-face. The paleness receded before him, pulling in behind so that the cliff-top soon became obscured and then vanished altogether. Shenty followed at his heels as usual, still keeping a little distance between herself and her master after the incident a couple of weeks before.

Stepping onto the sand, the hound leapt down beside him and bounded off towards the surf, disappearing from sight. Thomas smiled and made his way to the back of the cove, noting that the storm had altered the face of the beach and revealed a jagged spine of rocks, like a partially buried reptile lying in wait at the base of the cliff.

He fetched down the net from its storage shelf and headed out towards the receding tide as Shenty began to bark. 'A jellyfish or the like washed up during the storm, no doubt,' he commented to himself with a faint smile.

He clambered up the rocks to the right of the beach. Reaching the pool, he found that the tide had already retreated to such a degree that its waters no longer replenished the contents.

'Shenty,' he called, letting out a sharp whistle as the hound continued to bark.

The sounds fell silent and shortly after she came bounding out of the mist. Shenty scrambled up to join her master, tail wagging as she made her way over and around the rocks.

Thomas crouched and fussed the dog for a short while. Straightening, he built the required momentum before throwing the net out across the rippling waters, the surface suddenly disturbed by movement and revealing the presence of fish within the cold depths. The weights splashed and took the net from sight. He waited for the floats to bob near the far end and then began to pull on the ropes attached to the four corners.

Slowly and surely, he pulled in the net. Thomas then drew it up out of the water like a cradle, two mackerel jumping and writhing upon it as water dripped back to the surface of the pool.

Pushing Shenty back a couple of steps, he took each fish in turn, holding their tails and bringing their lives to an end against the rocks. The diminutive hound sniffed at the catch as Thomas took a folded piece of tanned leather from his coat and laid it flat, placing the fish upon it. Folding the bottom and then the top over them, he tucked both ends and slid the package into his pocket.

'There will be mackerel for both of us this night, my friend,' he said to the hound while roughing her head.

She licked at his hand as Thomas glanced down from their position, looking at the small stretch of sand that was visible through the mist to the left. He turned his attention back to the net and reached to gather it up.

His brow suddenly creased as something registered in his mind. Thomas looked back to the sand. He thought he had seen a ghostly shape lying in the surf, but now that he scanned the edge of the mist there was naught to be seen bar the occasional piece of seaweed left by the waves upon the beach.

The mist thinned as he stared in furrowed puzzlement. A vague shape was revealed, long and pale with a dark shadow about its landward end.

'A dolphin?' he pondered doubtfully as the form was hidden from his sight once again.

Shenty barked and looked at him expectantly.

'Aye,' he replied, looking at the hound and scratching behind her left ear. 'You go investigate, my friend.'

She barked again and then scampered across the rocks to the beach below. Thomas watched until she was no longer visible and then gathered up his net, slinging it over his left shoulder, drops of water running down the leather.

He made his way down the rocks towards the sand, careful with his footing while occasionally glancing to the indistinct form lying in the surf. The mist continued to shroud it in mystery as Shenty went to stand beside it, barking and whining a little.

Thomas' pulse quickened as he reached the beach and moved closer. The figure was revealed to be that of a woman lying upon her back and clothed in a thin white gown which clung to her body, her nakedness apparent beneath. Her legs lay within the caress of the waves, the waters moving about her prone form with each breaking tumble. The tangles of her long dark hair were woven with seaweed, her face deathly pale.

Shenty nuzzled at the woman's neck as if trying to awaken her. Thomas came to a stop beside her and looked down. His eyes widened, mouth running dry and feeling his pulse throbbing in his neck. Her features were those of the mermaid he had carved and she bore a deep gash upon her left temple, as she had in the dream.

Slowly crouching, he studied her alluring features, pools of shadow gathered about her eyes. She looked to be in her early twenties, around ten years his junior with skin as soft and smooth as rose petals.

Thomas looked to her chest, her small breasts visible through the thin fabric of her gown, but could see no sign of breathing. He reached towards her cheek, noting that his fingers were trembling. Barely daring to touch her for fear she may fade like a dream after waking, he found her skin to be cold and clammy.

Leaning forward, Thomas put the side of his face above her mouth, her lips slightly parted. A gull called out in the mist as he waited and Shenty watched in silence.

The faintest sigh of warmth brushed against his cheek. She was alive, her life stowed somewhere deep within.

Shenty gave a sharp yap as she looked to him, clearly expectant of some action on his part. Thomas glanced back towards the cliffs, the mist concealing them. There was a moment of indecision; should he fetch help or attempt to traverse the steep track with the woman in his arms?

The hound licked at his hand and then turned to the woman.

'Aye, she cannot be left here,' nodded Thomas before gathering her into his arms. Her head rested against his left shoulder as she lay cradled in his careful hold. She was light and no more than five foot tall, a good four inches shy of his own height.

He began to carry her to the path ascending to the cliff-top. His mind swum with the impossibility of her face, one that seemed to have called to him across space and time, one that held such great appeal in its soft vulnerability. Shenty trotted at his side, glancing up regularly as if showing concern for the woman's condition.

'We will take her to Bersaba,' stated Thomas, the hound nodding and letting out a short bark of agreement as they neared the foot of the climb.

13

His expression showed the strain as he carried the woman through the grassland at the foot of the moor, arms aching, shoulders burning. She had made no sound and shown no sign of life.

Thomas paused and adjusted his hold. He looked at her face, as he had so many times during the journey from the cove. He was unable to comprehend how he could have carved and dreamt of the woman in his arms, one who stirred his heart despite being no more than a stranger.

Gritting his teeth and hoping the old healer may be able to put an end to his bafflement, Thomas continued towards the location of her hut. He noted that Shenty remained by his side instead of gallivanting across the bleak and misted landscape, as was usually the case. Wondering at the dog's wish to stay close, he looked ahead as the mist began to thin a little. A wind was rising from the east and growing in strength, slowly clearing the moisture from the air.

Shenty suddenly stopped and let out a brief whine as she stared ahead of them. Thomas slowed his pace, glancing back at the hound.

'What is it?' he asked, unable to make out anything untoward.

Taking a few more steps, The Old Man of the Moor was unveiled by the mist and his expression became one of surprise. Seated upon the stone was a hunched form wearing a hooded cloak of dark green.

Thomas' steps faltered and he came to a halt. He stared at the figure, thinking it may only be a figment of his imagination.

'Good day to thee, Young Thomas,' came a familiar voice from within the shadows of the hood.

'Bersaba?' he enquired. 'Is that really you?'

''Tis I,' she replied.

Pausing, Thomas then walked over to her. The mist drew back and Elowen was revealed ten yards further across the grasses and rocks, nodding her head in greeting. Shenty kept her distance, as she did near the old healer's hut, watching the woman closely.

'It is fortuitous that you are here, for I was coming to seek your help after finding this woman upon the beach.' He paused and looked down at the unconscious form in his arms. 'It may be that she is a siren or mermaid who found ill fortune in last night's storm. She had washed up on the sands of Treen Cove.'

''Tis not mere good fortune that brings this meeting, for I have been waiting for thee, it seems,' she replied, pulling back the hood to reveal a kindly smile upon her lined face, narrowed eyes sparkling as she looked up at him.

Thomas' expression became confused.

'I knew I must to the moor with my bag of tricks,' she explained, glancing at the hide bag beside her bare feet. 'The feeling arose deep and strong, though its reason only made itself known when thou stepped from the mist.'

Bersaba rose and moved closer to study the woman cradled in Thomas' arms. 'I cannot say as to her origins, but I know we must quickly away to thy cottage. It will not be long until the mist clears as the wind rises and it would be unwise for others to see thee with her.'

'My cottage!' he exclaimed in surprise.

Bersaba looked up and nodded, the wisps of hair falling about her head stirring in the breeze. 'Thee thought to leave her with me,' she said, her words a statement rather than a question. 'She hast come to thee, Young Thomas, not I. She is thy ward now and this is by no accident.'

'I cannot nurse her. I know naught of the healing arts,' he protested.

'Did ye not help nurse thy mother in her final days?' she asked. 'I seem to recall a boy beside the cot who was eager with questions and earnest in his wish to lend his aid.'

The image of his weakened and emaciated mother lying upon her deathbed began to take form and he felt emotions stir in response. He stared at the rough grass at his feet, quickly blinking the vision away before it had time to take hold.

'That I did,' he said softly, not wishing to dwell on those dark times when Bersaba had often visited in order to tend the ailing wraith beneath the covers, 'but I only cleaned her body and kept her comfortable as she faded from this world.'

'Ye need only do the same in this instance. She will awaken or she will not. All ye need do is clean her and make sure she is warm.'

'What about the injury to her head?'

'I shall see to it. I have all I need with me,' she said, turning to pick up the bag. 'Come. We must away from here,' she added as she set off down the slope.

'But there is more I would tell you,' he called after her.

'It can wait until we are within the concealment of Ocean Mist,' replied the old crone without looking back, the mist taking her into its arms.

Elowen snorted and nodded her head as she looked at him. She then followed after the old woman with a graceful stride.

Thomas glanced back at Shenty. She let out a whine and then barked. He sighed and then began after Bersaba, the ache in his arms almost forgotten as he pondered her presence upon the moor.

Shenty took a step forward as she prepared to follow after her master and then suddenly fell still. Looking down the slope, she saw a figure fading into the mist beyond the first of the stone walls that enclosed the fields below. She let out a low growl and watched as it disappeared from sight.

Marrek walked across the small field towards the gate in the corner, his cattle resting on the grass about him. His pace was quickened by what he had seen and heard as he made his way back to the village.

'A mermaid,' he whispered to himself as he shook his head and exited the field.

14

Thomas entered the cottage and laid the woman upon the cot, Shenty and Elowen electing to remain outside. Straightening, he flexed his aching shoulders as Bersaba shut the door and set her bag down. There was still no sign of life inhabiting the pale body lying upon the furs.

The healer sat on the edge of the bed and took a small earthenware bottle from her bag. Holding it in her left hand, she took out a small ball of wool as Thomas watched in silence.

Bersaba unstopped the bottle and the gentle sound filled the hush. She tipped it onto the wool, which glistened with the pale green balm contained within. Leaning over the prone form beside her, she applied the liquid to the gash, following the cut downwards with gentle strokes.

'May Dor Dama bless thee and grant thee the will to return to the world of the living,' she mumbled.

'I know her face. I carved its likeness on the figure of a mermaid only recently,' commented Thomas as he watched.

'Indeed,' said Bersaba as she continued to administer the potion.

He looked at the back of her head, wisps of pure white hair hanging to her shoulders. 'How can that be so?'

The old woman paused her activity and looked at him over her shoulder. 'We exist in this time, in this moment, but there is more that exists beyond. It sees the past, present and what is yet to come. Sometimes memories of the future arise within us because we are part of it.'

His brow creased as he thought on what she had said. 'Future memory?'

She nodded before turning back to the patient lying upon the furs. 'Future memory,' she confirmed as she put the stopper back in the bottle and held it out to him with the ball of wool.

Thomas hesitated and then took them from her.

'Make sure to keep the wound clean and apply the tonic at least twice a day,' she instructed while peering inside her hide bag.

'What ingredients are within?' he asked, holding the bottle beneath his nose and sniffing.

''Tis healing water from Madron's sacred well infused with herbs of my choosing,' she replied while taking out a small wooden box and placing it upon her lap. Opening the lid, she took out a needle of an inch in length and made of bone. It had been whittled down to a mere splinter with a point at one end and a hole at the other. Bersaba then produced a coil of catgut. She took one end and threaded it through the hole. Securing the thin cord in place, she bent over her patient and began to sew up the wound with quick stabs and gentle pulling.

'It will heal in time, but she will bear a scar to mark the wound,' she commented as she sewed. 'Ye will need to move the bed closer to the fire. Have thee any waxed leather to place beneath her so that her waste may be collected and cleansed with ease?'

Thomas nodded despite the old crone's gaze being concentrated on the work at hand. 'Will she live?'

Bersaba took a small blade from the wooden box and cut the catgut, offering him no answer as she did so.

'Will she live?' he reiterated with greater volume, thinking that she may not have heard him.

'That is not thy concern, Young Thomas,' responded Bersaba as she placed the needle and catgut back into the box and closed the lid. 'What will be will be,' she added, looking up at him.

'Do you know?'

There was a look in her eyes that answered his question without need for words. 'We all die, in the end,' she responded obliquely. 'Ye should not think on such things. Tend thy patient and allow the future to unfold as it will.'

53

'I cannot remain at her side. What about my traps? Shenty and I must eat.'

'Indeed,' she said with a nod. 'As must she,' she nodded towards the woman. 'Ye need not be at her side at all times.'

'What if she wakes while I am out?' asked Thomas.

'Then so be it,' she replied, bending down and putting the box back into her bag. 'Doest thou have rags with which to wash her?'

He stared at the old woman and then nodded.

Bersaba stood and took up her bag. 'Do not fret. I will visit and check on her whenever I pass. If ye are not in I shall leave some sign so that ye know I have attended her.'

'Surely she would be better cared for at your home?'

She lifted her withered right hand and placed it upon his shoulder. 'Thou art the one that fate has entrusted her to, Young Thomas. Thy discovery was by design, for there are no accidents in truth.'

'By design?'

She nodded and removed her hand, stepping to the door. 'I will take my leave now. Be sure to move the bed near the fire and cleanse her.' She opened the door. 'And apply the tonic twice a day,' she added with a glance at the bottle in his hand.

Thomas glanced at it and then looked back to the door to see the old woman step out.

She turned on the threshold. 'Heed my words, Young Thomas. Thy deeds are written into the waters of time and shall create ripples that last for eternity.' Bersaba held his gaze a moment and then set off along the path.

'May Dor Dama bless thee,' she said over her shoulder in parting. 'Come Elowen,' she called as she walked away, the deer grazing upon the long grass of the front garden.

He stared at the open door, hearing her diminishing passage along the path. He turned to the sight of the face which was so familiar. The woman seemed fit for the grave and if it were not for the faint breath he had felt upon his cheek he would have believed her dead.

'Who are you?' whispered Thomas with a shake of his head.

Shenty came trotting into Ocean Mist, stopping just inside the door and glancing at the woman upon the cot to her left. She moved to stand beside her master, sitting and looking up at him with pleading eyes.

He crouched and scratched behind her ears. 'It seems that we have a guest,' he stated as she licked at his hands enthusiastically, her tail wagging.

15

Night had fallen and the interior of the cottage was filled with a smoke haze which diffused the firelight. Thomas had moved the cot closer to the flames at an angle to the south-facing door, the head by the woodpile and foot facing the entrance to the Old Pen. The woman's simple gown hung over the cooking frame between the fire pit and far wall, the rags he had used to wash and dry her laid on the earth beneath.

He sat in the chair, hands upon the oaken arms, and stared across at the mysterious figure lying beneath the furs. The warm pulsing glow of the fire hid her paleness, leant a life that she did not possess in truth. He could not deny her beauty, his gaze drawn to the soft features and gently pouting lips.

'Maybe she truly is some siren of the sea,' he said into the hush as Shenty lay curled upon his lap and the fire crackled.

Thomas sat for a little longer, transfixed by her presence. Shaking his head and blinking, he turned to the hound. ''Tis time we had our fish,' he stated, rubbing her head affectionately.

He shifted forward a little and Shenty leapt down and trotted into the Old Pen. Rising, he followed after her.

Thomas stopped in the doorway and quickly looked back at the woman. He had been overcome by the feeling that he was being watched, but her lids remained closed. He stood and stared, but there was no movement.

Disconcerted, he continued into the small enclosure and found Shenty already seated before her bowl. She looked over her shoulder at him as she waited for her supper.

'It will not be long, my friend,' he stated, stepping to the table and taking the parcel of fish from the pocket of his coat as it hung over the back of one of the chairs.

The scent of the mackerel wafted to him as he unfolded the leather. Taking the knife from his hip, Thomas then sliced open the gut of the smallest and began to take the bones from its carcass, pulling away the spine with its ladder of ribs. Shenty moved to sit by his feet, looking up expectantly and licking her lips.

'You will have your supper soon enough,' he said down to her, fingers slipping as he removed smaller bones and laid them on the waxed leather with the others.

Thomas' hands suddenly fell still and he turned to the doorway. Staring out, he listened intently, but heard only the gentle crackle of the fire.

'Did you hear that?' he asked, looking down at the hound, who simply stared up at him as she waited for her food.

He stepped to the door and peered to the right. The woman was still and silent, resting beneath the furs just as she had been when he vacated the living space. His brow creased as he stared at her, sure he had heard a soft moan arising from the room.

Dismissing it as a trick of his mind, he went back to the table. Removing a few stray bones, he then stepped towards the seaward door and placed the fish on Shenty's bowl, the hound following his every move and then tucking in hungrily.

Going to the counter before the window, he went to rinse his hands in the dinted bowl that rested there, its contents having been refreshed from the wooden butt outside the door after he had cleaned his patient. He stared down at the vague reflection visible in the water, his features faintly illuminated by the firelight from the other room. Though his face was but a collection of shadows, Thomas could see that he had grown into his father's likeness, the growth of hair upon his face adding to the similarity which was apparent.

'You have returned,' he stated to the shadowy form, watching the mouth of the image before him move and imagining it to be a greeting from father to son. 'Mother will be pleased.'

Images of his wasting mother came to mind as he stared vacantly down at his likeness. With a blink, he plunged his hands into the chill water, the ripples warping his image and pushing the sad memories back into the haunted vaults of his mind.

Thomas went back to the table, taking up the remaining mackerel. He made his way into the living space, walking past the back of the chair to the cooking frame. He took the woman's gown from it and placed the simple item of clothing over the head of the bed. Hanging his half of the morning's catch in its place, he moved the frame over the edge of the fire to both cook and smoke the fish.

Straightening, he went to the bedside and carefully seated himself, reaching out and taking the woman's right hand, cradling it in both of his. With gentle voice, he began to sing The Lay of Ailla, all the time staring at the face that he felt he knew so well.

Shenty came through from the Old Pen, her snout glistening with the remains of her meal. She sauntered over and leapt onto the foot of the bed, where she sat and proceeded to clean herself as her master sang softly into the night.

16

Thomas woke in the dead of night. He shifted in the chair, the wood creaking as he winced, twinges of pain in his lower back. The room was faintly illuminated by a glow emanating from beneath the ashes of the fire as he stared across at the figure beneath the furs, noting Shenty's vague shape curled at the foot of the cot in the gloom. The remnants of a dream receded from his mind like a gentle tide. He had found his father washed up on the shore and dragged him from the surf. As he carried him from Treen Cove the figure had transformed into that of his mother, her face filled with the gathering shadows of coming death.

He began to shiver, the chill having taken hold during his slumber. Rubbing the small of his back as he got to his feet, he went into the Old Pen and retrieved his long coat from the back of the chair. Donning it, Thomas wrapped it tightly about himself, but found his trembling becoming uncontrollable, teeth gritted against the bite of the cold.

Returning to the other room, he passed along the length of the bed and went to the woodpile in the far corner. Selecting a few small branches, he moved beyond the head of the cot and back to the fire.

Crouching by the cooking frame, he used the end of one of the branches to reveal the burning embers and then placed the wood upon them. He bent forward and blew gently until a weak flame took hold, flickering in the light drafts circulating about the cottage.

Thomas returned to the seat and tried to make himself comfortable as his back continued to ache. He reclined his head and hoped sleep would come upon him soon.

The fire spat, a few sparks arcing out of the pit and scattering about his boots. He watched them fade into darkness. 'Mother,' he whispered, tears glistening in the flickering light.

A soft groan lifted into the air. His gaze moved to the woman lying on the other side of the fire pit, seeing an expression of discomfort upon her face.

Sitting up, Thomas stared at her. No further sounds issued forth, her features sinking into lifelessness once again.

Slowly rising, he stepped around to the bedside, his shadow falling across her midriff as he felt the faint heat of the fire against the back of his legs. Thomas pulled back the furs to reveal her nakedness, Shenty raising her head and watching his activities.

Turning her away from him at the hip, he saw that she had not soiled herself and then let her body settle back onto the waxed leather upon which she rested. He looked to her face and stood transfixed for a few moments before slowly sitting on the edge of the bed.

Shenty got up and went to him, nuzzling his neck and licking his ear. Thomas distractedly rubbed her head as he continued to stare at the woman, the flickering light casting deep shadows on the left side of her face.

His expression fell. There, in the shadows, he saw the semblance of his mother's wasted visage.

'Mamm,' he whispered, eyes glittering as he turned away.

He abruptly stood, barely daring to glance at the figure upon his cot. The illusion was gone and in its stead the enigmatic woman's features had returned.

With pulse easing, Thomas made his way back to the chair and sat heavily. He did not heed the temptation to look across at the woman. Instead, he placed his left elbow on the arm and rested his head upon his hand, closing his eyes and wishing for the morning light to come quickly and vanquish the gloom within which he was cloaked.

17

Thomas removed the snare from where it had tightened about the large rat's shoulders. Resetting it at the base of the stone wall, he then tied the beast to his hip with another that he had already found in one of his smaller traps. He looked at the brace of rodents and frowned. He did not relish the thought of having to dine on them that night and hoped that he would have time to cast his net at Treen Cove.

Shenty sniffed the gatepost of the small field in which he stood as Thomas absently watched her. Marking it with her scent, she then looked over at her master.

He began to walk towards her, his sight turned within as he wondered about the woman lying within the confines of Ocean Mist. He had intimate knowledge of her physical existence, but no clue as to what lay beneath, what past she carried with her and who she really was. She remained a mystery and would do so until such a time as she awoke.

'I do not even know the colour of her eyes,' he mumbled to himself as he drew close to the gateway and Shenty trotted into the adjacent field, a thin mist clinging to the grass, but the sky above clear and a yellow glow to the east announcing the immanent arrival of the winter sun.

Exiting the second field, Thomas went left up the slope. He raised his sight to the rocky moor. Many were the times he and his father had ventured up to that peak, sat and looked eastward across the rolling landscape, Zennor north-east of their position, resting in the fold of the land below. He had sat with the weight of his father's arm about his shoulders and unyielding rocks at his back as he listened to tales of boekkas; goblins that his father said lived beneath the hill and scrambled out from amidst the rocks at night, emerging grey and clawed from their lair. They would hunt in the moonlight, eyes large and milky white. Woe betide any traveller lost on the moor on such a night.

Thomas shook his head sadly and turned from the moor, looking for the withered remains of a tree which marked the location of another of his traps. Seeing its sorry form, which was no more than a stump with feeble branches reaching east, he began to make his way along the slope towards it.

The call of home suddenly arose from deep within. His steps faltered and he looked over his shoulder, staring down the hillside.

The sound of Shenty's barking gave him a start and he came to a halt. Thomas looked up the moor to see her standing alert and facing homeward.

'You feel it too,' he said curiously as the sensation persisted, feeling like an invisible cord was tugging at his gut and attempting to draw him back to the cottage.

He looked at the stunted tree, the urge to check the trap keeping him in place as he fought with indecision. 'It would be foolishness to turn back when I am so close,' he stated to himself, moving forward, his stride quickened by the feelings calling him home.

He reached the tree to find the snare lying empty near its trunk, a smear of blood on the ground marking where crows had feasted on whatever creature had been caught within. With a frown, he crouched and reset the trap with quick fingers, the desperation to be on his way fuelling his haste.

Thomas stood and set off with purpose towards Ocean Mist. His hurried steps took him north along the grassland beneath the moor, Shenty trotting ahead.

The roof of the cottage come into view as he followed a gentle upward slope on the hillside, the modest dwelling gradually revealed as he rose to its small tableland. He could see naught that hinted as to his need to return and stared ahead in puzzlement.

Shenty came to a halt before the front gate despite her usual habit of leaping over the low and rotting structure. Thomas hardly noticed, taking hold and swinging it open without ceremony so that it jammed into the grass and remained in place at his back, the hound standing on the path, but making no move to approach further.

Ignoring the tree arcing over the wall to his right, he made for the door. Entering, his gaze immediately settled on the cot. The woman rested there as she had upon his departure, eyes closed and face pale.

Thomas stared at her, feeling the dampness of sweat beneath his arms after his swift journey home. The faint rise and fall of her chest was almost imperceptible, but it was now in evidence as the life which had been stowed deep within began to take back its domain from the darkness that had threatened to snuff out its light altogether.

'Good day, Young Thomas Carrow.'

Thomas jumped, heart skipping a beat. He turned to the healer as she stood in the doorway to the Old Pen. A smile rested upon her lined face, the wisps of white hair framing her features stirring as a breeze passed through the house, the seaward door open as Bersaba aired the interior.

'I trust thy endeavours have met with success,' she stated while stepping to the foot of the cot.

Thomas looked at her without comprehension.

'Thy traps,' she stated, nodding to his waist.

He looked down and then realised what she was referring to. 'A brace of rats only,' he replied, pulling aside his coat to reveal the vermin hanging beneath. 'I did not have time to check all the snares and so it may be that they are full.'

'Did not have time?' She looked at him quizzically, noting the perspiration glistening on his forehead and the redness of exertion upon his cheeks.

'I felt...' He sought the right word. '...*Called* home.'

Her eyebrows rose. 'Indeed,' she replied with a nod.

'How does she fare?' he asked, moving to the side of the bed and looking down upon the woman, noting that Bersaba had placed more wood on the fire, the flames dancing on the far side of the cot.

'She improves,' replied the healer simply.

'You will tell me no more?' said Thomas, his gaze remaining on the woman's face, the wound on her temple beginning to heal.

'There is no more to tell, Young Thomas. She is as she is. Ye can see as well as I what progress she makes. Life is awakening within her and stirring her body from time to time.'

He lifted his eyes to the old crone. 'You have seen movement?'

Bersaba nodded once again. 'A Little.'

'She moaned during the night, but when I saw her so still and pale this morning I believed it to be a fancy of my mind.'

'It was no fancy. She has spoken since my arrival.'

'Spoken!' He looked at her in shock.

'Mere mumblings, but if I am not mistook, they were words of a sort.'

'Of a sort?' His brow creased.

'They were not of our tongue,' she stated, casting her gaze over the patient lying before her.

Thomas continued to stare at the healer as her response sank in. He turned back to the soft visage of the woman beneath the furs, studying her as if trying to undo a riddle, but without success. 'Then it is as my mind whispered, she is not of the human world.'

The sound of Bersaba's chuckling surprised him and he turned back to her.

'Do you mock me?' he asked.

She smiled at him, crow's feet deepening. 'No, Young Thomas, only find amusement in thy words. Be not so quick to judge. There is more yet to be revealed by time's passing.'

'And yet you will tell me no more,' he replied, holding her gaze.

'I have told thee enough,' she said, her smile fading. 'If I have a mind to tell thee more I shall do so in good time.'

As Thomas looked at the healer he recalled what his father had once said to him. 'How much did you see in the entrails?'

Bersaba's laughter lifted into the air, eyes briefly closing as her skeletal hands moved to cradle her distended stomach.

'Do not believe all that ye hear of my doings, Young Thomas,' she replied when her mirth had faded to a mere smile.

'Then how do you come to know such things?'

She took a deep breath as she considered whether to enlighten him. 'Stones,' she stated. 'I have a pouch of such which were taken from these hills. I need only cast them to the ground and consult their design to see what is to come, though sometimes they will not reveal the future's secrets even unto me.'

'Stones?' he echoed with a doubtful look, her revelation diminishing his boyhood imaginings of her activities.

'Aye, 'tis so,' Bersaba confirmed with a nod.

The woman stirred beneath the cover. Movement took to the muscles of her face, which became pinched with pain. Her lips tightened and she let out a groan from behind them.

Thomas and the healer stared at her, gazing at her eyelids. They remained closed.

She shifted her head to the left and then right. Another moan lifted as her left foot kicked out and appeared from under the furs, her slender toes curling.

'Does she wake?' asked Thomas in a whisper.

'I think not. 'Tis but life returning and discovering the aches within her as it stretches itself through muscle and nerve.'

'Is there naught we can do to relieve her suffering?' He looked at Bersaba, his expression filled with concern.

'We are doing all there is to be done. Only time and the grace of Dor Dama can do more,' she replied.

He turned back to the woman. Her face was twisted into a look of such pain and anguish that his heart ached as frustration grew. Sitting on the edge of the bed, he carefully cradled her head in the crook of his right arm and brushed aside strands of dark hair from her forehead.

'Shhhh,' he said softly. 'It will pass.'

Bersaba stood silently watching as Thomas stroked the woman's cheeks with the backs of his fingers, her expression softening a little in response to the sight.

'You are safe and I will tend to your needs,' he stated, seeing movement beneath her eyelids and noting that her look of pain was replaced by confusion, the tightness of her skin falling away a little.

'The worst is over,' he added as the urge to bow his head and kiss her lips came over him with astonishing strength.

Feeling disorientated by the sensation, Thomas laid her upon the cot and rose to his feet, feeling heat in his cheeks as he stepped back from the bed.

Bersaba studied him. 'What troubles thee, Young Thomas?'

'She is some siren of the sea,' he whispered, 'some temptress washed from the rocks who now weaves her enchantment about my heart and mind.'

'No.' Bersaba shook her head. 'Thou weave thy own enchantment.'

He looked to her. 'You do not see and feel it?'

'She is not as ye say,' she replied, shaking her head again. 'Thy mind is a trickster Thomas, and long has it been so.'

It was his turn to shake his head. 'I feel her spell winding about my very soul.'

'There is a spell being woven, but not of her casting.' Bersaba's gaze glittered with unspoken knowledge.

'You speak in half-truths and riddles,' he stated with a touch of annoyance as the woman became still beneath the furs once again.

'I only speak what needs to be spoken.'

Thomas frowned at her. 'What *you* believe needs to be spoken,' he corrected.

'Think what ye will, Young Thomas. I have no need or wish to explain my ways further. All ye need know is that what I do is for the greater good, for the good of all.'

'Aye, so say you,' he said with a touch of bitterness.

The healer reached down and took up her bag from where it had been resting by the foot of the cot. 'I will bandy no more words with thee today,' she stated, stepping past him to the south-facing door.

Thomas watched her pass out onto the path, his body filled with tension. 'Will you return on the morrow?' he asked, his voice softer.

She paused and turned to him. 'Aye, and I shall hope to find thee in kinder spirits,' she replied. 'May Dor Dama bless thee.'

His head bowed as the healer stared at him and then set off, her hunched form held within Shenty's wary gaze as she backed away from the gate. She drew to a halt ten yards away and stared as the old crone exited.

'Ye can enter freely now,' stated Bersaba with a soft smile before continuing on her way, Thomas watching her departure from within the cottage.

18

He stared at the wooden plate set before him on the table. He had managed to eat the turnip and leeks, but could not stomach the small cuts of rat meat which still lingered there.

Thomas' expression of distaste remained as he looked at the net hanging over the seat opposite. He had gone to Treen Cove after Bersaba had left, wishing to escape the pressure that had built within the house due to their exchange and the call of the siren's lips. The tide pool had offered up no fish, but he had noted that one of his early attempts at mending a hole had come apart.

He remembered his father's patience when teaching him to cast it into the pool, Shenty barking and snapping at the glittering droplets that fell each time he heaved it back out. Even then the net was somewhat shabby, numerous repairs in evidence after having been passed down from his grandfather. He recalled that one of the weights along the bottom had been newly attached, bright and untainted, the others dull and discoloured by their time in the waters.

Thomas sighed and lethargically got to his feet. Taking up his plate, he emptied the contents into Shenty's bowl, giving a little whistle to call her in. Much to his surprise, she did not come trotting into the room.

'Shenty,' he called, standing by the seaward door and looking across the room.

She still did not make an appearance.

Frowning, he placed the plate by the bowl of water before the window. Stepping to the table, he dragged the net from the back of the chair on the far side and rested it upon the top, hunting down the break.

Thomas glanced at the doorway, wondering whether he should sit in the chair as he made the repair, but deciding against it as the image of the siren's face swam into his mind.

He had no wish to be near her, was made uncomfortable by the urge that had come upon him earlier and he once more considered the possibility that she was a creature of the sea. If that be so, then there would be more trouble for him if the folk of Zennor discovered her presence within Ocean Mist.

His frown deepened as he turned to the bench along the back wall of the Old Pen, stray pieces of rope hanging over its edge and beneath which the sacks of vegetables were gathered. Briefly glancing through the doorway into the living space, he then reached for a lidless wooden box resting amidst the selection of items gathered before him. Looking at the contents, he saw a spare float resting atop the coils of cord within.

Thomas took the box over to the table as the sound of the fire spitting lifted into the subdued gloom of the interior. The possibility of the bed cover catching light passed through his mind fleetingly as he set the box down.

He seated himself heavily and then took out a length of rope, drawing the net closer so that it hung down to his lap. With slow deliberation, Thomas began to mend the hole, angling it towards the doorway and the illumination of the firelight that spilled into the room.

He sat alone in the Old Pen without even his hound for company. She was curled upon the bed, choosing to remain by the feet of the creature occupying his cot. A feeling of rejection heightened his loneliness, the task at hand unable to distract him from feelings of isolation as he tried to concentrate.

Thomas took his time completing the repair, lacking the will, but knowing it must be done. Finishing, he lay the net on the table and turned to the doorway. He stared at the foot of the cot. The light of the fire had diminished, the soft flicker that permeated the gloom of the Old Pen caught in his sorrowful eyes, writhing there like the ghosts of his past.

He sat for a while with the shadows deepening about him. The images of his parents drifted through his mind, glimpses of his childhood that held more pain than they did pleasure.

Feeling the chill, he finally rose from the chair and made his way into the living area, boots soft upon the compacted earth. Thomas moved along the far side of the bed from the fire, forcing himself to glance down at the woman resting there. His gaze fell on the wound upon her temple and he knew that Bersaba's ointment still needed to be applied that night despite his wish not to venture near her.

He took a few logs from the woodpile in the corner of the room, tucking them in the crook of his arm. Passing beside the head of the bed, he crouched before the dwindling flames and placed them on, hearing a slight sizzle as the heat drove away the dampness which had settled in the bark.

Warming his hands, Thomas then stood and moved around to the far side of the cot. Bending, he picked up the small bottle and ball of wool from where they rested beneath. He pulled out the stopper, tipping a little of the salve onto the fibres. Leaning over, he began to apply the ointment, keeping his sight focussed on the wound so as to avoid the call of her lips.

The liquid glistened in the firelight as the flames steadily grew once again, the heat only faintly reaching him, its touch like a breath upon his cheeks. He ran the wool along the length of the sewn gash one last time and then straightened, pain in his lower back causing him to wince.

Stopping the bottle, he rested it on the ground beneath the head of the cot, placing the wool beside it. He glanced at Shenty as she lay curled by the siren's concealed feet, the hound not even deigning to lift her head during his activities, showing no interest in his presence.

He passed along the bed and to the far side of the fire, shoulders sagging as he seated himself in the chair. The wood creaked as his weight was brought to bear and Shenty's eyes opened.

'Here, Shenty,' he said, patting his lap.

She stared at him and then her lids lowered.

Thomas sighed. The fire crackled and its warmth radiated against his shins as he considered beginning a new carving to pass the time.

Rising again, feeling agitated and ill at ease, he went to the bench cluttered with wood in the rear right corner of the room. His gaze temporarily rose to the mermaid watching him from the lower of the two shelves above. He glanced over his shoulder at the woman upon the cot, wondering at the likeness and the possibility that she was a creature of the sea.

Shaking his head, he turned back to the driftwood. He picked up numerous pieces, scraping a chicken dropping from one length of timber and sighing heavily. None whispered of their desire to be transformed.

Thomas finally spied a piece of wood which already had the rough outline of a bloated fish and took it back to the seat. He rested it on his lap as he withdrew the small knife from his hip. With sharp cuts, flecks of wood falling to his legs, he began to whittle, allowing his mind to drift and finding a small degree of contentment in the consuming activity.

19

He woke to the darkness of her eyes. They called to him across the fire pit, a few tendrils of smoke rising from the ashes as the morning gloom illuminated the room. She was studying him with confused curiosity.

Thomas hardly dare breathe as they held each other's gaze for long moments. Silence pressed in. Naught moved.

She blinked. Thomas felt his heart pounding as he shifted on the chair. He felt movement at his lap and looked down to see the carving he had started during the night fall to the floor, landing on the earth with a dull thud.

Looking back at her, he found the woman watching his every move, curiously glancing at the object which had tumbled from his knees.

''Tis a carving of a fish,' he informed her. 'I must have fallen asleep with it still upon my lap.'

Her brow furrowed as she looked at him in puzzlement.

Thomas looked down and spied his knife resting on his coat, which was tightly drawn about him in order to ward off the chill. He took it in his right hand and held it up. 'I was carving,' he reiterated.

Her eyes widened, expression becoming one of worry as she stared at the small blade glinting in the dull light.

He quickly placed it in its scabbard and then held up his hands to show their emptiness as he slid forward on the chair and slowly got to his feet. Her fear intensified and she bunched the bed cover in her fists, pulling it up beneath her chin.

'I mean you no harm,' he said softly. 'I found you upon the beach and have been nursing you. My name is Thomas Carrow.'

The fright evident in her dark eyes was coupled with a lack of comprehension. She stared at him, shrinking back as he made to step towards her around the fire.

Thomas became still, seeing that she was scared and not wishing to worry her unduly. 'It must be a fearful thing to wake in the company of a stranger and unfamiliar surroundings,' he said, trying to reassure her with the gentle tone of his voice.

Seeing that his words had no effect, Thomas decided against going to her side. Instead, he crouched by the fire pit and took up the burnt end of a branch, poking at the ashes in the hope there were still embers by which to rekindle the flames. He had ne'er enjoyed the labour of striking flints and had sliced open the tips of his fingers on numerous occasions as a boy.

She slowly relinquished her grip on the cover. Her nostrils flared a little as she smelt the sweat of her body and the general mustiness of the cot. She slid her right arm from beneath the stitched patchwork of animal pelts and carefully touched her temple, discovering the wound and following its length, her fingers trembling with the effort of movement.

'Bersaba tended to the cut,' stated Thomas, watching as she explored the injury with her fingertips. 'She is a healer who lives hereabouts.'

She turned her gaze to him once again.

'It will not be long until the stitches can come out.'

She made no reply.

Thomas rose and she watched his every move. He stepped around the fire to where his tinderbox rested by the woodpile, picking it up and then taking a handful of kindling from the sack beside.

Making his way back to where he had been crouching between the pit and chair, he placed the handful of twigs and dry grass beside the fire pit. Shifting the ash from the centre with the burnt branch, he revealed a piece of granite set in the earth beneath, its roughness ingrained with soot. The kindling was placed atop the stone and then he removed his flints from the box.

'My father taught me how to light the fire and his father taught him,' said Thomas as he held the flints before the dried glass and began to strike one against the other.

'When you are recovered enough to walk we can visit the tidal pool where I cast my net for fish. That skill was also passed down.'

He glanced over at the woman to find her watching him, but she offered up no words. Shenty rose from her resting place, seating herself and nipping at her right flank.

A spark took, the resulting flame stirred into life by the drafts circulating around the dull interior. He watched it begin to devour the kindling and then got to his feet. The woman cowered beneath the covers, staring up at him nervously.

'I would not have nursed you if I wished you ill,' he said in a reassuring tone, holding his hands up once again.

She shifted further away from him, her taut expression showing the great effort required for such simple movement as she continued to recover from her ordeal.

Thomas sighed and went around the fire, passing between the pit and the granite wall where the cooking frame rested. Going to the wood pile, he took up a selection of large and small pieces of wood and took them back to the fireside by the chair.

Placing the thinnest upon the consuming flames, he listened to the crackle and hiss as he searched for words that may bring her some confirmation of his good nature. None were forthcoming and he poked at the fire with one of the branches, a touch of irritation showing in his sharp actions and not lost on the woman in the bed.

The sounds of Shenty's grooming and the burning of the fire filled the hush as Thomas moved to the chair, picking up the carving before seating himself. Glancing at the woman, he wondered if he should offer her food or something to drink.

Deciding to leave her in peace until her trepidation abated, he turned his attention to the piece of wood, withdrawing his blade in readiness. The point dug in, defining the scales, small flecks of wood falling as he concentrated on the creation and tried to clear his mind of all other thoughts. The Lay of Ailla came without bidding to his lips and he began to sing, the woman looking at him in mild surprise as the tune rose into the paling day.

20

Jago stood by the stable door of the old forge, the top open and its hinges creaking as the sea breeze gently banged it against the outside wall. The sound of wood tapping against granite was almost lost as dark clouds passed overhead and released a heavy downpour, water streaming from the top of the doorframe to mingle with the mud and horse manure of the track beyond.

'Marrek says there be a storm a coming,' he said, turning to the blacksmith, who stood to the right with sleeves rolled up his thick forearms, black hair clinging to the perspiration on his forehead and long beard woven into two braids.

'Marrek always says there be a storm a coming. I think those cows of his are just plain lazy, they be always sitting down,' replied Gerens as he brought his hammer down on the glowing horseshoe held in tongs upon the anvil, a few sparks skittering across the flat of the metal and falling to the blackened earth within the gloom.

Jago stared north along the rutted track passing through the village, seeing rain clouds interspersed with blue sky. His gaze then wandered west and he looked over the roofs of the homes across from the forge, tucked in the bottom of the shallow vale in which the settlement was located. Staring south-west over the patchwork of fields rising up the far hillside, he thought he could spy a thin trail of smoke above.

He looked back to Gerens as he smote the horseshoe once again and then turned it over, hammer rising into the air. 'Marrek also says he heard Carrow speaking of a mermaid. He spied him on Trewey Hill one misty morn and there was also mention of Bersaba.'

'Marrek likes to tell tall tales,' stated Gerens as he brought the hammer down. 'Do you remember when he swore boekkas had stolen one of his calves? He swore on the lives of the twins that them goblins had thieved it during the night and taken it into the hill.' He laughed and shook his head. 'I think the mead speaks on his behalf many a time.'

Jago nodded as he watched the smith at his work, the soot blackened walls and cluttered workbenches framing him in darkness. 'Aye, I recall it well,' he said, running a hand through the dishevelled mop of mousy hair that fell to his shoulders.

'He found the calf a wandering the next day,' said Gerens, the hammer swinging down again and followed by the sharp sound of metal upon metal.

'Then there were the time he said he heard the spirits whispering at the cairn and fetched people out of their beds to listen,' added the blacksmith, wiping his brow with a filthy rag, a smear left in its wake.

'It were the easterly wind,' responded Jago with another nod of his head.

'Aye, that and the mead.' Gerens turned to the rangy man standing by the door as the rain continued to pour. 'His cheeks are not made ruddy by the wind alone, Jago. He knows not when to still his hand and stop his drinking.'

'Tis true,' he conceded, rubbing his thin nose, 'though his words on the mermaid did hold conviction.'

The hammer swung again. 'As did his words on boekkas and spirits,' replied Gerens, pushing the shoe into the hot coals gathered in the fire pot standing on three legs to his right.

'There were the gleam of truth in his eyes,' stated Jago.

'The gleam of mead, more like,' countered Gerens.

'I did not smell it upon his breath nor notice its slur in his speech.'

The blacksmith shook his head as he drew the horseshoe out of the coals and placed it on the anvil. 'Even if he did hear Carrow speaking of a mermaid, what of it?' he asked, bringing the hammer down.

'You have heard the rumours.'

'Aye, made up by men who have naught better to do with their time than act as women with their loose tongues. I will

77

hear no such unguarded words here,' he stated firmly, the hammer falling once again.

There was a brief silence as the passing shower abated, the drips falling from the top of the doorframe lessening. The hammer struck a regular beat as Gerens turned the shoe and beat it, sparks flying as weak rays of light slanted in through the small back window, its open shutters stained by soot.

Jago looked out of the door, glancing up at the perpetually green sprig of oak fastened to the outside of the wooden lintel, a drop of water gathering and then falling from the stem. It had been placed there by the smith's father, so it was said, and its colour had ne'er faded.

His gaze moved to the hill where he knew Ocean Mist to lie hidden from sight. 'Carrow has not been the same since returning five years hence.'

Gerens paused his beating. 'I see no change other than that of age, but even if what you say is true, what harm is there in it? Has he given any cause for complaint or concern?'

Jago shrugged his narrow shoulders. 'That time may yet come if we do not act now.'

'Act!' He gave Jago a stern look. 'There is no reason to act. We should leave him be, allow him to live in peace upon the hill.'

'You may the rue the day,' stated Jago, raising his right eyebrow.

'Then so be it,' replied Gerens. 'I say he is no threat and will have no part of any action others may deem fit to take in his regard for it would be the action of fools.'

'Fools you say. What if I were to tell you that Father Blyth has spoken of the need to cast out Carrow's evil from among us?' Jago looked at the blacksmith, a smug expression upon his long face, feeling that he had won some victory of words.

'He said such? In church?' Gerens was clearly taken aback.

Jago's crest fell and he looked to the darkened earth. 'No, not in church. We were speaking on it yesterday over the wall to the graveyard.'

'He sees evil in any who do not attend Mass. Carrow is no more evil than I,' he said firmly. 'What is more, he is not among us and so there is no cause to cast him out.'

'I think you twist his words. You are well aware of what he means,' countered Jago.

'Aye,' nodded Gerens, 'and I like it not.' He lifted the horseshoe and placed it back in the fire pot as he shook his head with disapproval. 'He will need the consent of the village to act against Carrow.'

Jago nodded. 'True, but there are few who would speak against such.'

'Then I shall have to be the loudest voice.'

'You may shout until your mouth runs dry, but it will be no good. The folk have been wary of Carrow since his return.'

There was another brief silence. Gerens used the bellows on the contents of the fire pot, the coals glowing brightly with each puff of air.

'You may attend church every day, but I know the truth,' stated the blacksmith with a hard edge to his voice. 'What if I were to take exception to the rites you perform at Giant's Rock when the moon is in her fullness?'

Jago looked at him in surprise, unaware that his activities had been known to Gerens.

'What if Father Blyth were to discover your true beliefs?' The threat in his words was thinly veiled. 'I am certain some would use your adherence to the old ways in the same way you would use mere rumours of Carrow.'

Jago stood silent for a while as he thought on what had been said. He nodded slowly. 'What you say has its truth,' he conceded with his head bowed, 'but I cannot stop what already is in motion. Mark my words, the time will come when Carrow's presence will be challenged. It may not be tomorrow or even next week, but it will come as long as he lingers nearby.' He looked to the blacksmith. 'It is inevitable.'

Gerens' frown deepened. 'I fear you are right, though I would not wish it.' He stared down at the coals and occasional flames that licked at the air about the horseshoe resting there.

'He has already endured much, but for some there seems no peace.'

Taking the shoe in the tongs, Gerens placed it on the anvil and hammered it, the blow carrying the weight of his vexation, sparks showering about the hammer's head. He struck again, venting his feelings on the heated metal, the left curve of the shoe becoming dinted and bent.

'I will take my leave before the next shower blows in from the sea,' stated Jago, glancing out of the door and seeing dark clouds gathering to the north.

The blacksmith merely nodded his farewell as he continued his work.

'Mind how you go, Gerens.' Jago watched for a few moments, time beaten out by the clang of metal against metal. Turning, he opened the bottom portion of the door and stepped out onto the mud and manure, shutting it behind before setting off along the track to the south.

21

Thomas stepped down from the steep path and onto the sand of Treen Cove, the fishing net hanging over his shoulder. Anticipating the leaping arrival of his hound, he sidled to the right, but she did not land beside him as usual.

Wiping damp strands of hair from his forehead, he found Shenty still halfway up the incline, a sense of dejection about her demeanour. He was certain it was not the shower that had briefly engulfed them which had soured the dog's mood. Upon finishing the carving, he had discovered that his ward had fallen into the arms of a fitful slumber, Shenty curled at her feet. Thomas had needed to persuade the hound to vacate the cot before leaving, an event unheard of previous to that day. She displayed no enthusiasm and there had been no rushing off over the hills in search of something to chase or a suitable place to leave her scent. She had stayed at his heels with her tail low, as if scolded for misbehaviour.

'Come on, my friend,' he said, patting his thighs.

Shenty stared at him, her fur wet and eyes appearing sad. She slowly made her way down towards the sand, coming to a stop at the foot of the path, staring downward with sorrowful disinterest.

Thomas crouched by her side and roughed her head a little, hoping to perk her spirits, but she gave no response, not even licking at his hands in gratitude. 'Will you not snap and snarl at the surf?' he asked, pointing at the incoming tide, small waves tumbling and rushing in.

Shenty continued to stand at his side with head bowed. He frowned and scratched at the increasing growth of hair upon his face which was fast becoming a beard suited for the colder winter months that were drawing in.

Standing, Thomas began to move across the sand towards the ocean, hoping that the hound would eventually find the will to follow and frolic as usual. He approached the waves and then began the climb towards the tidal pool. Seeing something pale amidst the rocks in the periphery of his vision, he turned to the left, spying some material snagged on one of the uneven stones.

Thomas went over to investigate and found that it was a tatty piece of linen. Tugging, he pulled the cloth free and held it up, a few patches of damp sand clinging where it had collected during high tide. He could see that by trimming the ragged edges it would be a useful piece a good four yards square.

Thomas rolled it up, pleased with the find, and looked about the rocks for more. His sight settled on splintered wood lodged between the stones, the likes of which was unmistakable.

'A ship,' he whispered to himself, glancing down at the roll of material in his hands. 'She must have gone down in the storm the other night.'

Memories of the fateful day when his father and grandfather had been lost at sea arose from the depths of his mind as he wrung out the cloth, seawater dripping to the rock upon which he crouched and patting on his boots. His grip was tight, all colour pushed from his knuckles. His teeth were gritted and his eyes glistened, brow creasing and he twisted the linen as if trying to wring the memories which tormented him from his mind.

A thought suddenly came to him, its revelation gratefully chasing away the painful recollections. 'Was she upon the ship or did she sing it to its doom?' he asked, looking out to sea and wondering if his ward held her silence due to the possession of a siren's voice.

There was no answer bar the collapse of a wave upon the shore and the distant cry of a gull. He looked to the sky and placed the roll of linen over his left shoulder, where it lay over the repaired net.

Thomas made his way to the tidal pool. It came into view and he went still, his stomach knotting. He stared wide-eyed at the corpse floating face-down in the water and felt his pulse race, heart thunderous.

Body trembling, he forced his legs to take him forward, finding them weak. He came to a halt on the high nearside, the waves washing in at the far end.

The body was close, dark hair floating on the surface. It was dressed in brown leggings and a pale shirt. The left arm was shattered and bobbed loosely by its side. There was a large cut along the forearm, the sleeve torn and lying open to reveal the wound, the tatters of pale skin about it showing evidence of having been nibbled by fish.

Thomas swallowed hard. His heart was in uproar, mouth going dry and perspiration building upon his worrisome face.

'A sailor from the sunken ship,' he said quietly, hoping the sound of his own voice would bring some calm.

He looked over his shoulder in the hope of seeing Shenty close at hand, feeling ill at ease alone on the rocks with the corpse resting before him in the grip of death's eerie stillness. There was no sign of his hound and he presumed she sat waiting at the foot of the path leading from the cove.

Glancing around, he spied a length of timber to his left. Clambering over the rocks, Thomas retrieved its splintered form, tar darkening the wood. He tested its weight as he moved back to the pool, averting his gaze from the body that moved with each wave that washed into the far side, its head butting the rocks by his feet as he came to a stop.

He took a breath, bracing himself for what he must do. Tightly gripping the three foot timber, he bent and pressed the rough point to the small of the man's back. He pushed against the tide, moving around to the side of the pool with the progress of his task.

The body bobbed in the water and the wood came loose. He quickly stabbed down before the movement of the waves could take it back to the landward end. Putting too much strength behind the motion and missing the mark, Thomas caught it in the side and it turned.

He let out a yell and fell back onto the rocks, the timber loosed from his hand and clattering to the stone. The corpse

83

bore his father's face. The skin was drawn tight over its cheekbones, beard glistening and sightless eyes to the dark clouds as another shower drew in from the north.

'Son.' The whispered word issued from the corpse's mouth.

Thomas looked fearfully at the body as he scrabbled away. His boots fought for purchase on the slick rocks, hands lifting his rear from their hardness and aiding in the rapid retreat. The sound of his hide leggings tearing rose into the air before his back thudded into the cliff behind him.

'Son.' The word was soft and gargled.

'NO!' Thomas got to his feet and rushed from the scene, the image of his father's face peering back at him from the deep waters of his mind. He hurried over the rocks, feet slipping, cracking his right knee against one of the boulders in his haste to be away.

Face flushed with pain, he reached the sand. He ran for the path that would lead him from the cove, but could not deliver his escape from the sight that was now carried within. The tails of his long coat snapped at his back like some pursuing beast as the rain began to beat upon him.

Shenty stood alert at his sudden approach. Her hackles rose in response to her master's haunted look. She bared her teeth and growled at the diminishing stretch of sand beyond him as the tide drew in. The hound then began to bark, hoping to ward of the danger lurking somewhere out of sight.

The raindrops patted and splashed upon the rocks as Thomas hurriedly made his way up the path. It was awash in the deluge, streams of water cascading over the sides and running down its steepness as he gripped the guide rope. Shenty followed, glancing over her shoulder at regular intervals, the hair along her spine still raised as her coat began to drip and the wind howled against the cliff beside them.

His feet slipped on numerous occasions, but no fall came. He reached the carved steps and hurried up to the cliff-top, feeling great relief at escaping the confinement of the cove.

Rainwater blurred his vision as he strode along the coastal path without looking back. Wiping it away as best he could, he decided to check at least a couple of his traps, not relishing the thought of being contained within Ocean Mist, of having time to dwell or be caught in the spell of the siren lying in his cot.

Veering off the track to the right, he set off up the gentle slope. Shenty trotted by his side, still looking back from time to time as the shower passed and a pair of gulls glided overhead in watchful silence, making their way towards the cove.

22

He felt the weight of the rabbit hanging beneath the coat as he opened the gate to the front garden, the regular beat of the smith's hammer rising on the wind from Zennor. Shenty trotted up the path to the door, displaying some eagerness now that they had returned. Following after her, Thomas took hold of the handle and frowned at the canine before opening it.

He fell still. His ward lay upon the floor before him. She was lying face down upon the earth and had managed the drag the patchwork of furs from the cot in order to cover herself as best she could, her pale legs still remaining bare.

She tried to raise her head, but it fell back onto her left arm. A soft moan of anguish arose as Shenty looked at the woman and then glanced over her shoulder at her master.

Thomas shook his head and blinked, freeing himself from the paralysis of shock. Quickly shutting the door, he went to the woman's side.

She turned her head, looking up at him apprehensively, clearly not comfortable with his closeness as she lay helpless and vulnerable before him. Her eyes continued to exhibit fear, but there was also frustration at her own fragility.

Thomas pulled away the furs to reveal her nakedness, her expression falling further and tears glistening as she lay enfeebled. He carefully manoeuvred her onto her back, her left arm weakly moving to cover her small breasts, face tightening as she tried not to weep as a result of the predicament she found herself in.

Putting his arms beneath her, he raised the woman and gently placed her back onto the waxed leather upon the cot. He gathered up the patchwork of furs and quickly covered her, seeing her discomfort.

'Did you fall from the cot while sleeping?' he asked while straightening.

She looked at him tearfully. Taking her left arm from beneath the furs, she pointed at the wooden bucket in the corner of the room beside the door.

'You are too weak,' he said with a regretful shake of his head, feeling empathy as she struggled with her helplessness. 'It will be a day or two until you can use it, but even then it will be with my aid.'

She looked at him pleadingly, but still voiced no words. He reached forward to brush away stray strands of dark brown hair from her face, but she drew back from the approaching fingers as best she could, the fear redoubling within her eyes.

Thomas sighed and let his arm fall back to his side, his heart heavy as he recalled tending his wasting mother in the same way. He glanced over his right shoulder at the waste bucket and then turned back to her. 'We shall try,' he conceded, bending towards her in order to pull back the furs and pick her up.

She did not attempt to cover herself as her nakedness was revealed once again, her strength waning and surrendering to the humiliation of her predicament. He took her in his arms and she inhaled between her teeth in response to the aches and pains that filled her body, which hung limply in his grasp.

Thomas walked the short distance to the bucket with care. Lowering her feet to the floor, he took a firm grasp beneath her arms, feeling the sweat gathering in the dark hair of her pits as she suffered the situation and fought against the pain she was feeling.

He settled her on the bucket, but did not dare release his hold for fear she would topple. Standing bent-backed before her, he tried to adopt a blank expression as she briefly glanced at his face.

Bowing her head in misery, the woman began to relieve herself, the sounds filling the interior of the cottage and seeming thunderously loud in the hush. After a couple of minutes they fell silent and she nodded bleakly, not able to bring herself to look up at his face.

Thomas adjusted his grip, his arms aching. Lifting her, she tried to take some of her own weight, but her legs hung limp and useless.

He took her into his arms once again and carried her back to the cot, laying her down and smiling disarmingly when she glanced at him. Pulling the cover over her, he went into the Old Pen and fetched the bowl of water, along with a handful of rags that had been resting beside it on the counter before the seaward window.

She saw him approach with the items in hand and her brow furrowed. She took a deep breath to bolster herself, understanding what he intended to do. Thomas put the bowl on the floor beside the cot, glancing over at the fire on the opposite side and noting that it was in need of stoking.

Folding back the cover, he rolled the woman onto her side so she was facing away from him. He took one of the strips of cloth and dipped it in the clear water, squeezing the out excess before setting to the task of cleaning her. He did so with careful haste, not wishing to prolong her ordeal.

Satisfied that she was clean, he took a dry rag and rubbed the moisture from her skin. He noticed her body quaking and heard her sniffling. She was weeping.

Swiftly finishing, Thomas covered her. She did not turn, but continued to quietly cry as Shenty leapt onto the foot of the cot, circling a few times before settling down beside the woman's shins.

He straightened and looked down at her sorrowful profile, his heart reaching out to her. Without the intervention of hesitant thought, he bent forward and stroked her cheek with the backs of his fingers, seeing the glistening of tears as they spilled over the bridge of her nose.

'I am sorry,' he stated, his voice filled with the warmth he felt towards her despite the possibility that she may be a creature of the sea. 'At least you have your life.'

He continued to stroke her for a while, seating himself on the edge of the bed. Her sobbing abated and she closed her eyes as his fingers caressed her skin like gentle waves washing upon pale sands.

23

The cooking pot hung above the flames, a rabbit stew within. Thomas sat in the chair as the woman slept in the bed across from him with Shenty at her feet. He stared southward out of the window beyond the cot. They were at the edge of night, the blue of the sky steadily deepening as the first stars made their presence known.

A gentle knock sounded at the door as he considered rising to close the shutters on the chill. The woman did not stir as her body continued to recover its strength and the hound was equally lost in slumber.

Thomas got to his feet and stepped around the foot of the bed, passing along its length. He opened the door, Bersaba's hunched form revealed beyond.

'It is late to be passing,' he commented quietly as he stepped back to allow her across the threshold, Shenty looking up and letting out a low growl when she spied who was entering.

The old healer stepped past Thomas and moved to the bedside. 'The colour is returning to her cheeks,' she commented as she bent close and inspected the wound on the woman's temple, the hound loyally remaining on the cot despite feeling uncomfortable with Bersaba's closeness.

Thomas shut the door and moved around to the other side of the cot, his back to the fire and shadow falling across the furs. 'She woke for the first time on this very morn.'

Bersaba looked up at him. 'Indeed. What did she say?'

The hound growled again, lips curling back.

'Shenty!' snapped Thomas, giving the dog a hard stare. 'She has yet to speak a single word,' he stated, turning back to the old crone.

'She has not spoken?' she asked as if disbelieving her own ears, staring back down at the patient lying between them.

Thomas shook his head and followed her gaze, seeing the woman's eyes moving beneath her lids as she dreamt. 'She holds her silence, but for what reason I cannot tell.' The image of the body floating in the tide pool came to mind and his chest tightened as he recalled his visit to Treen Cove.

Bersaba glanced up at him. 'What are thee not telling me?'

He took a breath. 'I found evidence of a shipwreck. There was a piece of torn sail, timbers and a...' He licked his dry lips. '...A body.'

'A body, ye say?'

He nodded again. 'It was caught in the tide pool at Treen Cove.'

'Which is where thee found thy mysterious guest,' she added, turning back to the woman.

'Be she a siren, Bersaba?' he asked, his pulse elevated.

'This I cannot tell,' she croaked without looking at him.

'Cannot or will not?' He stared at the old woman, the wisps of pale hair shifting restlessly as they hung thinly about her head.

'Cannot,' she stated firmly.

'Then I fear for the time when words issue from her lips. What if I am spellbound and forced to do her bidding? What if the folk of Zennor discover the presence of such an enchantress here?'

'What if? What if?' she repeated with a shake of her head. 'Thou must act on what is, not what may be, Young Thomas. Ye were full of such questions as a boy when thy mother first began to ail.'

'But if she be a siren of the sea I could become enraptured by her voice,' he replied with obvious concern.

Bersaba turned her attention back to the woman. 'Why doest thou presume she will wish thee harm? Surely there will be a debt of gratitude for bringing life back from the depths into which it had been driven?'

Thomas thought on her words.

'Why doest thou think ill of her?' Bersaba turned to him.

'I...' He pondered further. '...I have heard stories.'

90

'We have all heard stories, but that is not enough to condemn her.'

'But the sirens call sailors to their doom,' he protested.

'So 'tis said, but ye are no sailor and she is not upon the rocks. What stories are there of sirens washed upon the shore and living upon the land?' she asked with her right eyebrow raised.

Thomas bore an expression of confusion. 'None.'

She smiled faintly. 'Then this story has yet to be told and it may be a tale of wonder.'

Thomas became thoughtful once again and nodded to himself after a few moments. His gaze returned to the woman lying oblivious upon the cot. His heart stirred and he recognised its increased vigour. He had felt it when looking upon her face for the first time in the cove and even before, when carving the figure of the mermaid, but had not wanted to admit the presence of his feelings for fear of her true nature. Bersaba's words had calmed the fear and the cage it had placed about his heart was weakened.

'It will only be a few days until the stitches can be removed,' commented Bersaba.

Thomas blinked. 'I beg your pardon?'

'The stitches,' said the old crone, looking across at him. 'The wound is not far from being closed beyond risk and they can be removed in a few days.'

He nodded. 'Should I continue to apply the ointment you left with me?'

'Aye, until the redness about the injury has faded to naught.'

'Then I shall need more. What remains in the bottle will not last much longer.'

'I will bring more,' she stated as she sniffed the air. 'Rabbit,' she said, eyeing the cooking pot.

'You are welcome to join me for supper,' he offered. 'It is a stew that simmers and will soon be fit for eating.'

Bersaba looked at Shenty, who was eyeing her unkindly. 'Ye have my thanks, but I shall be on my way before the storm comes.'

91

'There is a storm coming?'

'Aye,' she nodded. 'I feel it in my bones. There is always an ache before the winds and rains come and today the ache has been great.'

Thomas glanced at the shuttered seaward window as it rattled in place and thought he could hear waves crashing against distant cliffs.

'Take care, Young Thomas Carrow. I shall call again soon.' She went to the door and opened it, stepping out and looking back at him over her shoulder. 'If she speaks, do not give a care to thy fears, but follow what I see in thy heart. May Dor Dama bless thee both.'

His eyes widened in response to her perception of his feelings and he gave a nod. 'Safe journey, Bersaba.'

The healer closed the door and he heard her padding steps recede into the darkness beyond. A moan rose from the cot and he looked down to see the woman stirring with wakefulness.

Her lids lifted, gaze settling on his. He fell into her dark waters, swam in the depths that glittered with the warm glow of the fire behind him and was momentarily lost.

Blinking, her spell was broken and he took an involuntary step back. He stumbled, heels upon the soot covered stones ringing the fire pit. For an instant it seemed as though he would fall back into the flames and the woman reached out her right hand to him. Thomas felt surprise at her kindly action as he regained his balance without need of taking hold, Shenty watching from her position on the cover.

Standing by the bedside, he looked curiously upon her, wishing to unravel the mystery surrounding her origins and identity. 'What is your name?' he asked.

She looked up at him without comprehension, drawing her hand back beneath the furs as the fire crackled.

'My name is Thomas,' he said, placing his right hand to his chest. 'What is your name?' he asked again, indicating for her to answer.

Still she seemed not to understand his words.

'Thomas,' he stated, pointing at himself before pointing at her and raising his eyebrows expectantly.

Her expression changed as she fathomed his meaning. Her lips moved, but the word was beyond hearing. Clearing her throat, she tried to speak once again.

'Rosita,' she said quietly, the qualities of her voice hidden within the whisper.

'Rosita?' he echoed.

She nodded against the pillow.

'That is a name I have not encountered before, but it is one of beauty,' he said with a disarming smile.

Her brow furrowed as her look of bewilderment returned and she shook her head apologetically.

'You do not understand my tongue?'

She stared up at him blankly.

Thomas' smile faded. If she could not speak his tongue then she was not of Kernow. More than that, she was not of the country entire and he would have no way of discovering her truths.

He frowned as he looked upon her with contemplative seriousness. She would remain a riddle and her identity hidden in all but name.

Glancing at the door, he wished for the presence of the old healer, sure that she would have some solution to offer him. 'Maybe I should go after her,' he pondered aloud.

Shaking his head, Thomas moved to the window and closed the shutters on the deepening darkness, seeing no sign of Bersaba on the hillside beyond. He passed around the fire and seated himself on his chair. Peering over the flames, he found the woman watching him. A faint smile appeared on her pale face, a regretful look in her dark eyes.

'It is no fault of yours,' he stated, returning her gesture.

After a moment, he picked up the fish carving and withdrew his knife. He began to mark lines along both sides of its tailfin, carefully drawing the tip of the blade back towards him with steady hands. Trying not to dwell on thoughts of the woman's background, Thomas began to absently sing The Lay of Ailla, Rosita continuing to watch him and listening to the soft tune that seemed hauntingly familiar.

24

He ripped at the long grass of the front garden, grasping handfuls and tearing the blades away to then place them in the reed-woven basket resting to his right as he crouched on the muddy path. Water ran into his eyes as the persistent rain patted on his long coat. Memories of the herbs and vegetables his mother had once grown within the protection of the walls came forth. He recalled helping her cut sprigs or dig out turnips for cooking or bartering in Zennor.

He turned to the solitary tree in the far left corner, the inland sweep of its branches passing above the wall. It was the only plant remaining of those his mother had set down. A testament to the passing of his father and grandfather, it was the last mark of her presence in the world other than his own existence.

Looking to the grass he had collected, he blinked away the tears which had begun to gather. Deciding he had enough, Thomas took hold of the basket that his mother had woven during long winter nights many, many years before. He straightened and looked about the rolling landscape. Dark and heavy clouds concealed the tops of the moors both south and east of his position as the strong wind disturbed his coattails.

Staring south along the hillside towards the location of Bersaba's hut, he wondered when the healer would pass by again. It had been three days since last she visited and he sorely wished to speak with her in regards Rosita's origins.

Frowning, he made his way to the door. He reached for the handle, but his hand paused before taking hold, the feeling of being watched coming over him.

Thomas looked to the left, scanning the grey hillside rising above the cottage. His gaze fell upon a small figure, indistinct behind the thin curtain of rain.

'Elowen,' he whispered as the deer stood motionless.

Though he could not be certain, he felt that the creature was watching him. He looked beyond in search of Bersaba, expecting the hunched figure to come into view along the brow of the hill, but saw no sign of the healer.

Elowen suddenly bolted westward, rising towards the moor with strong leaps and bounds. Despite her speed, there was a grace to her passage as she passed over rock and grass.

Movement caught his eye as she vanished from sight. A figure had risen from behind one of the stone walls marking the fields upon the slope. It was Golvan, one of the local farmers, the bow in his hand being lowered behind the concealment of the wall.

The farmer touched the front of his cloth cap in greeting, giving a vague nod towards him. Thomas felt a touch of anger tighten his jaw as he saw an image of Elowen pierced by an arrow.

'Take your bow and do your hunting elsewhere, Golvan,' called Thomas, his anger adding heat to his words and silencing the voice within that gave warning to hold his tongue.

A look of surprise passed across the farmer's bearded face, his expression then hardening. 'Where I hunt is of no concern of yours, nor is it of your choosing.'

'I am making it my concern.'

'Do you threaten me, Carrow?' asked Golvan, facing his adversary squarely as he stood behind the wall, puffing out his chest and shoulders wide.

Thomas' stare faltered as his flare of anger faded and he regretted his outburst. 'I make no threats,' he conceded.

'That be a wise choice,' called Golvan up the slope. 'There is talk enough against you in the village without need of adding fuel.'

Thomas visibly sagged, wishing for the concealment of the cottage's interior, to hide from the world which had taken against him so.

'Heed my words, Carrow, for it would not take much on your part to turn that talk into action.'

96

Head bowed, he entered Ocean Mist, feeling the farmer's gaze weighting upon his back. Gratefully shutting the door, he found Rosita sitting upon the bed, looking over her shoulder with a curious expression after hearing the exchange of unfriendly words.

'It is naught for you to be concerned about,' he stated despite her inability to understand, forcing a smile that was shown to be a lie by the pain in his eyes.

Moving around the head of the cot, Thomas set the basket by the fire so that the grass within would dry and could be used as kindling in the days to come. Crouching, he checked the broth in the cooking pot suspended over the flames. Steam rose to his cheeks as bubbles stirred its watery contents, the basis of which had been the remains of the rabbit stew from the night before.

'I will have to go to the cove on the morrow and try to catch some fish,' he said as he straightened.

Trying not to dwell on the words of the farmer, he went into the Old Pen and fetched a pair of wooden bowls and a large wooden spoon. He set them down on the ground before his chair as he knelt beside them, wrapping a cloth about his left hand and gingerly removing the cooking pot from the blackened frame.

Half-pouring, half-spooning some of the contents into each bowl, a few drops falling to the earth, Thomas then reset the pot above the flames. He rose with a bowl in each hand and took one to his ward, who took it with a look of concern on her face as she studied his expression.

'Eat,' he encouraged with a nod.

Rosita looked down at the unappealing broth and raised it cupped in both hands. Sniffing it, she found no appetite awakening in response to the smell of the offering.

Thomas stepped around the fire pit and settled on his chair as Shenty looked at Rosita's bowl expectantly. Lifting his bowl to his lips, he briefly blew across the surface of the broth and then sipped it, finding it hadn't much taste or body, only a few shreds of meat and leek in evidence.

He watched surreptitiously as his ward took a sip and her small nose wrinkled in response. He sympathised as he consumed a little more and then sighed while staring at the food, lowering it to his lap, where the warmth of the bowl seeped through the hide of his leggings.

Thomas looked through the doorway to the Old Pen. 'There is a little bread left,' he commented, 'though it has begun to go green with mould. I will have to take a brace of rabbits down to the village and get some more when the occasion arises that I find such in my traps,' he added, looking over at Rosita.

She studied him and then glanced over her shoulder at the waste bucket resting in the shadows, turning back to him with an apologetic expression. He nodded his understanding and got up.

'Shenty,' he said, placing his bowl on the ground.

The hound leapt down from the cot and went to it. She sniffed the broth and then lapped at the contents despite the heat still contained within.

As Thomas made his way to the far side of the bed, Rosita placed her bowl on the cot beside her and weakly drew back the covers on her nakedness, the embarrassment she had initially felt having vacated during the few days since regaining consciousness. She had come to accept her condition and the limitations it imposed upon her existence.

Rosita carefully manoeuvred her legs over the side of the cot. He helped her rise, quietly impressed with the progress of her recovery, the strength steadily returning to her body.

With his left arm about her shoulders and her right about his waist, they made their way to the bucket. Her steps were short and stumbling thanks to her weak state, but her legs were able to take much of her weight.

Thomas helped her settle on the bucket and paused beside her as Shenty climbed back upon the bed, looking expectantly over. Rosita had no need of his support whilst sitting anymore and he was unsure what do to as she began to relieve herself.

'I found something for you,' he stated, recalling the item discovered while checking the traps earlier that day.

He walked away and into the Old Pen. Taking the tree branch from the table, he moved to stand in the room's entrance and held it up.

'I thought this may come in useful when you begin to walk without my aid,' he stated, taking one end in his hand and putting the other to the earth, taking a step to indicate the meaning of his words and then pointing at her.

Rosita nodded and managed a faint smile as the sounds beneath her came to an end. Thomas leant the branch against his chair and then went over to her.

She was soon resting back upon the cot, head sinking to the pillow as Shenty curled by her feet. He fetched the bowl of water from the Old Pen and placed it beside her, gathering the rags scattered on the ground beside the fire and handing them to her with a smile.

She looked up at him in welcome surprise. This was the first time she had been entrusted with cleaning herself and the relief showed in her expression.

'I am here if you need help,' he said, hoping that she could glean the meaning of his words.

Moving to the woodpile, Thomas took up his chopping axe from where it leant against the wall as Rosita began to wash herself. He stepped around the fire pit and picked up the branch he had found for her. Passing beyond the chair, he crouched and rested it on the ground before the seaward window. With careful aim, he cut away the stumps of smaller branches that jutted from its length.

Thomas gathered the off-cuts and took them to the fire, throwing them into the flames. Seeing that Rosita had finished, he went over and removed the rags and bowl. Placing the former back on the ground on the far side of the fire, he left the bowl beside them, eager to begin carving and knowing that its position would serve to remind him to change the water within its dented tin.

He sat and put the branch upon his lap, taking out his small knife. 'I was gladdened by this find,' stated Thomas without looking up as he began to cut the bark away in curling shaves. 'It meant my journey was not a wasted one.'

Rosita settled on her side after placing her cooled and unwanted broth on the floor beside the low cot. She looked across the flames at him as he whittled the branch, her dark eyes filled with the dancing light as night began to take hold beyond the shuttered windows.

'I cannot recall the last time I found all the traps empty,' he continued, the sound of his voice extricating him from what would otherwise be a palpable silence between them. He hoped that his ward also found some comfort in the sounds and glanced up to find Rosita watching him, her expression relaxed and drowsy.

'It was my grandfather who taught me how to set traps,' he stated. 'I must have only been around the age of four, but I recall his kindly face. It was long and weathered, skin marked by sun and age. His eyes were filled with kindness and wisdom, set in deep wrinkles that added to their warmth. His beard was streaked with bristles of the purest white.'

Thomas quickly glanced to the right after seeing movement in his peripheral vision. Finding naught but the gathering shadows within the Old Pen, his attention returned to the branch upon his lap and he turned it slightly before continuing to remove the bark.

'Just a mouse,' he mumbled to himself.

As he worked he began to speak more on his early memories of his grandfather, his feelings of loneliness and isolation lifting as he did so. Rosita watched him, tiredness eventually weighing down her lids as the fire flickered and kept the chill of the night at bay.

25

Gerens stopped his hammering, the large metal pin that was to be used to repair the roof of Marrek's barn glowing as he held it on the anvil with the tongs. He could hear men's voices and barking outside and looked to the door, both portions shut on the cold wind, drafts stirring the sooted spider's webs hanging from the eaves.

Listening intently, he recognised the voice of Jacob Trewey, but could not place the others. With brow furrowed, he placed the pin into the coals of the fire pot, rising from his stool and then striding to the door, hammer still held in his hand.

Opening the top portion, he peered out, the chill immediately ushering the heat from his face and the sky thick with grey cloud. Old Jacob stood ten yards along the track to the right, his small flock of half a dozen ewes bleating from time to time as his dog stood at his side. Before the aged farmer was a man that the blacksmith did not recognise, a knot of five other men standing a few yards further down the muddy track, two carrying spears and wearing leather armour.

Opening the lower part of the door, Gerens stepped into plain view. 'Is all as it should be, Jacob?' he asked loudly, holding the hammer in both hands.

The farmer focussed on the smith as he leant on his staff, barely four and a half feet tall and his lack of height accentuated by the presence of the other men. He nodded. 'All is fine, Gerens. These men are from Carrack Looz En Cooz. They seek answers to a riddle of sorts,' called the old man in his rasping voice.

'Gerens, there, likely knows more than I. Many are those who frequent his smithy,' stated Jacob to the man before him, who then turned to stare at the blacksmith, his face covered in a tightly cropped black beard and his leather coat darkly stained and studded.

'My thanks for your time,' said the man without turning back to the diminutive farmer.

He moved through the flock, the sheep baaing and a couple of their number eating the thick grass growing at the foot of the stone walls which flanked the track. The men behind followed as the wind swirled smoke about the track, drawing it up from the buildings below, their rooftops and the trees thereabouts misted by the fumes.

Gerens watched their approach, his grip on the hammer tightening. 'How can I help you?'

The leader of the group came to a stop five yards away, boots caked in the mud of the track. 'I am Arranz and I come seeking news of the coastline north of here,' stated the man. 'A ship carrying pilgrims was expected at Carrack Looz En Cooz some days ago, but its arrival ne'er came. We fear the worst and search for sign of its wreckage.'

'You are from St. Michael's Mount?'

'I have said it is so,' confirmed Arranz with a curt nod.

'Tell me, be it true that a giant resides with the monks there?' asked Gerens, having heard many rumours of the beast living with the monks atop the Mount, which rested off the coast a few miles south-east of Zennor.

The man glanced back at his comrades. 'Aye, of sorts,' conceded Arranz.

'I hear the merest sight of the creature is enough to strike fear into the hearts of even the bravest man.'

'I am not here to talk of such fancies,' stated the man with a touch of irritation. 'Have you heard tell of any wreckage being sighted upon the rocks north of here?'

Gerens looked at the man for a moment, disappointed that he was not to hear more of the giant, especially as the rumours of its residence had been confirmed. 'No,' he replied eventually, shaking his head. 'There has been no word of such from any who have called into the forge, though many are the rocks to which no man can go unless from the sea. Treen Cove is one of only a few places where there is a way down.'

'Treen Cove?'

'Aye. It lies in the eastern lea of Gurnards Head. There be a path leading down, but only one man takes its cursed route to the sands.' He looked at the hillside across the shallow valley to his left and pointed. 'Thomas Carrow.'

Arranz scanned the slopes as more palls of smoke swirled up from below and Jacob continued to stand with his sheep, listening to the exchange as best he could and hoping to question the blacksmith about it once the men had moved on.

'I see no dwelling,' stated the man as he turned back to the smith.

'It is there, upon a small table of land and hidden from the sight of Zennor.'

'Thomas Carrow, you say?'

'Aye,' nodded Gerens. 'It is said he goes to the cove almost daily despite it being a place of ill fortune.'

Arranz looked at him, deciding not to ask about the supposed ill fortune of the cove. He did not wish those who were with him to be unsettled nor cause their search to falter due to the superstitions of simple folk. 'I give you my thanks for your assistance and wish you good day,' he stated, making to turn to his men.

'There is something else I have need to tell you,' said Gerens with a touch of regret, his expression showing his discomfort. He had no wish to put voice to that which was the subject of many loose tongues within the settlement, but knew the men of the Mount must be made aware.

'Carrow is not...' He sought the right words. '...Not a normal man. He sees and hears things that others do not and can oft be heard talking to himself as he wanders upon the hill.'

Arranz looked at him questioningly, the two men with spears exchanging a glance.

'There are those that say he has been touched by his time up-country, for he lived in Truro for some years. Others say he has always been so,' expanded the blacksmith.

The expression of the man before him darkened. 'Your warning is heeded,' he stated, wishing to waste no more time

103

hearing foolish notions from such insular folk. 'We will take our leave and give our thanks for your time.'

Arranz went to his men. They exchanged a few mumbled words and then set off along the path, moving past the sheep as they headed north out of the settlement. Gerens and Jacob watched them march through the thick mud and then the old man wandered over, his dog padding at his side and glancing back from time to time as the ewes continued to graze the verges.

'Did I hear tell that the giant be real?' rasped the farmer.

Gerens nodded. 'Aye,' he responded as he watched Arranz lead his mean onto a track heading west, disappearing from sight behind Lacy Lugg's cottage on the left.

'I heard talk of Thomas Carrow.'

'Aye, that you did,' confirmed Gerens, not wishing to discuss the matter, aware that if he revealed what had been said it would soon be known to all, such was Jacob's way.

The old farmer looked at him expectantly. 'And?'

'And I must to my work. The pins for Marrek's roof will not hammer themselves,' replied the smith, stepping to the door. 'Take good care, Jacob,' he stated before entering the forge and closing the door, knowing that his actions would be deemed inhospitable, but wishing to forego further questioning.

Jacob stared at the wood with a sour look on his wrinkled face. He glanced up at the sprig of three oak leaves fastened to the lintel beneath a bent nail while pondering the recent events, noting a yellowing touch to their edges.

One of the sheep bleated loudly and he turned to his small flock. 'Come Blackberry, let us go where we are more welcome,' he said loudly, walking back along the track and patting his leg for his hound to follow.

26

Thomas dragged the rotten tree trunk across the hillside, the rope tied about its girth grasped tightly in his hands as it dug into his left shoulder. Its weight was increased greatly due to being waterlogged and he was struggling as the stump of a broken branch dug into the earth and carved a furrow in its wake, catching on stones and grass. The palms of his hands were sore and a layer of perspiration was building on his forehead despite the winter chill as the clouds pressed upon the landscape.

A murder of crows flew overhead. He looked up as they called out to one another, briefly circling and weaving before continuing their flight inland.

'To empty my traps, no doubt,' he mumbled to himself unhappily, wiping his forehead with the back of his hand.

Hearing voices carried on the wind, Thomas looked down the slope and spied a group of men walking up a farm track passing between the fields. Seeing the spears carried by two of their number, he felt the need for caution and slowly lowered himself into a crouch so that only the points of the weapons could be seen.

He looked across the hillside, able to see the smoke rising from Ocean Mist and wondering whether he should try and make for the concealment of home. He turned to the trunk, its bark patchy and the wood beneath pockmarked with rot.

'I could return for it later,' he said to himself.

Thomas glanced at the spear-tips and felt a touch of apprehension. The course on which the men were set would take them close to the cottage and he worried that Rosita's presence would be discovered. A woman delivered onto the sands by the sea would be looked upon with suspicion at the very least and he shivered at the thought of what trials she may have to endure as they sought out her true nature.

Keeping low, he set of with haste. The wind ruffled his hair as he kept a watchful eye on the progress of the men. The cottage came into view over a small brow and halted. The men were drawing close and there was no opportunity to reach it without being seen.

His body tensed as the man leading the group took hold of the gate leading to the humble abode. Arranz began along the path to the door, the men with him filing through the gate behind.

'HEY!' called Thomas, quickly standing and waving his arms in the air as he began to run towards them. 'HEY!'

Arranz turned and stared, bringing the group to a stop barely four yards from the door.

'What is your business here?' asked Thomas breathlessly as he closed on their position, unable to hide the look of alarm upon his face.

'Are you Thomas Carrow?' asked the man with the black beard and studded coat.

'Who be asking?' replied Thomas as he stopped at the gate, placing his left hand to the cold stone of the wall beside and catching his breath.

'My name is Arranz Calder. We are seeking any news of wreckage upon the rocks north of here.'

'Wreckage?' He glanced down, hiding his eyes from the men before him in the hope they would not glean the truth.

Arranz studied him and then moved around his men, closing the distance between them. 'What do you know?' he asked, his tone filled with certainty.

Thomas lifted his gaze momentarily. 'I know naught of any such wreckage,' he said, the image of the body coming to mind.

'From your manner, I swear it is not so.'

Thomas looked to the cottage, smoke being drawn from the hole in the mossy thatch, the shutters thankfully closed upon the cold day. The longer the men lingered the greater the chance of Rosita's discovery, and it was this thought that loosened his tongue. 'I have seen broken timbers in Treen Cove,' he conceded, 'and the remnants of a sail.'

Arranz nodded, satisfied with his ability to detect a lie. 'Where is this cove that you speak of?'

Thomas pointed north. 'It lies east of Gurnard's Head.'

'What is this Gurnard's Head of which you speak?'

''Tis a headland that reaches into the sea beyond all others along this part of the coast. You will find a steep path that leads down the cove's east cliff.'

'You do not offer to guide us there?' asked Arranz pointedly.

The sound of Shenty barking arose from the cottage and Thomas looked over with a pained expression, fearful that the shutters of the window would open to reveal Rosita beyond. Arranz studied him curiously and briefly glanced at the low building.

'Will you accompany us?' asked Arranz.

'I...' Thomas shifted and scratched at his beard, which was nearing its winter fullness. 'I have timber that needs to be taken in. It was left upon the hillside when I saw your approach.' He glanced back the way he had come.

Arranz continued to hold him in his gaze, wondering at the strangeness of his behaviour. He briefly considered asking to look inside the cottage, thinking that maybe Thomas was concealing some booty found amidst the wreckage, but the words of the blacksmith came to mind. Gerens had warned him that Thomas was not as others.

He looked to the cottage once again while he debated his course of action.

'We should be on our way if we wish to search the cove and return to our lodgings before nightfall,' said one of the other men.

His thoughts disturbed, Arranz nodded and then turned back to Thomas. 'We shall continue with our search, but be warned, if you have not told us all there is to tell then the occasion may arise when we return to question you further on this matter.'

'I have told you all,' said Thomas, forcing his gaze to meet that of the man before him, pulse racing.

107

There was a moment of stillness and then Arranz stepped towards the gate, Thomas moving out of the way and letting him pass. The other men followed, one of those carrying spears pausing in the gateway.

'Be sure you have told us all, my friend, for we will not be so accommodating should we have to return,' he said in a low growl.

'That is enough, Uriens!' snapped Arranz.

Uriens snarled and walked on, the men making their way around the right-hand side of the cottage. Thomas watched as they vanished from sight and then began up the path, taking deep breaths to calm the beating of his heart.

He rushed into the cottage, Rosita craning her neck to look up at him with concern as she lay upon the cot. He was grateful to see that the shutters were closed over the seaward window and placed a finger to his lips as he glanced down at his ward.

Thomas hurried to the far side of the interior and peered through the small gap between the shutters. He could see no sign of the men, but believed he could hear the vague sounds of their diminishing steps.

Going into the Old Pen, he went to the seaward door, the chicken perched on the table clucking as he hurriedly past by. Hearing no evidence of the men's presence, he opened it a little and looked out. They were barely visible, their bodies hidden by the slope of the hillside as they descended towards the northern coastline.

He stood and watched as their heads sank from sight, feeling relief and hoping that their threat of possible return was an empty one. A nagging doubt whispered in his mind. Had Arranz been convinced that he had no more to tell?

Thomas shook his head, trying to cast the unsettling question aside. He shut the door and glanced down at Shenty's bowl. The traps had been empty once again and he had not found the time to fish at the pool.

Going into the other room, he stood just inside the doorway. 'Did you call the ship to the rocks?' he said softly, the question asked of himself rather than the mysterious woman lying beneath the furs before him.

She cocked her head to one side and looked at him quizzically.

Thomas studied Rosita's gentle features. He found it almost impossible to conceive of her causing anyone harm. The idea seemed contrary to the fragility that she exhibited, though it was a fragility at least partially enforced by her condition.

'I must fetch the wood before it is taken by someone else,' he stated, wishing for the distraction of activity.

Going to the door, Thomas glanced back at Rosita before leaving the cottage. He walked along the path to the gate as the first drops of rain began to fall and took the chill air deep into his lungs as he turned his deliberations to matters of sustenance. He hoped that the chickens had laid at least a couple of eggs or it would only be vegetables for their supper, the last of the previous day's broth only fit for Shenty's consumption.

Fastening his coat as the rain became persistent, Thomas bowed his head to the heavy clouds and made his way back to where he had left the tree trunk. The wind strengthened, gusting about him as a soft howl sounded from the moor.

He looked up at the rocky heights and memories of his father immediately surfaced. 'Always close at hand,' he mumbled, his parents ne'er far from mind, lingering in the shadows and ready to come forth at the slightest prompting.

Reaching the glistening trunk, he stared down at its rotted length, the head of his axe buried in its upper side so there was no need for it to be carried. 'Corpses everywhere,' he whispered.

Thomas stooped and picked up the rope. Holding it in both hands, he took it over his shoulder and began to haul the wood back to Ocean Mist.

27

He woke with a start and sat bolt upright in the chair. The night was filled with screaming. Shivers raced up his spine as his pulse was set to a gallop.

Thomas stared across the fire pit. Rosita writhed like one possessed, the red glow of the smouldering embers upon her skin. Her screams continued to fill the cottage as Shenty cowered at the foot of the bed and stared at the wide mouth from whence the fearful sounds issued.

Rising hastily, Thomas went to the far side of the cot as his ward's body continued to convulse, arms and legs flailing wildly. Her eyes were wide open. He waved his hand before them, but her sight was elsewhere.

Her head snapped from side to side upon the pillow and he feared that she would do herself an injury. Seating himself beside her, Thomas gathered Rosita into his arms, holding her close to ease her violent movements as best he could.

The screaming stopped abruptly. There was a sudden gasp before her body went still and fell limp against him. She whispered a few words of her alien tongue, breath upon his neck.

'You were dreaming,' he said as he held her at arms length and sought out her eyes.

She looked at him, face glistening. He saw fear retreating from her gaze, the tension fading from her expression.

Rosita put her arms about him and drew herself close once again. She began to weep against him, the shudders of her outpouring causing him to hold her tightly as if to encourage the tears to empty from her.

Thomas stroked her dark hair as Shenty sat at the far end of the cot and watched. Her tears slowly abated, body falling still within the comforting warmth of his embrace as the shadows deepened and the embers of the fire began to blacken and fall cold.

Continuing to caress her hair, Thomas began to sing The Lay of Ailla, as his mother had done when he woke from bad dreams as a boy. The half-sung, half-spoken words filled the gathering gloom with their gentleness, soothing the last of Rosita's night terror.

The song came to its sad end and he continued to hold her close, a thoughtful expression upon his face. 'I think the sea brought you to me,' he said. 'It heard my song of loneliness and washed you upon my shore.'

There was a gentle snore from his shoulder and he realised that Rosita had drifted into slumber. Hoping that she would find sleep without disturbance, he carefully laid her on the cot. He bent over and picked up the bed cover, standing and spreading it over her.

'Rest well, Rosita,' he said quietly, stroking her cheek before making his way back to the chair on the other side of the pit.

Seating himself, Thomas looked over at his ward for a time, only the faintest light illuminating her presence. Leaning his head against the high back, he felt grateful that his grandfather had made such a chair.

He closed his eyes, but found no weariness within his body or mind, only an aching in his shoulders as a result of dragging the trunk home earlier that day. He shifted in the seat, unable to find any comfort by which to encourage rest.

After a while, Thomas opened his eyes once more. The screams to which he had woken had caused his fatigue to take flight. Glancing down at the fire, the trunk resting to the left as it dried and the cooking frame in its place beside the wall beyond, he decided to continue carving the walking stick.

He slipped from the chair, taking care to make as little noise as possible. Moving over to the bag of kindling, he took out a large handful and then crouched beside the ring of blackened stones. The last few embers were uncovered with a small branch and he placed the dried grass upon them, blowing gently until flames took hold.

Thomas went to the much diminished woodpile and selected a few of the smaller pieces. Setting them upon the fire, he sat on his haunches and watched the spellbinding flicker, the licking dance of the growing flames reflected in his wide pupils.

The light finally enough to work by, he returned to his seat and took up the branch, its bark removed and the nubs of smaller stems cut away. He studied it, turning it over in his hands as he waited for its whispers. There was a large knot near the top which pleasingly marked the boundary of the grip, giving the lower edge of the bearer's hand something to rest on.

Thomas smiled thinly as the wood spoke to him and he knew what should be carved upon it. Laying the stick across him, the upper portion raised by leaning it upon the right arm of the chair, he took out the knife and began to carve.

Time was marked by the slice and cut of the blade. He hummed The Lay of Ailla when at first he began, but it softened and faded as he became lost to the task. The fire crackled and the wind grew stronger, rattling the shutters at the seaward window behind him. One of the chickens clucked briefly before settling back down as it roosted upon the corner of his table of driftwood. Rain came pattering, seeping beneath and between the shutters to run down the wall and darken the earthen floor.

The dim light of morning slowly made itself known through the crack beneath the southern door, the rain still beating its steady rhythm. Thomas' lap was covered in shavings as he finished the last of the shoal of small fish that circled the handle of the stick.

Lifting it to eye level, he turned it slowly and smiled contentedly. Slipping his knife into the small scabbard, he rose and went into the Old Pen, hunting out a pot of wood stain that he knew to be stowed upon the bench there. Finding it amidst the oddments stored above the sacks of vegetables, he took it to the table, the pungent smell filling his nostrils, one laced with the odour of the rotting vegetation used to create the thick liquid. His uncle had shown him how to make it and put much faith in its ability to protect and strengthen both leather and wood.

Laying the walking stick before the pot, he seated himself and then began to rub the stain into the wood with his right hand. There was a sense of satisfaction as his slick palm passed along the wood and he wondered if he should have smoothed it with sand from the beach, as his grandfather had done when making the arms for the chair in the living space.

He shook his head as he dipped his hand in the stain and let the excess drip back into the pot. There was need of smoothness on the arms, but no such need in regards the walking stick.

Completing the task, Thomas stood the stick by the seaward door in order to dry. Washing his hands in the bowl of water placed before the window, he listened to the rain on the shutters and watched water seeping down the wall. There was another task he wished to perform, one that had drifted into his mind as he carved.

He wiped his hands on his leggings as he went back into the other room. Pausing to smile at Rosita's sleeping form, he moved to the right, crouching before the old chest that still rested in its position by the wall, one that would have found it beneath the cot before the woman's arrival.

Lifting the lid, he looked at the clothes within. Some had been his father's and were retained due to their similar build. His mother's clothes had been bartered by his uncle prior to leaving for Truro, exchanged for foodstuffs both for them and the mule that pulled the cart upon which they had travelled.

Ushering the ghosts of his parents from his mind, Thomas rummaged through the scant offerings. He selected a woollen shirt of deep green and a jerkin which had seen better days, the leather worn and tainted by white mould. A pair of tatty boots which he knew to have a hole were taken out and placed on the earth. Finally, he removed a pair of hide leggings, the stitching coming undone in places and the single pocket hanging loose.

Draping the clothes over his arm, he closed the box and straightened. Stepping to the bed, he laid the items upon the

113

covers at its foot. Rosita was recovered enough to start gaining her autonomy and it would not be long until she wished release from the cot's confinement, but the gown in which he had found her would be of little use in winter's chill.

Thomas stepped to the south-facing window and opened the shutters on the grey day. Rain dripped from the granite lintel, but did not gain entry thanks to the northerly wind, which passed by with barely a breath reaching into the cottage.

Taking in the fresh air as a thin haze of smoke was drawn out about him, he decided to make the journey to Treen Cove while his ward still slept. He would check the traps on his return and hoped that enough meat would be found to last a good few days.

28

The pocket of his coat bulged with a parcel of fish as he bent to check the trap at his feet. Thomas had caught five mackerel in the tide pool despite reservations about visiting the cove, thankful to find no sign of the men who had passed by the day before. A rabbit hung at his hip and he was pleased with the fruits of his labours. He and Rosita would have plenty of meat to sustain them for a week or more and half of the traps were still to be checked.

His smile faded as he pulled aside the wet tufts of grass that hid the small snare. There, lying upon the stony ground with its fur matted by rain, was a weasel. The cord was tight about its midriff, pulled in above the bulge of its narrow hips.

He looked sadly upon its still form, recalling his mother telling him that they were creatures of magic, able to transfix their prey with a strange dance. None had ever been caught in his traps before and he suspected this was due to their magical nature rather than their diminutive stature.

He sighed and reached to take the corpse from the trap. The weasel suddenly turned and sank its teeth into his index finger, biting down hard.

Thomas let out a yell of shock and pain as blood dripped from the wound, the beast keeping its jaw clamped tight. It had seemed dead, but there was clearly fight left in it yet.

Overcoming his surprise, he reached down and prized its jaw from his finger, quickly removing both hands from within its range. Looking at the puncture wounds, he felt a flush in his cheeks. He turned to the animal, which struggled against its restraint, the cord pulling tighter about its body.

His left hand darted down, grasping its neck. He pushed it against the ground, limiting its ability to scratch and bite. Taking out the small knife which was habitually at his waist, he took it to the snare with as much care as he could. The creature squealed and fought, but he managed to cut the cord without inflicting a wound.

Releasing the weasel and moving hastily back, he watched as it scampered away and vanished in a scattering of rocks further up the slope, apparently uninjured by its entrapment. He stared for a moment and then tucked the knife away. He could feel his pulse in the pain of the bite and a wash of watery blood ran down his palm as the raindrops diluted its crimson.

Thomas frowned and looked to the cut snare. Crouching, he tied the ends together as best he could and then reset it. He stared at the small hoop and wiped rainwater from his eyes as the grasses about him shivered in the wind.

Standing, he scanned the hillside. His gaze was attracted by movement down the slope to the north. Bersaba was walking in his direction through the grassland that rested between the high moor and fields below as she headed inland, presumably to her hut.

Thomas began towards her. The healer looked up and a smile deepened her wrinkles as he approached.

'Good day to thee, Young Thomas,' she called in her croaky voice.

'Good day, Bersaba,' he replied as he stopped before her.

'I have just visited with thy ward.'

'Rosita.'

'Rosita,' she echoed with a nod, the wind toying with her thinning white hair. 'From whence does she hail?'

'This I cannot tell you for she does not speak our tongue,' replied Thomas, wiping a drip from the end of his nose.

'So 'tis certain, she is alien to these lands,' said Bersaba thoughtfully, addressing herself rather than the man before her.

'Then you know not of her origins?'

Bersaba shook her head. 'I left a bottle of ointment upon thy table,' she stated, changing the subject. 'I do not think she is in need of it. The wound heals well and the stitches can be taken out when thee are ready to do so. It may be thou art in

116

need of it more than she.' The old crone glanced at the bite upon his finger.

Thomas looked down in momentary confusion and then returned his gaze to her. 'Aye, a weasel in one of my traps fooled me into carelessness.'

She chuckled to herself. 'They are wily creatures, Young Thomas, as are many that dwell in these parts.'

'I have sorely learned my lesson.'

Bersaba laughed again. 'Indeed,' she responded, her eyes sparkling. 'Have thee more to tell of Rosita?'

'She gains strength daily and it will not be long before she can walk without my aid. I have made her a stick by which to guide her steps when that time comes.'

'Aye, I spied such by the seaward door. The fish are a touch I am sure she will admire,' she said with a knowing smile. 'It shows thy truth.'

Thomas looked at her quizzically. 'What be your meaning?'

'Words are mere trifles. ''Tis in deeds that we reveal ourselves. Sometimes our deeds reflect our words, sometimes they are contrary, but always they show the truth of our nature.' She smiled at him warmly.

'So ye see, Young Thomas, it matters not that thee do not share the same tongue. Thy care and consideration is shown in the carving upon the stick and the gift of the clothes upon the cot. In such ways thou shalt also discover her truth.'

He pondered what she had said and nodded. 'She has given me no cause for concern as yet,' he stated, 'though she suffered a terror during the night and I was woken by her screams.'

'We all suffer bad dreams.'

'Even you?'

Bersaba chuckled once again. 'Even I,' she said with a nod. 'I am not so different from any other, despite what some may say about dark arts and magic. Ignore rumour and think on my deeds, Young Thomas, for there lies my truth also.'

She briefly looked past him. 'It seems I am being summoned.'

He glanced back and saw Elowen. The deer stood at the bend which took the track westward to the healer's abode. 'She needs to take care in these parts, there are some who like to go hunting upon the hills.'

Bersaba stared up at him, her kindly smile still in place. 'Of this she is well aware,' she replied, 'though thy concern is duly noted.'

She placed a withered hand upon his right shoulder. 'Thou art a good man, Young Thomas. Rosita will see it clear enough.'

'Why do you say such a thing?'

The old healer chuckled and moved her hand to his chest. 'I see thy heart and find its growing warmth echoed in thy deeds and thine eyes, as will she.'

He felt heat in his cheeks and turned his gaze to the stony ground at his feet. 'Are my feelings truly that plain to see?'

'What did I say to thee only moments ago? Look to the deeds and all is clear. The walking stick and the clothes say much, as does thy care during her time of need despite concerns as to her nature.'

He sighed deeply. 'I still have those concerns. I fear hearing her voice and the spell it may put me under.'

'I think thou art already under her spell,' responded Bersaba with a grin.

''Tis true,' he said. ''Tis a spell I have been under since first I set eyes on her.'

'Then it may be that she is a siren of sorts, but not of the likes that should cause thee undue worry.'

There was a soft bark from along the track behind him.

'Elowen calls me home,' said the healer, taking her hand from him and stepping past.

'I hope to see you soon,' he said in parting.

'I am sure thee will,' she said without turning to him, a certainty to her tone. 'May Dor Dama bless thee.'

Thomas watched her hunched form diminish, the deer no longer visible. He noticed that her feet were bare despite the cold and wet. A thin smile curled his lips as he wiped rainwater from his forehead. Moving up the slope, he made for the next trap of those he had yet to check.

29

He walked along the path to the door with the weight of three rabbits and a large rat at his hip, the parcel of fish still bulging in his pocket. Thomas smiled, feeling well disposed towards the world for the first time in recent memory. Dor Dama, Earth Mother, had truly blessed them on that day.

Opening the door, he found Rosita perched on the near edge of the bed wearing the leggings he had left upon the furs. She was fastening hoops of wool about their corresponding wooden toggles at the front of the green shirt, both items a loose fit. Shenty was sitting on the floor a couple of yards in front of her, observing every movement with interest.

Looking up at him, she smiled brightly, brushing her ruffled mane of dark hair from beneath the collar to tumble down her back. She said something in her native tongue, her voice causing him to think of warm honey, tones rich and deep.

'I am glad the clothes meet with your approval,' he replied, the meaning of her words apparent in her expression.

'I have caught a good many fish and the traps gave a good yield today,' he stated while shutting the door. 'We will have meat aplenty for the next week, even after I take two of the rabbits down to Trewey Farm to trade for bread and salted butter.'

He pulled back his coat to reveal the beasts hanging from the leather ties at his hip and she nodded before picking up the jerkin he had left for her. Her strength beginning to fade with the effort of dressing, she weakly placed her right arm through and then struggled with the left.

Thomas stepped forward and helped her. 'There,' he said.

She glanced down at herself and then looked up into his face. 'Gracias,' she said with a nod of gratitude, her eyes becoming hooded as weariness came upon her.

Rosita glanced at the waste bucket in the corner, her smile fading as she pointed at it.

'Wait,' instructed Thomas, holding his index finger in the air to indicate that she should remain where she was.

He went quickly into the Old Pen. Collecting the walking stick from beside the seaward door, he found that the stain had almost dried, merely a little tacky in places.

Going back to stand beside Rosita as she continued to sit on the edge of the cot, he held it out to her. She stared at it, sight settling on the shoal of fish circling the grip. She slowly took it from him and moved the carved handle closer, studying the scales and fins of the fish while turning the stick in her hands.

Lifting her gaze to him, she reached for his right hand and gave it a gentle squeeze. She placed the end of the stick to the floor and readied herself to rise, gathering her strength. With her hand still in his, she got to her feet, gripping the staff tightly.

Rosita moved away from him, steps foreshortened by her condition. The sound of the walking stick against the earth marked her slow progress as she covered the relatively short distance to the bucket. Leaning the aid against the wall and pulling the leggings down to her knees, she carefully lowered herself.

Thomas made his way back into the Old Pen and took the rabbits and rat from his hip, the latter suitable for Shenty's supper. He withdrew the parcel of fish and placed it beside the bounty of his traps on the tabletop, looking upon the array of foodstuff with an expression of satisfaction.

'I shall take the rabbits down to Zennor on the morrow,' he stated, 'and tonight you shall…' His words fell silent when he turned to find that Shenty had not entered the room despite thinking that he had seen her in the periphery of his vision. He was momentarily puzzled, staring at the patch of earth where he had expected to find the hound.

Shaking his head, he heard the creak of the cot as Rosita returned to its confines. He stepped to the doorway to find her sitting on the edge, the white of her thigh visible where the stitching was coming apart along the seam of the hide leggings.

'We will be having smoked mackerel tonight with boiled vegetables,' he said to her with a kindly smile.

Rosita looked at him, strain evident in her expression and a layer of perspiration glistening upon her forehead. Pulling the patchwork of furs over herself, she then settled and lowered her head to the worn pillow, the tension in her face visibly diminishing as she rested.

'I shall leave you in peace.'

Rosita forced a smile before closing her eyes. Thomas stood and stared at her awhile. The urge to walk over and kiss her suddenly came over him and he was taken aback by its force.

Moving back to the table, he could feel the quickened beat of his heart. Putting his hand to his chest, he felt its thunder against his palm. He took a couple of deep breaths and steadied himself, allowing the urge to pass in the rush of blood.

His sight settled on the mammals and parcel of fish. He forced his thoughts onto matters of preparation and preservation.

Thomas stepped to the bench along the back wall and hunted out a lidded wooden box of a goodly size. He rested it beside the catches and took off the lid. Within its confines was sea salt which would be rubbed into the meat in order to preserve it once the skinning and gutting had been completed. Taking the knife from his hip, he took hold of the rabbit that he would be keeping and made his first incision.

30

Golvan reached the top of the fifteen foot ladder, placing his hammer onto the wall before him, the granite dusty and cobwebbed beneath the eaves of the thatched roof. He looked at the strut to his left and then glanced down at the barn floor. 'Mind yourselves,' he called.

Giving the strut a hard push, its rotten length tore loose from the pins that secured it to an angled roof support and one of the main rafters, both of which were mere tree branches peeled and cut to fit. The strut tumbled through the air and thumped to the floor with a hollow sound, damp shards scattering about it. Taking the hammer, he then beat the rusted pins into the beam and rafter in turn.

'Ready,' he called down, glancing over his right shoulder at Marrek and Gerens as they stood below, Old Jacob behind them at the door, the thick fog beyond swirling through the opening like a ghost seeking entry.

'What do you want first, the new timber or the pins?' asked Marrek, his voice echoing slightly in the emptiness of the small barn.

Golvan looked at the beams as he pondered a moment. 'Pins,' he replied.

Marrek turned to the blacksmith and Gerens handed him the four large pins that had recently been made. The farmer stepped to the foot of the ladder and made his way up, the wood creaking under the combined weight of both men who clung to its length.

'Here,' he stated, keeping his face as far back from Golvan's muddy leather boots as possible, the smell of manure thick in his nostrils.

Golvan returned the hammer to the top of the wall and stretched down, taking the pins, Marrek almost dropping one as he handed them over.

'Been at the mead already, Marrek?' asked Jacob with a rasping touch of amusement.

Marrek gave the old man a sharp look over his shoulder as he descended the ladder and leapt the last rungs to the floor, boots thudding upon the earth.

'Should I carry the new beam up to him?' asked Gerens, bending to pick up the three foot length of rough timber, its bark removed.

'I have not touched a drop and am able to do so myself,' said Marrek with clear irritation, quickly moving to take up the strut.

Placing it over his shoulder, he began up the ladder once again, holding on tightly to its right rail. He reached the other farmer's boots and passed it up, hands to the bottom as Golvan took a firm grasp.

'Where are you going?' asked Golvan as Marrek began to descend. 'I am in need of someone to hold it in place while I hammer in the pins.'

Marrek looked at the ground, heights having always created a disturbance within him, legs weakening and finding he had to force his body to move. 'I...' He felt his pulse becoming elevated.

'It will not take long,' said Golvan, seeing the flush on the other man's face. 'Besides, I shall be the one balancing on the top rungs while you lean against the ladder.' To illustrate his point, he moved upward until his feet were on the uppermost rung, the new timber over his right shoulder as he gripped the roof support and stood with back bent, dark hair brushing against the underside of the thatch.

'Take a care, Golvan,' said Marrek, the mere sight of the balancing act above making him feel more unsettled.

'I could climb up and give my aid, if thee so wishes?' asked Jacob with a mischievous tone, winking at his younger brother, Golvan smiling in return.

Marrek ignored the old farmer's comment and climbed further up as Golvan moved his feet to the edge of the top rung to allow more space. He then put the strut in place against the beam and rafter.

'Hold it there,' he stated firmly, seeing the inner turmoil in Marrek's eyes.

Marrek forced his hands to release the rails with great effort, leaning his body against the rungs. Reaching up, his saw that his hands were trembling. Gratefully grasping the strut, the action hiding the shaking of his fear, he tried to steady his nerve as Golvan took up one of the pins and the hammer from the eaves.

'I saw Carrow speaking to himself upon Trewey Hill yesterday,' said Golvan, trying to distract the other man from his obvious discomfort.

'Was there mention of mermaids?' asked Jacob, recalling the claims Marrek had made in relation to Carrow.

'No,' said Golvan as he began to hammer the first of the pins into the upper end of the strut. 'He was conversing as if to another, but there was no other with him.'

'As if to another?' Marrek looked up at him.

'Aye,' nodded Golvan without turning his attention from the task, the wood splitting as the pin dug deeper and the hammer beat a regular rhythm. 'It were a peculiar sight indeed. He stood upon the old path leading to Bersaba's hut and held a conversation with himself as the rain beat down.'

'We all talk to ourselves from time to time,' stated Gerens, uncomfortable with the topic of conversation.

'This was different,' stated Golvan, reaching for the second pin and holding it near the bottom of the strut in order to secure it to the angled beam.

'Different?' asked Jacob.

Golvan nodded again and brought the hammer to bear. 'It were one-sided, as if someone were talking with him.'

'Are you sure there was no one else upon the hillside?' asked Gerens.

'Certain.'

'Long have folk said he sees things that others do not,' said Jacob thoughtfully. 'It may be he converses with the dead.'

Golvan stopped his hammering in order to look down at the other men. 'I tell you in earnest, as I watched him a chill

125

settled upon me and reached deep within, as if his very presence was a poison to my soul,' he stated, looking from face to face. 'Thomas Carrow is unnatural and his evil should not be allowed to endure here.'

'Evil?' Gerens shook his head. 'I think you overstate yourself.'

'I think not,' replied Golvan firmly as Jacob glanced out of the door behind him with a touch of nervousness, taking a couple of steps closer to Gerens and drawing his fur cloak about his small frame.

Golvan began to hammer the second pin once more. 'We should cast him out from among us.'

'As I have said before, Carrow is not among us. He is removed upon the hill and of no threat,' stated the blacksmith.

'No threat?' said Golvan incredulously. 'Only recently he threatened me when I was...' He caught himself before openly admitting to his poaching activities. '...Walking upon the hill.'

Gerens looked up at him with an expression of disbelief. He was well aware of the farmer's habit of exaggeration, having heard many a tale from his mouth and then the bare truth from another, the accounts differing greatly. 'I think you add a flourish to serve yourself,' he stated, ne'er fearful of speaking his mind.

'I do no such thing.' The farmer hammered the pin one last time, its head becoming flush with the wood. 'You may make your way down now, Marrek.'

'We should speak with Father Blyth on the matter,' said Jacob with concern.

'You should do no such thing. Loose tongues are the only threat here,' said the blacksmith.

'The presence of Carrow casts a shadow over us all,' said Golvan. 'I warn thee now, one day he will prove me right and enact a great evil.'

'Aye, Golvan, and it may be that our pigs take flight from their sty one starry night,' stated Nonna as she appeared in the doorway, giving Jacob a start and receiving a sour look from the man upon the ladder at which the sarcastic remark was aimed. 'How goes it with the repair?'

'It is all but finished,' said Marrek to his wife, a stained apron tied about her wide hips and a grey and homely woollen dress beneath.

She nodded her approval. 'How goes it, Gerens?' she asked, the two of them sharing a bond since the days of their youth, when they had spent many a day playing on her father's farm.

'It goes well, Nonna. How are the twins?'

'They would do well to mind how fast they grow. We need new clothes by the week, is seems,' she replied with a smile.

Gerens returned the gesture.

'We have bread and a little broth should any of you require something to eat when the job is done,' she announced.

'That is a kindly offer,' said Jacob, 'but I must to my sheep before day becomes night.'

'Finding them will be a trick in this fog,' she replied.

''Tis so,' he replied with a grave nod, looking beyond her at the thick moisture moving through the air, stirred by a gentle breeze. He felt a chill, not relishing the idea of walking into the concealing arms of the fog after his younger brother's disturbing words.

'It will not be the first time you have had to venture out in such conditions and certainly will not be the last,' said Gerens, noting the look on the old man's weathered face.

'You are wise enough not to take note of your brother's words,' said Nonna. 'We have heard the same many times before.'

'Have you no control over your wife's tongue, Marrek?' asked Golvan with annoyance, staring at the other farmer.

'My tongue is not his to control,' she responded with bite, crossing her arms over her ample bosom and glaring up at him.

Marrek winced at her reply.

'Of that I have no doubt,' said Golvan. 'It is a tongue that none could control without cutting it from your unseemly mouth.'

127

The other men looked up at him in shock as he stood atop the ladder, the forcefulness and bile of his words striking them with a physical force. Nonna's mouth fell open and she stared up at him before turning to her husband, hoping that he would come to her defence. Marrek remained silent, head bowing beneath the pressure of her gaze.

In a rush of movement, Nonna went to the ladder. Grasping the rails, she yanked the bottom away from the wall, the top sliding rapidly down the rough granite.

Golvan cried out in alarm, dropping the hammer, which thudded to the floor as he made a desperate grab for the support beam. He managed to take hold, pain searing in the palm of his left hand as it slid down the angle of the wood and a large splinter dug into his skin.

'You bitch!' he said loudly as Nonna stormed from the barn, vanishing into the fog beyond.

'Golvan!' exclaimed Gerens, staring up at the man as Marrek hurried to right the ladder, hoping to smooth the waters his wife had roughed.

'You all saw what she did,' stated the farmer, his face reddened by effort and pain.

'Aye, and we also heard your words that came before,' replied Gerens.

Marrek placed the ladder to the wall and Golvan found the top rung with his boots, a look of relief briefly softening the anger apparent in his expression.

''Tis interesting that you speak in her name and not her husband. Marrek knows better than to try and defend the indefensible.'

Gerens stared up at him, but held his tongue despite the words that rested upon its tip. He knew there would be no dissuading the farmer of his opinion, his stubbornness well known throughout the settlement.

'I shall take your silence as admission that she went beyond the pale. Though maybe I should take it as a sign of guilt,' said Golvan, raising his right eyebrow.

'Take it as you like,' replied Gerens before turning to Marrek. 'I will take my leave,' he said flatly, walking away.

The blacksmith glanced over his shoulder as he exited the barn. 'Good day to you,' he said in parting, gladly walking into the dampness that waited to enfold him.

'And good riddance,' said Golvan, glaring out of the door for a while as the other two men remained silent and glanced at each other awkwardly.

'I had better go to the house,' said Marrek with a touch of embarrassment, knowing that the men of the village mocked him for his servility to his headstrong wife.

'You had better hurry or there will be no supper for you tonight,' said Golvan with a tone of mild amusement.

'Take good care, Marrek,' said Jacob.

Marrek nodded and walked quickly from the barn.

'Do not forget to bow and scrape when addressing your lovely wife,' called Golvan after him.

''Tis not his fault,' said Jacob as he looked up at his brother.

'No?' Golvan raised his brows. 'I would say it is entirely his fault. If she were my wife she would know her place.'

Jacob did not respond as he rubbed the back of his neck, which was beginning to ache as he looked up at his kin. Golvan stared down at the hammer lying on the earth below and then turned to the new strut.

Taking hold of it, he pushed and pulled, finding that it was firmly in place. He subtly took up the two remaining pins and slipped them into his jerkin while his brother's attention was taken by seeing to the pain in his neck. Satisfied that his actions had not been noticed, he began to climb down.

'What did thee mean by "guilt"?' asked Jacob as his brother neared the ground.

Golvan stepped down and picked up the hammer, his back to Jacob as he grinned to himself, glad that his snide comment had not been wasted. Replacing the grin with a look of utmost seriousness, he faced his brother and sighed with exaggerated concern. 'In truth, I should not say,' he stated.

Jacob stepped closer. 'I shall not tell another soul,' he said, lowering his voice.

Golvan feigned indecision, fully aware that anything spoken to Jacob would be spoken to many others, such was the looseness of his brother's tongue. 'I fear it is more than friendship that brought Gerens to Nonna's defence so readily when her husband remained silent.'

'Truly?' Jacob was genuinely shocked.

Golvan nodded solemnly. 'I am afraid it is so. Did you not note the way they looked at each other and how she greeted him with singular interest.'

Jacob pondered and then nodded. 'It is as ye say, Brother. She did indeed pay him special heed and now that I think on it there was something that passed in the looks between them.'

'It is poor Marrek that I feel sorry for,' said Golvan, shaking his head. 'Not only does his wife treat him with disrespect, but one of his closest friends is bedding her behind his back.'

'I wonder how long they have been conducting their affair?' said Jacob, more to himself than his brother, glancing over his shoulder to the paleness beyond the entrance to the barn.

Golvan grinned again. The seed was sown and there was little doubt that it would grow strong and bare fruit. 'I should take my leave and you must to the fields to find your sheep,' he said, his vindictive nature sated.

'Mmm,' nodded Jacob, deep in thought, not truly having heard what had been said.

'I will see you anon, Jacob.' Golvan stepped to the doorway, leaning the hammer against the wall to the right, the pins in his pocket clanking dully against each other as he did so and making him wince. Turning to his brother, he could see that the noise had been lost on him, but that his aspersions most certainly had not.

'Take good care, Brother,' he said as he stepped out of the barn.

'Aye, and thee,' came the distracted reply as Golvan walked into the fog with a wide smile of self-satisfaction upon his face.

31

Thomas walked along the farm track and went right when he reached the more substantial path that ran through Zennor. Lacy Lugg was cutting herbs in her small front garden, the old woman's back bent as she took her knife to the plants growing there.

She glanced over her shoulder and a look of disdain appeared upon her rounded face. She straightened and made her way through the front door with a hand to her lower back, the sound of it slamming following soon after.

He looked over to the church on the left, its tower watching over the village. His frown deepened as he recalled the altercation at the entrance to the small meadow resting beside it that had occurred on the feast day of Guldize.

Thomas passed the forge, hearing the hammer beating against the anvil. His boots sank into the mud as he continued beyond the scattering of buildings which were the heart of the settlement, passing the stream in which the women did their washing.

Trewey Farm lay ahead at the top of a gentle incline in the track. A thin mist hung over the fields about the granite buildings, which seemed huddled together so as to fend off the winter chill. The sun held little warmth as it perched above the hill which rose behind the farm and shared its name, Ocean Mist hidden upon its north-western slopes.

He walked through the entrance and past a small tumbledown barn which was overrun with ivy, the roof and near wall fallen into disrepair. Reaching the main buildings, he stopped and looked about the courtyard. Directly before him was the low bulk of the farmhouse, smoke rising from a hole in the thick thatch. To the left was a large barn where feasts and celebrations were held during inclement weather and opposite it rested a cowshed, lowing arising from within.

Listening for signs of activity, Thomas heard naught that hinted as to Jacob's location. He strode across the yard, a feeling of being hemmed in by the granite walls adding pace to his steps.

Reaching the front door, he rapped his knuckles upon the wood three times and waited. Glancing at the buildings to either side with nervous agitation, he shifted on his feet and hoped he would find the old farmer at home.

The sound of the door opening made him jump and he turned to find Jacob's diminutive wife, Conwenna, standing upon the threshold. Her wrinkled expression became one of surprise when she set eyes on him and she took an involuntary step back into the smoky gloom, wringing her hands together and looking distinctly perturbed.

'Is your husband home?' he asked.

Conwenna shook her head, grey hair tied back and a dusting of flour on the front of her dark woollen dress. 'He be with the sheep,' she replied nervously, seeing the restless look in his eyes, the rumours about his strange activities having been eagerly related to her by her husband.

'I have a brace of rabbits for bread and butter.' Thomas pulled his coat back to reveal the conies hanging from his hip.

'I...' She struggled in the face of his unsettling presence. 'I do not interfere with my husband's affairs.'

'It is only one loaf and some salted butter. I am sure he would not mind. Many are the times we have traded such,' encouraged Thomas, attempting to smile but the result showing the strain of his uneasiness.

Her expression became pinched as he lingered before her and she wished for his departure. 'I do not think we have butter to spare. I could perhaps give thee some clotted cream in its stead?' she asked hopefully.

'I have no use for cream,' replied Thomas, his thin smile falling away.

The sound of barking caused him to look over his shoulder, finding the old farmer's hound at the entrance to the yard. Jacob came into view with crook in hand, his gaze falling on the visitor.

132

'Hush now, Blackberry,' he stated, pausing beside the dog and stroking her back.

The barking became a low growl.

He made his way towards Thomas. 'Ye may leave us to our business, Conwenna,' he called, seeing the distress in his wife's expression that immediately became relief as she hurried into the depths of the farmhouse.

Thomas turned to the farmer's approach. 'Good day, Jacob.'

'Good day to thee, Thomas. I see thou hast some more rabbits for my cooking pot,' he said with a nod towards the animals.

'Aye, but your good wife tells me you have no butter.'

'I am sure I can find some to spare,' he replied. 'Wait here a moment.'

Jacob moved past him and went into the house. Thomas tried to follow his progress, peering into the smoke-filled gloom. The bleat of a goat issued from within and he wiped stinging tears from his eyes before turning from the vagaries of the interior. Blinking away the fumes, he looked back to the dog still growling on the other side of the courtyard as the mumble of voices came to him.

Shortly thereafter, the sound of Jacob clearing his throat issued from behind him. He turned to face the old man, looking down on his frail form and finding that he held a loaf with a knob of muslin-wrapped butter resting atop it.

'Here,' stated Jacob, holding them out.

Thomas pulled aside his coat and began to untie the conies.

Jacob studied the man before him while his face was down-turned. 'Any visitors of late?' he asked, trying to make the question appear nonchalant.

Thomas looked at him, a hot flush rising to his cheeks as he immediately thought of Rosita. 'Visitors?' he asked, throat constricting and mouth going dry.

'Aye, there were men seeking word of any wreckage found along the coastline. They did not call on thee?'

The alleviation of his tension was clear as his shoulders lost some of their tightness. 'They called,' he replied with a nod, finishing the task of taking the rabbits from his hip.

'And did thee have knowledge to share?' prompted Jacob as they exchanged the items being traded.

Thomas nodded again. 'I saw broken timbers and a torn sail at Treen Cove,' he confirmed. 'This I told them and they were on their way.'

'They did not visit again?'

'They had no need,' said Thomas.

Jacob looked at him thoughtfully. 'How goes it upon the hill?'

'As well as ever it has,' he replied evasively, wishing to be free of the courtyard walls.

'I recall when thy grandfather finished building the cottage. Many of the villagers gathered there and Trevedic hosted a celebration. Thy father cannot have been more than ten.'

'You have told me of this before,' said Thomas, having heard the same tale numerous times. 'My father placed the last stone in a gap left by my grandfather in the southern wall for that very purpose. It was this stone that completed the build.'

'Ye remember well what I have said,' nodded Jacob. 'Doest thou also remember visiting the farm as a boy before…?' He found himself unable to finish the sentence, unsure as to how the other man would react to the words which had nearly spilled from his tongue.

'Before my parents died,' finished Thomas with regret, his tone deepening. 'Aye, though it seems as if in another lifetime.'

'Ye would come with thy friend.' He studied the face of the man before him.

'Elowen,' said Thomas softly.

'Aye, that was her name. Doest thou still spend time in her company?'

He shook his head and was beginning to feel uncomfortable under the old man's scrutiny, wondering why

Jacob was probing and suspecting there was more to his words than mere reminiscence. 'I must be away,' he stated, turning before there was chance of another enquiry.

'My thanks for the bread and butter,' he said over his shoulder, his pace brisk as he kept a watchful eye on the hound which continued to stand to the left of the courtyard entrance, growling as he approached.

'Blackberry!' admonished Jacob loudly.

'Take good care, Thomas,' called the farmer in his rasping voice, watching as the other man hurried from the yard and thinking back on Golvan's words. There did not seem to be aught of evil about him, but his mind was undoubtedly touched by an unnatural hand.

32

Dark clouds were drawing in from the west as the wind took breath and ushered the low mist from the fields. The tails of Thomas' coat stirred and his hair was messed as he glanced upward, the promise of rain carried on the air. His boots set a faster rhythm upon the muddied grasses of the track as he made his way between the stone walls of the fields up the slope, the growing gusts against his face.

Reaching the edge of the fields, he went right and made for the cottage. His mood had been darkened by clouds within, the wind on which they had arrived being the words of the old farmer. Something was amiss, of that he was certain. Many were the occasions when Jacob had shared memories, but few were the times when he had delved into his affairs. What reason lay behind the questions he knew not, but he felt sure that something festered there.

He reached the front gate and hurried up the path as the first drops of rain patted upon the leather covering his shoulders, carried ahead of the clouds by the wind. He entered Ocean Mist and came to a halt just inside the doorway.

Rosita was standing before his bench of driftwood and the two shelves of carvings above. She was staring at the mermaid resting central to the figures on the lower shelf, her gaze fixed on its face.

He closed the door and she slowly turned to him with a curious look, the walking stick supporting her and Shenty sitting on the earth beside. She pointed at the mermaid and spoke a few honeyed words in her native tongue.

Thomas could guess their nature from the tone, believing that she was asking as to the likeness of the carving's face. 'I carved it before I found you upon the sands,' he said slowly, hoping that somehow she would understand, but seeing that comprehension did not come.

He walked over to stand beside her, placing the bread and butter on the clutter of wood arrayed upon the bench. Reaching for the mermaid, Thomas took the figure down from the shelf. Looking at the similarity, he then held it out to Rosita as an intuitive feeling took hold. 'I carved it for you.'

She stared at the mermaid and then looked up. She spoke a couple of alien words, the intonation once more indicating a question was being asked.

Thomas nodded.

Rosita reached out and took the carving into her delicate grasp. She caressed it with her fingertips, studying the gentle curves and soft features. Holding it to her breast, she looked to him with eyes glittering.

She took a teetering step toward him and rose to place a kiss upon his left cheek. 'Gracias,' she whispered.

She looked back to the figure, taking it from her chest and following the contours of its face. A single tear rolled down her right cheek and captured their reflections in its impermanence.

Thomas fought the urge to gather her into his embrace. He stood motionless for a moment as he battled within and Rosita held the mermaid in her hand and her fond gaze.

Taking up the bread and butter, he made his way into the Old Pen, moving out of her line of sight before coming to a stop at the far end of the table. He put the foodstuffs on the battered top and then leant against it, right palm upon its grain as his heart pounded and he took steadying breaths.

He stared out of the open shutters of the window before him as the world was darkened by the heavy clouds, the rain becoming persistent and heavy. The wind banged the shutters against the granite as its strength grew, reaching in and stirring the dust. The sea beyond the cliffs in the middle distance was deep grey and topped by white horses that marked the choppy swell.

He watched the crests prance and rear as his pulse calmed and the need to hold Rosita abated. The soft patting of her walking stick upon the earth drifted from the other room and was followed by the creak of the cot.

'I had better light the fire,' he stated to himself, moving to the window and closing the shutters on the downpour beyond.

33

Thomas opened the south-facing door of Ocean Mist and looked out across the hillside, the window shutters already open and welcoming in the light despite the distinct chill in the air. There had been barely a break in the cloud for weeks and the blue sky was a welcome sight. The low sun hung watery and weak in the sky before him, as if unwilling to wake fully from its oceanic slumber on the winter solstice.

He turned to the sound of Rosita's approach, the walking stick in her left hand, but her pace much improved in comparison with her initial wanderings about the interior of the cottage. This was to be her first journey into the open air and his stomach was churning, muscles tight. He feared that one of the village folk would spy them upon the hill, a sight that was sure to raise questions and suspicions. He had not visited Zennor since enduring the questions of Old Jacob and had no wish to encourage any to be roused to the cottage by their curiosity.

He scanned the fields and hills, but found no evidence of anyone loitering close by. He picked up the reed-woven basket from where it had been placed beside the door and stepped out onto the path. Shenty padded past him, coming to a halt a few yards ahead and looking over her shoulder as she waited for Rosita to make her timely exit.

Thomas watched as his ward paused in the doorway, wincing against the glare of the sun as she savoured her liberation from the confines of the house. Many were the times she had sat upon the chair made by his grandfather and stared out through the seaward window of the living area, absently caressing the carving of the mermaid with her fingers as it rested upon her lap. Even when the rain fell in wind-blown torrents and patted upon the floor below the sill, she would still sometimes sit with her gaze to the horizon. The sight always set Thomas to wondering about her origins, the words of The Lay of Ailla coming to mind as he considered the likelihood that she was not of the human realm, that the ocean called her home.

He offered his left hand. She smiled and took a short step forward, shutting the door before taking hold. They began to make their way to the gate, Shenty trotting ahead.

'My mother planted that tree in memory of my father and grandfather,' he said, pointing at its barren and windswept form.

Rosita glanced at the tree, but his words washed over her without leaving any imprint bar the tone of his voice. They reached the gate and he led them through, letting Shenty exit first and closing it after them.

'We shall follow the path until the slope becomes less steep. Then we will make our way up and pass over the hill. There is a small wood on the far side where I can collect firewood as you rest and regain your strength for the return journey,' said Thomas as they began to follow the hillside, knowing that she could not understand, but needing to fill the silence between them.

They walked fifty yards along the track and then Thomas began to lead them up the hillside to the right, Shenty sniffing rocks and tufts of grass as she explored. It was the hound's first outing from Ocean Mist for a long time. Though Thomas had given her encouragements whenever he ventured out, she had stubbornly remained by Rosita's side.

The going became increasingly slow and the strain upon her stamina was apparent in the tightening of her grip on his hand. He glanced at her face, seeing the tension there, her eyes downcast as the walking stick clipped against the stony ground.

Looking over his shoulder, he feared being spied from below. The crest of the hill was still some distance above and he hoped she would be able to carry on till they were over its concealment before needing rest. He tried to think of words that would spur her on despite her lack of understanding, but none came to mind as his nervousness constricted his chest.

140

She began to fall a couple of steps behind, the link of their hands becoming the means by which she continued, pulled up by his desperation to be hidden as her legs began to feel as though they would soon buckle. Rosita gritted her teeth, feeling dizzy and her sight passing in and out of focus as they neared the hilltop.

They reached the brow and began to walk down the western slope. She stumbled, legs suddenly giving way under the pressure of the descent.

Their hands tore loose as Rosita fell to her knees. She let out an exclamation of pain as a stone dug through the hide leggings and her wrist twisted back due to her grip on the walking stick.

Thomas turned, finding her kneeling upon the ground with head bowed and face drained of colour. She cradled her wrist as her eyes rolled back and she fell forward with fearful inevitability.

Dropping the basket and quickly stepping to her, Thomas stooped with his arms open. She collapsed into his supportive embrace, head coming to rest against his left shoulder.

'Rosita?' he said quietly.

There was no response bar her soft breath upon his neck. Thomas took hold of her shoulders and gently pushed her away from him, ducking to look up into her face. Her eyes were closed, but the lids flickered and then lifted slowly.

Rosita looked at him in temporary confusion as she came to, her brow knitting as memories of her recent past laboured to the fore of her mind. The tension dissipated, her time in Ocean Mist gaining clarity. She held his gaze and was softened by the light she saw shining there.

'You passed out,' he said as she wearily lifted her head.

Thomas rested her upon the ground and she let out a groan. Looking to her left knee, he saw blood through a tear in the hide. He inspected the wound more closely to find that it was not much more than a deep scratch and wiped some earth away from the cut with his thumb.

''Tis not serious,' he said, with a comforting smile.

Rosita managed a smile in response, but it soon fell away from her lips. She tried to rise, moved onto her elbows and then attempted to push herself further with her hands. Letting out a yell of pain, she fell back to the earth and rough hillside grass.

'What troubles you?' he asked with concern.

Rosita glanced at her wrist and said a few words in her native tongue, having grasped the meaning of his words. He moved to her side and carefully lifted her arm. He delicately felt her wrist with his free hand and she winced, inhaling sharply.

'I think it no more than a strain,' he said, laying the arm back upon the ground. 'You will have to hold the stick in your other hand until it heals.' Thomas picked up the walking thick and placed it by her right hand, knowing that his words were lost on her.

Sitting back on his haunches, he looked at her pale and weary face. Without forethought, he reached out and tenderly brushed strands of dark hair back behind her ear, eyes following the action with unveiled desire.

Rosita took hold of his wrist, drawing his palm to her lips and kissing it tenderly. Their eyes locked and she released her hold, Thomas' hand slowly falling away from her face. They existed in a pocket of total stillness as the westerly breeze stirred the grasses on the hillside about them. They dove into the depths of each other's gaze and became one with the waters, lost in the eternal moment as all else faded to naught but whispers.

Thomas leant forward, lips tingling as they neared hers. His body trembled with anticipation, heart filling his chest with thunder.

The sound of a partridge taking flight was followed by Shenty's barking. Thomas quickly straightened. He looked wide-eyed down the slope, worried that someone else was upon the hillside, but finding no evidence of another as the partridge flew west. His racing pulse echoed the urgent wing beats of the vanishing bird, heart fluttering with a mixture of desire and fright.

142

He turned back to Rosita. She was smiling at him, but the moment in which they had been captivated was lost, stolen by the sudden disturbance.

'It may be that I should visit the wood while you remain and gather your strength,' he said, getting to his feet and glancing over his shoulder. The ragged copse lay a few hundred yards down the slope to the left, due south-west. He was certain she would not find the strength to make the climb back even if she could manage to reach the trees.

He was left with two choices; either leave her upon the hillside while he set forth to collect firewood or help guide her steps home and return without her. The woodpile was much diminished and would soon be exhausted. If he did not collect more there would not be time for it to dry beside the fire before the flames went out.

'I will take you to the cottage and then return,' he stated as she raised herself on her elbows once again.

He helped her to unsteady feet. Picking up the walking stick, Thomas passed it to her, watching her slender fingers curl about the shoal of fish forever swimming about its grip. He placed his arm about her waist and they turned in the direction from which they had come, Shenty joining them, sniffing Rosita's leg before looking up at her with concern.

The going was tortuously slow and he felt their presence made naked to the world as they reached the hilltop and stood in plain sight. Rosita found any increase in their turn of speed to be too much during the easterly descent, stumbling and finding her legs threatening to fall away from beneath her. Thomas was forced to keep the pace to a crawl despite his anxieties. He stared at Ocean Mist as it rested below, willing them closer, drawing them back to the concealing safety offered within the granite walls with the pull of his gaze.

34

Nonna knelt on the grass before the stream. She vigorously rubbed the linen bunched in her glistening hands on the washboard leaning against her knees. To her left knelt two other women from the village, the three of them regularly visiting the bank-side together.

'Do the twins fare well?' asked Breaca, her face rounded by youth and brown hair braided beneath the pale veil that covered it.

'Aye, though the rains set an itch in their feet. They were restless and boisterous within the confines of the cottage.'

'Such is the way with boys,' said Morvoren, glancing around Breaca, her sockets hollow and cheeks sunken as she recovered from a cold which had kept her to her bed for two weeks, many saying she was lucky to still be in the world of the living.

'This I am starting to learn,' replied Nonna, looking over with a smile.

The three women knelt side by side in silence for a while. They took clothes from the baskets at their sides, dipping them in the cold waters and wringing them tight, water running over their fingers, which were reddened by the activity. Morvoren used a washing bat to manipulate the items she placed into the stream, beating out the stains and then rubbing the clothing on one side of the simple implement.

Breaca gave the older woman a nudge and nodded sideways at Nonna. 'Ask her,' she mouthed.

Morvoren looked at her, a strained expression on her face. 'Really?' she mouthed back.

Breaca nodded her affirmation.

Morvoren sat forward and turned to Nonna once again. 'We...' She took a breath, glancing at the young woman between them, who nodded vaguely. 'We have something we wish to ask you,' she stated, her voice made uneven by nervousness.

Nonna rubbed the shirt in her hands down the board and looked over, seeing the tightness of Morvoren's expression and feeling her pulse quicken. 'What is it?' she asked worriedly.

Morvoren swallowed hard and glanced at Breaca again. Returning her attention to Nonna, she gathered her courage with another deep breath. 'Are you having an affair?'

Nonna was taken aback by the enquiry, mouth falling open as she regarded the two women beside her. 'An affair?'

Breaca gave a nod as the woman beyond her bore an apologetic look after seeing her friend's reaction to her enquiry.

'Why would you ask me such a thing?' asked Nonna with a wounded tone.

Breaca glanced at her confederate when no more words were forthcoming and found Morvoren tightly lipped. 'We have heard that you and Gerens have been...,' began the girl after turning back to Nonna.

'Gerens!' Nonna shook her head sadly as she stared down at the hurrying waters of the stream, eyes filled with the sunlight dancing upon the ripples.

'Do you believe these rumours?' she asked while continuing to look at the ribbons of snaking light.

Breaca looked back at Morvoren with a questioning look. The older woman shrugged, her shoulders sagging with the weight of guilt as she saw the hurt contained in Nonna's fallen expression.

'Of course not,' stated the girl with as much conviction as she could muster, looking to the downcast woman on her right. 'We simply thought you should know what is being said about you.'

Nonna shook her head again. 'I cannot believe that you would take such rumours to be the truth,' she said, hearing the lie within Breaca's response.

There were a few moments of stillness and silence. The babble of the stream rose to them as Morvoren diminished in the face of the tension that hung thick in the air. Breaca shifted position, feeling awkward and wishing there were some way to retract her words.

Nonna got to her feet in a flurry of movement, the item of clothing she had been cleaning still clutched in her right hand as the wash board toppled forward and fell into the stream with a splash. Without pause, she made for the track twenty yards behind them with hasty steps. The sodden hem of her grey dress clung to her legs and she raised it higher to enable greater speed, wishing to be away from the other women, who watched her departure with regretful expressions.

With tears gathering within her grey eyes and spilling upon her cheeks, Nonna hurried home. The twins were playing rough and tumble upon the grass in front of the cottage, taking little note of her passage as she hastened to the front door.

Stepping inside, she shut the door on the sunlight, the relative gloom of the interior taking her in its welcoming embrace. She closed her eyes and leant against the wood, taking a deep breath, body shuddering as the flow of tears slowed.

'What be the matter with you?'

She looked to the far side of the fire pit in surprise, finding her husband seated upon a stool before the small window, shutters creaking in the breeze. 'Why is it that you are home?' she asked, sniffing and wiping her cheeks with the back of her hand. 'I thought you to be out in the fields all day.'

Marrek raised the cup of mead resting upon his lap. Taking a long swig, he lowered it again while smacking his lips. 'I saw Carrow upon the hill,' he stated.

'So? That is not a sight to have chased you home,' she replied, regaining her composure as their conversation distracted her mind from what had been said upon the bank of the stream.

'There was someone with him, someone that I have only seen once before this day, though I thought my eyes may be deceiving me upon that first occasion.' His gaze rose to meet hers. 'There is something I did not tell you of the time when I

146

saw him in the mist,' he admitted. 'The time I heard mention of a mermaid.'

'What did you not tell?' she whispered, the volume taken from her voice by his haunted look.

'The figure that appeared to be carried over his shoulder had not legs, but a tail.'

'What?' She stared at him, aghast at his answer.

There was a short silence as he took another swig of mead. The sound of their children's laughter drifted in through the open shutters of the front window as the twins chased each other to the recently repaired barn on the far side of the grass.

'I had no wish to mention it before,' said Marrek. 'I know my reputation well enough and know what the folk would have said if I had stated such, but I swear to you, my wife, that the creature over Carrow's shoulder had a white tail. It hung limply down his back. It is that same creature that I saw with him today, I am sure of it.'

Nonna stood in stupefied silence as she looked at her husband. The slight slur of his words spoke of more than one cup of mead passing between his lips since his arrival home, but the look in his eyes was one that held no knowing lie.

'I told others that Carrow had made mention of a mermaid upon the hill that day and they made light of it. Imagine their reaction should I have revealed more,' he added, shaking his head as he turned his sight to the last of the mead within the cup.

'A mermaid?' said Nonna, still wrestling with what he had told her.

'As time passed I believed it may be that the mist played tricks upon my mind, but now I am sure of it,' he responded. 'She had legs when I spied her this morn, but could not walk a step without the assistance of Carrow and a walking stick, so unnatural it is to her nature.'

'Had you drunk of the mead before leaving?' she asked, searching his gaze.

Marrek shook his head. 'It was not until I returned that I felt need of its warmth. My report is honest.'

147

Nonna blinked away the last residue of her tears. She walked over to her husband and knelt before him, taking his left hand in both of hers. 'You must not tell another soul of what you have seen.'

'Should they not be warned that such a creature watches over us from the hill? I feel her presence looming over us and it unsettles me greatly.'

She pondered a moment. 'Proof,' she stated. 'We must have proof before we take such news to the village.'

'What proof do you suppose we can find?'

Nonna sighed. 'It may be that it is I who needs proof,' she admitted. 'Though I am certain your words hold no lie, it is hard to believe such a creature dwells with Thomas Carrow. I will see her for myself before we tell others that she resides on the hill.'

'You will go visit with Carrow?' He looked at her in surprise as she remained upon the earth before him, his hand still cradled in hers.

'That I will,' she nodded.

'Under what guise?'

'This I do not know as yet. I shall think on it and find some reason by which to call upon him and discover the truth for myself.'

'I have already told you the truth,' he grumbled, frown deepening.

'Would you not need to see something so fantastical as to defy belief for yourself, even if your most trusted friend told you of its existence?' She gave his hand a squeeze. 'I do not doubt your words. It is just that I must see her with my own eyes.'

Marrek continued to look hurt as he lifted his cup and drained the last of the mead within.

'Swear to me you will tell no other of the mermaid until I have seen her for myself,' said Nonna, tightening her grip on his hand so as to draw her husband's gaze.

He sighed. 'I swear,' he said with a curt nod.

The sound of one of the twins wailing as they approached the house caused her to release Marrek's hand. She rose to her

148

feet, readying herself to deal with the cut or scrape that had been suffered during the boy's boisterous play.

35

Rosita lowered the bowl of fish broth to her lap as she sat on the edge of the cot. She turned to the fire before her, the lively dance of the flames adding a warm glow to her skin.

'Have you had your fill?' asked Thomas from the chair as he peered across the fire pit. During the nights the seat was placed before the flames, but in the days he moved its position so that it faced the seaward window. There Rosita would sit and stare to the far horizon or sew the shirt she was making with the sail cloth he had found upon the beach.

She looked over at him, the heat rippling the air above the fire pit between them. She lifted the bowl and took another sip, clearly not enjoying the thin broth which had been boiled from the bones and skin of a mackerel he had caught a few days before.

Thomas saw the distaste expressed in the wrinkle of her nose and creasing of her brow, the scar left by the gash on her head not overly apparent. A sense of guilt mixed with his sense of duty. He hoped that the traps would provide a rabbit or two on the morrow and wondered whether to visit Jacob with the collection of pelts that hung in the Old Pen in order to trade them for some bread.

She leant over the side of the cot and placed her bowl upon the earth, Shenty looking over from her position upon the patchwork of furs. The hound leapt down and wandered over, sniffing the steaming contents. The sound of her eager lapping soon followed.

Rosita settled on her side, face upon her hand and the carving of the mermaid held to her chest despite the slight swelling of her wrist. The flames writhed and leapt in her eyes, the stain of weariness darkening her sockets as her lids began to fall. The journey to the top of the hill had sapped all her strength and now the sleep of rejuvenation beckoned.

Thomas cradled his bowl upon his lap as he watched her succumb to the embrace of much needed slumber, her eyes closing and breathing becoming light. Shenty finished the last of the broth before making her way back to the foot of the cot, circling and settling once she had padded the furs.

The carving slowly tumbled from Rosita's hand as her grip was loosened by sleep's arrival, teetering on the edge of the cot before falling to the ground with a soft thud. Thomas rose to the crackle of the fire and creak of the chair. He held his bowl in his right hand as he passed around the fire to the bedside.

He crouched and picked up the mermaid. Studying it a moment, he then tucked it beside her before taking her bowl from the floor and straightening. He paused to look down upon her face, feeling the distemper within his heart that caused it to ache with longing.

With a sigh, Thomas took the bowls into the Old Pen, the deep shadows within its confines waiting for the fire to die and their time to creep forth and fill the interior of the cottage with their pitch. He placed the bowls on the table and faced the shutters of the seaward window to his left as they bumped against their fastening.

'If only she could tell me of her origins,' he said to the night. 'If only my heart did not hold her dear.'

He glanced at the simple white gown hung over the chair on the far side of the table. It appeared as if aglow in the gloom, containing magic within its strands. 'Who are you?' he whispered.

36

Lacy swept along the aisle, the switches of the broom scraping over the stones. Motes of dust stirred in streams of sunlight slanting through the windows as she mumbled to herself. The whispers of her words echoed in the chill hollows of the small church as she moved towards the altar, back bent with age and covered in thick furs.

She sneezed, the sound thunderous in the confines and reverberating about the empty pews regimented to either side.

'Bless you.'

Lacy jumped and peered over her shoulder, finding Father Blyth walking into the aisle after having entered through the main door along the south side of the building. Right hand to her chest as her heart fluttered, she turned to approach and leant on the broom. 'Father,' she said with a sigh. 'I did not hear thy arrival.'

His footsteps rang out as he walked towards her and came to a halt a couple of yards away. 'How goes it, Mistress Lugg?'

'Nearly finished, Father.'

He nodded.

'Is thy mass ready for the morrow?' she asked, rubbing her hooked nose with the back of her hand as dust continued to irritate her nostrils.

Blyth gave another nod, an expression of stern thoughtfulness upon his lean face. 'I could not help but overhear a little of your talk upon my entry. I believe you were speaking of an affair? Did I gather your words correctly?'

Lacy shifted with discomfort and turned her gaze to the hickory switches at her feet, not wishing to be known for a wagging tongue. 'Aye.'

'Wilt thou not tell me more?' His tone held a touch of incredulity. 'After all, I am the spiritual leader of the community.'

She took a deep breath. 'Nonna Trelawny and Gerens the Smith,' she stated. 'It is they who are engaged in such activity.'

'You know this to be true?' Blyth's eyes narrowed as he studied her down-turned face.

'I cannot be sure of it,' she admitted.

'Who told you of such a thing?'

'Matthew Sithny. He was told by Jacob Trewey.'

'Did no one think to tell me?' said the priest with a touch of irritation.

''Tis not my place to give voice to rumour or cast shadows over the good names of others,' replied Lacy.

'Hmm,' said Blyth as he rubbed his chin and pondered the old woman's words, gaze wandering to the altar beyond her stooped form. 'Such would not surprise me at all. She is a woman who yokes her husband and he a godless man,' he muttered to himself.

Lacy glanced up at him.

Blyth blinked and looked at her as if forgetful of her presence. 'You may take your leave now, Mistress Lugg.'

'I have yet to finish my sweeping,' she responded, wanting to complete the job in readiness for the mass celebrating Christ's birth that would be held the following day.

Father Blyth gave the flagstones a perfunctory glance. 'It is well enough,' he said with a forced smile.

Lacy stared at him and then nodded. 'I shall see thee on the morrow, Father,' she said as she shambled past him.

'On the morrow,' he replied, watching her walk along the aisle and then turn right towards the door, the broom still clasped in her withered hands as she passed between the pews. The sight reminded him of the witches in tales his mother had told him as a boy, his expression darkening.

'Folklore and foolishness,' he mumbled to himself with a shake of his head.

153

As the sound of the door closing echoed about the interior of the church, Blyth turned his thoughts back to the affair of which Lacy had informed him. He recalled the voices of Gerens and Nonna being raised in support of Thomas Callow during the feast of Guldize and saw it as a sign of their sinful collusion.

'Their own evil was shown in their support of evil,' he said to himself with a nod, turning to the altar and staring at the cross resting upon its red cloth between white pillar candles. 'And evil must not be allowed to endure.'

37

Thomas watched Rosita sewing, Shenty curled on the ground by her feet. She had discovered a bone needle much like Bersaba's upon the rear bench in the Old Pen, along with a coil of catgut. The shirt was all but finished, only a little stitching required and the cross-threading of the cord that would secure the front.

'We could take another walk while the village attends church,' said Thomas into the hush. He sat on the edge of the cot, elbows upon his knees as he attempted to warm his hands before the fire, its heat barely able to penetrate the chill. It seemed that Rosita had regained her strength. A short and less arduous walk would be good for her spirits and help her confidence return after the events of a few days previous.

He turned to the shutters covering the south-facing window. A slim shaft of sunlight slanted in through the gap between, specks of dust glittering as they drifted lazily through its golden beam.

'It seems to be a good day for it,' he commented to himself as he pushed off from the bed and got to his feet, his body filled with aches brought on by the cold and sleeping in the chair. He had contemplated building another cot, but had decided to wait until spring. He knew not how long Rosita would reside with him and had begun to fear her departure. Her company was highly valued despite not being able to converse and she would be sorely missed should she leave.

Thomas stepped over to the door and opened it, allowing the sunlight entry. 'Will you walk with me?' he asked, gesturing out of the door.

She paused her stitching and nodded, smiling warmly at him from the other side of the room. Saying a few words in her strange tongue, she then continued to sew the last seam.

He watched, guessing at her meaning and seeing that her task was almost done. One of the chickens walked past him, head bobbing to mark each step as it wandered out into the garden.

Thomas looked to the fire and wondered whether to douse the flames, but they were already diminishing and would soon be replaced by the fading glow of embers. Turning back to Rosita, he studied her face, followed the gentle contours and caressed them with his sight. Her expression was one of concentration as she passed the pale needle through the linen and drew the thread after it. She bit off the catgut, snapping it between her teeth.

Securing the end, Rosita held the shirt up. She examined her work and nodded to herself before noticing the direction of his gaze and lifting her head. 'Terminado,' she said with a smile, both the gesture and the word filled with warmth.

Her meaning was easy to discern and Thomas smiled in return. 'I am glad,' he stated.

Placed the shirt over the left arm of the chair, Rosita got to her feet. She stretched and yawned before taking the walking stick from where it leant against the seat and making her way over to him, Shenty looking up with interest. Crouching, she temporarily rested the stick on the ground and donned the old boots, which were a good deal larger than her feet required. The hound padded over and passed them both, exiting the cottage.

Thomas stepped back so that Rosita could vacate the cottage. She glanced at him as she passed and affectionately smoothed her hand over his chest. His pulse quickened in response as she took a few steps along the path and then waited for him to follow.

Taking a breath, he closed the door and went to her side. She reached for his hand and entwined her fingers with his as they began to move away from Ocean Mist, the chicken clucking as it moved hurriedly out of their way.

They followed the path along the hillside, heading further inland. Their progress was steady but slow, the sound of the walking stick against the earth marking each step.

'As long as you have the strength, we will visit with Bersaba and then return home once you have had a little rest,' said Thomas, having developed the habit of breaking the silence between them with his words despite her lack of understanding.

The pace remained constant and Rosita's stamina showed no sign of waning. Thomas regularly glanced to the left, looking past her to the fields below. He saw no sign of any of the folk of Zennor and felt confident that they were at worship within the confines of St. Senara's Church.

They rounded the bend in the track and made their descent down the southern slope. The healer's hut soon came into view with its discoloured thatch and copse of whispering yews, Shenty coming to a stop twenty yards from the simple abode.

'She will ne'er go closer,' commented Thomas.

Rosita glanced at him curiously and drew to a halt beside the dog. Thomas took a couple more steps, but was brought to a standstill as the bond of their hands pulled tight.

'Will you not visit with Bersaba?' he asked, turning to her.

She looked at him with an expression of puzzlement, head cocking to the side and brow knitted.

'Come,' said Thomas, giving her hand a gentle pull.

Rosita shook her head.

Thomas looked into her eyes. 'You wish to wait here?'

She made no reply and gave no sign of comprehension.

He made to release her hand and continue to the hut, but Rosita retained her grip. She shook her head again and attempted to draw him back to her.

'What is wrong?' he asked, starting to feel unnerved.

She said a few words in her native tongue, but their meaning was lost on him.

'Is it the whisper of the trees or the tingling of your spine?' he asked. 'Such things are commonplace here. This is a place of natural magic.' He smiled warmly and wished she could understand his words.

'I will visit with Bersaba. You may wait here and rest before the journey home,' he said. 'You will have Shenty for company.' He nodded towards the hound.

Rosita glanced down and then frowned at him, reluctantly relinquishing her grip on his hand.

'I shall not be long,' he stated, filling his tone with reassurance in the hope she would glean at least a little comfort from his words, comfort by which to lessen her perplexing uneasiness.

He walked to the hut, glancing back before reaching the door and seeing that Rosita continued to stand, Shenty seated by her feet as both looked on. Rapping his knuckles upon the wood, he listened for evidence of the old crone's approach.

He was given a start by the sudden opening of the door and stared down at the aged healer as she stood hunched before him. 'Bersaba,' he greeted with a nod as he steadied his heart.

'Good day to thee, Young Thomas Carrow. How goes it?' She grinned up at him.

'Things go well. Rosita is upon her feet and walking.'

'As I see,' she replied, looking beyond his left shoulder. 'She does not approach.' It was a statement rather than a question.

'Like my hound, she finds her legs will not bring her to your door.'

'She is a woman,' stated Bersaba as she looked back at him.

He studied her face questioningly.

'Women are more sensitive to…' She looked upward thoughtfully. 'I suppose thee may call it "natural magic",' she finished. ''Tis powerful in this place.'

'Of that I have no doubt,' replied Thomas, glancing at the watchful yews.

'Indeed, but thou doest not have the same instinct for it as she. Men are preoccupied with their stature and their legacy.'

He opened his mouth to protest, but saw the sparkle of mischief in her eyes. 'You jest?'

'In part,' she admitted with a nod. 'Will ye come in?' Bersaba took a step back.

'I had better not linger. We have journeyed out while the folk of Zennor are at church and would be best served by returning to the cottage before they regain their freedom. I would not wish for us to be spied upon the hill.'

'Doest thou still fear the truth of what she may be?'

Thomas shook his head. 'There is no longer any fear, only idle thought.'

'But there is something that I see gnawing,' she stated, looking deep into his eyes.

He sighed. 'My mind turns to her departure.'

'She has indicated that she wishes to leave?' Bersaba was taken aback.

'Not as such,' he replied, 'but surely there will come a time when she will follow the call of home, wherever it may be.'

The healer gave a shake of her head and looked at him as though viewing a child. 'Young Thomas, thou casts thy thoughts to a time that may ne'er come to pass. Why doest thou not enjoy the time that is and leave the future to its own devices?'

'I can see the sense of your words and know their truth, but acting upon them is difficult.'

'Because of thy feelings,' she responded knowingly.

Thomas nodded. 'Aye. They grow stronger daily.'

'And hers towards thee? Doest thou know if there be fondness within her heart?'

'Sometimes I think it may be so, but how could such a woman love such a man?' He frowned and bowed his head dejectedly.

Bersaba took his chin in a withered hand, raising his gaze to hers. 'Listen to me, Young Thomas, such thoughts are as poison. They are a creeping darkness that will only do harm. Cast them out and stay true to what lies within thy heart,' she said firmly. 'Doest thou love her for who she is or for what she can give in return?'

'I said naught of love,' he replied weakly.

She raised her right eyebrow incredulously as she regarded him. 'Doest thou think I am a fool?'

Thomas shook his head within her grasp. 'I love her for who she is,' he said.

'So it matters not if she gives thee aught in return. Ye love her for being her, not in order that she must love thee.' Her expression softened and she smiled, lowering her hand from his face. 'Savour the present, Young Thomas, and savour thy time with her. It is a blessing to love another, whether that love is returned or otherwise.'

He stared at her as he pondered what the healer had said. 'They are words easy to say, but hard to follow.'

She nodded. 'Indeed, but remember them and try to hold to their truth.'

'I shall,' he replied with a nod. 'Your guidance is gratefully received, Bersaba.'

'I am glad to hear it is so,' she grinned. 'I would not like to think I have wasted my breath, for this aged form has little to spare on wasted words.' The healer winked at him. 'Now, ye must be away before the church empties.'

'Aye, it will take some time to reach the cottage. Our passage is slowed by Rosita's need to conserve her energy.'

'Take good care, Young Thomas, and remember what I have said to thee.'

He smiled. 'There is little danger of forgetting. I hope to see you soon, Bersaba.'

'May Dor Dama bless thee,' she said in parting.

Thomas turned back to Rosita and began to walk away. He glanced back over his shoulder and waved farewell, the healer raising her hand in response before shutting the door and vanishing from sight.

Coming to a halt before his ward, Thomas found her studying him inquisitively, lines of concern gathered between her brows. His smile faded as he tried to grasp the meaning of her expression, feeling discomforted by her bewildered gaze.

'What worries you?' he asked, voice restricted to a whisper and knowing his question had little point for she would not be able to answer.

160

Thomas nervously glanced back. The door of the hut remained closed and there was no sign of Bersaba as the yews continued to converse in their hushed manner.

'We should go,' he stated, the hairs on the nape of his neck tingling as he reached for her hand.

Rosita withdrew it as if fearful of his touch.

He looked at her in surprise. 'Rosita?'

She stared at him and then tentatively offered her hand. Thomas took it within his gentle grasp.

'I will not hurt you,' he said, finding no explanation for her behaviour other than the unfathomable belief that he would bring her harm.

Thomas raised his free hand and tenderly brushed a few stray strands of hair from her forehead. He saw the tightness about her eyes and felt the additional strength of her grip, both betraying her tension.

He scanned the location of the hut yet again before turning his attention to the southern slopes of Trewey Hill. He could find no evidence of anyone or anything that could have unsettled her so. It seemed that her behaviour was due to naught but his presence and this disturbed him greatly.

Knowing that they had to make their way to Ocean Mist before the congregation emptied from the church, he began to lead them back the way they had come. Shenty padded on the far side of Rosita, apparently also wishing to keep her distance. They made steady progress in strained silence, passing up the track and around the bend before making their way along the hillside. All the time his mind searched for answers, but found none. Thomas could not conceive of why she should behave in such a way towards him.

Passing through the front gate, Thomas glanced to the right and saw a patch of russet and white feathers amidst the long grass near the base of the windswept tree. He stopped and frowned, Rosita coming to a halt beside him and following his gaze. A pair of pale feathers lifted into the air, circling each other in a dance stirred by the breeze before settling back to the ground.

'El Zorro,' said Rosita.

'Zorro?' Thomas turned to her. 'Is that what you call a fox?' he asked, hoping she would get the gist of his question and that the act of sharing words would lessen the tension still lingering between them.

She looked up at him. 'Fox?' She made a snapping motion with her mouth.

'Aye. A fox,' nodded Thomas.

'Ah,' she said, nodding in return.

Thomas felt a little relief, glad for the brief exchange. He led them towards the door and was grateful that they would soon be hidden within the cottage. Taking hold of the handle, he hoped they would quickly settle back into the soft comfort of each other's company.

Nonna sat with shoulders hunched, as much against the collective glances of those gathered behind her as against the chill within the church. She had been made late by trying to rouse her husband. Marrek had been unable to rise after consuming too much mead the previous night, his eyes bloodshot, hand to his head as he lay on the cot and moaned. She had arrived during Father Blyth's opening words and discovered only the foremost pew on the left to be empty. Many had been the looks cast in her direction as she hurried to be seated with the twins in tow, holding their hands tightly as she suffered the combined scrutiny of the congregation.

She sat and endured the weight of those behind her, the breeze whispering in the eaves and a pair of pigeons cooing, much to the priest's glancing annoyance. He stood before the altar at the front left of the congregation, Nonna sitting closest to his hawkish position as he looked out over the gathered villagers and spoke of Christ's birth.

His words were lost on her as she tried to hold herself in place, her legs filled with the urge to make haste from the church and return to the privacy of home. She knew those behind her would be pondering Marrek's failure to attend, their thoughts turning to the rumours that had been circulating in regards her infidelity. She was also certain that when the sermon came to an end there would be whisperings and mutterings, though whether any of the folk would find the courage to openly voice their questions was doubtful.

Nonna tried to focus her attention on Father Blyth, glad to discover he was giving the benediction that indicated the service was near its end. The Latin words echoed about the interior as Jowan began to shift upon the hardness of the pew to her right. She glanced down at him and lowered her brow, the boy frowning up at her, but bringing his agitated activities to an end.

'Amen,' stated Father Blyth with a bow.

She took hold of the twins' hands and brought them to their feet, making for the aisle.

'Mistress Trelawny,' Blyth's voice lifted from amidst the sound of worshippers rising to their feet.

A hush descended and stillness reigned as Nonna turned to the priest.

'You may all go home now,' he said pointedly, looking to the congregation.

The folk of the village began to make their way to the southern door, glancing over their shoulders as they made as little noise as possible, hoping to overhear what was to pass between the two figures standing in front of the altar. Blyth moved to stand before Nonna. He glanced at those exiting the building as they stepped out into the sunshine beyond.

'I would have a private word with you,' he said once satisfied that the church had emptied enough so that his words would not be overheard.

Nonna's grip on the twins' hands grew tighter, finding security in the contact and their closeness. 'What word would you have?' she asked, sure of what the priest wished to speak with her about.

Blyth looked to the boys, briefly wondering whether he should ask that they be sent away, but certain she would not heed such a request. 'I spoke of faith during the sermon,' he stated.

Nonna nodded. 'Aye?'

'I also spoke of remaining faithful to Our Lord and the laws He set down, for He remains faithful to us despite our sinful ways and sent his only Son in order that these sins could be forgiven.' He held her gaze meaningfully.

Nonna merely stared at him, hoping to make his castigation as awkward as possible and not wishing to take the lead of his words by admitting she knew what they related to.

Blyth took a deep breath and his frown deepened. 'We must also remain faithful to those with whom we have been

164

bound in the eyes of God,' he stated, raising his eyebrows as Daveth and Jowen started to become restless, looking longingly at the open door to the church, the latter swinging his mother's arm back and forth.

'I do not take your meaning,' she lied, donning a look of bafflement.

His expression soured. 'To stray from your husband is also to stray from the path of God,' he said, being as direct as he dared before the boys.

She gave the priest a hard look. 'Does wisdom come from God?' she asked.

Blyth looked at her in confusion, her response being far removed from what he had anticipated. The woman before him seemed to feel no guilt, but to have grown in stature as a result of his thinly veiled comments. 'Aye,' he replied simply, wary of where she was leading the conversation.

'Then those who claim to be His servants should use this wisdom and not listen to the talk of idle tongues,' said Nonna with a challenging tone that caused both boys to look up at her curiously.

'Idle tongues?' balked Father Blyth.

'Aye,' she nodded. 'There is not a grain of truth in what you have heard.'

He pondered for a moment. 'Then where is your good husband? Should he not have been seated by your side?'

'Indeed he should, but the mead he took last night was to his detriment this morning,' she replied.

'Why does he drink so?' Blyth and noticed a flicker pass fleetingly across her face. Something was afoot.

Nonna glanced downward. 'It is a habit that has long been his and one which grows worse.'

'There is no more to it than that?'

She raised her gaze to his once again. 'Seek and ye will not find, Father, for there is naught hidden here.'

His jaw tightened at her manipulation of the Biblical quote. 'Tread carefully, Nonna,' he said, purposefully using her first name, 'for you step close to blasphemy.'

'I only speak the truth.'

'That remains to be seen,' he replied, wondering at the look that had passed across her face. 'Your sins will find you out for God knows all and sees all.'

'Then I have naught to fear, for I have not strayed.'

Father Blyth studied her. There seemed no lie in her eyes.

'May we leave now or are there more words you wish to share with me?' she asked, her tone laced with impatience.

'You may leave,' he said with a dismissive wave of his hand, a contemplative look upon his face as he tried to un-riddle the flicker of concealment which had shown in her expression when he had enquired about Marrek's consumption.

Nonna turned without words of parting and led the twins along the aisle between the empty pews. They then went left and made for the door, the boys eager to be at play.

'One last thing,' called Father Blyth.

Nonna paused, the boys staring longingly at the sunshine only a few yards before them.

'You will wear a veil next time you attend my church.'

'I do not cover my hair,' she replied.

'It is not a request,' he stated coldly, believing that the lack of headdress was an outward sign of her wayward nature, the woman lacking the servility suited to her sex.

Nonna glared at him defiantly and then led the twins from the building.

The pigeons cooed in the rafters and Blyth looked up at them absently. 'I will find out your sins,' he muttered. 'Of that you can be certain.'

39

Thomas sat in the shifting gloom of the Old Pen, the fire burning brightly in the next room. He chopped the last of the turnips for the stew, palms dusted with dry earth that had rubbed from the skin of the vegetables. Scooping up the pieces, he dropped them into the cooking pot to his right and they splashed into the water held within.

Pushing the back the seat, he stood and wiped the off-cuts of rabbit they lay upon the tabletop into his hand. He stepped over to the seaward door and bent to place them in Shenty's bowl, glancing at the entrance to the living space over his shoulder in expectancy of her arrival.

'Shenty,' he called as he straightened.

The hound did not make an appearance.

The sound of melodious humming drifted to him and he recognised the tune immediately. It was The Lay of Ailla, a song that Rosita had heard many a time during her stay at the cottage. He stood and listened, her wordless rendition containing a light which his had ne'er carried, a touch of warmth which was not evident in the story the lay told, but which was woven into the harmonies by her kindly nature.

Thomas smiled sadly as he moved back to the table and picked up the cooking pot. Rosita glanced up as he entered the living space, her eyes sparkling as she paused the task of threading cord at the front of the shirt she had been making, the tune momentarily faltering.

He went to the fire, a pile of twigs and branches drying on the far side of the pit. Crouching, he hung the pot from the frame that was already in place over the lively flames. He stared at the leap and flicker as the lay concluded, the sound of Rosita's humming seeming to whisper about the interior after the tune had come to an end.

Thomas slowly turned to find her smiling. She lifted the shirt and motioned it towards him, saying a few words in her strange tongue.

'For me?' He stared at her in surprise. He had not suspected for an instant that she was making the garment for him. He knew that the woollen shirt he had given her irritated her skin and believed she had been making another as its replacement.

Rosita nodded, gaze filled with affection. She held the shirt out further, clearly eager for him to try it on.

He hesitated, still held in place by his surprise. Thomas then reached for the shirt and took it from her, holding it up to himself.

Turning to the bed on his left, he carefully rested it on the patchwork of furs. He took off his jerkin and the woollen shirt beneath, placing them over the foot of the cot. Lifting the gift, he drew it down over his head, feeling the relative comfort of the linen as the warmth of the fire caressed his bare back.

He looked down at the front of the shirt, his beard brushing against his collar bone. Pulling the cord, Thomas drew the front together, the ends hanging loosely from the top. He lifted his arms and studied the airy sleeves. Though the style was one he was unfamiliar with, it was comfortable and would be perfect when the warmth of spring arrived.

'My thanks,' he said, turning to her and nodding. 'It is a wonderful gift,' he added.

Rosita gave a short laugh and clapped her hands together in delight, her smile wide and beaming. She could see the pleasure upon his face and that the shirt was a good fit.

Thomas perched on the edge of the cot, not wishing to take the shirt off for the time being and thankful that the warmth of the fire was keeping the night's chill at bay. 'You are precious to me, Rosita,' he stated, looking to the flames once again as emotions churned within and his heart swelled.

He turned to her. 'Very precious,' he restated, hoping beyond reason that their time together would ne'er end.

40

Jago walked southward along the muddy track as he made his way through Zennor Churchtown. Smoke swirled across his path as it drifted up from the cottages beyond the stone wall to his right. He glanced down at them, a haze of fumes wrapped about their presence and the scattering of trees in which they rested. Scrabbling sounds issued from the cage swinging beside him as he gripped its handle and it rubbed against his leg. Teca was lively, the pale ferret anticipating what was to come.

He turned his attention to the forge which lay ahead on the other side of the track. The blows of Gerens' hammer issued from within, the top portion of the door open to the dull day. The rumours of the smith's salacious activities immediately came to mind, as did the threat Gerens had made not so long ago, Jago prickling in response to the memory.

He drew level with the door and stepped over, boots sinking into the mud. 'How goes it, Gerens?' he called loudly, looking into the gloom as the smith beat the blade of a scythe that rested on the anvil.

'It goes well,' replied Gerens, glancing over briefly, 'and with you?'

'Aye, well indeed.'

The blacksmith nodded as he hammered the blade and sparks flew. 'What brings you to my door?'

'I am called for at Trewey Farm. Old Jacob is in need of my assistance.'

'Of this I am not surprised. The week of rain we have endured will have brought many a rat in from the fields.'

'In the hundreds, by his account,' confirmed Jago, 'and it looks as though the rain may soon return,' he added, glancing up at the heavy clouds.

''Tis no surprise in winter,' responded Gerens with little interest as he thrust the blade into the glowing coals within the fire pot.

Jago watched for a while, feeling Teca's movement within the cage at his side. 'I hear ye have been enjoying Nonna's company of late,' he said with a knowing tone, studying the smith's reaction to his words.

'What?' The question was sharp and accompanied by the quick turn of Gerens' head as he looked to the man standing outside the door.

'Oh come now, Gerens. It is common knowledge amongst all the folk,' said Jago with a conspiratorial grin.

'I know not of what you speak and would have you tell me plainly rather than dally with unnecessary words.'

''Tis apt you use such a word, for I speak of the dalliance between you and Nonna Trelawny.' Jago raised his brow accusingly.

Gerens' visibly stiffened and his glare gained a hardness matching that of his anvil. 'You accuse me of conducting an affair?' he asked darkly.

'It is not an accusation, it is knowledge,' retorted Jago.

The smith shook his head. 'Your knowledge is limited to rodents and little else, Jago. Now be gone before my anger sees fit to make itself known with greater force.' His grip tightened on the hammer.

'I recall the threat you made the last time I stood at your door, smith,' he said, the last word said with distaste. 'It seems your threats are easily made, just like Nonna,' he added with vicious self-amusement.

Gerens rose from his stool with purpose, hammer clasped in both hands. Jago stepped back from the door, right boot slipping in the mud and temporarily unbalancing him.

'Do not let your shadow darken my door again, rat catcher,' growled the blacksmith.

Jago spat upon the wood before him and then set off towards Trewey Farm once again.

Gerens went to the door. Stepping out, he found the rat catcher hurrying away and already at some distance from the

170

forge. He battled the urge to hurl insults at Jago, if not his hammer. Breathing heavily through flaring nostrils, he tried to calm himself, his thoughts turning to Nonna and wondering whether he should visit with her in order to give warning in regards the rumours.

Shaking his head, knowing that if he were seen his visit would be misconstrued, Gerens slowly turned. His gaze lifted to the sprig of oak leaves above the door. His eyes narrowed as he studied them. The edges were growing brown and curling in upon themselves.

He stood with an expression of concern as he stared upward for a while, wondering at their diminished vitality. Returning inside, he went back to his stool, the scythe still tucked in the coals. He seated himself, taking the blade in the tongs and then beating it upon the anvil as he pondered both Jago's words and the ominous change evident in the leaves that had remained green for so long.

41

She moved low upon the path between the stone walls, trying
to make as little noise as possible. The roof of the cottage
came into view above and to the right. Nonna could see
smoke rising from the hole in the thatch and hoped it
signalled that Carrow was in residence.

Reaching the end of the walls that marked the field
boundaries, she hesitated on the threshold of the open
grassland ahead. Another step and she would be in clear sight
should Carrow or his supposed guest look from the south-
facing window. She had found no suitable excuse by which to
call upon him and so had decided to simply climb the hillside
and spy out the cottage in the hope of gleaning answers and
satisfying her curiosity.

Nonna tried to think of a reason for her presence should
she be seen, but naught came to mind, as had previously been
the case. Frowning as a magpie gave out its rattling call, she
stepped from the concealment of the walls and moved with
stealth up the slope towards the cottage.

Nonna barely dared blink as she stayed low and
approached with haste. She reached the gate and ducked
behind the stones of the garden wall beside. She would not
risk the creaking of hinges and so moved to the right, passing
beneath the branches of the windswept tree. Moving around
the corner, she kept as low as she could without crouching.

Nonna came to a halt once again when she reached the
side of the building. She listened for evidence of occupation,
but there were no sounds bar the call of gulls at the coast.

She brushed a few windblown strands of sandy hair from
her face and made her way to the north side of the cottage, her
back to the granite. Reaching the corner, she peered round,
finding no one in evidence.

Nonna went down on her hands and knees. She crawled beneath the first of the seaward windows, the shutters closed on the chill breeze. Rising on the far side, she attempted to look between them, seeing naught but darkness through the small gap.

She crouched beside the water butt by the seaward door and wondered at her next course of action. She had not the courage or excuse to simply knock, but did not want to return home until her thirst for the truth was quenched.

Sitting on the ground, she decided to wait awhile. She pulled her fur cloak tighter about her frame, the wind brushing against her lower shins as they were revealed beyond the hem of her woollen dress.

Time passed slowly and she felt the dampness of the ground rising through her clothes. The first drops of rain began to fall and her thoughts turned to home. If she lingered much longer she would likely catch cold, something she could ill afford with the twins, her husband and the house to maintain, not to mention the chores about the farm she had to see to when Marrek was too impeded by drink to carry out his duties.

Nonna looked to the right and readied herself to crawl back to the corner of the cottage. She began to make her way, the shutters above beginning to stir in the growing wind as she planted her hands and knees upon the wet grass, feeling the plaint earth sinking beneath her weight.

'We will be in need of more firewood soon.'

She became motionless at the sound of Carrow's voice, listening intently for a reply.

None came bar the sound of the shutters against their fastening.

'I will take the basket and pass over the hill to find more after checking the traps on the morrow.'

Nonna risked rising to the shutters once again, her head cocked towards them. She waited for some response to the words spoken by the man whom she had known to be unusual even as a boy. They had grown up around Zennor at the same time, Carrow only a year older than she. Though they had rarely crossed paths, she knew him to be afflicted by a strange malady, one that seemed to remain with him if the evidence of her ears was aught to go by.

Staying in place a moment longer, Nonna then began to make her way back around the cottage. She heard no other words issue from within as she reached the south side of the building and paused. Checking that the way was still unwatched, she followed the wall of the garden and then moved down the hillside as the rain became heavier, beating against her back as if hurrying her home.

42

Father Blyth got to his feet. 'May the Lord watch over you and keep you,' he said, crossing himself as he looked upon Lacy Lugg through the smoke haze. She lay beneath the covers of her cot, skin ashen and cheeks sunken. A stream of mucus oozed from her nose, making its way down the near side of her face.

She tried to speak, but the soreness of her throat brought only fearful coughing, her eyes closing and tears forced from them.

Morvoren moved to crouch beside her mother and wiped the glistening mucus away as best she could with the encrusted rag in her hand.

'I will take my leave,' said Blyth, pushing back the stool upon which he had been sitting. He passed around the fire pit and stepped to the door of the small cottage. The glow of flames was captured in the fumes filling the air and brought to mind images of hell.

With great relief, he opened the door and felt the bite of the wind upon his cheeks, remaining just within the threshold as the rain beat down beyond. It dripped from the lintel in a steady curtain of dully glinting droplets and he saw the orange glow behind him in their fall.

'Father?'

Looking over his shoulder, he found that Morvoren had followed with the filthy rag still in her hand. He turned to her, hawkish nose wrinkled and barely able to hide his disgust. Of all the homes in Zennor, this had always been the one he least liked to visit, the pungent smell of herbs always hanging thickly in the air, ragged bunches hung about the walls.

'Will she recover?' asked Morvoren, holding the piece of cloth in both hands and wringing it with concern that was echoed in her expression.

Blyth glanced past her at the sorry figure upon the cot. 'By the sight of her, it does not look good,' he admitted, turning his gaze to the woman before him.

'Is there no more you can do for her other than offer up prayers?' she asked with a pleading tone.

'Prayers are the best medicine, Mistress Nan. It is by the Will of God that they be answered or otherwise, for He sees all and knows all. Your mother will recover if it is Our Lord's bidding.'

She stared at him in dissatisfaction, but put no voice to it.

'If there be naught else, I will take my leave and bid you farewell,' he stated.

Morvoren simply nodded her response, taking hold of the door handle in eagerness to close it upon him.

Father Blyth turned to the curtain of rain. Seeing movement at the edge of his vision, he peered to the right. Gerens was skulking through the downpour, coming along the track some hundred yards away and making his way towards the forge. He watched as the smith reached the door, glancing around as if hoping he had not been seen.

Blyth stepped from the doorway. The men's eyes met as Morvoren closed the door behind him.

Gerens stared at the priest, his dark hair and braided beard dripping with water. Adjusting the position of the parcel held beneath his left arm, he opened the door to the forge and quickly made his way inside.

Blyth watched the smith vanish into the gloom as the rain soaked into his black vestments and a pall of smoke swirled down from the roof of Lacy's cottage. He looked to the church on the other side of the track, narrowing his eyes against the fumes. Thinking for a moment, the image of Gerens sharp in his mind, he decided to visit Trelawny Farm and discover whether the words spoken by Nonna two days before were in fact the truth.

The priest moved to the rotting gate that hung permanently open and would soon come away from its hinges. He walked out of the small garden and onto the track. Turning left, he tried to hurry through the rain, but his shoes slipped in the slick mud and hampered his progress.

Reaching the turn that led to the farm, he passed westward and walked down the gentle slope between stone walls that bordered small grazing meadows. The entrance lay thirty yards ahead, the farm no more than a ramshackle collection of huts and a small barn resting at the bottom of the shallow valley, the cottage where the couple lived set back to the right.

Nearly losing his footing, Blyth slowed his pace. He looked up the slope that rose beyond the farm to find a figure making its way down the track towards him. His eyes widened as he realised who it was and the image of Gerens before the door to the forge came to mind.

With as much haste as he could manage, he moved out of Nonna's line of sight. Walking over to the entrance of the barn, he stepped inside and moved to stand by the wall to the left of the doorway.

He stared out, able to see the cottage from his vantage point. Listening for any sign of her approach, he hardly dare breathe for fear of alerting her to his presence. His mind swam with thoughts of the clandestine meeting that had no doubt recently taken place. He envisioned the harlot and the smith entwined in the rain beside of one of the field walls and his expression became pinched with distaste.

Nonna suddenly appeared from the left, moving swiftly as she headed for the cottage. Father Blyth moved from his hiding place, stepping into the doorway, but careful not to leave the shelter of the barn.

'Good day to you, Mistress Trelawny,' he called after her.

Nonna visibly jumped and spun round to face him, immediately recognising his nasal tones. 'What reason have you to be loitering in our barn?' she asked a little breathlessly, her pulse elevated.

'From whence have you come?' he replied, ignoring her question.

She glanced over her shoulder at the cottage as if thinking of attempting a retreat. 'That is my business,' she replied.

Blyth shook his head. 'To think I was nearly convinced of your innocence. Now I find your list of sins growing longer. You are both an adulteress and a liar.'

She blanched at his words. 'I know not what causes you to find me this way, but you find me wrong.'

'You have just returned from a meeting with Gerens, have you not?' He raised his brows as if daring her to disagree.

'I have not,' she stated.

'Then where is it you have been?' he insisted.

Nonna turned her gaze to the ground as she considered her response. She feared for her husband. If she mentioned his assertions of a mermaid living upon the hill then he would likely become a laughing stock. His drinking was already beginning to consume him and it would only become worse should he face such derision. On the other hand, if she were to reveal what she suspected of Carrow then he would surely suffer a cruel fate at the hands of the folk.

'Where I take myself is none of your concern. I need not seek your say so nor your pardon. Only my husband has right to know where I choose to go.'

'Well then, shall we go and ask him?' Blyth walked out into the rain and began towards her.

She held up her hand and shook her head. 'He recovers from another night lost to the mead and not will look kindly upon the intrusion.'

He halted a few yards in front of her. 'I would be the judge of that.'

'I am his wife and judge well enough his needs,' she said coldly.

There was a moment of stillness. The sound of the front door opening caused her to turn.

'Shut the door, I will be along shortly,' she said, waving the twins back inside as their pale faces peered from the gloom beyond.

'My family is need of me,' she stated to the priest as the boys vanished back into the cottage and the door was closed.

He held her in his cold gaze.

Turning, Nonna walked away.

178

'I will be sure to speak with you again,' said Blyth with menace, watching her for a little longer before making his way back through the rain.

A chill ran the length of her spine in response to his tone. It did not bode well and Nonna was certain this would not be the last of it. However, she could bear the brunt of the priest's words, whereas her husband would not be able to bear the ridicule of the village and Carrow would suffer far worse than mere words should the truth out.

She entered the cottage with her mane of sandy hair matted and dripping, boots encased in mud which had also spattered her lower legs and the hem of her grey dress.

'Daveth says you were speaking with Father Blyth outside?' said Marrek from his stool by the fire, the intonation of the statement carrying with it a question.

'Aye, he spied me coming down the hill and wanted to know my reasons for such.'

'Did you tell him?' he asked as the boys sat upon the earth in the far left corner, Jowen poking a stick at the funnelled and dusty cobweb where they knew a large spider to dwell in the hope it would mistake the movement for a fly and scurry into sight.

Nonna shook her head as she walked over and crouched beside the fire, gathering her long hair and wringing it above the flames to the hiss of watery demise. 'It is not his business to know.'

Marrek stared down at his wife and leant forward, elbows upon his knees. 'What did you discover upon the hill?' he asked, lowering his voice so that the boys would not hear.

'I think you were mistaken,' she replied, removing the fur cloak and placing it over the empty stool to her right so that it may dry.

'I heard Carrow speaking, but there was no reply. It may be that the friend he had as a boy remains with him to this day.' She settled on the ground and savoured the heat, closing her eyes as the water upon her face glistened in the firelight.

'Friend?' Marrek looked at her without comprehension.

179

'Aye, do you not remember? Many are those who spoke of it when he first returned from Truro.'

Marrek shook his head.

'He had a friend, though I cannot recall the name they went by. Some said she was a girl, others a deer, but none could see her other than Carrow. He would talk freely to her and play upon the moor.'

Marrek nodded slowly as a memory came to the fore of his impeded mind. He recalled Old Jacob telling of Carrow's boyhood visits to Trewey Farm. The lad was said to speak to someone who was not in plain sight and the farmer would offer slices of buttered bread to both him and his imagined friend.

'But I saw her with my own eyes,' he protested.

'You *thought* you saw her in the mist,' she stated with emphasis on the second word. 'As for the other sighting, the mead may be playing tricks on your mind, as it has before.' She looked at him knowingly. 'I recall when you saw your father at the foot of the cot and the time you heard your mother calling your name.'

'This was no imagining, Nonna, this was a mermaid as real as you or I.'

'A mermaid?' enquired Daveth, looking over from the corner of the room.

'Let us speak no more of this now,' she said, glancing meaningfully at the boys as they rose and made their way over.

'What mermaid?' asked Jowen as they drew alongside their father with inquisitive expressions upon their youthful faces.

''Tis no concern of yours,' stated Nonna, her tone indicating that the matter was closed and there would be no more talk of such.

The boys glanced at each other and then frowned. They looked to their father, hoping that he would satisfy their curiosity, but he stared at the flames before him and paid them no heed. Dejectedly wandering back to the spider's web, they slumped upon the ground as the interior of the cottage was filled with a wordless hush.

43

Thomas sat upon the chair his grandfather had made and whittled the thick piece of driftwood held in his left hand. His leggings were covered in shavings as Rosita sat on the earth between the seat and the cot, warming herself before the flames as the fire's heat held back the evening chill.

This was the second evening he had spent working on the new piece. The wood had whispered to him and he could clearly see the shoal of overlapping fish that wished to be carved. He was absorbed in the task, investing little thought as the blade cut and sliced.

Rosita coughed and he looked up, finding her watching him. She smiled, though he could see restlessness in her eyes and a plea tucked within the creases of her expression. She had been confined to the cottage for some time and was hankering for the wide open spaces beyond.

'I should teach you to carve,' he said, glancing at the driftwood.

He pointed at her and then at the wood before lifting the knife meaningfully.

Her features softened and she shook her head. Rising to her feet, Rosita held her hand out to him. Thomas stared at it and then tucked the knife into its scabbard, taking hold and smiling up at her.

With a gentle tug of effort, she pulled him to his feet. Wood shavings scattered about his boots and upon the ring of stones surrounding the fire pit. Speaking a few words of her native tongue, she nodded towards the Old Pen.

Thomas did not grasp her meaning, but allowed Rosita to lead him into the other room as he continued to clutch the new carving. She took him to the seaward door and went to open it with her free hand.

'You want to go outside?' he asked. 'But it is dark and the night is cold.'

'Outside,' she said with a nod, grasping the handle.

He glanced over his shoulder at the warm glow spilling into the Old Pen, hesitant to leave, but wishing to make her happy. 'Wait,' he stated, holding up his hand.

Releasing himself from her grip, he quickly went back into the main living space and placed the carving on the chair. Stepping over to the cot, he took up the patchwork cover and then returned to the door where she waited, Rosita smiling brightly when he re-entered carrying the fur.

'This will keep you warm,' he said, going to her and draping the cover over her shoulders.

'Gracias,' she responded, pulling it about her and then opening the door.

They walked out to find that the cloud of earlier had cleared. A sickle moon hung in the sky as it waned towards newness. Rosita took a few steps and then drew to a halt, craning her neck to stare up at the multitude of stars that blinked and flickered above them.

Glancing at him, she lowered herself to the lush grass. Taking the patchwork from her shoulders, she covered herself with it as she lay down.

Thomas stared at her as she patted the ground to her right.

'Come,' she whispered simply.

He moved to her and rested upon the grass, a good yard between them. She shook her head and chuckled lightly before moving over so their shoulders touched, pulling the cover over him in order that they could both benefit from its insulation against the chill.

They lay side by side and looked up to the heavens, the starlight falling into the deep pools of their eyes. Rosita pointed at the brightest of the lights above, Thomas nodding in response as a fox barked upon the hillside to the south.

She shivered and drew in closer to him. He placed his left arm beneath her shoulders and felt her hair against the side of his face and she moved her head to his.

'Hermosa,' she sighed while continuing to take in the sight of the glittering sky, a swathe of stars more dense than any other directly overhead.

Thomas was overcome by a sense of contentment the likes of which he had ne'er felt before. Rosita snuggled into his side as the minutes passed in the distant wash of waves. A gentle breeze caressed their cheeks with its cold touch, the fox barking once more, its call further inland as it hunted in the darkness. Thomas could almost hear the sound of the stars singing, such was their presence above. It was like a song at the very edge of his hearing, a potential held in the air.

'I love you,' he whispered into the night.

She shifted against him and he turned to find that her eyes were closed, a tranquil look upon her face. His gaze followed the gentle curves of her nose and dark lashes, passed over the smooth skin of her cheek and took in the slight pout of her lips.

'I think this may be a dream,' he said softly, looking back to the stars hung in the firmament.

Rosita snuffled and gently smacked her lips as she slept beside him. Letting out a moan, she buried her face against his neck, hiding from the chill. Her breath caused his skin to tingle and a tremor of response ran through him as he drew her closer within the embrace of his arm.

The minutes passed in the succulent whisperings of the night. The cold began to bite, his nose becoming painful and cheeks stinging. He felt Rosita begin to shiver beside him and decided it was time to go back into the relative warmth of the house, hoping that the fire would not need relighting.

Shifting from her side, letting her head rest upon the grass, Thomas then gathered her into his arms with the cover still upon her. She stirred, eyes opening but remaining hooded. She draped her arms about his neck as he stood, leaning into his chest and curling there.

He took her back into the cottage and through to the main living area, setting her upon the cot. Moving to the woodpile, he selected a few slender branches and took them over to the weak flames that still struggled against the invasive touch of winter. Placing them in the pit, he remained crouching at its side, holding his hands above and trying to bring warmth back to his fingers.

Rosita sat up and yawned. She looked to him, a sweet smile upon her face though she continued to shiver.

Pulling the patchwork about her, she slipped from the bed to sit on the earth beside him. Thomas lowered himself and placed his arm about her thin shoulders. They watched as the flames took hold and the fire slowly regained its strength, vanquishing the damp that remained in the wood with which it had been stoked.

'On the morrow I shall begin to teach you to carve,' he commented, the growing warmth beginning to ease the pain in their cold-reddened faces.

44

Stepping out of the seaward door to Ocean Mist with the waste bucket at his side, Thomas paused as he yawned, eyes still puffed by sleep. He walked to his left and passed around the corner of the cottage, the tails of his long coat fluttering in the cold wind. He emptied the contents of the bucket between the building and the buttressed timbers that held the hillside in place, the ash emptied from the fire pit absorbing much of what he threw down.

Noting a spill of earth upon the ground, he looked to the higher timbers and saw that part of a rotting plank had given way after the recent rains had added weight to the soil. With a touch of worry, he surveyed the wood. In many places it was crumbling in damp shards and it would only be a matter of time before a serious collapse threatened the cottage.

Going back to the northern side of the house, he moved to the water butt on the far side of the door. Crouching, Thomas placed the bucket on the grass before the wooden barrel and then pulled out the stopper near the bottom. Water gushed out and he swilled it around the inside of the bucket as he continued to think about the possibility of a landslide.

Stopping the butt once again, the fingers of his right hand dripping, he stood with the bucket in his hands. He made to pour out the water and suddenly went still, his gaze fixed on what appeared to be vague footprints.

Thomas settled onto his haunches. Placing the bucket beside him, he leant in close and studied the imprints, scanning the ground and discovering more leading around the corner. He followed them along the eastern side of the cottage, walking with back bent and eyes narrowed as he looked for traces of disturbance. The prints became increasingly vague, finally vanishing from his sight in the high grasses that grew upon the hillside beyond the garden wall.

Thomas straightened and searched for any sign of someone skulking upon the hillside, first looking to the moor and then to the fields below. A feeling of discomfort came upon him. He glanced over his shoulder at the gate, the urge to beat a hasty retreat building within.

Movement caught his eye and he looked to the moor once again. Elowen's small form was silhouetted against the pale clouds as she stood upon the hilltop.

Thomas blinked. She took fright and fled from sight, as if his meagre movement had set her hooves in motion upon the rough ground.

He stared after her for a while before retracing his steps alongside the house and making his way back to where the waste bucket rested on the far side. He looked at the prints and noted that they were most apparent beneath the window.

Guessing at the purpose of whoever had been sneaking about the property, Thomas stepped to the shutters and attempted to peer through the gap. He was relieved to find that he could spy naught but darkness.

A gull cried out as it flew overhead and he glanced up before looking down the hillside. His sight settled on the church tower below as he pondered what reason had given cause for someone to prowl about the cottage. Only one answer came to mind.

'Rosita,' he whispered.

His expression tightened. 'Are there some below who suspect she abides here?' he asked, the wind taking his hushed words.

Glancing around nervously, Thomas picked up the bucket and tipped out the water as the nape of his neck tingled. Stepping to the door, he walked into the Old Pen and gratefully shut it behind him.

He put the bucket upon the earth and picked up the chair resting on the right-hand side of the table. Leaning it against the door, he wished for something more substantial by which to bar any unwanted entry.

Hearing Rosita shifting on the cot in the living area, he turned to the doorway with a deep frown. He could not bear the thought of losing her to either the place she called home or the people of the village below. Her presence had to remain a secret.

Thomas took the bucket through to the other room, placing it in its usual position in the corner by the south-facing door. Rosita sat up, drawing the furs about her shoulders, Shenty disturbed as she lay curled at the bottom of the cover.

'I shall light the fire for you and then go to the cove in the hope of catching a fish for our supper,' he stated, managing a weak smile.

She cocked her head as she regarded him, clearly aware that something had unsettled him.

'Do no worry yourself,' he said with a dismissive wave of his hand.

Thomas collected his tinder box from beside the woodpile and moved to the fireside. He took out the flints and began to strike them violently together, the imprints beside the cottage lingering in his mind and accompanied by a distinct sense of foreboding.

45

Nonna crouched beside the cot in the far right corner of the farm cottage and stared at the sleeping visage of her husband as the twins tussled with each other by the front door. Strings of saliva clung to the bundle of furs upon which Marrek rested his head, his mouth agape and gentle snoring issuing forth.

She took hold of his shoulder and shook him. "Tis time for church,' she stated.

He did not stir.

'Marrek,' she said as she shook him again.

Still her husband did not wake.

'MARREK!' The word was shouted and she shook him with greater vigour than before.

An expression of annoyed confusion dawned upon his reddened face. His eyes opened a little, the whites heavily veined with the affects of the previous night's drinking.

Marrek placed his hand to his forehead, cupping it as his brow creased in response to the pain that throbbed there. 'I shan't be coming,' he said, voice thick with phlegm.

'You have not attended Mass on many an occasion of late,' she replied, frowning at him. "Tis Sunday morning and the most attended service of the week.'

'It cannot be helped.'

'It can,' she said curtly. 'If you could resist the call of the mead then you would be at my side, as you should be.' Her tone had a hard edge and he winced in response.

'I have no wish to suffer the glances of the village by attending without you,' she said, 'as I have before.'

Marrek licked his lips, tongue thick and a foul taste in his mouth. 'Sorry,' he whispered, closing his eyes and massaging his temples with his fingertips.

'That word has no meaning without action.'

'Ouch! That hurt,' said Jowen loudly.

Nonna's head snapped to the right. 'If you cannot play nicely then you will not be playing at all,' she scolded.

'Why do we need to go if Tas does not?' asked Daveth.

Nonna glanced at her husband and raised her eyebrow. 'This is what your drinking begets,' she said before turning back to the twins. 'Your father is unable, not unwilling,' she replied.

The boys looked at each other knowingly.

'The mead,' said Jowen.

Marrek attempted to raise his head, but lowered it again almost immediately, letting out a moan of pain. 'It is no good,' he said with a vague shake of his head as he swallowed back against a rising surge of nausea and took deep breaths.

The sound of three loud knocks upon the door gave Nonna a start. She rose to her feet and walked across the room, passing the darkened fire pit.

'Who do you think it is, Mamm?' asked Jowen as the boys moved aside.

'I have no way to tell until the door is opened,' she replied, taking hold of the handle and opening it as she turned from her son.

A look of surprise dawned and she was taken aback by the sight that greeted her. Golvan stood before her and was flanked by Father Blyth and Jago. Beyond them were two other men of the village. On the right stood Morvoren's husband, Benedict, who bore an abashed expression as he stared at the ground and shifted uncomfortably. To the left was Arthur Pendle, an elderly resident who had an unfortunate look, one side of his face hanging limp and lifeless after suffering a seizure some years before.

She looked at the men before her door in utter bewilderment. 'What is the meaning of this?'

'You are to come with us,' stated Golvan forcefully.

'Why?' Her heart began to pound fiercely as the twins peered out from behind her.

'You are to be secured upon the cucking stool beside the church door so all can see your shame,' said Father Blyth sternly.

'The cucking stool!' She looked at them in horror.

'Aye, and may it purify you of temptations of the flesh,' replied the priest.

'But I have done naught to warrant such punishment,' she protested, her cheeks flushing and placing her hand to her chest, grasping the wool of her dress tightly over her heart.

'You have committed adultery.'

'I have done no such thing.'

'Come,' said Golvan, reaching for her arm.

Nonna stepped back.

'It is no use resisting. Your punishment has already been decided upon.'

'By what proof do you pass judgement?' she asked.

'All the folk know of your activities,' said Jago, 'and Father Blyth caught you returning from meeting with the smith.'

'That he did not,' she said with loud incredulity.

'Enough of this,' snapped Golvan, taking a step and grasping her right arm, pulling it from her chest as he tried to take her into his custody.

Nonna slapped him across the face with her free hand, the sting of the blow heard in its sharp sound and seen in the release of his grip. He stared at her as his shock passed to anger.

Golvan raised his right hand and cast a swiping blow upon her cheek, his knuckles jarring against bone. She staggered to the side, banging into the door. Her hand rose to her mouth as blood began to weep from a split in her lip. Her cheekbone ached, mouth hanging open as she looked at him with a victim's dismay.

He prepared to strike her a second time, the gleam of pleasure in his eyes.

'Stay your hand, Golvan,' said Blyth sternly.

191

He glanced over his shoulder to find the priest looking at him disapprovingly. Slowly lowering his hand, he looked at Jago as he stood to his left. 'Bind her hands,' he ordered.

Jago stepped forward, taking a coiled length of rope from the top of his leggings.

'Marrek!' called Nonna, her word edged with panic as she looked back and blood dripped onto her dress, pain creeping beneath her right eye. He was asleep upon the cot.

'Leave Mamm alone,' stated Daveth, stepping around his mother and planting himself between her and the men beyond.

'Move him aside,' instructed Father Blyth, looking back at Arthur.

The old man moved forward and gathered the boy into his arms.

'Let me down,' said Daveth as he struggled and beat Arthur's shoulders with fists unequal to the task of freeing himself.

'Leave him alone,' yelled Jowen, rushing over.

Benedict moved to intercept the boy and took hold of his wrists, holding them firmly. Jowen tried to wriggle them from the grasp, but lacked the strength.

With rope uncoiled, Jago walked towards Nonna, Golvan stepping to the side.

With sudden movement, she spun round and made to run over to the cot. Golvan's hand shot forward, grasping her sandy hair. He yanked her back, her legs buckling beneath her so that she hung in the air from his painful grip.

'Quickly,' he stated to Jago as he took hold of her hair with both hands.

The other man moved forward and grabbed her arm, twisting it behind her back and tying one end of the rope about her wrist. He took hold of the other arm and repeated the process as she set her feet on the ground and tried to rise.

Her hands securely tied, Jago stepped back. Golvan retained his grip on Nonna's hair with his right hand, turning her to face him and pulling her head back so her throat was exposed and constricted. He drew her to him and grinned.

"Tis time your learnt your place, bitch,' he whispered, savouring his revenge.

'Enough!' exclaimed Father Blyth, seeing the sadistic satisfaction in Golvan's expression and sickened by the sight, his nose wrinkling. 'We must take her to the stool and secure her there before the service is to start.'

Golvan glanced at the priest and then held Nonna in his gloating gaze for a moment before releasing her hair. Her head fell forward, blood still oozing from the split in her top lip. She stared at the dark stains down the front of her dress as tears began to fall, her right cheek swelling and eye pulsing with the pain of bruising.

Jago took hold of her arm and began to lead her away as her sons watched helpless, Arthur and Benedict still holding them securely as Jowen began to sob. Father Blyth followed behind Nonna, Golvan lingering momentarily as he savoured the sensations of power that filled him.

'Today your sins will be exposed and absolved,' said the priest as he drew alongside her, 'and what better day to be cleansed than on the eve of a new year? You can start afresh on the morrow.'

Nonna did not reply as her tears flowed silently. They fell to the ground beneath her bowed head, marking her passage from the cottage as she was led away.

The twins were released as she was taken beyond the barn and left along the path. Jowen ran into the cottage, weeping loudly as his brother stood dumbfounded, staring wide eyed at the diminishing form of his mother.

Arthur and Benedict caught up with the group as they reached the main track through the village. Nonna's boots slipped in the mud as the cold wind stirred the hem of her faded green dress and Jago kept a tight grip on her arm.

She was taken through the entrance to the churchyard and up the path to the church. Lifting her head, she blinked away her tears and saw the cucking stool resting to the left of the door as they drew close.

'Sit,' commanded Jago as he drew her to a halt before the simple seat.

193

No fight left, she did as instructed, sitting on the stool, the creak of its timbers welcoming her. Jago produced another length of rope and tied her ankles to the front legs, the twine hanging between.

Nonna kept her head lowered as he checked that the bonds were secure and then stood. He stepped out of the way and Father Blyth took his place as the other three men looked on.

'Now your shame is for all to see,' he stated as she heard others entering the churchyard as the time for the Sunday morning Mass drew close. 'I advise that you use this time to think on your duty to your husband, for it is straying from this duty that has brought you to this place.'

He remained before her for a few moments and then stepped to the church door as more of his congregation approached along the track, whisperings arising in response to the sight of Nonna bound to the stool. She kept her head low, gritting her teeth against the pain in her cheek as she shivered.

'What of Gerens?' asked Jago as Father Blyth stepped into the building. 'Surely he cannot go unpunished.'

Blyth looked back at him. 'I will speak with him later. Now I have my flock to attend to.'

'Speak to him? He belongs in the stocks.'

'Would you be the man to restrain him so?' asked Golvan, whose courage knew its limits.

Jago glanced at him and then sagged, looking to the mud. He had hoped to see the smith humiliated and to be part of the action taken against him.

The sound of Father Blyth's steps marked his passage into the Church, Jago lingering with his disappointment as the other three men went inside. The folk of the village began to pass as they entered, Nonna enduring the weight of their stares and the half-heard words that passed between them. Her thoughts were elsewhere as she considered taking the boys east to her sister's. She would leave Marrek to his mead and begin afresh beyond the reach of those who sought to punish her.

As the door to the church was shut on the last of those to arrive, she lifted her head and looked up at Trewey Hill to the south-west. Should she have told Father Blyth that he was punishing her for the very thing he believed she had strayed from, that it was her duty to her husband that had caused her to be seated on the cucking stool?

Nonna shook her head and sighed. There was little to gain in telling the truth now. She would take the punishment and, even though the temptation to leave was strong, she was resigned to staying in Zennor with the man to whom she had been bound in the eyes of God. Thoughts of going were mere flights of fancy conjured by her mind as it balked at the treatment she had received. She doubted whether she had either the will or the wings to leave.

46

The blade passed slowly along the whetstone. A few flakes of rust fell from the nicked edge as Thomas drew it away from him. He sat at the table in the Old Pen, the shutters of the seaward window open despite the chill wind, letting in the light so that he may clean the knife which had belonged to his father. Its wooden handle was darkly stained by sweat and grime from his father's hands and he could feel the residue of life still clinging to the wood. It was rare that the knife was left behind, but on the fateful day that had claimed his life, his father had gone to sea without it.

He glanced into the living area to his right as the sound of Rosita stoking the fire came to him. His gaze settled on her back as she crouched before the flames and he frowned. When her request to accompany him to Treen Cove had been refused she had been visibly perturbed. She did not understand his caution in light of the prints discovered that morn, but instead found his refusal to be a bewildering rebuke.

Thomas shook his head and sighed, hoping that his gift of the knife would mend the small rift between them. He looked to the window as the shutters thumped softly against the granite and stared at the heavy clouds beyond. His shoulders were tight and he had spent much of the time at the cove glancing over his shoulders. He had felt as though he were being watched and worried that someone may approach the cottage during his absence. His nerves were jangling and he expected a knock to sound upon the south-facing door at any moment.

Turning his attention back to the sharpening, he made good the old blade so that she may learn to carve. He checked the blade against his thumb, finding that it was fit for purpose.

Rising, he stepped to the window and closed the shutters on the wind. He made his way into the living space and moved to crouch by Rosita's side as she sat on the earth by the fire pit.

'Here,' he said, holding the knife out to her.

She glanced at the implement and then looked at him in puzzlement.

'Take it.' Thomas motioned it towards her.

After a slight hesitation, she took it from him, adjusting her grasp on its worn handle to find comfort. He straightened and went to the cluttered bench against the wall. Scanning the driftwood, he picked a small piece and dug his nail in, finding that it was soft and would be easy to cut.

Thomas returned to her side, looking to the gap beneath the door to check no lurking shadow was in evidence beyond. Seating himself on the ground, he passed her the piece of wood and realisation dawned upon her face. Rosita smiled at him and then stared at the timber clasped in her left hand. It was smoothed by the sea and paled by the bleach of the sun. A few grains of sand were embedded in its surface and she ran her thumb over them in contemplation of what she would carve.

He watched. There was care and softness in her handling of the driftwood, as if she held something precious and sacred. Her face was lit by the flames of the fire and the light of thoughtfulness. Her brow was creased, the scar upon her temple a constant reminder of the misty morn when he had first found her lying in the surf.

Rosita's expression changed, the flicker of a smile passing across her lips and her eyes widening almost imperceptibly. He recognised the change. The wood had whispered to her.

The blade of her knife moved to the surface of the driftwood and made its first incision, a shaving falling to her leggings. Thomas watched her work for a few minutes, feeling a deep affinity with the enigmatic woman. She had heard the wishes of the wood and her creative spirit had been stirred into action in response. It was something he had

197

experienced many times and which strengthened their bond despite the lack of words that passed between them.

He got up, Rosita glancing sideways at him for only an instant before returning to the gentle thrust of the blade. Going to the chair, he picked up the fish carving that rested on the ground beside it. He did not seat himself, but moved back to sit by her side, settling before the fire and taking out his knife. Taking pause to consider the wood in his hand, he composed himself before setting the blade to its potential.

47

'Gerens the smith.'

He turned and looked at the door to the forge, poker stilled in the fire pot. The nasal voice of Father Blyth was unmistakable, though there was an edge to the holy man's tone that he had not heard before. 'What need do you have of me?' he called back.

'I would speak with thee about a matter of some importance.'

Gerens pulled the poker from the coals and hung it on the wall to his right, the faint glow at its end quickly fading to black. He rose from the stool and walked to the door. Swinging open the top portion, he discovered Blyth standing on the muddy track with Golvan and Jago flanking him, both having requested to be present and the priest accepting their company for the sense of security it brought him.

'It would seem you need an escort in order to speak your words,' he said, 'and a poorly chosen one at that.' He glanced at Jago on the left, whose expression darkened.

'I care not of your opinion, smith.' Blyth's words carried a greater chill than the wind. 'I come to tell thee to leave this place and ne'er return.'

'Leave?' Gerens was taken aback. 'What reason drives you to such a demand?'

'Adultery,' stated the priest.

'I have committed no such thing. You pay too much heed to rumour and not enough to truth.'

'I live in truth,' counted Blyth with a touch of condescension. 'You live in godlessness.'

'You know not of what you speak. Rather than one god, I find godliness in all things. You see one face of God. I see all faces.'

'Blasphemy is unwise,' said Blyth's coldly.

'Is it blasphemy to see God in all things when all things come from God?' asked the smith. 'Is your God in one place or every place, Father?'

'You know the answer well enough, Gerens.'

'Aye, He is in every place.'

Blyth nodded. 'That is so.'

'Then He must be in rock and stream, in beast and bird, even in the rain,' said the smith. 'We revere the same essence, only with different words.'

'I did not come to endure your sacrilegious words. Your pagan beliefs cannot be compared with the sanctity of the Church,' said the priest heatedly.

'No, you came to make demands based on ignorance. You have not the wit between you to see that talk of an affair is merely the dripping of loose tongues that congeals in the minds of those foolish enough to take heed.' Gerens looked at the three men and shook his head.

'Mind your words, smith,' said Jago with a scowl, taking a step forward.

'Your confidence is misplaced,' said Blyth. 'Even now Mistress Trelawny sits upon the cucking stool before the church due to the sins you have committed together.'

The blacksmith looked at him in shock. 'Nonna is upon the stool?'

'Indeed she is,' nodded the priest. 'Her shame is public and your shame is known to all.'

Gerens looked along the track, leaning out of the door and spying the edge of the churchyard wall. 'You must release her. We have done naught wrong.'

'We *must*?' Golvan sneered, a club fashioned from blackthorn root gripped in his right hand, its shaft misshapen by burls and its end bulbous.

'It is too late for your protestations,' said Blyth. 'Your guilt has already been deduced and judgement has been passed.'

'You have no authority over me.' Gerens' expression darkened and he opened the bottom portion of the door, stepping out onto the mud.

Golvan moved to block the path leading to the church and readied his club, believing that the smith may attempt to make his way to Nonna. Though he did not relish the idea of tussling with the stockier man, he knew that such action would rally the entire village against Gerens and his expulsion from Zennor would not be in doubt.

The smith looked to Golvan and then glanced past him to the wall of the churchyard. He was well aware of what would happen if he tried to free Nonna. Her place upon the cucking stool was seen as punishment, as the metering of justice. If he interfered there would be no allies to be found amidst the folk.

'I tell you again, there was no affair,' he said with cold certainty.

'What proof do you offer?' asked Blyth.

'How can I offer proof when there is naught by which to offer it?' he replied in exasperation.

'As I thought,' said the priest with a look of disdain.

'What proof do you have that such transgressions took place?' Gerens fixed him with a demanding stare.

'It is written all over your face,' responded Jago. 'You carry the weight of your guilt for all to see.'

'That which you read upon my face is not guilt, only despair at those who blindly hound the innocent, and with apparent relish.' He held the priest's gaze. 'Did you know that one in your company has an axe to grind in regards Nonna Trelawny and the other against me?'

'Do not try and muddy the waters with your forked tongue,' said Jago.

'That is of no consequence,' said Blyth. 'Neither man forced you to indulge in elicit activities, and that is why we are here.'

'And yet you have no proof.' Gerens shook his head sadly, turning his gaze to the mud.

'I saw both you and she returning from a clandestine meeting only the other day.'

The blacksmith's head lifted and he regarded Blyth in confusion.

'I had visited with Lacy Lugg and spied you before the forge.'

Gerens thought back, his expression becoming one of realisation. 'Had I a parcel beneath my arm?'

'Aye,' nodded Blyth. 'Some token of your meeting, no doubt.'

The smith showed clear signs of relief. 'It was salted beef,' he stated. 'I had been to Trewey Farm to deliver the mended blade of a scythe and the meat was my payment.'

Golvan glanced at Father Blyth, whose brow furrowed as he pondered what had been revealed.

'Can Jacob confirm this?' Blyth bore a look of concern, the image of Nonna bruised and battered as she sat on the cucking stool coming to mind.

'Aye. We should to the farm right away.' Gerens stepped to his left, Jago quickly moving to block his way.

The priest thoughtfully rubbed the bridge of his nose. Though he had long held the smith in contempt and wanted rid of him, he could not risk expelling him only to have Old Jacob undermine his reason for doing so. If Nonna had been wrongfully punished his position would already be weakened and he dare not take action against the smith without checking his claim.

'Even if what you say is true, that does not mean you are free of guilt,' stated Jago, seeing that the holy man was wavering and hoping to stiffen his resolve.

'Aye,' said Golvan. 'The entire village knows of your seedy activities.'

'The entire village *knows* naught of the matter,' replied Gerens.

'We should go speak with Jacob,' said Blyth, shaking his head, unhappy with himself for jumping to conclusions based on village gossip.

'What point is there in that?' asked Jago, starting to feel the situation turning to the favour of the smith. 'Gerens and Nonna may have met before or after he visited with the old man.'

'Aye, what Jago says is true enough,' added Golvan.

202

'Do you not hear the axes grinding, Father?' Gerens looked meaningfully at Blyth.

The priest glanced at the men to either side of him. 'Gerens and I will go to Trewey Farm alone,' he stated firmly.

Jago opened his mouth to protest, but Blyth held up his hand to silence him.

'Go back to your homes. Your presence is no longer required,' stated the holy man.

Jago and Golvan glanced at each other and in that glance they knew defeat. They hesitantly withdrew from the priest's side and began to make their way northward along the track, the club hanging limply at Golvan's side.

'Do not concern yourself,' mumbled Jago as smoke from the buildings below swirled about them. 'His time here is almost at an end.'

Golvan glanced questioningly at the rakish man to his left.

'Did you not see the yellowing of the oak leaves above his door? It is an augury. His time at the forge is coming to a close. Dor Dama's blessing is no longer upon him there.'

'Do not speak to me of such things,' stated Golvan coldly, 'for I put no faith in them and neither should you.'

'Mark my words, whatever the result of this day, Gerens will soon be gone.'

Golvan ignored the rat catcher and picked up his speed, not wishing to hear more of his talk.

48

Nonna raised her head to the approach of muddied steps. Her eyes widened at the sight of Gerens walking side by side with Father Blyth, a sight she had ne'er thought to behold.

'We have come to release you,' announced Blyth as they drew to a stop before her shivering form, dark bruising beginning to make itself known about her right eye, cheek and lip angry with swelling.

'Release me?' she asked in confusion.

'Aye. It seems that I was mistaken,' admitted the priest, Gerens' claims having been confirmed by Old Jacob during a brief exchange at Trewey Farm. 'I am sorry for that which has been unfairly inflicted upon you.'

Relief showed in Nonna's beaten expression. Gerens moved before her and went down on one knee, reaching for the bond about her left leg.

'Wait!' exclaimed Father Blyth as the smith made to untie it.

'What is it?' asked Gerens over his shoulder.

Blyth's brow furrowed as he thought on the sight of the blacksmith gently brushing Nonna's pale shin with the backs of his fingers. It was not the touch of strangers, but one of familiarity and affection.

'You almost had me for a fool, but you have undone your own deceit,' he said after a few moments of contemplation, staring coldly down at the smith.

Gerens looked at him in puzzlement.

'I saw the caress of your fingers. It said far more than all thy words,' he stated. 'She will not be freed and you will not escape justice.'

'I know not of what you speak,' replied the smith with mock innocence.

'Oh, but you do, Gerens,' said Blyth. 'I will listen no more to your pleas or complaints. I know your guilt as sure as I know day follows night.'

Gerens glanced at Nonna, hopeful that she may find words which could undo the betrayal of his fingers. She remained silent, expression falling.

'Leave her be and vacate these sacred grounds before you sully them with your heathen presence,' instructed Blyth with icy hardness.

Gerens slowly rose to his feet, looking regretfully at the woman tied to the stool before him. He turned to the holy man, knowing that there was little point in arguing his innocence. His touch had revealed all. Golvan had stumbled upon the truth by hap of chance and soon Blyth would make sure rumour became knowing.

'I will give you five days grace in which to leave the village,' stated the priest. 'If you remain beyond that time you will be forcibly evicted.'

'I was born in that very forge,' he replied, not as protest, but in sad reflection.

'You cannot make him leave,' said Nonna, straining against her bonds.

'There is one other choice,' said Blyth, ignoring the woman upon the stool.

'What may that be?' asked the smith as he stared at the holy man.

'We could take you into custody and give you over to the authorities in Lostwithiel, though I fear their punishment would be more severe, especially when I inform them you tried to free the harlot.'

Gerens sagged. 'I will be gone by the fifth day,' he conceded weakly, his gaze to the ground as he began to walk towards the churchyard entrance.

'You cannot do this,' moaned Nonna.

Blyth turned to her. 'Further words would be ill advised,' he said. 'Use this opportunity to think on where your loyalty should truly lie.'

'With my husband?'

'Aye,' he nodded as Gerens reached the track and turned left, his head bowed as he made his way back to the smithy.

'He is not my husband,' said Nonna. 'My husband drowned in a cup of mead many years ago.'

'He is the man to which you are wed.'

'Man and woman should be joined by love, not ceremony,' she replied. 'Surely God sees within people's hearts and is in no need of such?'

'Marriage is God's sanction of that love.'

'And when that love has died?' she asked pointedly. 'What of those who marry for land and fortune and not for love?'

'True love ne'er dies.'

'Thus speaks a man who knows naught of such love.'

'I have given my heart to the Lord and such devotion should not be mocked,' he stated, a tone of warning to his words.

Benedict Nan came hurriedly along the track from the opposite direction of the forge, his face drawn. He looked over the wall and came to a stop, stepping to the stones. 'Father,' he called.

Blyth turned to him.

'Morvoren asks that you come quickly to the house of her mother. She fears the worst and wishes you to perform the last rites.' He glanced back over his shoulder, a sense of urgency to his voice and demeanour.

Blyth looked down upon Nonna as he ran a palm over his shaved scalp. 'Heed my words and repent, for thy soul is in need of cleansing,' he stated, pausing momentarily before turning and walking away with a long stride.

He passed out of the churchyard and made his way to Benedict. The two men then set off for the cottage, the priest bracing himself for the haze of thick smoke and strong smell of herbs as Nonna stared after them with tears in her eyes.

49

A few days had passed since Thomas had spied the imprints that whispered of someone lurking about the cottage. Each morning after taking out the ash and emptying the waste bucket he had checked for fresh signs of visitation, but had seen none. The fear of hearing a knock at the door had subsided, becoming only a shadow in the back of his mind. The shutters banging in the wind no longer drew his gaze.

He sat on one of the chairs from the Old Pen, which had been brought into the living area. Rosita sat in his favoured chair to the right, both seats facing the seaward window, the dull light of another cloudy day affording them the illumination by which to carve.

His mind was not set to the task. Instead, he wondered about the likely duration of her stay. He feared that she would leave when spring came, called back to the place that she called home, be that the embrace of the ocean or some faraway land. The cottage had been changed by her arrival. Where there had been gloom and loneliness there was now light and company. She had brought colour into his life and he dreaded the return of the dismal existence he had endured for so long.

Rosita cleared her throat and he blinked, shaking out the thoughts as he did so. He turned to her and found her looking at him with concern.

'Do not worry,' he said, adopting a thin smile. 'All is well.'

She continued to study him and then raised her carving, lap sprinkled with shavings. In her hand was a curled shell. Its wide entrance was hollowed and a groove circled the side, making its way to the centre, a gentle rise between its constricting passage. An ever shortening pattern of waved lines passed over the rise as it drew inward, like ripples upon the ocean.

''Tis beautiful,' he said, looking into her dark eyes, which sparkled with the pleasure and fulfilment of creation.

'Beautiful.' Rosita held his gaze, the word filled with the warmth of her accented voice. 'Hermosa,' she said in her native tongue.

'Hermosa,' he echoed with a nod.

Her smile broadened. She glanced at the shell and then held it out to him. 'Thomas,' she said softly.

A delicate shiver caused him to tremble momentarily. She had ne'er spoken his name before and the rich depth she afforded it made his heart ache. He slowly took the shell from her grasp, sparks akin to those from his flints arising as their fingers touched, the fire of his desire burning in response.

Rosita withdrew the mermaid carving from where she kept it tucked inside her jerkin. Looking down at it, she ran her fingers over its face with a delicate appreciation before turning and regarding him with affection.

'Te adoro.' The words were barely a whisper.

She rose from the seat with dreamlike slowness and stepped over to him. Thomas looked up at her as a tear fell upon her left cheek. He stood and wiped it away with the back of his hand as they stared into each other's eyes.

Rosita put her arms about him, drew him close and held him tightly. He returned the embrace, the shell still clutched in his hand as she leant her head against his shoulder. They stood for long minutes, lost in the warmth and closeness.

She took a step back from him. Reaching for his hand, Rosita took him to the seaward door in the Old Pen and opened it, motioning that they should go outside.

Thomas frowned. Though much of his nervousness relating to the prints had faded, he was still apprehensive about journeying out in the open with her.

Rosita's gaze contained a plea for liberty, one that he found impossible to refuse after the embrace they had so recently shared. He nodded his agreement and her smile immediately shone.

Giving his hand a thankful squeeze, she rested the mermaid upon the table. With a spring in her step, she went back into the other room and collected her walking stick, taking it out of fondness rather than need. The full recovery of her strength was almost complete and the strain of her ankle but a memory.

Rosita returned to the Old Pen, Shenty trotting in with her and letting out an excited yap. Draped over her arm was his coat, along with a moth-eaten fur cape which she had recovered from the small chest of old clothes. She handed the coat to him and flung the fur about her shoulders with a flourish, Thomas smiling in response to her enthusiasm.

Taking his hand once again, she led Thomas out of the cottage and into the fresh north-westerly, Shenty following and then bounding ahead.

'We shall walk to the cliffs and then return before I go and check the traps,' he stated as she looked to the grey sea and the calls of gulls lifted to them.

They set off down the slope at a steady pace, Thomas not wishing her stamina to be sapped unduly. She had spent weeks with little need for physical exertion and it would take time for her to gain enough vigour by which to accomplish greater distances or make her way over more demanding terrain, the latter a lesson hard learned.

He enjoyed the sensation of her hand in his as they made their way between the few fields that lay upon the hillside. Glancing over, it was clear that Rosita was happy to be out in the fresh air and he suspected that the sight of the ocean also gave her pleasure as they drew closer to the shore.

It was not long until they arrived at the cliffs, the wind ruffling the grasses and thrift that hung precariously over the edge. Thomas brought them to a halt five yards from the edge and they stood beside each other while staring out over the rolling waves that stretched to the horizon.

Rosita let out an exclamation and pointed to the left. He followed her gaze and saw the white sails of a distant ship. It bore three masts and was making its way south-west, soon to pass from sight as it made its way to the currents that met beyond the rocks of Land's End.

'I wonder to what destination they sail,' he pondered aloud.

Rosita released his hand and stepped to the edge of the cliff. He felt his stomach flutter with nerves at the sight of her so near the drop and had to resist the urge to pull her back to safety. Shenty sniffed a tuft of grass nearby and then moved to stand by her side, the hound raising her face to the wind and sniffing.

Rosita watched the rollers tumbling and thrashing thirty feet below. They frothed over the rocks, spray rising and drawn to the east by the wind, a few droplets caressing her cheeks. The last verse of The Lay of Ailla came to Thomas' mind and he became fearful that she would dive down to the waves, rejoining the ocean from whence she came. His heart beat against his ribcage and a feeling of nausea arose in the pit of his stomach, his mouth running dry.

She sought out the ship with her gaze, but it had passed into the west. Scanning the horizon, she then turned to him, the low sun breaking through the clouds as they became ragged, its light settling upon her face and illuminating the faraway look in her eyes.

He studied her expression and wondered at her thoughts. Did she think of home? Did the sea call to her soul?

Her smile returned, though without the vitality it had exhibited before. She walked over to him, the tapping of the walking stick marking her steps. Taking his hand, Rosita led them back up the gentle slope to Trewey Hill and Ocean Mist, Shenty wandering about the hillside before them, her explorations disturbing a partridge which took to the sky and fled into the west.

50

They moved through the thick fog upon the moor. The previous day had been one of light mist, but it had thickened and drawn in, visibility reduced to a few meagre yards. Rosita stayed close as they made their way to the next trap, the fur cloak pulled tight about her shoulders.

Thomas glanced over his shoulder, as he had many times before, checking that she was not tiring. She smiled at him, content to be upon the hillside despite the moisture gathered about them.

He smiled back and then turned his attention back to seeking the marker that would inform him of their location. Though the fog concealed them from the fields and village beyond, it also concealed the landscape through which they passed and hampered their progress.

Thomas saw the dark shape of The Old Man of the Moor and nodded to himself. A partridge called somewhere in the mist and he heard the skitter of disturbed stones as an animal fled from their approach.

Coming to a stop beside the rock, he rested his hand on its slick coldness as Rosita stopped alongside him, the tap of the walking stick falling silent. Shenty appeared out of the pale and wandered over. She sniffed the rock and relieved herself at its base before vanishing from sight once again.

The distant clash of metal arose from below and was accompanied by the faint creak of wood, the fog carrying the sounds and lending them a sharper quality than if the day had been clear. Thomas looked into the paleness down the slope, briefly wondering at the noises and then setting off once again.

As they neared the site of the trap he heard something that he did not expect. The urgent flapping of wings rose into the still air and he could hear the scrape of feathers upon shingle.

The fog retreated from his approach and revealed a jackdaw struggling to be away, its wings wide as they beat upon the ground, right foot tangled in the snare. Upon seeing him, the bird's attempts to flee became more desperate and it chattered in alarm. A couple of small black feathers rose into the air before settling upon blades of grass, held their by moisture, a bluish sheen apparent in their softness.

Rosita slowly moved past Thomas. She talked softly in her native tongue, the grey plumage about its neck and the back of its head ruffled as it turned to her approach. It jabbered and flapped it wings at her, hopping back and pulling the cord of the snare tight.

She crouched, but made no further motion toward the bird. The jackdaw's calls became less frequent as her warm words lulled it and its fear abated. It cocked its head to the side and observed her. Tucking in its wings, it let out a gentle call, all sense of alarm now absent.

Rosita calmly reached out with measured patience. The jackdaw shifted on its feet, watching her hands intently but showing no sign of undue distress as she continued to speak to it.

Thomas realised he was holding his breath as he watched the enchanting sight and fell under the spell of her words. He doubted any would be able to resist their soporific effect and wondered if he not be dreaming as the fog shifted about them as if stirred by her magic.

She took the bird into her hands without struggle. It let out a call as she took it to her breast and cradled it there while freeing its foot with her right hand.

Rosita's words continued to weave their tranquillity as the cord came loose and fell to the ground. She rose with grace, stroking the back of the jackdaw's head as she did so.

Once again taking it in both hands, she raised it into the air. There was a moment of stillness as Thomas watched, the image of Rosita standing in the paleness with her arms on high and the bird resting within her gentle grasp filled with a strange beauty.

She released the jackdaw and it took flight, quickly vanishing into the fog with a parting call. She stared after it for a while and then turned to him with a kindly smile that held more warmth than any fire.

'I do not want to leave, Mamm.' The protestation drifted up Trewey Hill, the voice that of a boy.

'Hush!' came a woman's sharp response. 'We must go quickly and quietly.'

Thomas looked towards the voices, judging their owners to be some way down the slope and there to be no risk of his and Rosita's presence being discovered. 'We must check the last of the traps and make our way home,' he said, keeping his voice low and indicating that they should move on with an ushering motion.

She nodded and he led them through the fog, her walking stick marking their passage across the hillside. He patted the brace of conies hanging beneath his coat, satisfied that they would have enough to eat for a few days and hopeful that the final trap would have ensnared another.

51

Jory passed the stool to Gerens, the smith placing it on the cart resting in the fog before the forge. His belongings were piled into its damp confinement, the fire pot emptied, the flames of his life in Zennor put out.

'That be the last of it,' said Mathey, walking out of the building and dusting off his soot-blackened hands as he came to a stop beside the young farmhand who played the rote on feast days.

Gerens nodded as he regarded the two men before him. They were the only members of the village to offer their help despite the years he had dwelt there and served the needs of the community, no others having the courage to give aid and face the disapproval of those few who had set themselves against him.

'There is one last thing,' he stated.

'I saw naught else,' responded Mathey.

Gerens walked past them, moving into the gloom of the forge. Jory looked at Mathey questioningly, the other man shrugging in response.

The smith returned with a tatty scabbard in his hand, its leather stained with the pale green of mould and the hilt of a sword rising from its shabbiness. He moved back to stand before the others.

'I could not leave without this,' he stated, pulling the blade partway out. The metal gleamed and it was clear that the smith took great care in maintaining it. 'It was hidden in the thatch.'

'Did you hide it there?' asked Mathey.

'Aye. It has been handed down from generation to generation,' he said, turning his gaze to the weapon. 'When my father gave it to me he told me it was from the time of

Arthur and The Merlin, that it had seen battle against retreating Romans on Bodmin moor.'

Mathey and Jory regarded the sword with admiring wonder.

'That is indeed a precious heirloom,' said Mathey.

Gerens nodded. 'One day I hope to be blessed with a son to whom it can pass,' he stated while continuing to stare at the blade.

There was a short silence, the solemnity of the occasion beginning to weigh upon them.

'I have heard that the tenancy is to be given over to Jago,' commented Jory in order to break the hush. 'Though his skill with a hammer could ne'er match yours,' he added with a flush of embarrassment when the smith abruptly slid the blade into the scabbard and his expression darkened.

Mathey glanced at the young man with brow furrowed. 'It is fortuitous that you do not have to journey far in this fog.'

'Fortuitous?' said Gerens. 'There is little fortuitous in this.' He looked to the possessions piled upon the cart, most of which related to his work in the forge.

'Will they have need of a smith in Mousehole?' asked Jory.

Gerens shrugged. 'That I do not know, but can only hope, for I have no stomach for the sea and would be of little use upon a fishing boat,' he replied. 'It may yet be that my cousin cannot put me up.'

'What then will you do?'

'I shall to Bodmin from where it is said my ancestors came,' he replied, glancing at the sheathed sword once again before looking up at the two men before him.

He stepped forward and extended his hand to Mathey. 'My thanks,' he stated as they grasped each other's wrists tightly, having grown up together and been friends since boyhood.

'You will be sorely missed.'

Gerens moved to Jory and gripped his wrist in parting. 'I will miss your rote playing,' he said with a sad frown.

Myrtle whinnied and shifted upon her hooves, the cart creaking in response.

'It seems as though it is time I took my leave,' said the smith with a glance at the mule.

'Fare ye well, Gerens,' said Mathey. 'May the journey lead you to better times.'

The blacksmith nodded. 'My thoughts will oft linger here,' he responded, looking at the old forge. 'I wish you both the best of fortunes.'

He glanced at the withered remnants of the oak leaves above the door and then walked to the front of the cart, placing the sword on the seat before pulling himself up. The vehicle creaked as he sat and took up the reins. Turning, he raised his hand in parting, both of the other men responding in kind.

Snapping the reins, Myrtle strained against the yoke and began to pull the laden cart along the track, its wheels digging deep into the mud. The timbers moaned and the belongings clanked as the cart passed over the uneven ground.

Gerens glanced back one last time, finding that the fog hid the forge beyond his sight, veiling his past and leaving him to the uncertainty of what lay ahead. With a deep frown, he set his face south and pulled his fur cloak tight as the mule plodded on.

Long minutes passed, the fog thickening. Naught was visible beyond a few yards, the walls beside the track mere shadows. He felt utterly alone as he glanced to the left, a winter thicket coming into view and then fading back into the paleness that drew back in behind the cart.

'Gerens.' His name was spoken quietly.

He brought Myrtle to a halt and looked to the right, seeing the vague presence of someone on the far side of the wall. 'Nonna?'

'Aye,' she replied, her voice a whisper. 'We are coming with you.'

'We?' He could see no one else.

'I have the boys with me. We will come to the gate a little further up the road,' she stated.

Gerens watched her insubstantial form vanish into the pale and then flicked the reins, the mule straining against the weight and setting off once again. He stared ahead, narrowing his eyes as he searched for her. She drew out of the fog, the twins holding her hands with heads bowed as they came to a stop upon the rough grass of the verge.

Bringing the cart to a creaking standstill once again, he looked down upon them. 'This is foolishness,' he said with a shake of his head. 'You cannot leave for they will only come after you.'

'I will not stay with Marrek any longer. I have endured enough.'

'And if those in Mousehole discover you are married?'

'Can you not be my husband? How would they know otherwise?'

Gerens glanced at the sullen boys. 'Word would reach them, of that I am certain. There are those here that would not rest until you were found.'

'Then let us go somewhere beyond their reach,' she said, looking up at him pleadingly. 'We could leave Kernow, seek a new life beyond its borders.'

'I do not want to leave Zennor, Mamm,' moaned Daveth as he stood to her left and looked up at his mother.

'Would you rather come with me or stay with your father?' she asked.

'I want to stay here with you,' he replied.

'I will not stay, Daveth,' she said with certainty. 'Even if Gerens will not take us, we shall not return to Zennor.'

The smith stared down at them. 'You mean to leave even if I refuse?'

She nodded.

'Where would you go?'

'I know not. All I can be sure of is that I am done with this place and the man to whom I am unfairly bound. He is not the man I married and therefore not my husband,' she stated, the conviction clear in her tone and expression. 'I thought to go with you, that the love we share would be enough for you to overcome the fear of discovery.'

Gerens glanced back over his shoulder as he pondered her request to join him. The punishment would be severe should the truth be brought to light. Mousehole was too close and there were those that knew it was his intended destination.

'We could to Bodmin,' he suggested. 'I doubt the reach of those set against us extends so far.'

'You will take us?' she asked, the words filled with hope and the fulfilment of her desire to leave with the man she loved.

Gerens nodded. 'That I will,' he replied, managing a thin smile. 'Now climb aboard, for we must away before your absence is noticed,' he added, sliding over to the far side of the bench.

'Up you go, you two,' she said, releasing the boys' hands.

They did not move.

'Go on with you.' Nonna put her palms to their backs and gave them both a gentle push.

Without enthusiasm, Jowen and then Daveth climbed aboard the cart, which greeted them with soft groans. Nonna followed them up and found no room to sit.

'One of you will have to sit on my lap,' she stated.

'I will, Mamm,' said Jowen, standing on the footrest as his brother sidled up beside the smith.

Nonna seated herself and gathered Jowen to her lap. Daveth grimaced as he shifted upon the bench and turned to see what was bringing him discomfort, his eyes widening as he picked up the sword.

'Is this yours?' he asked as he held it before him in both hands.

'Aye,' nodded Gerens as Nonna looked at him in surprise, the possession of such an item ne'er being mentioned during their times together.

'And it was my father's before me. It has been in my family for hundreds of years and saw battle in the time of Arthur.'

The boys looked at the sheathed sword in awe.

'It is even said that it was used to help drive Tewal-Tan back into his liar long, long ago.'

'The dragon?' whispered Jowen in wonderment.

'Aye, the dragon,' replied Gerens.

Daveth withdrew the blade a little, resting it on his lap and running his fingers over the cold metal. 'There is no blood on the blade,' he commented.

Gerens chuckled and shook his head, glad to be distracted. 'It was wiped away many years ago.'

'Have you ever used it?' asked Jowen, looking over at him from his mother's lap.

The blacksmith shook his head. 'Though there have been times when I have been sorely tempted,' he replied, glancing at Nonna meaningfully, gaze lingering on the fading bruise beneath her right eye.

'Can you tell us more about the time of Arthur?' asked Jowen, looking expectantly at Gerens.

'Let us be on our way first,' he replied.

'There is one last thing before we set off,' said Nonna.

He looked at her in confusion. 'What may that be?'

She leant across and kissed him tenderly. 'Hello,' she said with a smile while sitting back, the boys glancing at each other, but making no comment.

Gerens returned her smile and then took up the reins. Giving them a flick, he set Myrtle to the task of pulling the increased load along the muddy track, ne'er to go back to the village that lay hidden in the fog at their backs.

52

The mourners were shrouded in mist as they stood about the grave. Most of the village had gathered to pay their last respects, Father Blyth standing on the left-hand side, the church tower rising behind him as the Latin words of his final prayer lifted into the stillness. The heads of the villagers were bowed as he commended Lacy Lugg's soul to God after she had finally succumbed to the winter chill.

'Amen,' said Blyth, crossing himself and opening his eyes.

Those gathered at the graveside lifted their heads as the priest stepped to the pile of earth at its head. He took up a small handful and threw it down upon Lacy's body, watching it scatter upon the pale cloth in which the old woman had been wrapped, a few pieces tumbling into the shadows of death surrounding her.

One by one the folk followed suit, casting their farewells into the gloom and then stepping aside. Conwenna Trewey took up two handfuls, one on behalf of her husband. He had been struck down by the same fever to which Lacy had succumbed and was ailing in his cot, unable to attend despite his sincere wish to do so. She let the earth tumble into the grave, her pale lips moving as she offered up her own prayer, one which pleaded for her husband's return to good health.

The gate to the churchyard banged against the stones of the wall as it was flung open. All heads turned and all eyes settled on the form of Marrek as he leant again the gatepost for a moment and then staggered forward unsteadily.

'Damn you all,' he said vehemently, spittle leaping from his lips. 'You drove my wife away.'

'Golvan,' said Father Blyth, nodding over to the drunkard who could barely stay upon his feet as he tried to make his way over the glistening grass.

Golvan stepped away from the other mourners and strode purposefully towards Marrek. The inebriated farmer sneered, blinking as he tried to focus on the face of the man who approached, mouth hanging open.

'You drove her away for sins she did not commit,' he slurred, Nonna and the twins having disappeared three days before, most believing she had fled with Gerens the smith.

'You are drunk and know not what you say,' stated Golvan as he halted before the other man. 'I will take you home so that you may sleep off your intoxication.' He reached for Marrek's shoulder.

The farmer spun away from the hand attempting to take hold with drunken exaggeration. The sudden movement unbalanced him and he fell to the ground with a hard thud.

'You struck me!' he exclaimed.

'He did no such thing,' said Blyth with authority.

'You struck me and drove my wife and children from my side,' he said as dribble fell from his loose lips and he shook his head, hands and knees upon the earth.

Marrek tried to rise, but his boots slipped on the slick grass and he collapsed in a heap. He began to weep, mucus streaming from his nose and into the dark hair on his upper lip. Smothering his face in his hands, he mumbled words that could not be discerned as the rest of the village looked on in stunned silence.

'Come, I will take you home,' stated Golvan as he stepped up to the snivelling wretch and put his hands beneath Marrek's shoulders, straining to lift him to his feet.

'I have no home,' sobbed Marrek. 'I have no life. It took flight in the face of your lies.'

'The only lies were contained in your wife's denials,' stated Golvan. 'She and Gerens…'

'LIES!' yelled Marrek, his face glistening with mucus and tears as he stared at the other man with fire in his bloodshot eyes.

He swung his fist and Golvan quickly stepped back. The punch passed ineffectively through the air and the momentum

221

sent him tumbling to the grass once again. The farmer gathered himself into a ball and began to cry bitterly.

'It is best you leave him be,' said Blyth.

'Lies. All lies,' moaned Marrek. 'She was seeking the mermaid.'

Golvan shook his head as he looked down upon the drunkard with an expression of disdain. 'I should fetch a bucket of water with which to sober him.'

'The mermaid,' sobbed Marrek. 'This is all her fault.'

'Leave him be,' stated Blyth. 'It is time you all returned to your homes. The service is over and there is naught else to see here,' he said to the other mourners.

The villagers began to make their way through the mist to the gate leading from the churchyard, keeping a wide berth of Marrek as he lay curled upon the grass, body wracked by sobs. As they filed out, glancing back and passing mumbled comment to each other, Father Blyth made his way over to stand beside Golvan.

'Give him a few moments and then try to get him to his feet once more,' he said, his tone dark as he pondered whether to punish Marrek for disturbing the burial.

Jago walked over after lingering to the rear of the departing mourners. 'Is there any news on the forge?' he asked the priest.

Blyth turned and stared blankly at him. 'I beg your pardon?'

'The forge. Ye were going to put in a good word with Lord Adeney.'

'Aye, the forge,' nodded the priest. 'I shall draft a letter of recommendation on the morrow if you will help Golvan take this miscreant back home to sleep off the effects of the mead.' He nodded down at Marrek.

'Of course,' nodded Jago.

The two men stepped forward, each taking hold of an arm as Blyth watched. Marrek made no protest as he was dragged mumbling from the churchyard. Turning right, Jago and Golvan moved through the mist, the farmer's legs trailing in the mud as he continued to talk to himself, all the words passing between his dribbling lips indecipherable bar one.

'What do ye think he means by "mermaid"?' asked Jago, glancing over at Golvan to his right.

'Who knows? His mind is addled by the drink and the departure of his wife and children.'

Jago nodded as he altered his grip on the farmer's furs and they turned off the main track, Marrek falling silent. Snoring soon arose from his limp form as they passed the barn and made for the empty cottage before them.

53

The shutters were restless and the doors rattled against their frames as the gale buffeted Ocean Mist. Flames writhed in the fire pit strong drafts circulating around the interior. Rosita sat cross-legged on the cot beneath the patchwork of furs, the mermaid resting upon her lap. She was watching the dancing tongues of yellow and orange, eyes reddened by the thick haze of smoke stirring in the air. Thomas sat on the chair opposite her, the shoal of fish he was carving resting on his lap while he wiped away stinging tears and considered abandoning the task until a time more conducive to its creation.

He looked over to the shutters of the window beyond the head of the cot, the woodpile tucked in the corner to the left and in need of restocking. The wind had been strengthening all day, finally ridding the land of the mist and fog in which it had been bound for a week, but bringing with it stormy seas and the promise of rain to come. Thomas could hear it howl as it rushed in from the west and passed over the moor. He recalled trying to sleep on such nights when he was boy, his parents telling him that the sound was that of spirits woken by the storms, howling at the wind to quiet down and allow them to rest in peace.

Rosita began to absently hum The Lay of Ailla as she stared into the fire. He turned to her as the gentle melody placated the spirits upon Trewey Hill and the shutters quieted their activity, her rich tones lulling the storm.

She looked over to him when the tune came to an end and he spied the glistening of tears. 'Yo de largo para el hogar,' she said softly.

He looked at her in contemplation. 'You pine for home?'

'Si,' she said with a solemn nod, 'home.' The word was filled with longing.

'Such thoughts are common on nights like this,' he said, glancing to the shutters as the images of his parents rose to mind. 'The wind stirs the soul and makes it restless.'

Rosita looked at him without comprehension.

'It is the wind,' he stated simply, nodding to the window.

She glanced over her shoulder. 'La tormenta,' she said, nodding once again.

He smiled comfortingly and then turned his attention to the cooking pot hanging above the fire. Shifting forward, Thomas placed the carving on the earth and then moved to crouch before the flames. Shenty raised her head as she lay curled on the ground between the chair and cot, as if unable to decide who to sit with and eventually choosing the middle ground.

Peering into the pot, he found the stew simmering and hoped the meal would provide Rosita with a welcome distraction from the storm and the thoughts it gave rise to. He stood and went into the Old Pen, fetching two wooden bowls and a spoon.

Wrapping his hand in his sleeve, he removed the pot from the cooking frame and set it on the ground to allow it to cool, stirring the contents and watching the slices of turnip and cuts of rabbit turn in the thickness.

'You will have to wait.' He glanced at Shenty, who was sniffing the air with interest. 'Once we have eaten you can have a little of the leftovers,' he added as he poured a helping of stew into each bowl with the encouragement of the spoon.

Setting the pot back over the fire, Thomas then took one of the bowls to Rosita. She nodded her thanks and cupped it in her hands, savouring the warmth against her palms as she raised it and pursed her lips, blowing upon its steaming surface.

He went back to his seat and rested the bowl on his lap as he made himself comfortable. Lifting the stew, he sipped it and felt the heat against his face. They ate to the crackle of the fire and occasional rattle of shutters and doors as the wind rose and fell with less fury than before. The howling lifted now and then, like a lone wolf upon the hilltop.

Raising the bowl at a high angle, he drained the last of the liquid and then looked down upon the pieces of vegetable and meat remaining within. Sliding them up the sides until they could be properly grasped, he ate the last of the simple supper. The clatter and crash of boulders being tossed against the cliffs by the violence of the waves could be heard in the distance as the tide drew in towards the land.

'On nights like this my father would say that two giants stood upon Zennor Head and Gurnards Head throwing rocks at each other,' commented Thomas before sucking the last juices from the ends of his glistening fingers, his fingernails blackened by dirt. 'They were brothers called Garath and Garoth, and they competed for the love of a beautiful siren who sung out to sea.'

He looked over at Rosita, who smiled despite her lack of understanding. Noting that she had taken up the mermaid and the bowl lay empty upon the furs, he rose and stepped around the fire pit, reaching for the empty vessel.

She reached out and took hold of his hand, drawing him down to sit at her side. Putting her arms about him, she cuddled in close, resting her head upon his shoulder as she looked back to the flames.

Thomas put his bowl beside him and placed his arm about her shoulder, feeling the brush of her hair against his neck. 'You sing to my heart,' he whispered as he savoured the closeness.

54

Thomas opened the shutters and looked down the hillside to the left. The fields were bathed in sunshine as a warm southerly breeze rippled the grasses above. It was akin to a spring day and he marvelled at the change since the storm during the night.

Rosita drew up beside him and slid her arm about his waist.

''Tis a beautiful day,' he commented with a glance, seeing that she remained naked after washing herself with water from the tin bowl, the stained rag which she had used still held in her left hand.

She smiled at him and moved to the door. Opening it, she stood brazen in the sunlight that spilled into the cottage.

'Someone may see you,' said Thomas as he stepped over and closed the portal.

She frowned at him and then picked up the walking stick from where it rested against the head of the cot. Lifting it, she then pointed outside.

He nodded. 'Aye, we can do that,' he stated, though in truth he did not wish to risk walking upon the hill on such a clear day. It was likely that many of the folk below would venture from their homes to check livestock, survey crops or make such repairs as the storm had caused need for.

An idea came to him. 'We shall go to Treen Cove,' he said, knowing that no other villager went near due to the perception of its accursed nature.

Rosita walked into the Old Pen, returning with the white gown in which he had found her upon the beach and the shirt which she had made from the sail linen. She went to the bedside and lay the shirt out, nodding towards it. He looked at it and then glanced out of the open window. It did indeed seem warm enough to wear such a garment.

She dropped the gown over her head and freed her long dark hair with a backward brush of her hands. Thomas took off his jerkin and the woollen shirt beneath as Rosita picked up his shirt and stepped to him.

'Los brazos arriba,' she said.

He looked at her blankly.

Rosita took his left arm and lifted it up.

'Ah,' he said with a nod, raising his arms.

She climbed up onto the cot, its wood creaking. Running her fingertips over his chest, she suddenly tickled his ribs playfully.

Thomas wriggled and stepped back, a bright smile upon his face as he lowered his arms. Rosita chuckled, eyes sparkling.

She beckoned for him to approach with her index finger, saying a few words in her native tongue which seemed to protest innocence in regards another assault. He raised his eyebrow in amused doubt, but still stepped to the bedside once again.

Rosita regarded him with a mischievous expression and then waggled her fingers. Thomas retreated quickly.

She laughed, the sound filled with simple joy. Beckoning again, he shook his head in response.

'To me,' she said.

He hesitated and then moved back to stand beside the cot, his gaze ne'er leaving her face. She looked at him expectantly and after a moment he realised what she was waiting for.

Thomas raised his arms and Rosita took the shirt sleeves over them, drawing the garment over his head and torso. She looked down upon him and her smile faded slightly as the look in her eyes changed.

She took hold of the cords hanging from the collar of his shirt and pulled him close. He wrapped his arms about her and their lips met in an embrace filled with longing, her hands moving to his hair, fingers running through its unkempt length.

Shenty barked and he glanced at the hound, finding her looking up at him as she stood beside the bed and wagged her

228

tail enthusiastically. Turning back to Rosita with a smile, he saw his feelings reflected in the depths of her eyes as he continued to hold her for a few precious moments.

She stroked his cheek affectionately as they parted and then stepped down from the cot. Hastily donning her boots, she then took up the walking stick and stood before him in anticipation of their departure, clearly eager to gain liberty from the confines of the cottage.

55

He led her down the path into the morning shadows of Treen Cove. His arm trailed back as he held her hand, their balance upon the steep ledge of rock strengthened by the bond as their right hands grasped the guide rope. They passed from the carved steps and approached a fissure in the path where the rock had been smashed away during the night's storm.

Thomas brought them to a halt and stared at the gap. It was passable with a short leap, but the landing would prove awkward on the sloping and slick rocks beyond.

He released her hand. 'I shall jump across and then catch you,' he stated, finding that he still had need to explain even though she could not understand his words.

He took a small step back and felt her presence immediately behind him. With a deep breath, Thomas then leapt over the scar in the cliff-face.

He landed on the far side, boots slipping upon the rocks and causing him to fall back towards the fissure. Rosita let out a yell of fright as his hands flailed in a desperate attempt to take hold of the rope.

Managing to grasp it, his descent was brought to a jolting halt, pain searing in his shoulders. The metal hoop immediately to the left was yanked loose and pulled from its placement.

The additional give in the rope caused him to fall further back. His body dangled over the edge as he held on with white-knuckled insistence and the hoop that had come loose slid down to smack painfully into the side of his hand.

Thomas hung there a moment. His gaze was firmly fixed on the next metal hoop that held the rope to the cliff and he prayed it would not share the same fate as the other.

Seeing no sign of movement, he carefully began to pull himself up and away from the drop. He gained purchase with his boots, finally straightening and feeling a little nauseous as his heart pounded.

He turned to Rosita, his legs a little weak as he took a few breaths to regain his composure. He wiped perspiration from his forehead and then gingerly moved to face her.

'I will catch you,' he stated, holding his arms out to her.

She glanced down at the fissure and then turned back to him, a nervous expression tightening her soft features.

'I will not let you fall,' he said, forcing a strained smile.

Stepping back, Shenty waiting patiently behind her, Rosita then made the leap. She entered his arms and they stumbled back against the rock face, Thomas holding her tight.

Rosita looked at him with relief. 'Gracias,' she said, giving him a kiss on the cheek.

She withdrew from his arms and began to make her way down. Thomas watched as she vacated his presence, feeling her heat lifting from him.

Rosita leapt to the sand after slipping and sliding to the foot of the path. Pausing, she removed the oversized boots and placed them on a rock, turning to him with a bright smile. She beckoned him down as Shenty made the leap and scampered by her master.

He pushed off from the cliff, the mysteries of the woman with whom he now shared his existence drawing him ever deeper into her enchantment without need of a siren's voice. He could not help but smile as she laughed to herself and skipped off across the sands towards the retreating surf.

'I shall fetch my net,' he called as he reached the boulder-strewn sands.

He stood and watched as Shenty ran by Rosita's side yapping and leaping. The woman's dark hair was brushed by the fingers of the sea breeze and her long white gown fluttered behind her as she made her merry way to the waves with a carefree spring in her barefooted steps, the shadow of the cliffs still falling across the cove as the sun continued to rise.

Thomas made his way to the rear, the chill of the night still lingering in the air beneath the cliff. Climbing up, he retrieved the net as the sounds of Shenty's playful barking continued to rise.

He came to a halt as he reached the foot of the rocks gathered against the cliff, the net slung over his shoulder. He watched as Rosita stood ankle-deep in the waters, lifting the hem of her simple garb as she kicked plumes of glittering spray in the air and Shenty leapt and barked. They stood beyond the shadows of the cliff and were bathed in sunlight, her gown bright and the scene a vision of joy. His heart swelled and the warmth within chased away the chill in the air as he stood in the shadows.

A touch of sadness suddenly arose. Thomas felt removed from the scene of brightness and vitality. He was merely an observer, forever lingering in the shadows of his past.

With a melancholy sigh, he began to walk towards them. He wished to become part of the spectacle, to feel all his yesterdays tumble from his shoulders and bring a lightness of being.

Thomas paused upon the threshold of the shadows. The sunlight lay upon the sand only a yard ahead and the promontory of Gurnards Head was bathed in gold to the left as the waves lapped against its dark rocks.

Stepping forward, he felt the faintly warming touch of the late January sun upon his cheek and closed his eyes, imagining a caring hand laid soft upon his face. His mother's image began to take form in his mind's eye and he quickly raised his lids to find Rosita studying him curiously.

Thomas forced a tight smile. He longed to join his ward and the hound in the waters, but found himself unable. Some unseen barrier would not allow him to release himself to the urge, but kept him bound and upon the sands.

With a sigh, he wandered over to the rocks on the right, climbing up and making his way to the tidal pool. He blinked away the image of the corpse that he had found floating there in winter's infancy as he drew to a halt before it, the tide already beyond the far end.

Hearing the approach of bare steps, he turned to watch as Rosita clambered up to join him. She smiled brightly as the breeze smoothed her gown against her slender form and she moved to stand beside him.

She stared at the pool and dipped her toes into the waters while holding onto his shoulder for balance. Turning to him, she spoke in her honeyed voice, her words lost to him but still singing to his soul.

Releasing him as Shenty joined them by the pool, Rosita pulled the gown from her shoulders and let it fall to the rock at her feet. She stood naked for a moment and then dived into the pool. An arc of glinting droplets marked her entry and he watched as her head surfaced near the far end.

Running her hands back through her wet hair, she then called him into the waters with a wave of her hand. Her face was glistening, shimmering as though she were a mirage summoned from the depths of his mind, one of beauty and light, a siren whose song was in the depths of her beckoning eyes.

Rosita waved again and then dived back beneath the surface, her naked form patterned by golden ripples as she swam downward and then circled back to rise once again.

She looked at him and smiled. With arms wide, she swept her hands forward and sent showers of water towards him as she laughed.

Thomas glanced over his shoulders and saw no sign of another upon the cliffs or within the cove. He unfastened the shirt she had made for him and placed it on the rocks to his right before crouching to remove his boots, revealing feet ingrained with dirt.

Straightening, he tucked his thumbs into the top of his leggings and hesitated. The inner bonds that kept him restricted suddenly drew tight, causing him to doubt his actions, chest tightening with misgiving.

She splashed water at him again, encouraging him to join her in the pool after noting his uncertainty. Her warm voice came to him as she briefly spoke in her strange tongue, the caress of the sounds calming his tension enough for him to break free.

233

With a flourish of movement, Thomas pulled down his leggings and kicked them loose to the side. He stood disrobed before her and took a deep breath before taking the plunge.

The water in the pool was shockingly cold, his body tensing in response. He swam towards the surface, the chill only abating a little as he rose to the light dancing upon the ripples. Rosita down and swam past him with a smile and a wave. He looked to her legs as she kicked by, but no tail had taken their place.

His head burst from the waters and he gasped for air, wiping his face and flattening his hair back. She appeared at the landward end opposite him, shaking her head and loosing a shower of drops about her, Shenty snapping at those cascading close to the rocks upon which she stood.

Rosita laughed and then dived once again. He watched as she remained close to the surface, seeing the flashes of small fish darting about her as if welcoming one of their own. She swam towards him and then circled as he trod water. Her right hand trailed across his back as she did so, shivers of delight stirred into life by her fingertips, his spine tingling.

She arose immediately before him, the wash of her arrival against his chin. Rosita moved to him and draped her arms about his shoulders as she smiled. She leant forward and kissed him tenderly.

'You truly are a siren,' whispered Thomas as their lips parted.

Her expression changed, smile fading and eyes becoming hooded. A look of need the likes of which he had ne'er seen before came upon her.

'Te quiero,' whispered Rosita as her legs kicked back and she pushed him to the edge of the pool.

Her lips pressed to his, urgent and devouring. Thomas drew her into a tight embrace, the flames within her gaze leaping to his heart and loins.

The water rippled about them as she placed her hands upon the rock to either side of his head and raised herself. She sank onto his eagerness with a gentle groan as Shenty watched briefly and then wandered off to explore the rocks of the shoreline.

They made love within the pool, soft moans arising from Rosita's lips between their passionate kisses, her right hand moving to his hair and fingers running through the damp tangles. Their eyes ne'er parted, locked in shared desire as a touch of virgin's blood stained the waters.

A flush rose upon her neck and face. She let out a low moan, eyelids fluttering as she looked so deeply into him that Thomas swore his soul was laid bare.

Sinking against him, her wet hair to the side of his face, their bond of sight was finally broken. He stared at the blue expanse of the heavens, heart tumultuous with a mix of emotion and exertion.

'Thomas,' she whispered into his ear, the warmly accented word sending chills of pleasure through every nerve of his being.

Rosita drew her head back from his shoulder and stared into him. Their lips came together again in a tender embrace that made his spirit soar.

He took her face in his hands. 'I love you,' he whispered before kissing the scar upon her temple in acceptance of all that she was.

She backed away from him a little, his arms falling away from her. Moving to his left, she climbed out of the pool, water running down her gentle curves. He looked over his shoulder as she glanced down at him, the smile having returned to her face.

Thomas watched as she made her way to a large rock and lay down upon its flatness. He pulled himself from the pool and went to her as if in a dream. Reclining beside her, he found the stone cold against his back, the weak warmth unable to chase away the winter chill that still clung to the world.

The breeze gently brushed their skin as Rosita took hold of his hand. He glanced at her, seeing water glistening upon her nakedness, captured in the hairs upon her limbs and those rising between her legs. Moving closer, Thomas felt a deep

235

sense of contentment as gulls called along the coastline and they lay together bathed in sunlight.

56

Father Blyth knelt before the altar, his knees apart and vestments open to the waist. In his right hand he clasped a small knife, its blade blunt and its point long ago broken away. Its jagged end was darkened and glistening.

'Oh Lord, cleanse me of these sinful thoughts,' he said as he stabbed the knife between his legs, face flushed with the heat of pain, eyes watering.

Images of Nonna tied to the cucking stool had come to him again and again. They had raised his arousal despite attempts to expel them from his mind. He saw the backs of Gerens' fingers caress her skin, saw her large breasts heave against the wool of her dress as she sat bound and helpless.

'Oh Lord, free me from her bewitching sinfulness so that I may serve you in purity and piety.' The blade was again thrust downward, his jaw tight and teeth gritted as it jabbed into his already scarred and mutilated genitals.

The sound of the church door opening caused him to quickly turn and look over his shoulder. With Lacy Lugg passed, he had expected no one to enter.

'Father Blyth?' asked a male voice that he recognised, though he could not discern their identity as they stood silhouetted against the sunlight in the doorway.

He closed his black robes and tucked away the knife as he rose, wincing with pain. 'Who asks after me?'

'Marrek Trelawny, Father.'

'What do thee want, Marrek?' he asked with annoyed sharpness, unhappy to have had his penance disturbed by the drunk.

The farmer glanced out of the door and then closed it behind him before making his way between the pews to the aisle. His steps rang out in the hollowness as he approached the priest, his head bowed, lank hair hanging before his downcast eyes.

'I have come to beg your pardon for the deeds of yesterday,' said Marrek as he came to halt before Father Blyth, unable to lift his gaze to the holy man. 'I do not remember all, but that which I recall brings great shame.' He wiped mucus from his top lip and stifled a sneeze.

'You interrupted a burial and accused us of driving your wife and children from thee,' responded Blyth, looking upon the wretched man with mild disgust, the farmer's cheeks sunken due to a chill that had settled during his drunken stupor. 'Your love of mead has led you astray.'

Movement caught Marrek's eye and he looked to the drop of blood which had fallen to the stone from beneath the priest's robes. 'Is all well, Father?' he asked, finally raising his gaze to meet that of the other man, seeing the flush of his face and tightness of his jaw.

Blyth glanced down. 'It is not of your concern,' he stated with a dismissive wave of his hand. 'The only thing that should be concerning you is the weakness that drives thee to the drink.'

'Father, Nonna is innocent of the wrongdoing she has been accused of,' said Marrek, sniffing and wiping his nose with the back of his hand.

'No, she is not,' replied Blyth with a shake of his head. 'It was confirmed to me without a doubt.'

'When she returned in the rain to our cottage,' stated the farmer with a nod. 'I tell thee, Father, she was not returning from meeting with Gerens. She was returning from the home of Thomas Carrow.'

The priest was taken aback, but quickly regained his composure. 'Why would she visit with him?' he enquired doubtfully.

'She was not visiting with him, but trying to ascertain the truth of what I have witnessed with my own eyes.'

'And that is?'

'A mermaid.'

Blyth's brows rose.

''Tis true, Father. A mermaid now dwells with Carrow upon the hill. I have seen her twice in his company, the first without legs, but with a tail in their stead.'

The priest studied Marrek and sniffed the air. 'I fear the mead speaks on your behalf.'

'I have not touched a drop this day,' protested Marrek. 'What I say is the truth. My wife heard him talking to her when she went to spy out the reality of the creature's presence for herself.'

'So even she did not believe you,' said Blyth pointedly.

''Tis so, but I implore you, go visit with him and you will find her there.'

'I will not waste my time chasing the shadows of your drunken imaginings, for I am certain they will retreat with every step.'

'But…'

The priest raised his right hand to silence the complaint. 'I will hear no more of it and, if you are wise, you will speak no more of it. Few are those who will listen to your ravings and fewer still those who may believe such delusions.'

Marrek stared at Father Blyth and then bowed his head in defeat.

'Now go home and think on your sins, for you have many to purge from your darkened soul. Cast aside the mead jug and ask that God will forgive your transgressions.'

'I will, Father,' responded the farmer, taking a few steps back before turning and making his way to the door.

Blyth watched him go with furrowed brow, the pain between his legs causing him to clench his teeth. He shook his head. 'A lost soul,' he said to himself, the words whispering in the cold emptiness.

239

57

Thomas rinsed the bowls in the water and then placed them one atop the other as he stood before the seaward window in the gloom of the Old Pen. The firelight offered scant illumination as it spilled through the doorway behind him and glowed in the smoke haze hanging in the eaves above the Pen's walls. He wore his long coat, the night still bringing the touch of winter's chill despite the surprising warmth of the day.

He glanced thoughtfully at the eating vessels, his and Rosita's naked forms swimming in the pools of his eyes. Thomas shook his head, barely able to believe what had transpired at the cove.

His life had been changed profoundly by Rosita's deliverance upon the sands. She had brought light and colour even in the depth of winter's darkness. The ghosts of his past had grown largely silent as her companionship blessed him with feelings of comfort and contentment despite the lack of words they shared.

'And all by hap of chance,' he said with another shake of his head, one of wonderment at the mystery of life.

Thomas made his way to the doorway and came to a halt when he spied Rosita looking through the pieces of driftwood collected on the bench that rested against the far wall. He went over to stand beside her, running the fingers of his right hand along the back of his chair as he passed.

She glanced at him and smiled before turning her attention back to the pieces of ocean-smoothed timber, a scattering of sand glinting upon the bench. He looked at the shell she had made, which rested at the centre of the lower shelf before them, taking up the position once occupied by the mermaid, his completed shoal of fish to its right.

Rosita held an oval piece in her right hand, thumb caressing its grain as she stared off into space, listening for the whisper of inspiration within. It arose, her expression changing, gaining vigour as she looked to the piece of wood and gave a vague nod.

Thomas smiled as he studied her profile. She turned to him and he saw the reflection of his own creative spirit in her fertile gaze. The smile that curled her lips was soft and spoke of a mind elsewhere, already lost to the urge to follow the whispers and begin carving.

She raised herself and kissed him upon the cheek before stepping around him and making her way to the cot. He watched as she was seated, listening to the creak the wood and flutter of the fire as she made herself comfortable, crossing her legs before pulling the furs over them.

Rosita looked over with an expression of frustration. Thomas followed her gaze and spied her knife on the corner of the bench, picking it up and taking it to her.

'Gracias,' she said warmly, taking the blade and adjusting her grip again and again until she finally felt she was ready. Its tip made the first cut, a shaving falling to her lap as her attention became focussed on the task.

Thomas returned to the bench and briefly scanned the driftwood. He did not reach for any of the pieces, but instead found himself distracted by the glittering of the sand. He stared at the small lights, his sight loosing focus as his mind drifted in mesmerised emptiness.

'We will be in need of fresh meat on the morrow,' he muttered to himself, giving voice to the first thought that entered his mind as he blinked and broke the spell.

He made his way to the chair and seated himself, finding that the will to carve did not awaken within. He watched Rosita's increasingly skilled whittling as he considered going back to Treen Cove the following day in order to cast his net into the pool. He had not done so after they had dried and dressed, but had a yen for some fish to break the monotony of rabbit.

'CARROW!' The fearsome bellow arose from the hillside to the south of the cottage.

Rosita visibly jumped, dropping the knife upon the patchwork cover as Shenty lifted her head from the ground beside the fire and began to growl. Thomas stared wide-eyed at the door beyond the angle of the cot, his pulse racing.

'CARROW!' The cry was thick with rage.

Slowly getting to his feet, Thomas stepped over the hound and made his way along the far side of the cot, staring at the door with trepidation. The sudden grasp of Rosita's fingers about his wrist caused him to turn in surprise.

She looked up at him with obvious concern and shook her head.

'I must,' he whispered in response to her silent plea. 'If I do not, then they may seek entry and discover your presence.'

Rosita shook her head in frustration, unable to glean the meaning of his words. She held on for a little longer and then reluctantly released his arm.

'I KNOW YOU ARE IN THERE. COME OUT AND FACE ME, DAMN YOU.' The words contained a drunken drawl.

His hand trembling, Thomas reached for the door and swallowed against the rising nausea brought on by fear. Opening it, he found a man leaning against the gate at the far end of the garden path. He narrowed his eyes as he felt the veins in his neck throbbing, his heart pumping furiously.

'Marrek Trelawny?' he enquired as Shenty moved to stand beside him and growled her warning at the dark figure standing fifteen yards away.

'Where is she?' he demanded, no longer shouting now that Thomas was in plain sight, but his voice still raised.

'Of whom do you speak?'

'Do not treat me as a fool, Carrow,' he said sharply. 'I have already been marked as such by those below and my gizzard will not take more of it.' Spittle dripped from the farmer's loose lips.

'I do not treat you as a fool, Marrek,' said Thomas with as much calm as he could muster. 'There is no one here other than me and my dog.'

'What of the mermaid?' The question was filled with knowing accusation.

'Mermaid?'

'Your denial mocks me,' said Marrek, his expression pinched with anger as he kicked the bottom of the gate fiercely.

'No mockery is intended. I do not know of any such creature abiding hereabouts, nor have I ever set eyes on one in all my years.' Thomas' words contained the waver of nervousness.

Marrek stared through the darkness as Thomas stood silhouetted in the doorway of Ocean Mist. He sniffed and wiped mucus from his top lip. 'Who was the woman I saw with you upon the hillside?' he asked with a hiss.

Thomas mused for a moment. It was clear that the farmer had seen him with Rosita and therefore would not leave without suitable explanation. 'My cousin,' he replied. 'She came to visit with me from Pendeen.'

'Cousin?'

He nodded. 'Aye, Mary.'

'Mary,' echoed Marrek as he tried to recall if Carrow's father had made any mention of cousins. They had been friends long ago and if it were not for a farrowing sow, it would have been him aboard the ill-fated boat rather than Thomas' grandfather. It was at that time that he had begun to hear the call of the mead.

'She stayed for a few days before returning and may well visit again,' called Thomas, sensing that the flames in the farmer's heart were being doused by the sobering chill of the night. 'You are welcome to come inside for some rabbit stew,' he added, seeing the farmer's uncertainty and hoping the invitation would make firm his deceit.

Marrek shook his head and peered past him as Shenty let out another low growl. He looked to the flicker of firelight, able to discern the edge of the cot, but sight blurred by the

243

mead which had given him courage enough to venture up the hill.

'Why did she need your aid by which to walk?' he asked, turning his attention back to Thomas and wiping his nose upon his sleeve.

'She twisted her ankle during the journey from Pendeen and was in need of my assistance. The strain prolonged her stay.' There was no longer a tremulous touch to his words, his confidence waxing as the farmer's anger waned.

Marrek sneezed and sniffed.

'It would seem that you are feeling the bite of winter. You should return to the warmth of your home.'

'There is no warmth there. It has been stolen away by loose tongues and lies,' said Marrek sadly, looking at the ground and shaking his head with drunken exaggeration.

'I do not take your meaning?'

'My wife and children departed with the mist. The house is empty and silent.'

'Nonna has gone?' said Thomas in surprise.

'Aye, though she holds no blame in the matter for there were wolves snapping at her heels.'

Thomas looked at him without comprehension.

'Beware the wolves, Thomas,' said Marrek, lifting his mournful gaze. 'Beware the wolves.'

The farmer shook his head once again and then turned from the cottage, sneezing as he did so. Thomas watched as he began to stagger away, teetering first right then left as he struggled to stay on his feet. He considered helping Marrek down the hillside, but was dissuaded from such action when he looked over his shoulder and found Rosita watching him with continued disquiet.

Lingering a little longer, he heard the farmer mumble to himself as he made his way beneath the stars. Thomas then shut the door, Shenty sniffing the wood and giving one last growl before slowly making her way back to the fireside.

He stepped to the cot and forced a smile. 'He will not be disturbing us again,' he said, reaching out and stroking Rosita's cheek with the backs of his fingers.

She took hold of his hand and drew him down to sit on the bed, putting her arms about him, seeking out the security and comfort of his closeness. They held each other for long moments. Thomas raised his hand to her hair and stroked it while shutting his eyes, the regular motion soothing them both.

He yawned and Rosita eased him away from her, studying his weary face. Shifting over, she then patted the cot beside her.

Thomas felt a swell of warm emotion. She was a kindly soul and he no longer had any care as to her origins. All he knew was that he loved her deeply and hoped she would ne'er wish to return to whence she came.

Standing, he took off his clothes, laying them over the end of the cot. He slipped beneath the covers as Rosita wriggled from the gown and placed it over the head, the mermaid carving lying next to the stuffed hide that served as a pillow. They snuggled together, savouring the warmth and touch of their intimacy, Shenty leaping onto the foot of the bed and circling before settling by their feet.

She rested her head on his chest, her leg draped over him as she placed her hand to his heart and felt its vitality. Thomas sighed contentedly, catching the stirring scent of her body and feeling truly blessed in her company. He leant his head against the top of hers and closed his eyes, yawning again as the flames of the fire dwindled and the night drew in about them.

58

Thomas watched as Rosita made her way over the gaping fissure in the narrow path of rock. She gripped the guide rope with both hands and found small footholds by which to climb back out of Treen Cove, just as he had done before her. Shenty had leapt across before him with surprising ease and had already vanished from sight at the top of the cliff, no doubt exploring the grasses beyond.

He held out his hand and she gratefully took hold. Pulling her to safety, he felt great relief as he tried to ignore the drop to the rocks.

'Gracias,' she said, giving his hand a gentle squeeze.

Thomas made his way up the last of the path and felt grateful to reach the carved steps, the ascent becoming much easier. Reaching the cliff-top, he moved a few yards from the edge, patting his left pocket to ensure the parcel of fish remained in place.

Rosita came up beside him and took his hand. She glanced up the hillside, eyes narrowed against the glare of the sun. With sudden enthusiasm, she began to lead them along the coastline, heading west rather than home.

'Where are you taking us?' asked Thomas in amused perplexity as he was forced to make greater haste by the skip in her step. He was gladdened by her brightness and spontaneity, his life made more vital and touched with the excitement of the unexpected.

She laughed with airy lightness, swinging his arm like a child as she led them onto Gurnards Head. They clambered around the eastern side of the rocky heights, making their way to the end of the promontory.

Finding an area of grass amidst the rocks, Rosita brought them to a halt and they stood looking out to sea. The breeze brushed against their backs, like a whispered encouragement to leap into the waves drawing towards the shore below. A squabble of seagulls rested on the undulating waters, occasionally lifting to flap and hover as a cresting wave passed beneath, settling back in its wake as they called out to each other.

Rosita looked about, taking in the view.

'That is Zennor Head,' stated Thomas, pointing east along the rugged coast.

He felt something tickling his cheek and reached up to brush it away. Rosita turned to the movement and stayed his hand, resting hers upon his forearm. She carefully removed the insect from his face, opening her palm so that he could see the ladybird resting upon it.

'It must have been woken by the unusual warmth,' he commented as it crawled up her thumb.

Reaching the tip, the bright beetle took to the wing, passing between them. They turned and watched it make its way over the rocky tor until they could no longer discern its whereabouts.

'Fly away home,' whispered Thomas, feeling a touch of melancholy.

Rosita placed her palm to his cheek and turned his face to her. She raised her lips to his and they kissed as the waves washed against the shoreline behind them.

She drew him down to the lush grasses and embraced him, moving atop Thomas and taking his face in her hands. 'Te amo,' she said softly, gazing into his eyes, the veil of her tumbling hair hiding the world about them.

She loosened the cords at the front of his shirt and slid her hand inside, stroking his chest. Thomas reached to her sides and pulled up her gown as their kisses became increasingly passionate. Undoing his belt, Rosita took down his leggings to his thighs as he raised his backside from the ground in assistance and his desire was freed.

Her lips pressed to his once more and they made love with tender urgency amidst the concealing rocks of Gurnards Head. The tide rising within their hearts washed upon the shores of their eyes as the sun hung low in the winter sky and the gulls took to the air, wheeling and calling above them.

59

Jago walked alongside the mule as they passed through the mizzle, the top of the church tower veiled as it rose to the left. The wheels of the simple cart sank into the mud, the vehicle no more than a platform upon which his meagre possessions rested, Teca contained within her cage to the rear.

He waved in greeting as Old Jacob approached in the opposite direction, his crook in hand and Blackberry at his side. They were driving his small flock of ewes to fields lying between Zennor Churchtown and the sea. The aged farmer responded in kind, calling instructions to the hound, which passed quickly around the sheep and brought them to a halt on the track.

'My thanks,' said Jago as he stopped the mule before the forge.

Jacob moved through the flock, which took to the grasses at the trackside. He spoke an unintelligible word to Blackberry, bending to her as he passed and scratching her head. She sat alert and watchful as he stepped over to stand before the mule.

'I see the tenancy has been granted,' commented Jacob, reaching up and stroking the side of the mule's face.

'Aye.' Jago went to the door and glanced at the brown and withered oak leaves above. He reached up and tore the sprig from its fastening. Tossing it aside, he stepped on it with vindictive satisfaction, enjoying the sensation of his boot sinking into the mud.

'What wilt thou do here?' enquired the farmer.

'It shall be a forge, as before,' replied Jago, putting his hand to the granite beside the door, glad to be moving from the wooden shack in which he had lived for far too long.

'I did not know thee art skilled in metalwork.'

'It takes no skill to beat metal, merely strength of arm,' responded Jago with disdain.

'I fear thee may be wrong in that, Jago. Many were the times I visited with Gerens' father when he was smith and it was more than strength that wrought shapes and sharpness out of the metal he worked upon the anvil. Doest thou know of the difference between working steel, iron and sometimes tin? Doest thou know of tempering?'

Jago deigned not to answer and opened the door to the forge with agitated force, causing it to bang against the wall. He peered into the dingy interior, catching the scent of soot. He looked around the blackened and cobwebbed walls, his sight settling on the door to the rear that led to a small yard and timber-built stable. Nodding to himself, he turned to the ferret resting upon the cart, her coat glistening as she moved restlessly within her confinement.

Stepping over, he picked up the cage. Raising it and leaning his head closer, he regarded Teca fondly as he sucked air between his teeth, making the squeaking sounds with which she was so familiar. 'This is our new home,' he said, turning the cage so that the ferret within could see the building in question. 'Now we shall be respected.'

'It be a shame the sun does not shine upon thy arrival.'

Jago's head snapped round and he stared at the farmer. 'What do you mean by that?'

'Exactly as I say,' replied Jacob, perplexed by the other man's reaction after the week of unseasonable warmth which had only recently been ushered away by westerly winds bearing cloud and rain.

'Be sure you do,' said Jago, his voice low and containing threat.

'If I have said aught to offend thee, I am sorry,' replied the farmer. 'I only meant…'

'"I only meant",' said Jago, mocking the old man's voice. 'I know what you meant. You were a friend to Gerens and I see thy purpose.'

'My purpose?' Jacob was taken aback.

Jago simply glared at him, the farmer shifting uncomfortably under the hard gaze. He then took Teca into the forge, vanishing into the gloom.

'Wilt thou still hunt out the rats from my barns when I am need of such?' asked Jacob, hoping to alleviate the tension in the air.

'I am smith, not rat catcher,' stated Jago as he came back out of the building and went to the cart. 'Those days are gone. No longer will I be looked down upon by such as yourself.'

'Not for one instant did I do such a thing.'

'No?' Jago looked at him with brows raised. 'I know what most think of me, but as of this day such thoughts will not be allowed to linger.'

'I think ye misjudge the folk greatly, for I have not heard a single word said of that likeness.'

''Tis not in words that it reveals itself, but in eyes. I see the way in which I am regarded and I tell you it will no longer stand.'

'Thou sees things that are not there in truth, for my eyes have ne'er held thee in low esteem,' said the farmer, shaking his head. ''Tis in thy mind only, not those of others.'

'So I am to blame? I am affected by some malady of mind,' said Jago with a hard edge to his tone as he hefted a large wooden box from the cart. 'You twist my words back to me, old man, and I will listen no more.' He stomped into the forge, the contents of the box shifting with his angry movements.

Jacob stared after him with his mouth agape, shocked by the other man's frostiness. 'Winter grips some harder than others,' he said to himself as he looked back at his flock.

'Drei, Blackberry,' he instructed the hound.

She immediately got to her feet and made her way to the far side of the ewes, gathering them together on the track and bringing them forth. Jacob stood still as they passed and then fell into step behind as Jago reappeared from the forge, choosing to ignore the farmer as he collected a stool from the cart.

Jacob's frown deepened as he passed the church, smoke drawing across the track from the buildings opposite and below his position. The sheep bleated on occasion as they were ushered onward and he noted the lowing of Marrek's cattle in their field upon the gentle slope that marked the beginnings of Trewey Hill. Their calls carried an appeal that caused him to seek them out with his gaze, the task made impossible by the thin rain that misted the landscape.

He came to a halt and listened. There was certainly something in the tone of the lowing that caused concern. His thoughts turned to Marrek and he tried to recall when he had last seen him. He had not attended church in many weeks and there had been no sight of him about the village or fields.

He looked ahead to the path that branched left and led to Marrek's farm. 'I shall make a quick call as I pass,' he decided aloud, nodding to himself as he set off, his staff marking each step.

'Synsi,' he said to Blackberry, instructing her to keep the flock where they were as they drew alongside the smaller path.

The hound moved round to the front, bringing the ewes to a stop as the old farmer turned off the main track. He made his way down the slope to the entrance of Trelawny Farm and veered off to the right, passing the barn and walking across to the cottage.

Reaching the door, he banged the top of his staff against the wood. 'Marrek?' he called.

There was no answer.

He took hold of the handle and slowly opened it, peering into the gloom. As his sight adjusted, he noted Marrek upon his cot in the far corner, his back to him as he lay on his side and faced the wall.

'Marrek?' he said.

The farmer did not stir.

'Lost to a drunken stupor no doubt,' mumbled Jacob as he stepped into the dull interior.

He made his way past the fire pit, the ashes darkened by moisture. The air was still and heavy with the scent of damp earth and thatch.

He came to a stop beside the cot. 'Marrek, your cattle are calling and in need,' he said, reaching forward and taking hold of the other farmer's shoulder, turning him onto his back.

Jacob let out a yelp of shock and quickly took a step away, eyes wide and pulse racing. Marrek grinned up at him, lips naught but ragged remains revealing uneven teeth. His sockets were bloodied hollows filled with deep shadows and the flesh had been eaten from the end of his nose, bone protruding from the grizzly wound.

The old farmer noted the smear of dried mucus upon Marrek's top lip and sunken left cheek. He covered his mouth with his hand, not wishing to succumb to the chill again so soon after recovering from its feverish tremblings.

He jumped at sudden movement beneath the fur that covered the corpse. A bulge moved over Marrek's stomach.

'A rat,' he whispered, his heart fluttering and hands shaking.

Taking his crook in both hands, he tucked its end beneath the top of the bedcover. He slowly drew the fur back, the tension within him building, arms quaking.

The rat leapt from beneath the cover, landing on the floor and scampering to the woodpile gathered against the wall opposite the cot. It vanished into the logs with the scrape of bristly fur and scrabble of claws.

Jacob stared at the gap into which it had vanished, his heart pumping furiously. He swallowed hard and felt a little faint as he set the end of the staff back on the ground and used it for support.

Glancing at Marrek's sorrowful countenance, he then hurried from the cottage. Closing the door behind him, he took a few steps away and then came to a halt, raising his face to the mizzle and welcoming its coolness upon his face. He closed his eyes and breathed deeply, the image of the other farmer's death grin greeting him as it lingered on the back of his lids.

253

60

Jowen vomited into the waste bucket beside the cot, perspiration glistening upon his face. Nonna was perched on the edge of the bed next to her son, arm about his shoulders and expression filled with a mother's worry.

Gerens looked over from the stool on which he sat by the fire, Daveth seated to his left as they forced down the thin broth he had made for supper. The sickness had taken Jowen a few days previous, coming upon him after the twins had returned from playing in a stream with some of the local children. It had begun with a fever accompanied by the runs, but his condition had steadily grown worse and he was starting to show signs of brain fever. His feet and hands had grown cold, he complained of pains in his muscles and could not endure bright light.

'Will he get better?' asked Daveth.

Gerens turned to him and sighed as he cupped his bowl in his large hands. 'I do not know,' he admitted, not wanting to give the boy false hope by promising a recovery.

Daveth looked fearfully over at his brother as he leant over the side of the cot and wretched. 'I do not want him to die,' whispered the boy, tears glistening in his eyes.

'Naught is certain as yet,' said the smith as the fire hissed, water dripping from a few holes still remaining to be fixed in the thatch of the wattle and daub cottage they had managed to rent.

He looked up unhappily as a few more drops fell to the fire, the rain outside becoming heavier. They had taken up residence soon after completing the four-day journey to Bodmin and the cottage had been their home for nearly two weeks. It was located on the outskirts of the town, surrounded by woods and set back from the track that led south to the capital, Lostwithiel. There was a barn included which was little more than a glorified shed, but would serve as the new forge once he had conducted the necessary repairs to its dilapidated roof and walls, repairs which had slowed since Nonna had taken to nursing her ailing son.

Gerens looked back to the mother and son upon the cot. In truth, he feared the worst. Jowen was sickening by the day and there had been no break in the fever.

Two knocks sounded at the door and he lowered his bowl to the floor. 'That will be Carantoc,' he stated as he rose from the stool.

He stepped over to the door, opening it to the fading light beyond. 'Good day to you,' he stated, stepping to the side. 'Please, come in.'

The rangy physician entered, cloak wet through and hood hanging heavy about his head. He stopped just inside the cottage as Gerens shut the door. Taking down his hood, he revealed his narrow face, cheekbones like blades and black beard woven into a long braid. He raised his hand and stroked along its length while regarding Jowen's shivering form, the boy still leaning over the edge of the cot as nausea came upon him in heated waves.

'I see he is no better.'

'We continued to apply the leeches as you did, but there has been no change,' responded Gerens with a downhearted tone.

'Hmm,' pondered Carantoc as he made his way over to the cot, coming to a stop a good three yards in front of it and covering his mouth. 'Blood-letting was the last resort and I know of no other course of treatment to administer.'

'But you are a physician,' stated Nonna as she looked up at him. 'Surely there is more you can do besides apply leeches?' she added with a look of disbelief.

'I have done all I can.'

'Which may as well have been naught,' she responded.

'Nonna.' Gerens' tone contained a warning. 'Carantoc is not to blame for Jowen's sickness.'

She glanced over at the smith, her expression filled with anguish. 'There must be more to be done. I will not simply sit by and watch him suffer in this way.'

Jowen let out a moan as he shivered uncontrollably beneath the fur covers, eyes tightly closed and jaw clenched.

'It be God's will,' said Carantoc with a nod of his head, his mouth still covered.

'To make my son suffer?' she responded in astounded horror.

'We cannot question His ways.'

'Will not, you mean,' she snapped angrily.

'God is not to blame,' stated Gerens from the other side of the cottage, 'only the sickness.'

'And who created such ailments?' she asked pointedly. 'What God could conceive of such terrible torments of a child's body and mind?' She shook her head.

'We cannot guess as His purpose for He sees all and knows all,' stated Carantoc. 'We cannot see to what ends such events may take us.'

'Go back to your leeches, for you are no use here,' she said with a sharp wave of her hand, turning her attention to her son.

Carantoc looked down at her briefly and then made his way back to the door.

'I am sorry,' whispered Gerens as he moved close to the other man.

'There is no need for apology,' replied the physician. 'I have endured much worse, I can assure you.' He raised his sleeve to reveal a large scar on his right forearm. 'A husband whose wife I could not save,' he stated.

Gerens nodded. 'Can the boy be saved?'

Carantoc glanced back to the cot where Jowen ailed. 'Truthfully?'

The smith nodded once again.

'No,' he stated flatly. 'I have seen this many times before. It is common for death to come knocking and find the door open, the illness having left naught by which to ward off the swing of his scythe.'

Gerens sighed. 'My thanks for your honesty and all you have done.'

'It is my duty,' replied Carantoc, holding out his right palm.

The smith looked at it in momentary bewilderment. He then took a small pouch from where it was tucked into his belt, taking out a penny and dropping it onto the physician's hand.

His fingers curled about the cold coin. 'I bid you farewell,' he stated, stepping around Gerens and exiting the house, pausing on the threshold to pull up his wet hood.

Shutting the door, Gerens turned to find Nonna weeping silently as she sat on the edge of the bed, hands covering her face. Daveth was staring at her as he remained rooted to his stool at the fireside, his gaze desolate and heart being wrung tight by the sight of his distraught mother.

Gerens strode over to her, gathering her up into his arms. Nonna's legs were barely able to take her weight as her body convulsed with sorrow. She buried her face into his neck, wishing she could simply melt into his stoic embrace, the ache within falling away like winter's ice from a spring bud, but the ache remained and her tears flowed freely.

61

'…Her body taken by the sea, her heart forever his to be,' finished Rosita in her heavily accented voice as she sat cross-legged on the cot.

Thomas clapped his hands together and nodded. Shenty let out a moan as she lay beside him, as if voicing her approval. He had been teaching her The Lay of Ailla for two weeks on evenings when the urge to carve did not come upon them and she had finally completed a successful rendition. She had melodiously spoken the lay with a soulful tone, as if fully aware of the tragic story it told despite not understanding the words issuing from her sensuous lips. He had been spellbound by her rich voice.

'Very good,' he stated with a smile.

Rosita sneezed.

'Bless you,' he said in response, noting the touch of redness about her eyes that he had believed a sign of weariness and now feared may be one of creeping sickness.

He rose from his position by the fire pit and went to sit on the edge of the bed beside her. Placing the back of his hand to her forehead, he frowned when he felt the heat of her skin. 'It seems you have caught cold.'

He glanced at the cooking pot suspended over the flames. 'The stew will soon be ready and you must make sure you eat plenty in order to bolster your strength,' he stated, wondering if she could comprehend any of what he said to her.

Thomas stood and went to the woodpile, which had recently been restocked with branches gathered to the west of Trewey Hill and dried beside the fire. Selecting a few, he took them over to the pit and placed them onto the flames. He looked at the stew, large bubbles forming on its surface and bursting in thick demise.

Wrapping his hand in his sleeve, he took the pot down and turned to his left. He poured stew into the two bowls he had already fetched from the Old Pen in readiness. It slopped into their confinement, steam rising, carrying the scent of rabbit as it brushed his face.

Leaving the pot on the ground, he took one of the bowls to Rosita. She took it gratefully and cupped it in her hands.

'Gracias,' she said with a thin smile.

There was a wan look to her face and he felt his chest tighten with worry. There was another rabbit hanging in the Old Pen and he would take it down to Trewey Farm on the morrow in the hope Jacob may have some bread and butter for exchange. He would also visit Treen Cove in order to cast his net while she remained dry and warm within the cottage.

He went back to the fireside and seated himself, absently taking up his bowl as Shenty looked at him pleadingly. 'There are already a few off cuts in your bowl,' he stated to the hound.

His gaze returned to Rosita and he found her watching him curiously. 'I was just telling Shenty that her supper has been served in the Old Pen,' he stated, nodding at the dog.

She glanced down and then looked at him blankly, clearly not following the gist of what he had told her.

'Eat,' he instructed, raising his bowl and looking at her meaningfully.

Rosita hesitated and then did as he said, a dribble of thick stock running down her chin. She sniffed deeply a couple of times and then took another mouthful of the stew.

Thomas ate in contemplative silence, wondering if he should brave the wet night and visit Bersaba. He was sure she would have some tonic to help, some concoction of herb and root that would serve to chase away Rosita's chill.

He looked to the shutters, listening to the soft patter of rain and seeing the darkness through the gap between. 'You are not so ill as to make it urgent,' he commented to himself, deciding to wait until morning light.

Rosita put her bowl on the earth beside the cot and he could see that it was still half-full. Shenty looked over at it before glancing up at him in request.

Thomas shook his head at the hound before rising and going back to sit on the edge of the bed. He scooped up her bowl and held it out to her. 'You must eat and eat well,' he stated.

She stared at the contents without enthusiasm. Reluctantly taking the vessel from his hand, she sighed and began to eat what remained of her portion.

'Good,' he said with a nod, smiling and brushing hair back from the left side of her face before lifting his own bowl to his lips.

Taking out the last pieces with his fingers, Thomas then turned to her. There were a few remnants in the pit of her bowl, but most had been consumed. 'Would you like some more?' he asked, glancing meaningfully at the cooking pot by the fire.

Rosita shook her head wearily.

'Take some rest and make sure to keep warm,' he said, pulling the furs over her.

He hesitated and then moved back to the fire pit to pour himself a second helping. Rosita settled upon the bed, resting on her side facing the flames. She drew the patchwork up and held it in place beneath her chin. Her pale and slender left arm was all that could be seen of her body as it cradled the mermaid against her in chest and Shenty leapt to the foot of the bed, padding before curling at her feet.

Thomas filled his bowl and then moved to his seat, the wood creaking as he rested upon it. He glanced across at her to find her staring into the fire. 'All will be well,' he said, more to allay his own concerns than for the woman on the other side of the pit.

Lifting the stew, he began to eat once again, savouring the warmth of the food. His gaze lay dreamily on the flickering flames as he thought about their time together at the cottage, seeing images of contentment and happiness.

'How much longer?' he whispered to himself as he chewed on a cut of rabbit and the rain beat harder against the shutters.

62

He came up the hill from Trewey Farm, the bitter wind whipping the rain into his face and cheeks stinging. A leather-bound parcel containing bread and butter was tucked under his right arm. Jacob had little to spare and so had not given much in exchange for the rabbit, though enough to ensure Rosita had something more to eat than merely the stodgy remnants of the previous night's stew. The old farmer had been polite and not overly inquisitive. Most of his words had been concerned with events in the village. He had spoken about his discovery of Marrek Trelawny's body and the funeral which he had attended earlier that day.

Reaching the grassland beneath the moor, Thomas went left and headed south as he thought about Marrek's drunken appearance at Ocean Mist. 'Beware the wolves,' he said to himself as he sought the track leading to Bersaba's cottage, but could not see it amidst the rocks and waving grasses. It was little more than an animal trail and the wind-stirred activity of the hillside kept it hidden from sight.

With head bowed, he walked on, water dripping from his hair and the raindrops beating against his right cheek. The wind was howling across the moor above, sending a chill the length of his spine as the tails of his coat snapped at his heels.

He passed around the southern end of the hill and soon found himself approaching the healer's rounded hut. The yews were whispering and he knew she was home.

Reaching the front door, he raised his hand to knock only to find it opening before his knuckles touched the wood.

'Good morning, Young Thomas,' greeted Bersaba with a wrinkled smile. 'I sensed someone approaching my door and am happy to find it is thee. How goes it with thy ward?'

'I fear she sickens with the winter chill,' he replied. 'Have you a tonic to sooth her?'

She nodded and stepped back. 'Come in and I will hunt it out.'

Thomas entered the hut, a fire burning in the pit and a thick haze of smoke in the air. The scent of herbs was strong and he could see that she had been chopping sprigs of thyme and rosemary upon the table to the right, having cleared a space amidst the selection of covered wooden bowls.

Shutting the door behind him, he watched her hobble over to the table, her feet bare as usual. She lifted the cloth from some of the bowls, peering beneath and bending to sniff out their contents.

'There is more that worries thee,' she stated as her withered hands took up a bowl and she turned to him.

He nodded. 'It is the same as last we met.'

'Thee fear her departure,' she nodded, taking up the small length of wood from the tabletop and stirring the contents of the bowl.

'I cannot be sure of it, but think she pines for home.'

'Indeed,' she replied, setting the stirrer down and then shuffling over to pull a wooden box from beneath the cot at the rear of the hut. 'Wouldst thou not pine for home under such circumstances?'

Thomas pondered a moment and then gave a nod as she regarded the selection of earthenware bottles and wooden stoppers contained within. 'Aye.'

'Then 'tis only to be expected,' she responded while trying a number of stoppers in one of the bottles, finally finding one of the appropriate size and leaving it in situ. 'But love is stronger than such things.'

'Love?'

She looked over at him and chuckled. 'Aye, Young Thomas, love. Ye know as well as I that thee now share such a bond. When we last spoke it rested in thy heart alone, but now beats in hers also.'

Bersaba stepped from the cot and settled herself on the opposite side of the fire. 'Come, sit with me before the flames,' she said, setting the bowl upon her lap and the bottle on the earth in front of her.

263

Thomas walked over and seated himself, pulling his coat beneath him and resting the parcel of food on the ground.

'Thou hast deep scars, Young Thomas,' she said without looking at him, pulling the stopper from the bottle and laying it aside.

'Scars?' He looked across at her without comprehension.

'Indeed,' she nodded. 'Ye have carried them for many years. The passing of thy parents was their cause and now they serve to heighten thy fears of being left alone once more.' She lifted the bowl and slowly tipped it over the bottle as she began to decant some of the contents.

'Thy isolation was thy shield. It protected thee from loss, but with Rosita's arrival ye were forced to allow someone into thy life. That is why I did not take her into my care, Young Thomas. I knew the effect her presence would have upon thee.'

'You knew we would fall in love?' He looked at her in surprise.

Bersaba shook her head and glanced over at him, the flames rising between them. 'No. I knew she would end thy isolation, one in which thou hast lingered with the ghosts of thy past, longing for the closeness and company of thy parents, but unwilling to seek such in the company of others for fear of being broken again.' She stopped pouring the thick liquid and set the bowl back upon her lap.

'Thou doest not wish to admit she loves thee because that will deepen the need, strengthen the bond.' She placed the stopper in the bottle and then held his gaze. 'Do not be guided by thoughts of hurts which may ne'er come to pass. Thou doest not know what the future holds and so to take guidance from such thoughts is to restrict thyself with the insubstantial wonderings of thine own mind. 'Tis illusion and 'tis folly.'

'What then should I do?' he asked in earnest.

She shook her head and laughed. 'The answer is simple, Young Thomas. Follow thy heart. Do not let it be ruled by fear and do not cast the net of thy mind into the future. Thy life is now. Be in this moment.'

'Your words contain much wisdom,' he stated.

'Indeed, but 'tis thee who must turn them into deeds,' she said with a meaningful look.

Thomas nodded. 'I will endeavour to do so.'

'Here,' she raised the stopped bottle. 'Make sure she takes a spoonful before she lays her head to rest.'

He picked up his parcel and got to his feet before stepping around the fire and taking the bottle from her. 'I give my thanks, Bersaba.'

'And a rabbit when thou hast one to spare,' she said with a grin.

He nodded again and smiled down at the old crone. 'It shall be done.'

Thomas walked to the door and opened it on the rain.

'The ghosts of thy past are leaving thee, Young Thomas, and soon it will also be time for my farewell.'

He paused and looked back over his shoulder in puzzlement, mouth open as he prepared to ask her meaning. Bersaba was not to be seen.

Glancing about the interior of the hut, he found no place in which she could be hiding. The hairs on the nape of his neck tingled.

Thomas quickly stepped out, closing the door behind him and making to set off. Feeling a watchful gaze upon him, he became still and looked to the left, spying a familiar figure amidst the yews.

'Elowen,' he whispered as the deer stood motionless and alert.

She suddenly took flight, bounding away through the rain. Thomas stared after her for long moments, his mind returning to the mystery of Bersaba's disappearance.

Shaking his head and blinking away the grip of bewilderment, he set off homeward. His thoughts turned to Rosita and he felt his heart's needy response, suppressing the fear that arose with it. 'My life is now,' he said as the rain beat upon him, the late morning with the feel of dusk as darker clouds drew in from the west.

63

Thomas opened the gate in the downpour, wincing at the creak of hinges as he entered the garden. When he had slipped from the cot at first light, Rosita had simply rolled onto her side and returned to her slumber. She was clearly in need of rest and he had no wish to wake her should she still be sleeping.

Making his way along the path to the door, he hoped that Shenty would not be roused and begin barking. With water streaming down his face, he reached for the handle and carefully opened it. His gaze went first to the bed and found it empty. Scanning the interior as he stepped in, he found no sign of her and was reminded of Bersaba's disappearance.

'Thomas?' The accented enquiry issued from the Old Pen a moment before Rosita peered from its entrance, a smile dawning upon her face.

He felt a touch of relief and closed the door as she walked over. She brushed a drop of water from the end of his nose and giggled as she took in his sorry appearance, the earth about him darkening as drips fell from his clothes.

Thomas noted that the redness about her eyes was no longer apparent. He contemplated the words Bersaba had shared with him concerning casting his mind into the future and smiled down at her, pleased that his fears of illness seemed to have been misplaced.

Quickly taking hold of her before she could withdraw, he drew her close and embraced her, purposefully shaking his head and loosing a small shower of droplets. Rosita laughed and struggled in his sodden grasp. He released her and she spun away from him, going back into the Old Pen with a backward glance.

She reappeared with the bowl of water from the bench before the window held in her hands, grinning at him mischievously.

'No,' he said, raising his hands submissively and backing towards the door.

Rosita grinned, approaching slowly. She made to throw the contents over him, Thomas wincing and making a show of shrinking back.

With a sudden lunge forward, he knocked the bowl from her hands, causing the contents to empty upon her, the bowl falling to the floor. She glanced down, her jerkin and leggings running with water and a small pool about her feet that was slowly absorbed by the ground.

She looked back up at him and her expression of surprise became into one of amusement. They both began to laugh and she went to him, eagerly seeking out his embrace.

Stepping back after a few moments, she began to remove her clothes. Thomas placed the parcel of bread and butter on the cot and then put the bottle Bersaba had given him beside it. He then began to undress as Rosita pulled down her leggings, straightening to stand naked before him.

She went to the other side of the bed and moved the furs aside, hanging her clothes over the edge beside the fire. Turning, she crouched before the flames, holding her hands out to warm her fingers.

Thomas soon joined her, their clothes still dripping as they hung over the side of the cot. He warmed himself for a while and then went to the woodpile, fetching more branches and stoking the fire.

Rosita got to her feet. She went around the bed and fetched the bowl that was lying upside down on the earth. Taking it back into the Old Pen, she returned carrying one of the wooden bowls in the crook of her left arm, a spoon in her right hand.

She settled beside him and Thomas glanced at the contents of the bowl, seeing that a couple of partly beaten eggs rested within.

'So that is what you were doing when I arrived,' he commented as she set to the task once again.

Thomas sat upon the earth. Its coolness against his flesh was in contrast to the warmth radiating from the fire, a warmth he savoured as it chased away the dampness of his skin.

Rosita finished beating the eggs and got to her feet once again after resting the bowl on the ground. She paused and grinned down at him before vacating the main living space. He heard her moving in the Old Pen and wondered at her activity.

She re-entered the room with the second bowl in her left hand. Carried in the other was a shallow metal dish, one that had been his mother's and upon which he kept a selection of stones and shells which had caught his interest during trips to Treen Cove. They had been removed and the dish, which was the width of a man's hand, had been wiped clean of dust.

Rosita moved back to his side. She tipped the contents of the second bowl into the first and mixed them with the beaten eggs, Thomas watching as the chopped onions and leeks were stirred into the thickness. Passing him the newly emptied bowl, she then reached forward and placed the metal dish upon the near side of the fire. She held the very edge and manoeuvred it, burning tree limbs collapsing beneath as she made it sit as flat as possible amidst the flames.

'What are you doing?' he asked, turning to her curiously.

Rosita simply smiled at him and then stared at the dish. After a couple of minutes, she licked the end of her index finger and reached forward, briefly placing it to the metal at the centre of the dish. Rosita then nodded to herself and took up the bowl containing the mixture of eggs and vegetables. She quickly poured some out until the dish was nearly brimming.

Thomas looked at the slick and slimy concoction with a dubious expression. The consistency of the mixture slowly began to change and he watched as it solidified, losing its transparency and becoming white before starting to yellow.

Rosita let out a brief exclamation and suddenly got up, rushing into the Old Pen. Thomas took in her carefree nakedness as she returned with a wooden spoon and sat beside him once again. She carefully turned the unusual cake over in the dish and Thomas could see that it had browned in places.

A couple more minutes passed and then she took the empty bowl from him. Slipping the spoon beneath the strange food, she carefully lifted it from the dish and settled it on the bowl, its edge rising out as the centre sagged into the hollow.

Rosita passed him the bowl and indicated that he should eat with a nod. Thomas felt its heat against his fingertips as he tore a piece off, steam rising as he raised it to his mouth, smelling the distinct scent of cooked egg.

An expression of pleasant surprise arose upon his face as he ate the morsel. He looked at her and nodded while making noises of approval.

'This is very good,' he stated after swallowing.

Rosita's eyes sparkled all the more. She leant towards him and kissed his cheek before turning her attention to pouring the last of the mixture. She used the spoon to scrape out the last drips and the dish was barely filled.

Thomas finished his food and licked his fingers before scratching his thick beard, his stomach grumbling its gratitude. She took the bowl from him when her food was ready, transferring it with the spoon once again.

Rosita held the bowl out to him. He looked at the steaming offering in surprise, a swell of emotion rising in response to her willingness to forego sustenance so that his hunger may be satiated.

He shook his head in response.

She stared into his eyes and raised her hand to his cheek, stroking it with her thumb. 'Thomas,' she said with gentle warmth.

The fire crackled and spat at their feet. They looked to the fading glow of the embers that had spilled upon the ground and Thomas quickly brushed one from his right leg, feeling the slight sting of a burn.

Rosita turned her attention to the food and set the bowl upon her bare lap before breaking the omelette apart and eating it piece by piece. Thomas reached behind them, pulling the patchwork of furs from the cot. He placed it about their shoulders to protect their backs from the chill as they sat naked beside each other and the rain continued to patter upon the shutters.

64

Gerens stood upon the short ladder in the growing gloom, chest leant against the top rung as he reached forward and tore handfuls of rotten thatch from the roof of the small barn. His mind was not on the task, but was instead distracted by Nonna's deep melancholy. It had been five days since they had woken to discover that Jowen had passed in the night. Her grief had been terrible to witness. He had hoped that after the burial the previous day it would begin to lift, but its weight still bore down on her, crushing out her light.

He ripped another handful of blackened straw from the roof, fingers slipping in the mould that coated it before he released it to his right, looking down to watch it tumble to the pile already upon the ground below. In his mind's eye he could see Nonna at the graveside, her loss beyond tears, face pale and lacking any sign of life bar the blink of her eyes.

Gerens sighed and shook his head. He felt helpless in the face of such pain.

Reaching further forward, the ladder shifting slightly beneath him as the ropes which bound it together strained, he roughly grasped more of the thatch, tearing it away with the violence of frustration. He clenched his jaw as tears threatened. He needed to stay strong for Nonna, could not afford to succumb to the tumultuous emotions within. The loss of the boy and the sight of the woman he loved so devoid of vitality were wringing his heart, as was her withdrawal from his attentions.

The clearing of a throat gave him a start and he looked down over his shoulder. An old man stood in the half-light by the pile of discarded straw and drew back the dark hood of his muddied cloak. Gerens looked at his face, his beard woven with white and eyes marked by wrinkles. A vague sense of recognition tugged at the back of his mind. 'Can I help you?' he asked.

'I seek work and was hoping thee may have some use for an old man,' replied the stranger as he adjusted his grip on the small cloth sack slung over his shoulder.

Gerens glanced at the thatch. There was much to do in order to repair it and there were also repairs to be done to the walls before the barn could become a forge, the last tenants apparently having been evicted over a year before.

'I have much use, but no pennies by which to pay,' he replied, looking back to the man.

'I will happily work for food and lodging.'

Gerens looked at him in surprise. 'You have no home?'

He shook his head. 'Though that has not long been my lot.'

The smith looked to the cottage resting with its back to the shadowy woods twenty yards to his left as he pondered, Myrtle stabled in a ramshackle shed built against the right-hand side and the cart resting next to it. 'It may be that another's company will break the mood,' he mumbled to himself.

'I beg your pardon?'

Gerens turned to the old man. 'I will take you into my employ if you are happy to sleep in here,' he said, patting the thatch. 'We can dig a pit for a fire so you may keep warm and with your help it will not be long before the roof is watertight.'

'Aye, any roof is better than none,' nodded the old man.

'Then it is settled,' said the smith as he climbed down the ladder. 'Gerens,' he introduced, wiping his hand on his leggings and then holding it out.

'Manow,' replied the old man, firmly taking hold of the smith's wrist.

'Mamm says that supper is ready,' called Daveth from the front door of the cottage.

Gerens turned to him, the boy's eyes surrounded by shadows that hinted at the nightmares which had been waking

272

him since the passing of his brother. 'I will be there shortly,' he called back.

'Thy son?' asked Manow.

'Of sorts,' replied Gerens. 'Come, you must join us,' he said, making his way across the muddy grass before the old man could enquire as to his meaning.

Reaching the door, the smith stopped short of taking hold of the handle and looked back at Manow with a frown. 'There is something I ought tell you before we go in,' he said, looking to the ground. 'We recently lost a child to a fever and my wife is not herself.'

The old man regarded him with sympathy. 'Art thou sure my company will not be an intrusion?'

Gerens raised his gaze to the old man, the touch of recognition arising once again. 'It will be a welcome intrusion,' he replied.

He took hold of the handle and entered the cottage. 'A guest is joining us for supper tonight,' he stated, looking to Nonna as she sat upon a stool on the far side of the fire.

She turned to him, all life stolen from her face, taken along with the life of her son. 'Guest?'

'This is Manow,' he said, glancing back and ushering the old man in with a wave and a nod.

Manow stepped in and Gerens shut the door behind him, the old man glancing back as he felt a little discomfort. 'Good evening,' he greeted.

'Manow, this is my wife, Nonna,' said the smith as he stepped over to the fire and warmed his hands, trying to act as if there were naught wrong.

'It is a pleasure to meet thee,' said Manow.

Nonna simply nodded at him and then stared blankly at the flames once again.

'And this is our son, Daveth.' Gerens indicated the boy seated beside his mother.

'I am not your son,' mumbled the boy belligerently, Nonna paying him no heed.

'Glad to make thy acquaintance, young sir,' said Manow with a strained smile.

'Come and sit by the fire.' Gerens nodded towards a stool beside him as he continued to stand before the fire.

Manow moved to the seat and sat down, placing his cloth sack by his feet before glancing across the flames at Nonna, a shiver passing along his spine. He ran a hand through his waves of greying hair and shifted on the stool, feeling distinctly uneasy.

'It would seem that supper is just a simple broth,' commented the smith, peering into the large pot suspended from three lengths of iron that leant over the pit and came together above the fire.

'If you are unhappy with such an offering then I suggest you expend the effort next time,' stated Nonna without looking up at him.

He glanced at her, his heart aching at the coldness of her words. Pulling the fourth stool up to the pit, he seated himself and hoped that Manow's presence would act as a distraction from the darkness that the firelight could not chase away.

'Have we met on some previous occasion?' he asked the old man sitting to his right. 'Only I feel I recognise you in some vague way.'

Daveth glanced over, studying the stranger's face but finding naught familiar, his interest immediately waning.

Manow pondered briefly. 'I think not,' he said, shaking his head.

Gerens nodded. 'It is likely you are right, for I am certain I would have remembered your name. It is not one that I have come across before.'

'That may be so, but Manow is not the name I was given at birth.'

The smith regarded him with puzzlement. 'What name did you bear and why did you seek to change it?'

'Alas, I know not what I was called and 'tis by chance that I go by this name.'

'By chance?' Gerens' brow was knotted in puzzlement.

'Aye, but let me not darken this evening with my sorry tale,' replied Manow. 'We should eat and then rest for I see there is much work for us to do on the morrow.'

The blacksmith glanced at Daveth as he sat morosely on the stool opposite and then looked to Nonna on the left. Neither seemed to be paying them any heed and it was likely that Nonna would refuse food or take only a little, as she had since Jowen's death.

'If you do not mind the telling, then I would be glad to hear your tale.'

'Art thou sure thee wishes to hear the ramblings of an old man?'

'I am,' stated Gerens with a nod.

Manow gazed at the flames before him and took a breath before beginning. 'Part I was told and the rest I know. I was found floating upon the sea and taken upon a fishing boat, half-drowned and thought dead at first. I came to during the journey back to port, unable to remember my name or my origins, the crew naming me "Manow et-an Mor".'

'Man of the Sea,' nodded Gerens.

'We docked at Falmouth, where I was left wandering upon the wharf. A kindly man asked if I would help him load bales of Spanish cloth he had purchased onto his cart, offering me a penny for my time. As I hefted the bales I told him my story, such as it was, and he took pity on me and took me into his employ. His name was Jeremiah and he was a tailor of fine garments for the nobility.'

'What misfortune has befallen you that you should be homeless and seeking my employ?' asked Gerens.

'King Edward,' replied the old man simply.

Gerens looked at him without comprehension. 'I do not take your meaning.'

'Jeremiah was a Jew,' said Manow. 'By edict of King Edward all those of Jewish faith were expelled from England in the year that recently drew to a close. I did not wish to leave with him, hopeful that my past would one day make itself known. I took over tenancy of his home, but his expulsion had cast a shadow over our association. There was no custom and no money by which to pay rent or taxes. I was cast out onto the street and all those I had known for nigh on twenty years turned their backs on me.'

'Twenty years,' echoed Gerens. With sudden revelation, the reason for his feeling of recognition came to him and he tried to conceal his surprise.

'Aye,' said Manow with a nod as he stared at the flames with a faraway look in his eyes. 'The life I led and the name I bore before that time are lost to me still.'

'Gerens?'

He turned to Nonna and saw the same realisation in her expression. It was the first time he had seen her face gain vitality for days and her eyes had lost their dull sheen, now shining with the light of astonished disbelief.

Glancing sideways and seeing the Manow's attention was focussed on her, he shook his head surreptitiously in the hope of warning her against putting voice to her insight. 'What is it?' he asked with mock innocence.

She thought quickly. 'Can we have supper now?'

He nodded and a thin smile passed fleetingly upon his lips. 'Aye, that sounds like a good idea,' he replied. 'What do you say, Manow?'

The old man also gave a nod. 'I have delayed supper long enough.'

'Nonsense, it was a story in which there was much of interest,' said Gerens. 'Let us hope that our meeting marks a change in your fortunes.'

'May that be so,' agreed Manow, nodding again.

'Would you have some mead?'

'Aye, that would be a welcome warmth indeed.'

Gerens rose from his stool and went to a bench resting along the left-hand wall of the cottage. 'Would you like a cup, my love?' he asked with a glance over his shoulder.

'I think I ought,' she said, the smith's brow furrowing at her response and Manow looking across at her with mild curiosity.

Gerens set three cups before him and then took up a jug to the rear of the bench. He unstopped it and poured the sweet honey brew into the vessels. Setting it back down, he carried two of the cups over to the fire, handing one to Nonna and then the other to their guest, studying Manow's face as he did

276

so, astounded by the unexpected arrival of a ghost from the past.

Fetching his cup, he returned to the seat as Nonna instructed Daveth to serve the broth. The boy rose with a reluctant slouch. He collected a ladle and pile of four bowls from the bench, dragging his feet as he went back to the fireside.

'So,' said Manow, 'how long have thee lived these parts?'

Gerens and Nonna glanced at each other.

'Too long,' mumbled Daveth as he set the bowls down, taking the top one and moving to the cooking pot with the ladle in his other hand.

'Many a year,' said the blacksmith, glad for the boy's dark comment and its seeming support of his lie, 'though it is only of late that we have taken up tenancy of this home. I am a smith and the barn will become my forge,' he said with a nod to the anvil tucked in the corner beyond the old man.

Manow glanced at the implement. 'That is a good skill.'

Daveth held out a bowl to his mother, the contents slopping over the edge.

'Our guest should be offered first,' she stated.

The boy rolled his eyes and passed the bowl between his hands before holding it out to the old man.

'My thanks, lad,' said Manow as he took it and held it upon his lap, waiting for his hosts to be served before starting to eat.

They were all soon supping the broth, which had little taste bar that of turnip. A thoughtful hush hung in the air, Gerens and Nonna sharing a few glances whilst also taking the opportunity to study the old man's face, as if needing constant reassurance that they were not mistaken.

'We should to the barn and dig a pit for your fire,' said Gerens after swallowing the last of his meal, putting his bowl upon the ground beside him.

'That would be most welcome. My stamina is not what it once was and rest I must,' responded Manow. 'My thanks for thy hospitality,' he said to Nonna over the fading flames.

'And thee for the serving,' he added, looking to Daveth with a forced smile.

Gerens and Manow rose from their stools. The smith went to the selection of tools gathered against the wall by the anvil and picked up a spade before stepping to the front door. He opened it and stepped out, finding that mist had gathered in the deepening shadows of the dusk.

'I bid thee good night,' said Manow as he paused in the doorway.

'I hope you will find sleep and wake well rested,' replied Nonna.

The old man nodded and vacated the cottage. Closing the door behind him, the two men then walked over to the barn as the mist moved sluggishly about them. They entered through the door that was located at the near end of the front wall and Gerens found he was barely able to see in the gloom. If it were not for the holes in the walls his task would have been all but impossible.

'Should I not dig the pit as its necessity is my doing?' asked Manow as he stood just inside the entrance.

The smith shook his head and made the first incision with the blade of the spade, pressing down on it with his right boot. 'I am happy to do so,' he replied as he continued with the task, slicing the earth in a small circle and then taking it up and piling it against the back wall.

It was only a few minutes until the task was complete and Gerens leant the spade by the discarded soil. 'I will fetch wood and a lighted branch from the cottage,' he announced. 'Will you be in need of aught else?'

'That will be plenty. I have a fur that serves as my bed and the bag serves as a headrest.'

Gerens nodded and exited the building, striding over to the cottage as the old man watched him from the doorway of the barn. The smith entered the cottage and made sure to close the door behind him. He found that Daveth had retired to his cot in the back left corner, though believed it unlikely that he already slept. Nonna was still sitting by the fire and looked up at him.

'Is that…?' she began with voice lowered.

'Aye,' he said with a nod before she could finish. 'Zethar Carrow, father to Thomas. Thought lost at sea twenty years passed.' He began to gather up a few branches to take out to the barn.

Nonna shook her head in disbelief. 'We must tell him.'

Gerens turned to her. 'No, we must hold our tongues.'

'But he must know of his true name and the life that was lost to him,' she said with a look of surprise.

'We cannot reveal the truth to him, my love. What do you think his purpose would be if we were to tell him? He would to Zennor on quick feet and those who would have us pursued and punished would soon discover our whereabouts.'

She sat in contemplation, her sight to the soft flicker of the flames as Gerens placed some smaller branches atop those already selected and held in the crook of his arm.

'We could make him swear to secrecy,' she stated, looking back to him as the smith moved to crouch by the fire before her.

Gerens shook his head and sighed. 'I wish there were some other way, my love, but we cannot trust to words. He is sure to be questioned and scrutinised.'

She frowned at him, but made no other protest. She knew he was right. The risk was too great and they had naught by which to move again in order to avoid detention and the punishment that would follow.

The smith took up a burning branch and rose to his full height. 'I know 'tis contrary to our natures to keep such hidden from him,' he said, looking down upon her with regretful fondness, 'but there is little choice. Fate has forced our hand in this and we are not to blame.'

Nonna nodded vaguely and turned back to the fire. Gerens stared at her and then stepped to the door.

'One day we may find it opportune to tell him,' he said with a backward glance, a thin smile of conciliation upon his face as he paused before opening the door and exiting into the night.

65

Thomas removed the pelt from the rabbit carcass and passed it to Rosita as she sat at the table to his right. Taking her blade to its underside, she began to scrape away any excess fat and flesh.

He made a cut along the stomach and the internal organs bulged out. Reaching in, he began to gut the creature, dropping the glistening entrails into the waste bucket resting on the ground near the seaward door.

Rosita put her knife down when she finished cleaning off the pelt and stretched forward to take a large pinch of salt from the wooden box before her. She sprinkled it over the skin and then began to rub it in to aid the drying process.

Thomas finished the gutting and smiled as he watched her for a moment. Picking up the bucket, he walked out of the seaward door and went around to the western side of the house. He tipped the slick contents onto the pile of ash and excrement before going to the water butt beside the door.

Crouching before it, he set the bucket on the ground and pulled out the stopper, rinsing the fluids and smears of blood from his hands as water tumbled into the vessel. Splashing his face and feeling the thickness of his beard, Thomas then stopped the butt and rinsed out the bucket, flinging the water to the left.

He rose and went back into Ocean Mist to find Rosita laying the pelt fur-down by the bowl before the window, the shutters open to allow the cool wind to circulate and dry the hide. Another pelt rested in the stretching frame leant against the base of the wall, having been tied into the simple square of rope-bound wood after drying for a few days.

'There will soon be enough for me to make you a coat,' commented Thomas as she moved towards him.

He took her at the hips and drew her close. She smiled, holding her glistening hands out to the sides so as not to soil his clothes.

They kissed and then parted, Rosita exiting the cottage in order to wash away the residue of her labours. He scratched his beard and listened as the water splashed. Thoughtfully stroking the thick hair, his sight fell on his knife as it rested by the rabbit on the table beside him.

Thomas nodded to himself and picked up the blade, taking it to the bowl before the window. Rosita entered and stopped inside the door, watching as he cleaned the knife in the water and then began to carefully shave beneath his chin.

She stepped to him and took hold of his wrist as he prepared to pass the steel across his skin once again. Her eyes were filled with warmth as she guided him to the table and manoeuvred him to sit on its edge.

Fetching the bowl, she set it down to the right and took the knife from him. With the gentle touch of her hand, she pushed his head back, his throat exposed. She lifted the blade and began to shave him, regularly rinsing it in the water as she revealed the freshness of his face beneath the growth of hair.

Rosita drew the knife over his skin with attentive care. He stared at her face, taking in every softness as she stood before him.

She turned his head with her fingertips, ran the cool blade down his cheek and along his jaw as he looked to the far corner of the room. Causing him to look in the opposite direction, Thomas stared out at the sea in the middle-distance, a scattering of white clouds drifting in the blue sky as the wind sent them east and gulls wheeled above the waves, their calls reaching the cottage.

Rosita turned his face towards her again, avoiding his gaze as she took the blade to his upper lip and he felt the slight tug as it passed over his skin. Leaning back, she regarded him and raised her hand to his face, stroking his cheek with the backs of her fingers.

She finally looked to his eyes, a smile replacing the expression of concentration. 'Terminado,' she said.

Thomas put his arms about her and pulled her close, their lips pressing tight. Her hands rose to his hair and ran through its growing length as they enjoyed the intimate embrace.

The kiss came to an end and she looked to his straggly fringe, running her fingers through it and looking at him suggestively as she held up the knife.

Thomas laughed and shook his head. 'When the warmth of spring arrives,' he said as she stepped away and his arms fell to his sides.

'Voy a tallar ahora,' she said in her native tongue, resting his knife upon the table and picking up her own blade. Seeing the fluids upon it, she quickly washed it in the bowl and then gave him a final fond glance before going into the main living area to continue with the carving of a seagull she had begun a few days before.

Thomas remained seated on the edge of the table as he stared after her and stroked his face. 'No longer the likeness of my father, but my father's son once more,' he said to himself with a smile, the ghosts of his past continuing their retreat.

66

Gerens stood before the wall at the end of the barn, the track to Lostwithiel a few yards behind him. He applied another handful of daub to the lattice of split branches which wove between stakes before him, his fingers numbed and the wind biting at his extremities as clouds laboured overhead. He and Manow had spent the previous day pulling away a large area of the old daub that was falling into ruin, cleaning the wattle down to begin anew. The repairs were nearly completed, only one section still requiring attention to the rear of the building.

He glanced to his right as the old man tipped more water onto the pile of earth, horse dung and old thatch straw which they had mixed by hand that morning. Manow had been unusually quiet and the atmosphere was subdued.

'If I be any judge, we will be finished on the morrow,' said Gerens, trying to fill his words with good cheer. They had been working every day for two weeks through rain and mist, February arriving in torrents that had hampered their progress.

'And when the work is done, what then?' asked the old man as he took up a handful of the daub and applied it to the lattice of wood.

'Then I can bring in the anvil and fire pot. It will not be long until my hammer is brought to bear and the name of smith is earned once more.'

'I mean, what then of me?' Manow turned to him. 'Am I to wander in search of work once again?'

Gerens stopped and looked at the old man. 'In truth, I had not thought on the matter,' he admitted, 'though I see no reason why you cannot remain in my employ.'

'What would thou have me do once the repairs are completed? I have no skill with metal and no charm with horses. The strength in my body wanes and I would be of little use.'

The smith smoothed his hand over the daub as he pondered. He could not allow Manow to wander homeless and destitute. There was guilt enough already as a result of keeping the secret of his true identity from him. It was a secret that would provide him with a home and answers to the riddles of his past, but one Gerens dare not reveal.

'I will find work for you,' he said before picking a piece of mud from his braided beard and bending to take up another handful of the thick paste matted with straw. He pushed it against the wattle, a few pieces falling to the ground at his feet, but most sticking to the wood as he smeared it into place.

'Why would thee do so when in truth ye have no need?' asked Manow, still holding the smith in his gaze, something in his tone making Gerens uncomfortable.

'I will be in need of assistance,' he replied without turning from the task.

'Did thou hast aid at your previous forge?'

He glanced at the old man as he bent to take another handful. 'No, but the work here will be more plentiful and create need for an extra pair of hands.' He rose to face the wall.

'What of thy son? He is of an age to begin working.'

Gerens turned to Manow, the daub in his hand. 'Surely my wish to continue our arrangement is to be smiled upon, not questioned so insistently.'

The old man regarded him in silence for a moment. 'When art thou going to tell me, Gerens?'

'What?' Gerens was taken aback.

'I saw the glances shared with thy wife when I told the tale of my life that first night. Thou be party to knowledge of my past, I am sure of it, and thy desire for me to stay even when the repairs are done has only served to strengthen this conviction,' he said firmly. 'For two weeks I have waited for thee to tell me, but I cannot restrain my curiosity any longer. 'Tis time to reveal what thee knows.'

Gerens considered protesting his innocence, but the look in the old man's eyes was that of a hound who had scented a fox. Denial would be of no use, for he would sniff out the truth whatever it took, so certain was he that it was there to be unearthed.

He released the handful of daub, letting it fall back to the pile between them. 'I know you,' he said. 'Or rather, I knew you in the life you led before being fished from the sea.'

Manow stared at him. 'My name,' he said breathlessly. 'What was my name?'

'Zethar Carrow.'

'Zethar Carrow,' repeated the old man, turning his thoughtful gaze to the wattle as he waited for the sense of recognition he hoped would come, along with the memories of his old life.

Naught stirred within and his disappointment was apparent in his expression. He had carried the expectation of a profound awakening through all the years since first waking without memory of his former life. He had believed his name would be the key to unlock everything that his mind kept imprisoned, but it seemed as though he was wrong.

'What more can thee tell me?' he asked.

Gerens glanced at the bare trees and nearby track. 'Let us not speak more of it here,' he said. 'We shall go into the barn and take some rest from the work. Once the fire is lit I will tell you all I know.'

'Aye, agreed,' nodded the old man before crouching and washing off his hands in the bucket of water, Gerens stepping over and following suit.

Gerens entered the cottage just after nightfall.

'How go the repairs?' asked Nonna as she sat darning a shirt by the fire, Daveth on the earth before her idly poking a stick into the flames and watching the end burn.

'They go well, my love,' he replied, unable to hold her gaze as he stepped to the pit and crouched to warm his hands. 'There is little left to do.'

Nonna rested the shirt on her lap and studied his profile searchingly. 'What is it that you do not tell me?'

'There is no more to tell,' he replied without turning.

'And yet you will not show me your eyes,' she said with a knowing tone. 'I may not be able to read the written word, but I read your face well enough, Gerens. There is something that you hide from me.'

The smith sighed. 'I hide naught, only struggle to put voice to what I must say.'

Nonna's expression changed to one of concern. 'Of what do you speak?'

'I must to Zennor on the morrow.'

Her mouth fell open and she was rendered speechless.

Gerens finally turned to her. 'Manow has known since the night of his arrival that we hid something from him. He held his tongue until now, but could retain his curiosity no longer and challenged me on the matter.' He sighed.

'I have told him all and he will travel west in the hope of rediscovering his old life. He would have gone this very eve if it were not for my offer to accompany him and insistence that we leave at first light.'

'But why must you go with him?' She stared at him worriedly.

'In good conscience, I cannot let him journey alone. The nights are still touched by the chill of winter and it is more than fifty miles. I will see him safely delivered to Zennor and then return.'

'Can I go with them?' asked Daveth, looking over his shoulder at his mother.

She looked down at her son. 'There is no reason for you to take the journey,' she replied.

'I want to see Tas,' he said with a sour look.

'You will stay here with me,' she stated firmly.

'You forced us to leave him,' he complained. 'Now I am a twin without a brother and 'tis your fault.' His words contained the heat of indignation and tears glistened in his eyes.

Nonna's expression fell and she took a steadying breath as her loss was brought to the fore by her son's words. 'I am sorry, Daveth,' she said. 'For what reason he was taken from us I know not, but I do know that I am not prepared to lose you, whether to sickness or to the call of a past which is best left behind us.'

'You are to stay here with your Mamm,' said Gerens, the boy glaring at him momentarily before suddenly standing.

'Then I shall go myself,' he stated, storming out of the cottage, the door slamming behind him.

'He will not go far.'

'And nor should you,' responded Nonna, briefly looking to the door.

'You know it would be wrong of us to allow Zethar to travel all that way alone, my love. What if some misfortune were to befall him?'

'What if it were to befall you both? You seem to forget that you will be a wanted man in Zennor.'

'I forget naught. I will not venture into the village, but will take him up to the cottage on Trewey Hill in which he once dwelt and where Thomas still abides.'

She shook her head. 'What of us? Would you leave me and the boy to fend for ourselves not knowing when or even if you will return?' she said, her heart aching at the idea of being parted from him. She had been forcibly parted from one of her sons only weeks before and did not think she could bare another loss so soon.

'Tomorrow is Wednesday, is it not?' asked Gerens.

'Aye, and the feast day of Saint Valentine,' replied Nonna.

'In which case, I shall be back by Sunday at the latest. With only two passengers and no load upon the cart, the journey will take half the time than before, if not less.' He forced a smile, hoping that the certainty in his words would bring some comfort.

The creaking of the front door caused them to both turn. Daveth entered, his head hanging low.

'It is to dark and cold,' he explained sullenly, 'but I am still going to leave in the morn.'

He plodded over to his cot tucked into the shadows in the far left corner. Nonna watched as he flung himself onto his bed, noting the redness of his eyes which spoke of the tears he had shed while outside.

A thought came to Gerens and he stood, going to the tools gathered beside the anvil. He searched for a moment before taking up the sword in its tatty scabbard. The smith made his way past the fire pit and over to the boy, Nonna watching him curiously.

'Daveth?' Gerens crouched beside the cot.

'What?' responded the boy, his back to the smith.

'I have something for you.'

Nonna's expression became one of surprised wonderment as she realised what Gerens was about to do. Her heart ached, a tide of warm emotion washing through her.

Daveth slowly turned over. His eyes fell on the sheathed sword and he looked at the smith in puzzlement.

'I always swore I would pass this on to my son,' stated Gerens. He held it out to the boy upon his palms. 'It is yours.'

Daveth's mouth fell open, eyes wide. 'Really?' he whispered.

Gerens nodded. 'Though there is one condition. You must stay here with your mamm. I entrust her safety and this blade to you.'

The boy sat up and stared at the sword, temporarily struck dumb.

'Will you guard her, my son?'

Daveth nodded slowly and Gerens lifted the sword to him. He reached out, fingers hesitating within a hair's breadth of the weapon and then curling around the leather of the old scabbard. He lifted it from the smith's palms and then rested it across his knees. Left hand grasping the hilt, he pulled the blade halfway out and stared at the firelight glinting on its polished steel.

Gerens reached forward and placed his hand upon the boy's shoulder. 'Son,' he said with a nod of confirmation, the word filled with feeling and spoken with firm assurance.

The boy stroked the blade for a moment.

With sudden movement, he sheathed and pushed it from his lap. It fell with a thud to the floor as he raised his raw gaze to the smith. 'You will ne'er be my father,' he hissed.

'Daveth!' scolded Nonna in shock, wiping away tears that had been brought forth by Gerens' actions.

The boy glanced at her and then pulled his cover over him, crashing to the cot and turning his back once again. The sound of sobbing arose soon after, his shoulders quaking with the strength of his outpouring.

Gerens slowly reached for the sword and picked it up. He rose to his feet, looking down on Daveth and wishing he could offer comfort, wishing the boy could have accepted his gesture and his love. Going back to the fireside, he sat heavily upon a stool with shoulders slumped.

'It will take time,' reassured Nonna.

The smith nodded as he stared at the flames, the sword gripped tightly in his hands as he fought back his own tears.

Nonna moved to crouch before him and looked up into his face while reaching for his left hand, holding it tightly within both of hers. 'Go with Manow on the morrow,' she said softly, 'and I will await your return with a warm and welcoming heart.'

He looked down at her. 'My thanks,' he replied. 'If it were not for my conscience I would ne'er make such a journey nor willingly leave your side.'

'I know,' she nodded, a sad smile curling her lips as she squeezed his hand.

They turned to the fire, Nonna seating herself on the earth beside him and resting her head upon his lap. Gerens stroked her long sandy hair as they sat in silence, both lost to dark thoughts of their immanent separation.

68

They walked hand in hand through the gathering dusk as they ascended Trewey Hill from the west. The regular tap of Rosita's walking stick marked their passage as they neared the peak and Thomas felt the weight of the three rabbits hanging at his hip. He was pleased with his decision to move his traps to the western foot of the hill, placing two along the edge of the copse where he often collected wood. Dor Dama had blessed them with many rabbits since the relocation and the cooking pot was ne'er in want of meat.

Reaching the bare rocks at the top of the hill, they paused and stared out over the darkening world spread before them. Thomas looked down the slope to the north-east, staring into the deep shadows pooled in the shallow valley in which Zennor Churchtown rested. He could see no firelight, the shutters closed on the growing chill.

Raucous laughter rose in the stillness. His brow furrowed as he listened, hearing many voices mingled in the mirth. He narrowed his gaze and saw the faintest touch of golden light at Trewey Farm.

'Today must be the feast of Saint Valentine,' he said after pondering for a moment. 'The village will be gathered in Old Jacob's barn,' he added, turning to Rosita and finding her looking down the hillside towards the sounds, the new fur cape about her shoulders.

They began to descend the moor towards the grassland above the walled fields. Shenty came bounding by after sniffing nearby rocks, a partridge taking to the sky in sudden alarm.

The thick grasses brushed against their legs as they went north, the dark shape of Ocean Mist coming into view as it was slowly revealed upon its small table of land set into the hillside. Thomas stared at the low building and an ominous feeling arose in his gut, which tightened and churned in response.

The high bark of a fox sounded on the moor at their backs as his steps faltered and slowed. He glanced at Rosita, but she showed no outward sign of feeling the same warning within. Sniffing the air, he smelt smoke, but could see none and knew that the fire within Ocean Mist had yet to be lit.

Reaching the gate, he placed his hand upon the top bar and hesitated before pushing it open. Shenty slipped past, apparently also unaffected by any sense of foreboding.

They walked up the path and Thomas glanced at the windswept tree that his mother had planted. For an instant it seemed as if its branches came alive, writhing like snakes as they arched over the wall.

He blinked and the unsettling movements were no longer in evidence. His pulse raced and he was filled with tension, one which built with every step they took towards the door.

Thomas looked to the shutters, but could see naught but blackness through the thin gap between. The crack beneath the door likewise offered no clue as to potential danger within.

Releasing Rosita's hand, he gripped the door handle in his left hand while his right sought out the hilt of the small knife at his hip, ready to draw it should the need arise.

With sudden movement, he flung the door wide. He stared into the darkness, heart furious and fingers tight about the knife's handle, seeing no sign of threat within.

Rosita moved to stand beside him and studied his face curiously, head cocked to the side as Shenty padded into the cottage.

He took a breath and turned to her. 'Do not worry,' he stated, the thin smile he adopted betrayed by the wild look in his eyes.

Entering the house together, Thomas left the door open to allow the last light of day to faintly illuminate the interior until the fire was lit, not wishing to close it and so deepen the gloom in which they found themselves. He went straight to the woodpile, taking up his tinder box and collecting a handful of kindling.

Crouching beside the fire pit, he placed the dried grass and twigs onto the ashes of the previous night. Taking out his flints, he struck them together, his movements filled with the quickness of urgency. He had no wish to linger in darkness for any longer than was necessary, the feelings of unease still stirring his stomach.

Rosita sat on the edge of cot nearest the pit and watched his desperation to set the kindling to flame. The fox barked upon the moor once again and a distant response followed shortly thereafter.

The grass took and Thomas carefully cupped the flames, blowing his encouragement. Putting away the flints, he took the tinder box back to its resting place and selected some slender branches from the woodpile, settling them on the young fire.

Watching until he was satisfied no more assistance would be needed in order to keep it going, he rose and went to the door, closing it on the night. He paused beside it, glancing at Rosita's back as she shifted forward and held her hands out to the growing flames, their heat as yet unable to push back the chill.

Thomas glanced about the interior. The feelings still lurked within him, but he could find no cause for their presence. The cottage was as they had left it.

Walking from the door, he passed along the bedside and went into the Old Pen. He untied the rabbits from his hip and rested them on the table before glancing at the seaward door, fighting the urge to place one of the chairs against it even though such action offered little security.

Thomas returned to the main living area and found Rosita crouched before the fire, rubbing her hands together above. He stood and watched her from the entrance to the Old Pen. He was glad for her company and felt his heart swell as his gaze followed the contours of her profile.

She looked at him over her shoulder. She was smiling. The firelight shone in her eyes, dark hair framing her face as it tumbled to her shoulders.

Rosita held out her hand.

He hesitated and then stepped forward, taking it and moving to crouch by her side. She took his hand to her lap as she settled upon the earth. Thomas seated himself, their bodies close as the fire crackled. They remained so for long minutes as the heat grew stronger and began to leech out the chill which had settled in their bones during the hours spent upon the hill and at its western foot.

Rosita lifted her face to the south-facing window as the sound of singing and music drifted through the shutters from the valley below. She turned to him questioningly.

''Tis a feast day,' he said, though no sign of understanding registered in her expression.

She released his hand and got to her feet, stepping beyond the head of the cot and opening the shutters, the volume of the merrymaking increasing. Leaning out, she looked down the slope of the hill, but could see naught but darkness beneath the company of stars that glittered above.

Thomas watched her, secure in the knowledge that the folk of Zennor would be gathered in the barn at Trewey Farm and no one would spy her presence at the window. He listened as the night fell silent for a few moments and then the sound of the rote lifted again, Jory playing a lively jig.

Rosita grinned at him. She skipped over and held out her hands.

'Vamos a bailar,' she said in her rich voice, beckoning for him to take hold by flexing her fingers.

Thomas reluctantly grasped them and she pulled him to his feet with surprising vigour. She began to dance backwards about the fire, her footfalls light and knees rising high as she lifted their arms in the air. He followed, trying to break the internal bonds of restraint brought about by his conservative nature. Shenty leapt upon the cot and began to bark excitedly, her tail wagging as she watched them.

294

Rosita released his hands and began to skip as she followed the circle of blackened stones about the flames. She bowed to the left and then to the right with the rhythm of her dance, waving her hands to each side as she did so. Thomas followed, the bonds beginning to break as he began to forget himself, lost to the sight of her graceful passage and the music drifting gaily up the hill. His cavorting became more enthused and the two of them pranced in energetic jubilation, turning and jumping, arms rising and falling as they circled the fire. It was like an ancient ritual, a celebration of life and love.

Face glistening with perspiration, Rosita led them away from the flames, took them out of the door and into the long grass of the garden, the hound enthusiastically following behind. They leapt and whooped, spun and skipped beneath the heavens, Shenty continuing to bark as she bounded about them.

Thomas was lost to the dance. He had ne'er felt so unfettered before and with this intense sense of freedom came greater expression as they frolicked in the darkness.

The music came to an end and he collapsed to the grass, coming to rest on his back and laughing at the sky. He was filled with joy, liberated from himself and completely existent in the present without thought of his past or future.

Rosita giggled as she walked over and settled beside him, Shenty wandering over to the tree and sniffing about its base. They turned to each other. Her laughter died away as she stared into his eyes. Leaning closer, she gave him a gentle kiss and then settled back onto the grass, smiling tenderly as she continued to look at him adoringly.

'Thomas,' she whispered with affection, taking hold of his left hand.

Resting it on her stomach, she then placed hers on top and stared at him meaningfully, her gaze filled with emotion.

He looked at her curiously for a moment and then his eyes widened. 'You are with child,' he stated breathlessly.

She nodded, understanding his meaning from his reaction and the tone of his words.

Thomas stared at her in shock as a new tune began in the vale below and was accompanied by singing. Rosita's expression was tightened by worry as she waited for his reaction.

He pulled her close and they embraced in the darkness amidst the long grass. 'I love you,' he said softly, tears running down his cheeks, barely able to believe he was to be a father.

He had long since believed he would remain alone and childless, and these beliefs had been made firm by being shunned by the villagers. Rosita had proved such dismal thoughts to be false. She was a blessed gift that had been offered up by the very sea that had claimed his father and grandfather, as if the waters wished to make amends.

'I love you so much.' He closed his eyes and clung to her warmth in the chill darkness.

They remained entwined for long minutes, Thomas' tears abating. He could feel her heartbeat against his chest and imagined the babe growing within her, sustained by the same pulse. He felt at peace. He felt whole.

'Mirar la luna!' exclaimed Rosita.

He drew away from her to find she was looking to the south-east and pointing into the sky. Turning, his expression became one of surprise. The full moon had risen over the darkened hills and was the colour of mead blushed by the honey of late spring.

Thomas sat up and stared in awe at the maiden of the sky as she rose in her dramatic gown of warm red. He had ne'er seen the likes before and was temporarily rendered speechless by the sight.

Rosita put her arm about his waist and cuddled into his side as they both looked to the heavens. Shenty plodded over and seated herself a couple of yards away before nipping at her left flank.

'I think it be a good omen on such an auspicious day,' said Thomas with a smile.

Feeling her shivering, he turned to find her cheeks rosy. He got to his feet and held out his hand. Rosita took hold and he helped her up, the two of them making their way back into the cottage with Shenty trailing behind them.

She moved to the fireside, the flames weakened but not having passed into the darkness of ash. Thomas shut the door and stepped to the woodpile, seeing that the window shutters were still open.

Taking hold, he paused to look at the reddened moon one last time. 'A good omen,' he whispered to himself with a nod.

Closing the shutters, he turned back to the wood and selected a few branches. Going to Rosita's side, he placed them on the fire and then seated himself on the ground, taking the fur from the bed and wrapping it about their shoulders as he had on previous occasions. They put their arms about each other, gleaning what warmth they could from their closeness as they waited for the flames to take hold.

69

''Tis an omen of misfortune to be sure,' said Old Jacob with a shake of his head as he stared up at the moon, vague clouds of breath marking his words.

'Aye, Brother,' nodded Golvan as the two men stood together in the yard of Trewey Farm and looked to the southern sky above the barn where the festivities were taking place. 'Tas told me of such a moon in the days of his youth. A "blood moon" he called it.'

'Aye, it was afore ye entered the world, but I remember it well.' Jacob glanced at his brother, whose birth had been the death of their mamm. 'The recollection gives me a chill greater than that of the night. Soon after it hung in the heavens half the village was struck down by a fever and half again ne'er arose from their beds.'

''Tis the bearer of bad tidings,' responded Golvan as light spilled from the entrance to the barn across from them and the sound of Jory playing his rote was accompanied by the clapping of hands. 'We should warn the rest of the village.'

Jacob looked at his younger brother as he stood to his left. 'And what would thee have us warn them against? We cannot foresee what will come.'

'They can be made wary and watchful,' replied Golvan. 'Besides, when the feast comes to an end they will see the portent of misfortune for themselves.'

'I am not so sure,' said the old farmer, turning back to the moon and pointing west. 'Cloud draws in and I think it not long afore she be veiled from sight.'

Golvan looked at the bank of cloud which had appeared beyond the top of Trewey Hill. 'So we leave them in ignorance?'

'Aye,' replied Jacob. 'We have no truth to give them 'cept the sight of the moon turned red. What good is there in causing undue worry when there is naught to do but wait and see what is revealed within the folds of time?'

Golvan looked at him doubtfully. 'Forewarned is forearmed,' he stated.

'And ignorance is bliss,' retorted the old man. 'Leave them none the wiser, for there is no preparation to be made and no action to be taken. We know not what comes or, in truth, if aught comes at all.'

'Something is coming,' stated Golvan, his tone grave. 'I feel it in my bones.'

'Thy feeling is not enough to warrant causing panic amongst the people, Brother,' responded Jacob with firmness.

Golvan stared at him, brow furrowing.

The aged farmer sighed. 'I cannot deny I feel it too, but there is little to tell and much to consider,' he said with a softened tone. 'What if our words cause the very thing we hope to avoid?'

'I do not take your meaning.'

'Think on it, Golvan. What would happen if one of the folk caught the chill that took Lacy and Marrek and almost had me away? Some would shut themselves away and others may even leave in hope of escaping the pestilence they perceive to have arrived. Even a sniffle or ache of the belly could set people to panic.'

Golvan looked to the mud as he pondered. 'Aye, I see the truth of yours words, though it still irks me that the village should be left blind to any signs of whatever ill wind is to blow, for it may be they would note it stirring and thereby warn the rest of us.'

'We will be watchful.' He reached up and placed his hand on his brother's shoulder. 'We will look for the signs and give warning when it is due.'

'So this is where thee hides thyself.'

Both men turned to find Conwenna standing in the entrance to the barn, her shadow falling across the yard.

'I retired for fresh air and a few moments of calm,' responded Jacob to his wife. 'Come, let us rejoin the feast,' he said to Golvan, patting him on the shoulder.

Golvan nodded. 'Aye, I could do with a cup of mead,' he replied with a deep frown, hopeful that his brother's sagely words would soon be forgotten and he would slip back into his loose-tongued ways, sharing the sight with his wife and others.

'Ye look to have as much cheer as the grave,' commented Conwenna as the two men made their way across the mud and drew close. 'What words have been spoken to give cause for such seriousness?'

'It is naught, my dear,' said Jacob. 'A passing melancholy brought on by the winter chill.'

She studied his lined face, unconvinced by his response, but knowing better than to enquire further. 'Then let us chase the chill away,' she said, taking hold of his hand.

He was led into the barn, which was lit by torches braced to its walls. Strands of ivy were wound about its roof beams and more hung like streamers of rich green from the rafters. The folk of Zennor sat about tables arranged along the sides or danced in the space between, Jory seated at a table in the left-hand corner, playing his rote and tapping his feet to the tune.

Golvan paused, watching the old farmer and his wife join the dance, the former forcing a smile as they continued to hold hands and circled first right and then left. He glanced up, leaning back in order to see the moon above the thatch. The bank of thick cloud was drawing across her, its leading edge illuminated by the red glow that spoke of ill fortune to come.

His face filled with shadows of concern, he turned back to the view of the barn's interior. He walked into the building and spied a jug of mead on the table immediately before him. Stepping over, he hoped its consumption would numb him to the feeling of approaching doom that knotted his stomach and his brow.

'What be ailing you on this fine night? You look as if death himself has come knocking,' asked Benedict Nan as he sat with his arm about Morvoren on the opposite side of the table, both of them smiling brightly and their cheeks coloured by their inebriation.

'It may be he has,' Golvan responded dismally as he picked up the jug and took it to his lips, drinking with gulping eagerness as a questioning glance passed between the couple and mead trickled down his beard to darken the earth at his feet.

70

Thomas emptied the waste bucket between the western wall of Ocean Mist and the hill, looking to the cloudy sky as he heard the chatter of crows. Their dark shapes passed overhead, heading west and soon hidden by the steepness of the slope.

Turning, he let out a gasp. Standing only ten yards away was Bersaba, Elowen beyond and keeping her distance.

'Did I startle thee?' she asked with a grin, eyes sparkling mischievously.

'Aye, I did not hear your approach,' he replied as his pulse returned to its usual rhythm. 'How goes it, Bersaba?'

'All goes well, Young Thomas.'

'Did you spy the moon during the night? She was in her fullness and the colour of springtime mead.'

'I did more than spy her presence. I danced beneath her at Boscawen Un.'

'The stone circle?'

'Indeed,' she nodded.

'My mother would tell of witches and druids conducting their rituals and dancing about the standing stones when the moon was full.'

'Thy mother did so herself in her youth.'

Thomas looked at her in dubious surprise.

''Tis true. She was amongst us in the days before she met thy father. He did not hold with the old ways and she put them aside in the name of love. If thy father had not been lost at sea it would not have been I that was called to her side when she ailed, for he would not have allowed it.'

'She was a witch?'

'If that is the name thee choose to use,' she nodded.

Thomas turned his gaze to the grass at his feet as he thought about what Bersaba had revealed. 'I recall little things,' he said. 'The caress of her hands upon the trunks of trees as we passed by, the silent blessings that fell from her lips, the respect she paid to the animals that came to our table and the whispered words spoken into my ears about the spirit dwelling in all things but not in truth divided.'

Bersaba nodded her head sagely. 'She may have put aside the practices of our number, but she ne'er turned her back on the wisdom that is the root of our simple ways, for it is the root from which the very tree of life grows.'

He stared at the old crone as snippets of memory flitted through his mind. All were touched with warmth and kindness, with a reverence for the natural world that gave rise to compassion and sensitivity.

'Thy life has been blessed by the Triple Goddess, Young Thomas, but now is the time of change,' said Bersaba, her words bringing his reverie to an end.

'Triple Goddess?' he asked in puzzlement.

'Doest thou not recall the many times we spoke of such things as we sat beside thy mother's sick bed?'

He shook his head.

'I speak of the maiden, the mother and the crone,' she clarified. 'Now the maiden becomes mother and it is time for the crone to take her leave,' she said pointedly.

Thomas stared at her for a moment. 'You know Rosita is with child?' he asked in surprise.

'Indeed,' she nodded.

'And you are leaving? Where does your journey take you?' he asked in bewilderment.

'Everywhere,' she replied cryptically as she smiled warmly at him, her narrowed eyes glittering. 'Fare ye well, Young Thomas, for we shall not meet again. May Dor Dama bless thee both and the babe that grows within her belly.'

Bersaba turned north as Thomas watched, temporarily struck dumb by her words and the wonderings they gave rise to. Her hunched form slowly diminished as she hobbled down the slope towards the ragged coastline, bare feet padding on the grass.

'Wait!' he called as a thought came to mind. 'What of the moon this past night? Was it an omen of some sort?'

'An omen?' she responded with a kindly chuckle and a shake of her head as she turned to look back at him. 'It was no more an omen than thunder and lightening. Do not choose the supernatural over the natural, Young Thomas, for to do so is to choose ignorance over knowledge. I have seen many such moons and they are to be taken simply as they are. Only fools find signs where there are none.'

'You said those words the night my mother passed away and the full moon hung bright in the sky,' countered Thomas.

'And I would say them again. Do not err in thy thinking and marry the two events, for there is no marriage in truth. There is naught more involved than hap of chance. Many moons have come and gone when naught followed bar the coming of dawn,' she replied. 'Fare ye well, Young Thomas, and may thy life be blessed.'

He wanted her to linger, to enquire further about his mother and benefit from her wise counsel, but she had always walked her own path and he knew she would not be bidden to remain any longer. 'Fare ye well, Bersaba,' he called after her. 'May Dor Dama bless you and your journey be a kind one.'

Thomas watched as she raised her withered hand and set off once again, her small form being slowly taken from sight by the slope as Elowen stood for a while longer and then followed after the healer. He felt saddened by her departure and wondered at Bersaba's destination.

He glanced at the cottage and then turned back to the hillside, finding no trace of the old crone. He smiled, the gesture touched with melancholy as he walked over to the water butt and crouched before it. Thomas rinsed out the waste bucket and went back into Ocean Mist, looking one final time down the hill before shutting the door behind him.

Taking the bucket through to the main living area, he stopped in the entrance to the Old Pen and stared down at Rosita with a soft smile. She still dozed beneath the furs, the cot having become a place of shared warmth and intimacy since the day they had swum in the tide pool.

'May our life together be blessed,' he whispered as his thoughts turned to the memories of his mother which had been awakened by Bersaba, memories filled with such delight and compassion that they held those of her sorrowful demise at bay.

71

Golvan glanced about surreptitiously, checking that none of the folk were evident in the fields before crouching beside the wall that ran alongside the track. He leant back against the stones and reached his left hand behind the small patch of gorse that grew before the wall, having to stretch, his shoulder to the thorny bushes. His fingers touched damp cloth and he leant in further so he could take hold.

He drew out the long bundle from its concealment and rested it across his knees as he remained crouched with his back to the wall. He pulled the grey cloth back to reveal a bow made of yew and a quiver of arrows. Taking up the bow, he plucked a slug from the wood and rested the weapon to his right, the quiver soon following.

Folding the cloth, Golvan tucked it back behind the gorse and then stood. He looked around once again, making certain that no one was in sight.

Satisfied that he was alone, he picked up the quiver and bow. He set off up the slope of Trewey Hill, holding them low so that the walls to either side concealed them from anyone north or south of his position.

Reaching the boundary of the fields that covered the lower slopes, Golvan crouched and moved slowly to where the track passed into the open grassland. He suddenly fell still, spying a deer fifty yards to the right. It was grazing on the grass near the garden wall before Carrow's cottage and seemingly unaware of his presence.

Tucking himself beyond the creature's sight beside the wall, he rested the quiver on the ground and withdrew an arrow from its confinement. Raising the bow, he placed the missile in readiness and then began to carefully move forward, keeping low and making as little noise as possible.

He peered around the corner, pulling back the bowstring as he did so. The small roe deer was looking away and the westerly wind ensured it would not catch his scent.

Golvan took a breath and then slowly let it out. The arrow was loosed.

A sharp cry of pain rose into the air and the creature toppled onto its side, legs twitching and then falling still. Golvan smiled and straightened, looking around once again to make sure his kill had not been witnessed, the punishment for poaching with such a weapon being severe.

He strode over to the deer and crouched beside it, the arrow's shaft rising from its breast. Taking hold of one of its antlers, he lifted the head and then let it fall back to the ground with a soft thud, its brown eyes staring blankly ahead.

The sound of quick steps caused him to turn. Carrow rushed from the garden and bore down on him. His expression was filled with fury after hearing the deer's cry and witnessing the farmer approach the body from the south-facing window of Ocean Mist.

Golvan began to rise. Thomas leapt the final distance and careered into him, sending him tumbling back. The farmer put his free hand out to soften the fall as he continued to grip the bow, letting out a yell of pain as his palm was sliced open by a stone hidden amidst the grass.

Thomas moved to the deer's side. 'Elowen,' he said in despair.

'You fool,' snarled Golvan as he remained seated on the ground, his heart pounding with the shock of Carrow's sudden appearance and assault. 'See what you have done.' He held up his hand, blood seeping from the wound and running down his wrist.

'Elowen,' repeated Thomas as he shook his head and gathered the deer into his arms, rocking her within their cradle.

'That is *my* kill,' stated Golvan angrily.

Thomas glared at the farmer. 'Your kill?' he hissed. 'Your kill. This is Elowen, friend to Bersaba and once friend to me.'

Golvan looked at him in confusion as he got to his feet. 'Bersaba?'

'Aye, and she will not be pleased that you have taken her life so coldly and so readily,' said Thomas, still rocking the deer in his arms.

Golvan glanced at the cottage and then began to back away, waiting until he was a good ten yards from Carrow before turning and hurrying towards the track.

Thomas looked over his shoulder and saw Rosita standing in the doorway. He turned back to watch Golvan's hasty retreat and his pulse began to quicken. Had he seen her?

He quickly rose with the deer held in his arms. Making his way to Ocean Mist, he glanced back to see the farmer pass down the track between the fields, his stomach tightening at the possibility that Rosita's presence had been noted.

Laying the deer upon the grass beside the door, he looked to the woman who carried his child with an expression of concern. She cocked her head to the side, her expression questioning.

Thomas forced a tight smile as Rosita continued to regard him. 'You must go inside,' he stated with an ushering motion.

She hesitated and then made her way into the gloom that was gathered within the cottage. Thomas stepped over the threshold and went to close the door, pausing to look at the track that led to the village, but no longer able to see the farmer. As the timber bumped against the frame, he was filled with the same ominous feeling he had experienced the previous day as he and Rosita had approached after checking the traps.

'Did he see you?' he said, turning to her as she perched on the edge of the cot, worry evident in her dark eyes.

72

Thomas agitatedly poked at the fire with the branch in his hand. He had been unable to settle since the recent confrontation with Golvan, the thought that Rosita had been spied in the doorway making him uneasy.

She sat upon the cot, the mermaid resting on the pillow beside her as she carved. Her hands became still as she glanced over at him and noted his expression of disquiet.

Rosita rose from the bed, a few shavings falling from her lap. Moving to crouch next to him, she looked at his profile as she set her hand upon his knee.

Thomas turned suddenly, as if having been woken from a dream. He looked at her and wondered whether they should flee. 'But where would we go?' he asked himself in a whisper.

Rosita was clearly frustrated, unable to understand his words or comprehend what troubled him. She raised her hand to his face and stroked his cheek, a thick growth of hair having grown since she had shaved him.

The sound of indistinct voices arose from outside and Thomas looked to the shutters, his heart immediately becoming thunderous. He got to his feet, her hand falling away from his face as she followed his every move with obvious concern.

He passed around the head of the cot and opened the window. Staring out, he saw a knot of five men coming hastily up the track along which Golvan had so recently departed. The farmer was at the head, his stride filled with purpose as he looked to the cottage and Father Blyth followed closely at his heels.

Thomas spun on his heels. 'Go,' he said with desperate firmness as Shenty leapt down from where she had been curled at the foot of the cot, going to the door and letting out a low growl.

Rosita looked at him in confusion.

'Go!' he exclaimed, stepping over and briskly getting her to her feet. 'You must leave. I will stay and delay them long enough for you to make good an escape.'

She shook her head in lack of comprehension.

He glanced back. They were nearing the top of the track.

Looking around, he spied the walking stick by the door. He rushed around the cot and picked it up, gathering her cape from where it hung over the head of the bed.

Going back to Rosita, he took hold of her left shoulder and forcibly turned her towards the other side of the room as Shenty began to bark. He began to push her to the Old Pen as she looked over her shoulder at him, tears in her eyes as confusion and fear filled her.

They passed into the other room and he took hold of her hand as the voices of the approaching men grew loader and he heard the creak of the garden gate.

'Please,' he begged, 'you must go.' He pointed at the seaward door and glanced worriedly back into the main living area, filled with tension as he anticipated the knock which would soon resound about the cottage's interior.

She raised her hand to his cheek again, eyes glistening. He took it in his and kissed her palm.

Three loud raps sounded on the south-facing door as Shenty continued to stand before it and bark.

'Go,' he whispered, passing her the stick and cape before giving her a gentle push away from him.

She stared at him with tears rolling down her cheeks, unable to grasp why he was not leaving with her.

He looked at her pleadingly, listening for any sounds of entry.

Three more knocks sounded.

'Carrow?' called Father Blyth.

Rosita went to the seaward door and opened it, lingering there and clearly reluctant to leave.

'What do you want with me?' Thomas called back, hoping to stall for time as he made an ushering motion to Rosita.

She stepped out. 'Te amo,' she whispered, hesitating a moment longer before shutting the door.

The sound of the other door opening caused him to turn away as he bit back his own tears.

'Carrow? Where are you?' demanded the priest.

'Here,' he responded, moving hastily to the entrance of the Old Pen.

He nervously faced the men entering Ocean Mist as they fanned out inside the door and looked about the interior. Blyth remained in the entrance as Jago and Golvan moved around the head of the cot beside the woodpile. Benedict Nan and Jory Meryn stepped to the right, the former glancing down at the waste bucket. Shenty backed away from them, her hackles raised and growling threateningly, lips curled to reveal her teeth.

'What reason do you have to enter my home in this way?' he asked, knowing the longer he delayed them the greater the chance of Rosita's escape.

'You know very well why we are here,' replied the priest.

Thomas licked his lips, mouth running dry as his body began to tremble in response to the rampant beat of his heart. 'I know not your reason and must protest at this intrusion.'

'You attacked Golvan with the knife at your hip and the evidence is upon his palm,' stated Jago as he moved between the fire and the far wall, keeping a wary eye on Carrow.

Thomas shook his head in confusion. He had anticipated questions relating to Rosita's presence, not accusations of an assault.

Jago drew to stop by the high-backed chair, the bench of driftwood behind him. Golvan stood between the cot and the fire pit, his left hand wrapped in a bloodied rag and his blackthorn club gripped tightly in the other.

''Tis also apparent that you are guilty of poaching,' said Blyth, Benedict and Jory shifting restlessly in anticipation of a struggle.

311

'Poaching!' exclaimed Thomas in surprise, Shenty moving to stand beside him and sounding an occasional growl.

'Aye,' said Golvan, 'and the evidence greeted our arrival.'

Thomas turned his gaze to the farmer and realisation dawned. 'I am not responsible for her death.'

'Do you know the penalty for poaching?' asked Blyth. 'You are going to be in want of a hand.'

'It was Golvan that took her life, not I,' he said, turning his attention back to the priest.

'We must also consider a befitting punishment for your of violence.'

'I committed no such act. He cut his open upon a stone. I can show you its position amidst the grass and you can witness the stain of his blood for yourself.'

Golvan looked at the priest with a touch of nervousness. 'He lies, Father. He is possessed by daemons.'

'What?!' Thomas stared aghast at the farmer.

Blyth looked across the cot at Golvan. 'Daemons you say?'

'Aye,' nodded Golvan.

'What brings you to such a grave conclusion?'

'After he inflicted the wound upon my hand, he spoke of seeing Bersaba this very morning.'

The priest's brows rose almost imperceptibly and he scrutinised Golvan's expression for any sign of deceit. 'Is this so?' he asked, his cold gaze returning to Thomas.

'Aye, I spoke of such. She came by to bid me farewell, though I know not where her journey took her.'

Uneasy glances passed between the men arrayed before him and Thomas felt his stomach tighten in response to the look in their eyes.

'Why do you look to each other in such a way?' he asked nervously.

'Benedict,' said Blyth, 'bind his hands.'

Benedict began to move forward, pulling a length of rope from his waist.

'Wait,' said Thomas, stepping back.

Jago stepped around the back of the chair and positioned himself in the doorway to the Old Pen. Thomas glanced back at him, stomach churning and perspiration upon his face. Something was wrong, terribly wrong.

'I would advise that you do not struggle,' said Blyth

'But I have done naught wrong. Golvan's palm was cut upon a rock and the deer was killed by his arrow.'

'And Bersaba?' asked the priest.

'I do not take your meaning,' said Thomas in confusion.

'Bersaba is long since dead,' stated Golvan.

'That cannot be so,' responded Thomas, his expression and tone filled with anxiety.

Benedict moved to take hold of his wrists, but he pulled them from the man's grasp.

'You lie. I have spoken to her many times,' said Thomas as Jago grasped him by the shoulders and Jory stepped forward to help Benedict, Shenty growling at them as they rounded on her master.

'He is indeed possessed by daemons,' said Blyth. 'We must away with him to the forge and drive them out.'

'NO!' shouted Thomas as Jory and Benedict grasped his arms and he struggled unsuccessfully against their tight grip.

'You can see the mania in his eyes,' said Golvan. 'The daemons cavort there in plain sight.'

'Aye, they can be seen by all,' nodded the priest. ''Tis clear evil lurks in this foul place and long I have suspected that Satan resided here.'

'You do not have the authority to do this,' said Thomas as Jory held his wrists and Benedict bound them tightly, the rope rubbing abrasively against his skin.

The priest's expression hardened. 'I have the authority of Almighty God, and there is no authority greater.'

'I am not possessed,' he protested, the bonds secure about his wrists.

'Bring him out of the house,' instructed Blyth. 'Jago, set a fire. We will raise this dwelling of daemons to the ground and pull down the remains stone by stone until there is no trace left in which they can linger.'

Jago nodded and stepped to the fire, taking up a flaming branch.

'You cannot do this.' Thomas struggled against the hands that took firm hold of his arms, digging his boots in as Benedict and Jory dragged him towards the open door. 'This is my home,' he said, face contorting as he fought to break free.

'See how the daemons show themselves,' said Blyth with a sorrowful shake of his head.

Golvan glanced down at the cot beside him. His gaze settled on the carving of the mermaid and he lifted it from the pillow. 'Look, Father, he carves images of unnatural creatures.'

Blyth stared at the figure and recalled Marrek Trelawny's ravings. 'Could it be that the daemons have granted you powers, that you have transformed this image into a living likeness by which to satisfy your base desires?' he asked as Benedict and Jory brought Thomas to a halt before the priest. 'It may even be that Satan himself has had a hand in this.'

'Of what do you speak, Father?' asked Golvan as Jago took the bag of kindling into the Old Pen in order that it aid in the task assigned to him.

'Marrek spoke of seeing this wretch with a mermaid on at least two occasions,' explained the priest. 'Only the dark arts of daemons could give breath to a carved image of such an ungodly creature.'

Blyth turned to Thomas with an expression of revulsion. 'Take him from my sight,' he snapped.

Benedict and Jory manhandled Thomas out of the door.

'Cast that abomination into the fire,' instructed the priest.

Golvan nodded and tossed the carving into the fire, its face wreathed in flame. Jago reappeared from the other room, a plume of thickening smoke gathering in the eaves visible above the rough walls that divided it from the main space.

He went to the bench of driftwood. Shenty began to bark again as she stood behind him and he cleared a space amidst the pieces near the wall, directly beneath the shelves crowded with finished carvings.

Ignoring the small hound, Jago placed a couple of large handfuls of dried grass and twigs in the gap he had made and lowered the end of the branch, the kindling flaring in sudden brightness as the flames took hold.

'That will do,' said Blyth.

Jago glanced over with a look of disappointment. He tipped the bag of kindling over the bench and then crouched, gathering up the chicken on the straw beneath and holding it in the crook of his arm as it clucked.

Walking across the room, he threw the lighted branch onto the patchwork of furs upon the cot, the smell of burning hair quickly rising. Shenty stood on the far side of the interior, her barking giving way to whining as she looked at the flames spreading about her, the eaves hidden by thick fumes which choked the hole in the centre of the roof.

Golvan and Jago filed out as the priest took one last look at the burning interior, the thatch above the bench of driftwood already starting to blacken. He nodded to himself, satisfied that the den of wickedness would soon be no more.

Stepping out, Blyth shut the door behind him. 'Take up the venison, Golvan. We shall not let it go to waste.'

The farmer tucked his club into his belt and took up the deer carcass. He placed it over his shoulders and held its legs to either side of his head as he moved a safe distance from the burning building, joining the others near the gate to the walled garden.

Thomas stared at the thick smoke pouring from the hole in the roof as Benedict and Jory continued to hold him. Tears streamed down his cheeks as the sound of Shenty's fearful whining was slowly enveloped by the roar and crackle of flames.

His legs gave way beneath the weight of his grief as he heard the hound's pained whimpers and desperate scratching upon the bottom of the door. He hung between the two men with head bowed, the sounds of Shenty's suffering finally falling silent as the thatch began to catch light.

Blyth glanced at the windswept tree. 'When the stones are scattered we shall chop down and dig out the tree for

315

firewood so no trace is left of this accursed place,' he stated coldly. 'Now let us to the forge so that we may vanquish the daemons that plague him.'

They set off, passing through the gate and across the long grass to the start of the track. Thomas was dragged by Benedict and Jory, a rag doll with no will remaining by which to resist, feet trailing as his head hung low and his heart was filled with anguish.

73

Jago opened the door and stepped back so that the priest could enter before him. Blyth walked in with the fledgling blacksmith following behind and looked around the dingy interior, nodding to himself as he stared at the soot-blackened walls.

'This is a place well suited for the driving out of daemons,' he said to himself as Golvan stepped in and set the deer down on a bench along the left-hand wall.

The farmer looked at the shaft still rising from its breast as Benedict and Jory dragged Thomas into the forge. He was waiting for an opportune moment to remove the arrow in order that it may be cleaned and returned to the quiver.

Blyth turned to the men carrying the dishevelled prisoner. 'Bind him over the stool,' he instructed.

'Over the stool?' asked Benedict.

He nodded. 'So that his torso rests upon it, his thighs and upper arms tied to the legs on either side. Then we shall exorcise the daemons by creating such discomfort that they will not wish to remain.'

Benedict nodded, feeling his stomach tighten as he guessed at the priest's meaning of discomfort. He looked to Jory and nodded at the stool on the right, the two men manoeuvring Thomas to stand before it.

'Here,' called Jago, tossing over some rope taken from a table at the back of the room. The lengths passed through the smoke rising from the fire pot and drew ragged ribbons of fumes in their wake.

Benedict caught them and nodded his thanks. 'Kneel,' he instructed, turning to the wretch on his right.

Thomas did not comply, but stood mute before the seat, his expression one of utter desolation and eyes raw. His mind reeled in the face of what was happening and that which had already transpired.

'I said, kneel,' said Benedict with more force, kicking the backs of his legs and sending him to the dusty and darkened earth, his knees thudding upon the floor.

Thomas was forcibly pushed forward so that his chest rested on the stool. The tops of his arms were roped to the front legs, both men crouching before him as they made secure the bonds. They moved round to the sides and bound his thighs to the rear legs as his head hung low, elbows upon the ground and wrists still tied before him.

'Jago,' said Blyth to the smith who still loitered at the rear of the forge as Benedict and Jory got to their feet and stepped back from Thomas. 'Heat the poker.'

Jago blanched. 'Me?'

Blyth nodded. 'You will act as the hand of God and I will be His mouthpiece.'

The smith stared at him in horror. 'I…' He swallowed hard. 'I cannot.'

'Cannot?' The priest held him in his hard gaze. 'This is God's work. Do you refuse it?'

'I shall do it,' stated Golvan, stepping forward.

Blyth looked over his shoulder at the farmer and nodded, indicating for him to take up position by the fire pot. Golvan moved past him and walked over to stand beside the smoking coals. He took up the large poker leaning against the wall and then turned to face the priest, the pot to his right and Thomas to his left.

'You must bring more heat to the coals,' said Jago.

'Then do so,' responded Blyth coldly, glancing unkindly at the man who had refused his instruction.

Jago quickly went to the pot, wishing a return to good favour. He picked up the hand bellows lying on the floor nearby and rested their thin mouth on one of the bands of metal that held the coals in place. Pressing the handles together, the blow of expelled air could be heard as the coals glowed.

'Benedict, bare his back,' said Blyth.

Benedict hesitated and then stepped over to Thomas, starting to feel nauseas at the thought of what was to come. He crouched beside the prisoner and began to pull up his jerkin and woollen shirt.

'That will be enough,' stated the priest when Thomas' lower back was revealed, his clothes drawn up beneath his shoulder blades.

Benedict gratefully retreated, moving to stand beside Jory just inside the open door, the chill wind reaching in and bringing some relief from his sensations of sickness.

'Golvan,' said Blyth with a nod to the glowing coals.

The farmer placed the end of the poker into the fire pot as Jago straightened, the bellows still held in his hands. An eerie silence settled as the metal was heated, cobwebs fluttering in the eaves as if agitated by the expectancy hanging in the air. Benedict, Jory and Jago all shifted anxiously, glancing at the sorry form bound to the stool and uneasy with what was about to occur. No such punishment had ever been enacted in Zennor before and its severity disturbed them greatly.

Golvan withdrew the tip of the poker, a faint glow to its blackened iron. He turned to his left, looking down upon Thomas, his sight settling on the pale skin of the prisoner's back. He took a few steadying breaths and looked to the priest.

Blyth nodded.

'Crux sacra sit mihi lux. Non draco sit mihi dux,' began the priest as Golvan moved the poker towards Thomas' back.

'Vade retro satana. Numquam suade mihi vana.'

There was a soft hiss as hot iron was laid upon flesh. Agonised screams filled the forge.

'Sunt mala quae libas. Ipse venena bibas,' finished Blyth, crossing himself.

Thomas' face contorted with pain as the heated metal was held to his lower back. His mouth was stretched wide, tears forced from his tightly shut eyes. The legs of the stool creaked as his taught body strained against the bonds holding him in place and cries of agony continued to issue forth.

Father Blyth nodded at Golvan once again. The farmer withdrew the poker and placed it back in the fire pot as Thomas moaned, the burn clear upon his skin, raw and blistering.

Benedict paled and quickly rushed from the building, doubling over and vomiting outside the door. Jory and Jago looked across at each other with expressions of pale horror.

'Again,' said the priest.

Golvan returned the poker to Thomas' back and the screams arose anew.

'I drive you out in the name of Jesus Christ. I cast you out in the name of the Holy Father,' said Blyth with firm authority. 'Be gone foul beasts and return to the abyss from whence you came. Be gone and ne'er return.'

He nodded at Golvan again, the poker being withdrawn, a shred of melted skin remaining upon its tip. Thomas' body quaked as pain seared his mind.

The sound of growling pierced the torment. He glanced to his left, vision blurred, thoughts swimming and indistinct. The vague figure of a small dog stood beyond the fire pot.

Thomas blinked and tried to bring order to his mind. 'Shenty?' he said thickly, still unable to focus.

Golvan looked down at him as he stood with the poker placed into the hot coals in readiness. 'He speaks,' he commented, looking over to Blyth.

The hound's low growl sounded again as she looked up at the farmer beside the fire pot.

'Shenty,' said Thomas in relieved surprise as his sight cleared. She bore no sign of her ordeal at the cottage and bared her teeth at Golvan.

'Who is Shenty?' asked Jago as he remained to the rear of the forge.

The men glanced at each other with expressions of bewilderment.

'It may be the name of one of the daemons possessing him,' said Golvan.

'Good day, Benedict.' The sound of Jacob's greeting caused the four men within the forge to turn to the door, finding the elderly farmer approaching with crook in hand and hound at his side.

'Good day, Jacob.'

'Are thee ailing? Thou art ghostly pale,' said Jacob as he studied the expression of the man leaning against the wall just outside the door.

Thomas moaned in pain, the sound drawing Jacob's gaze. He saw Father Blyth and his brow furrowed.

'What goes on here?' he asked, stepping to the door, eyes widening as he spied Thomas.

'An exorcism,' replied Blyth. 'Carrow is possessed by daemons and we seek to drive them out.'

'He has just spoken to one of the devils, which goes by the name Shenty,' added Golvan.

Jacob turned to his brother, noting the poker clasped in his hand as its tip rested in the fire pot. 'Shenty?' he asked, regarding his kin with an air of disappointment and disgust.

'Aye, he moaned the name not long before your arrival.'

'I have heard that name before,' said Jacob.

Father Blyth looked at him. 'You know of this daemon?'

Jacob shook his head as he pondered and stared at the glowing coals. Realisation dawned and he looked to the priest. 'It was the name of Carrow's dog when he was but a boy. She was aunt to Blackberry,' he said, looking down at the hound beside him, 'born to the same litter as her mother, Bramble.'

'Carrow's dog?' said Blyth in confusion.

'Aye,' nodded Jacob, 'but she passed before he left for Truro.'

The priest stared at the quivering form tied over the stool. 'His mind is addled by the daemons which abide there.'

'Shenty,' whispered Thomas, still looking to his hound.

Golvan checked the poker was secure in the pot and then released it. Crouching, he could see that Thomas was looking towards the back of the forge and followed his gaze, seeing only dark earth and the blackened granite of the wall.

He took the captive's face in his hand and turned it to him. 'Naught abides there,' he said. 'There is no hound.'

321

'I see her,' whispered Thomas, his face tightened by pain, brow knitted and perspiration glistening upon his flushed skin.

'She is not there. Your mind plays tricks and you see things that do not exist in truth, as with Bersaba.'

Thomas looked at him, eyes glistening and seeking out the lie he hoped to discover. He found only cold truth.

Golvan let go of his face and straightened, taking hold of the poker once again. 'The daemons still persist,' he stated.

Thomas looked back to his left, but found no trace of the hound. With teeth gritted against the pain, he strained to look over his shoulder, but still could not locate her.

'It has long been known that Carrow sees things that are not apparent to others,' stated Jacob. 'My brother knows this very well. Surly ye have all heard of the unseen friend that accompanied him as boy?'

Blyth glanced at Golvan as he began to suspect him of deceit and then shook his head in response to the question, expressions of vague recollection dawning on the faces of Jago and Jory.

'He said her name to me not long ago,' said Jacob as he stared up into the eaves and tried to recall. 'Elowen, I think it be.'

'Elowen?' Golvan stared at his brother. 'That be the name he gave the deer.'

Blyth turned to him with a dark look. 'The deer?' he said with brow raised. 'Be this the same deer of which you knew naught?'

Golvan's face reddened and he could not meet the priest's gaze. 'Aye,' he replied with a nod, his demeanour expressing his guilt.

'What is happening here?' asked Morvoren as she appeared behind Jacob in the doorway, four other woman of Zennor crowding beyond, their hands raw from washing upon the banks of the stream, hair veils fluttering in the wind.

'This affair is not of your concern,' stated Blyth.

'Oh, how so, Father? My husband is sickly upon the threshold and we were greatly disturbed by screams of such terrible agonies as we knelt by the stream.'

'We drive out daemons,' stated Jago from the shadows to the rear of the interior.

'The screams were those of the daemons which possess this wretch,' said Golvan.

'They appeared to be those of a man in torment.' Morvoren turned her gaze to the pitiful figure tied over the stool.

'Appearances are not always as they would seem,' countered Blyth frostily.

'What harm has Carrow done that ye should bring this upon him?' asked Jacob.

'He is possessed and that is reason enough,' said the priest.

'He attacked me.' Golvan raised his injured hand for all to see.

Morvoren looked at the farmer with disdain. 'For good reason, no doubt,' she said. 'You had a hand in the departure of Gerens and Nonna, and now I fear your part in this is far from innocent.'

Golvan glared at her. 'How dare you?!'

'I dare, Golvan. It is time someone spoke out against your machinations,' she responded, the sight of Carrow's tortured form filling her with indignation.

'You forget your place, woman,' said Blyth with a tone of warning. 'The cucking stool beckons should you continue.'

'Can you not see the truth of this man?' she asked, pointing at Golvan.

'Enough!' snapped the priest.

'Morvoren is right,' said Conwenna Trewey, moving to stand beside her husband, 'though he be kin and it pains me to say 'tis so.'

'I said, enough,' said Blyth loudly.

A hush descended, the only sounds those of Thomas' moans. The priest looked at the women and then to Golvan, who turned to stare at the ground. His gaze moved to the man bound to the stool as he pondered.

'We will make Carrow secure in the Trelawny barn while I consider what is to be done,' he stated eventually. 'I cannot deny there may be more in this than meets the eye,' he admitted, glancing at Golvan and then turning to those gathered in the doorway to the forge.

'I will take him to the barn,' stated Morvoren.

He regarded her briefly and then nodded. 'Jory, you and Benedict accompany her and make sure Carrow is left bound and unable to escape. It may yet be that he is in need of further exorcism.'

Jory nodded as he stood by those gathered in the doorway.

'I suggest you think on the meaning of yesterday's sermon,' he said, fixing his cold eyes on Morvoren. 'The feast day of Saint Valentine is one of devotion. This is not just to the Lord, but to your husbands and to the duties of your sex,' he stated.

She opened her mouth to speak, but remained silent when she saw his eyes narrow.

'Jory, set to thy task,' he instructed the rote player. 'The rest of you can go about your business. There will no more debate and no more to see here.'

Jory moved to Thomas, whose moans of pain had passed into silence as he hung limp over the stool, convulsions occasionally seizing his body. The three women in the doorway looked to each other and then moved away from the forge in order to return to their washing.

Jacob hesitated, looking to Thomas and wishing to ease his pain in some way, feeling a sense of guilt due to the involvement of his brother. Conwenna took his hand and the old farmer turned to his wife. She gave a sideways nod and he sighed, following her lead from the building.

'Should we not continue?' asked Golvan.

'It would be wise of you to hold your tongue,' said Blyth, turning to him with a stern look. 'I will root out the truth of this, Golvan, and if you be culpable in any way you can be sure thy punishment will come.'

'I assure you…'

The priest held up his hand to silence the farmer. 'Did you not hear the words that I just spoke?' said Blyth firmly. 'Leave. Your presence here is no longer required.'

Golvan hesitated, wishing to protest his innocence but seeing it would have no effect, the priest's expression as stone. He pushed the poker deep into the coals and made for the door, head low. He sneered unkindly as he passed Morvoren and his mind turned to thoughts of exacting revenge on the woman who had accused him so openly.

Jory untied the bonds about Thomas' arms, those binding his legs already removed. Thomas remained still and silent. The pain in his back brought fire to his mind and in the flames one thought flickered; if Bersaba and Shenty were merely conjurations, then what of Rosita?

'Benedict,' called Jory before covering the terrible wounds upon the prisoner's back, pulling down the woollen shirt to conceal their blistered rawness and hearing Thomas inhale sharply as the material brushed against them.

Benedict appeared in the doorway, his face drawn. He looked down at Thomas and was thankful that the burns were hidden. Stepping in, he made his way over to the prisoner's side, nodding over at Jory.

'Rosita,' mumbled Thomas, tears beginning to fall to the earth beneath his bowed head as he mourned what had been and yet in truth ne'er was.

Benedict and Jory took him by the upper arms and lifted him from the stool, his body a dead weight as his legs hung limp. They dragged Thomas from the forge, boots slipping in the mud as they turned right, heading along the track towards Trelawny Farm. Morvoren fell into step behind them as Blyth and Jago watched them leave.

'Rosita,' moaned Thomas, the word filled with a greater torment than mere physical injury, his heart constricted and wrung out by the truth of his self-deception.

74

Gerens pulled on the reins and Myrtle turned off to the left, the cart leaving the main track and passing onto another that was little more than a muddy cow path choked with bracken. He looked to the right, unable to see aught of the village bar the top of the church in the distance as it rested near the foot of Zennor Hill.

'Be that Zennor?' asked Zethar as he sat beside the smith, browned ferns brushing and scraping against the wheels of the cart.

'Aye,' nodded Gerens. 'I will not venture closer.'

'I understand,' replied the old man after being enlightened to the truth concerning Gerens and Nonna during the journey from Bodmin.

Myrtle was brought to a halt south of Trewey Hill, the track petering out and leading into a field where a small herd of cattle were grazing beyond the wooden gate that barred the way.

'We walk from here,' stated Gerens, climbing down, the thick foliage against the back of his leggings and fur cloak.

'To the cottage upon the hill that ye told me about?' asked Zethar.

'Aye. Your family home where your son, still abides,' replied the smith as he took his sword from the bench, the weapon wrapped in faded green cloth.

Gerens moved around the front of the cart, giving Myrtle a pat on the neck as he passed. He reached the far side as the old man clambered down with a grunt of effort, his sack slung over his shoulder. Zethar turned to the smith, who nodded towards a vague animal track which led to the hill through the thick growth of ferns.

Gerens led the way, wading through the undergrowth with the wrapped sword held tightly in his hand. He remained alert and watchful, his tension rising with every footfall. He could feel the settlement's presence nearby and knew that if he were seen there would be a pursuit in order to question him over Nonna's whereabouts.

They moved steadily towards Trewey Hill, skirting westward and passing through a copse of low and twisted trees resting within a bog, bark green with moss. Their boots sank deep and water seeped in to numb their feet. A magpie watched their progress between the trunks, its chattering marking their presence.

Gerens glared at the black and white bird, willing it to silence, but it continued to sound its call as they moved out of the boggy wood and into the bracken beyond.

'How much further?' asked Zethar quietly.

'We must head north along the hillside,' replied Gerens as they moved into a small fold near the foot of the hill, the bracken giving way to thick grasses which gently rippled in the wind.

The old man turned his gaze to a circular stone wall resting to their left, a few shrubs sheltered within its perimeter. His expression became one of contemplation as his steps slowed and he began to lag.

'Keep up,' said Gerens over his shoulder. 'I have no wish to linger longer than is necessary.'

'I know this place,' said Zethar, staring at the tumbledown stones as he came to a halt.

The smith stopped a few yards ahead and looked to the wall. 'It was the home of Bersaba, a healer who remained true to the old ways,' he stated.

'Bersaba,' echoed Zethar as vague memories stirred. 'There is something missing,' he said. 'Were there once trees about her abode?'

'Aye,' nodded Gerens, 'but they fell to the axe long ago. Bersaba passed less than a year after your wife.'

The old man looked back to the dwindling remnants of the hut.

'Come.' The smith waved Zethar onward and began along the vague path that wound up the southern slope of Trewey Hill, the old man pausing a moment before following.

A fine rain began to fall as they moved along the side of the hill, its thin veil drawing across the landscape from the west. Gerens found some relief in its partial concealment, only able to see the vague presence of Zennor below to the north-east and hopeful their passage would go unnoticed.

His steps faltered as he spied a plume of thick smoke rising before them.

'Is aught amiss?' asked Zethar from behind him.

Gerens stopped and looked back at the old man, his expression one of grave concern. 'The smoke rises from the location of your cottage.'

Zethar looked up the slight rise leading to the small tableland ahead, his pulse rising. 'What occurs here?'

'I fear ill fortune may have befallen your son. There are those below that sought to remove him.'

The old man's gaze settled upon him. 'Remove him? Why?'

'He is...' Gerens searched for the right word. '...Different.'

Zethar looked at him questioningly.

'Many recall the friend who accompanied him as a boy, but could not be seen by others. If that were not enough, his time in Truro with your brother Rumon made him a stranger to most, one to be avoided and viewed with suspicion.'

'He was an outcast?' The old man's tone echoed the sadness evident in his expression.

Gerens nodded. 'I am afraid 'tis so.'

Zethar turned back to the thick smoke.

'We must be wary,' said the smith, drawing the cloth back from the hilt of the sword and taking hold in readiness to unsheathe it should the need arise.

The two men approached, their faces glistening with rainwater and eyes set on the view ahead. The cottage was revealed, most of its roof collapsed and burning furiously.

Vivid flames rose from within the blackened walls, roaring and belching black palls of smoke into the air.

They came to a stop a few yards from the front gate and stared at the ruination of Ocean Mist. Zethar noted the wooden sign beside the doorway and felt a pang of recognition.

'What has transpired here?' he whispered in distressed confusion.

The two men peered down the slope, unable to see the village as the veil of mizzle thickened.

The tearing of timbers drew their attention back to the cottage. The last portion of the roof collapsed into the raging flames beneath, a swarm of orange sparks rising, but soon darkened by the moisture in the air.

Gerens pulled the cloth from the sword. 'You wait here,' stated the smith as he fastened the sheath to his belt and concealed it beneath his cloak as best he could. 'I will go to the village and search for your son.'

'And if ye do not find him?'

'I will find him,' replied Gerens firmly. 'I will not leave him to the wolves who dwell there.'

Zethar glanced at the burning cottage and then gave a nod. 'I shall conceal myself behind the wall,' he stated, taking a step towards the gate.

'I will return with Thomas,' stated the smith before setting off towards the track that led down the hillside.

75

He stayed low as he crept alongside the wall, the cattle in the field eyeing him with interest. Reaching the far corner of the meadow, Gerens peered over the wet stones. The main track into Zennor was on the far side and afforded him a view into the settlement.

He ducked down as Father Blyth stepped out of the forge fifty yards along the track to the left. The priest strode in the opposite direction and the smith watched for a few moments, the holy man becoming obscured by the mist as his vague form entered the graveyard and was then hidden from sight.

Gerens looked over his shoulder and considered retreating to the farm track that ran parallel to the one passing through the village, linking the main paths west. He shook his head, fearing that he may miss a clue as to Carrow's whereabouts if he were to remove himself from the immediate vicinity of the settlement.

Checking that no one else was in sight, the smith quickly vaulted the wall to his left and entered the next field. He crouched, clusters of thistles rising about him in the mist, their brown teasels hung with glistening cobwebs. He could see the vague presence of buildings beyond the far wall and made his way to the western side of the meadow in order to skirt around them.

As he passed from field to field, Gerens regularly glanced over the walls, looking and listening for any sign of Thomas' whereabouts, but finding no clue. The weight of the sword at his hip gave him little comfort as his body was filled with tension, muscles taught and ready to fight or flee.

He reached one of the farm tracks coming down from the soft slopes north of Trewey Hill. Slipping from the gateway of the field, he crouched beside it, the undergrowth beside the wall offering some concealment, the scent of damp earth and bracken hanging heavy in the air.

Looking towards the settlement, he saw Trelawny Farm thirty yards ahead, its barn on the left and cottage set a little further back, merely a shadow in the mizzle. He readied himself to rise, but fell still as two figures materialised from the farm entrance.

Crouching back against the wall, he watched the misted forms of Jory Meryn and Benedict Nan walk away up the slight incline to the main track. He waited until they had disappeared from view and slowly drew away from the wall.

Gerens crept along the track, hand moving to grip the hilt of the sword as he neared the farm and rainwater ran down his face. He became still as a pained moan rose into the still air. Dropping into a crouch, he stared at the barn, sure that the sound had issued from within.

Another moan arose and a shiver passed up his spine, the hairs on the nape of his neck tingling. He slowly moved forward, listening intently.

Gerens moved to the end of the building which abutted the track. Flattening his back against the granite, he was careful that the tip of the sword did not knock against the stones, hand resting upon the pommel.

He stood and listened for a moment. The gentle splash of water sounded from within and was followed by a groan.

The smith made his way along the wall and reached the corner of the building. He peered round and spied the entrance. No one was in sight.

His pulse raced as he stepped from the concealment, knowing that should anyone step from the barn his presence would be discovered immediately. He gripped the hilt of the sword tightly as each step took him closer to the doorway.

Stopping beside it, Gerens looked to the cottage on the other side of the patch of rough grass lying beyond the barn. He could see no sign of life and hoped that Marrek would not make an unexpected appearance.

Swallowing against the churning of his stomach, he slowly leant forward and surveyed the interior. More moans arose

331

from the left, hidden from his sight, and he fell still once more.

Craning his neck, Gerens looked around the frame. Morvoren was kneeling with a damp rag in her hands and a wooden bowl filled with water at her side. Curled on the ground before her was Thomas Carrow, his wrists bound and back bared to the woman. Two horrific burns blistered his skin and the smith's expression became one of shock when he recognised the indentations left by a poker.

Morvoren suddenly turned, sensing someone's presence at the door. 'Gerens!' she exclaimed in surprise. 'What are you doing here?'

Glancing over his shoulder, the smith then quickly slipped into the barn, making sure to move beyond sight of anyone who may approach the building. 'I came looking for Carrow. What has occurred to bring such ruin upon him and his home?'

She glanced at the wretch before her and sighed. 'Golvan claims that Carrow assaulted him and when they went to his cottage they found evidence of poaching outside his door. He has also been accused of being beset by daemons.'

Gerens looked at her in shock. 'Beset by daemons,' he said with a disbelieving shake of his head.

'Aye, but I fear the only daemon with which he has been beset is Golvan himself,' she frowned.

'In that he is not alone.'

'I thought as much,' said Morvoren with a nod. 'Is Nonna with you?' she asked with genuine concern.

'She departed Zennor at my side and is safe, though Jowen was lost to a fever not long after.'

Morvoren's expression fell. 'I am sorry to hear such sad news,' she said, shaking her head. 'There is more to tell of the village. Marrek has passed.'

Gerens was taken aback. 'How?'

'He caught a chill from which he ne'er recovered,' she replied.

Thomas moaned and they turned to him, Gerens blinking away thoughts of what Marrek's death meant to his life with Nonna.

'Take him away from here,' she said after a brief silence.

Gerens looked at her in surprise.

'He will only be made to endure more suffering if he remains and, if Benedict's account is true, he no longer has a home to which he can return.'

'I can attest to that,' nodded Gerens. ''Tis no more than a flaming ruin.'

Morvoren shook her head sadly once again. 'Come, help me untie his bonds.'

She bent over Thomas' sorry form and reached for his wrists. Fearful of more torment, he drew them to his body.

Gerens stepped over, crouching opposite Morvoren, the captive facing him. 'We are freeing you,' he said, keeping his voice low.

Thomas looked up at him, face filled with the tightness of pain. His mind was still lit by the searing of his nerves, but there was a place of clarity at its centre where the truth of his imaginings circled like crows, picking at the memories of Rosita's stay in Ocean Mist. His heart ached and he was filled with the despair of great loss, the realisation that Bersaba and Shenty were also merely illusions compounding his misery.

'I will take you to safety and away from this place,' said Gerens slowly and clearly as he released the hilt of the sword and moved his hands to the rope about Carrow's wrists.

Thomas nodded vaguely and did not resist. The bonds fell away, leaving rings of raw skin to mark their presence.

'Can you walk?'

Thomas did not speak, but pushed himself into a sitting position, wincing as his shirt fell to cover the burns. The smith put his left arm about Thomas' shoulders and helped him to rise upon unsteady feet.

'What will you say happened here?' asked Gerens as Morvoren stood.

333

She pondered a moment. 'I will claim he freed himself from his bonds while I washed his wounds and made good his escape after overpowering me.'

He nodded and took a step to the door with Thomas at his side.

'I will give you time enough for escape before making my way into the village and raising the alarm,' she added.

'My thanks, Morvoren,' nodded Gerens, stepping to the door.

'Please let Nonna know that I am sorry for her loss and wish her well.'

'I shall,' he stated. 'Fare ye well.'

'Fare ye well,' she replied, raising her hand as the two men moved out into the open, Thomas stumbling by the blacksmith's side.

76

Morvoren seated herself against the wall. Time drew out and she became increasingly agitated, picking up the length of discarded rope and running it about her fingers. With each second that passed the likelihood that one of the men would return and discover her duplicity grew greater.

Unable to wait any longer, she suddenly got to her feet. Dropping the rope, she went to the doorway and glanced out to check that no one was returning to the barn. She stared through the mist and felt her pulse quicken, hoping her attempt at deception would be successful.

Taking a deep breath, Morvoren ran from the building, the veil over her long hair fluttering with her hasty passage. She ran onto the path leading up from the farm, slipping in the mud and falling to her knees. Rising, she continued on and soon passed onto the main track.

'Help!' she called. 'Help! Carrow has escaped.'

She drew up to churchyard gate. 'Father Blyth,' she shouted.

The priest appeared in the doorway along the side of the church as Benedict and Arthur Pendle came hurrying up the track behind her.

'What has happened?' asked Blyth as he walked hastily to the gate.

'Carrow. He has escaped,' she said breathlessly.

'Escaped!' said her husband as he drew up beside her. 'Did he harm you?' He studied her face and then looked down to the mud upon her dress.

Morvoren shook her head. 'He managed to free himself as I cleansed the burns and then made good his escape.'

'Arthur,' snapped Blyth. 'Fetch Jago and any other men you may chance upon.'

The old man nodded and made for the forge.

'Benedict, go to Golvan's cottage and bring him with haste.'

'Aye,' he nodded in response before turning and striding back the way he had come.

Blyth turned his attention to Morvoren. 'In which direction did he go?'

'I was within the barn and did not see,' she replied.

He looked at her in puzzlement. 'You did not give chase?' There was a touch of disbelief to his words.

'Aye, but the mist concealed him.' Her eyes were downcast as she answered.

Blyth continued to stare at her, suspecting that there was more to the prisoner's escape than she would admit. The sound of footsteps drew his attention and he turned to find Arthur returning with Jago beside him.

Stepping through the gateway of the churchyard, the priest moved past Morvoren and stood before the approaching men.

'Is it true? Has Carrow escaped?' asked Jago as he and Arthur came to a halt.

'Apparently so,' replied Blyth, glancing at the woman who remained before the gate with her head bowed. 'We will start our search at his cottage. God willing, his attempt to escape justice will not meet with success. Come, let us begin,' he stated, turning north and heading along the muddy track.

Jago and Arthur set off after the priest and Morvoren watched them fade into the mizzle, taking a few breaths to calm the pounding of her heart. She was certain more questions would be asked of her, but that as long as her story remained consistent she would be safe from a spell on the cucking stool.

'May fortune favour you,' she whispered as she looked at the mist masking the hill to the west, wiping a bead of rainwater from her brow before turning home.

77

They walked through the grassland that bordered the fields upon the slopes of Trewey Hill. Thomas was slowly gaining greater autonomy, though he continued to need the blacksmith's assistance and his expression retained the tightness of pain. They moved up the gentle slope, heading southward as the mizzle concealed their passage.

Gerens turned to the left, looking to the shadow of the wall below their position. He could hear men's voices issuing from the settlement which was hidden in the paleness. The smith tried to discern their words, but could make out none.

'My home!' exclaimed Thomas as Ocean Mist came into view through the veil, the cottage shrouded in dark fumes.

Flashes of colour could be seen through the mist as tongues of flame licked at the air and the two men drew near. The seaward door hung from its hinges, much of its timber burned away. The shutters in the two windows were no more, the granite lintels blackened by the passage of smoke.

The sounds of pursuit could be heard over the consuming noises of the fire and Gerens picked up their speed. They remained at a safe distance from the cottage, skirting to the left and feeling the vague touch of heat radiating from the scene of devastation.

'How could they do this?' asked Thomas as they moved up to the southern wall of the garden, shaking his head as tears began to spill down his cheeks. 'How could they bring such calamity upon me without trial or warrant?'

Zethar rose from the other side of the wall. Thomas halted, startled by the unexpected presence, Gerens forced to a stop beside him as his arm remained around his shoulders.

The old man made his way to the gate as Thomas watched his every move with eyes wide, his heart thundering and stomach churning. He saw the likeness in the man's face, knew his features were reflected in his own.

Zethar drew up five yards before them. 'Thomas?' said the old man in gentle disbelief. 'My son?'

Thomas stood motionless, an expression of shock upon his face. 'You are not real,' he hissed.

'I have wandered for many a year, but have returned home at last,' said Zethar, stepping forward and reaching for him.

Thomas moved back, Gerens' arm falling from his shoulders. 'You are not real,' he repeated, turning his head away, but unable to tear his fearful gaze from the old man.

'After all these years, will thee not embrace me, my son?' pleaded the old man.

'You are not real,' said Thomas with growing force, raising his arm before his face to conceal the tormenting delusion.

'I am thy father,' said Zethar as he moved towards his son.

'YOU ARE NOT REAL!' screamed Thomas in fear and frustration.

With sudden movement, he reached for the hilt of Gerens' sword and drew it in a flash of steel before the smith had time to react.

Lunging forward, Thomas plunged the blade into the old man's chest.

Zethar's mouth fell open, eyes wide as he stared at his son in horror. He teetered and fell back to the thick grass. The sword rose from his body, legs temporarily twitching and then falling still.

The sounds of flames seemed to recede as Gerens looked to the old man in utter disbelief. Thomas fell to his knees and began to weep, covering his face in his hands. His tears were not for the man lying dead upon the grass, but in sufferance of the illusion he believed his father to be. He felt trapped within a mind over which he had little control. It played tricks upon him, conjured images that had become torments now that he was party to their falsehood.

Gerens heard men's voices coming up the hill and the sound broke the inertia of his shock. He moved to Zethar's side and put his fingers to the old man's throat, finding no pulse. His mind spun as he tried to think of a course of action. Glancing at the flaming wreckage of the cottage, an idea came to him.

He pulled the blade from the wound and quickly wiped both sides on the old man's shirt. Sheathing it, he rolled the body over and took off the cloak as hastily as he could, flinging it over his shoulder.

Grabbing Zethar's belt and the collar of his shirt, he rose to his feet and began to carry him towards the house, the old man's arms hanging limply at his sides. Passing through the gateway, he made sure that the old man's feet dragged on the grass as he moved along the muddy path, wishing to leave only one set of prints for those that were in pursuit.

Feeling the heat upon his face as he neared the doorway, he stared into the ruins. The door had come away from its hinges and fallen onto the burning roof timbers and thatch within, the flames still eager and billowing their fuming breath.

Standing before the door with perspiration building upon his rugged face, he took a breath in readiness. Raising the body so that its feet no longer touched the ground, Gerens swung it back and then tossed it through the doorway. It crashed amidst the carnage and he watched as the clothes rapidly caught light.

Turning, he spied Zethar's cloth bag by the wall. Making sure to pass over the grass, he quickly retrieved it.

Gerens took it to the cottage and tossed it over the wall into the centre of the fire, satisfied that it would soon be naught but ashes. The old man's cloak was taken from his shoulder and bunched before following the sack into the flames.

He made his way back out of the garden. 'Thomas!'

Thomas was lost to misery as he remained upon his knees.

Gerens went to his side, forcing him to his feet. 'We must leave,' he said urgently.

339

Thomas looked at him, his expression filled with anguish and eyes desolate. 'I am a prisoner of my own mind,' he whispered.

Gerens looked into the mist along the eastern slope beside the cottage, expecting the men from the village to appear at any moment. 'We must go,' he insisted, keeping his voice low but firm.

'It is still aflame.' The sound of Golvan's voice arose from the slope of the hill no more than fifty yards away.

Gerens grasped Thomas by the arm and propelled him towards the far wall of the garden. They made for the concealment, passing around the corner and ducking out of site. The smith pushed himself against the rough and glistening stones as Thomas buried his face in his hands.

Golvan walked through the mist, the cottage rising to his right. He scanned the paleness for any sign of Thomas as four shadowy figures followed behind.

The farmer walked up the last of the slope and came to a halt beside the garden wall, the barren tree arcing over the top to his left as he stared at the smouldering building. Father Blyth, Jago, Benedict and Arthur drew up at his back.

'Any sign of him?' asked Jago.

'None,' replied Golvan, moving around to the southern wall and walking to the gate as the other men looked about, squinting as they peered into the mist.

'He cannot be far. That was his voice raised only moments ago,' stated Blyth.

'There are fresh footprints,' called Golvan over his shoulder, moving through the gate and scanning the path to the house. 'They lead to the cottage.'

Gerens' grip tightened on the hilt of the sword, his body filled with tension as he listened intently. He glanced back, finding that Thomas continued to struggle with his inner turmoil as they remained crouched against the wall.

Father Blyth stood beside the garden gate with the other men gathered about him as they stared at the set of prints in the mud.

'It may be he left by another route,' commented Arthur.

'Aye, he could have vaulted the wall,' agreed Jago, looking to the far wall of the garden and the misty slope rising beyond.

Gerens stiffened and licked his dry lips, shifting the position of his feet in readiness to fight.

Golvan stared at the building and began to make his way over. His pulse suddenly became elevated as he set eyes on the grizzly sight resting beyond the blackened doorway. He swallowed hard as nausea churned his stomach.

The corpse lay face down and was wreathed in flame. Its skin was charred or absent, a few blackened shreds of cloth clinging to the remains. Blood and other fluids bubbled amidst the sinew and muscles that had been laid bare. The hair had been burnt from its head and portions of bone revealed by the fury of the fire.

Looking away, Golvan took a steadying breath. 'I have found him,' he said before swallowing again, fighting the constriction of his throat as the feeling of sickness grew.

The other men looked over and began to walk towards him.

'I would not advise it,' he said, holding up his right hand as he looked at the ground and cradled his stomach in the other. ''Tis not a sight you would wish to behold,' he added stepping over to the garden wall and resting his hand upon it, relishing the cool touch of the damp stones.

Gerens looked over his shoulder. He could see the farmer's fingers and the edge of his torso as he stood on the other side of the wall a few yards back. Thomas broke from the hold of his misery and reached for the stone lying in the grass before him, one he had knocked from the wall when vaulting it in the pouring rain many months before. He gripped it tightly, ready to use it as a weapon should the need arise, unwilling to be captured and unable to endure more pain.

Benedict and Arthur glanced at each other and halted their approach to the cottage, the former already having had his fill of horrors for one day. Jago glanced back at them and his steps faltered when he caught sight of the vague shape within the flames and noted its rawness.

Blyth continued, coming to a stop before the portal. He stared at the corpse and was apparently unaffected by the gruesome sight. 'So, 'tis done,' he commented with a nod.

'How can we be sure 'tis Carrow?' asked Jago.

The priest turned to him. 'Who else do you suppose it to be, some unfortunate traveller who happened to walk into a flaming ruin?' Blyth shook his head. ''Tis he, of this there can be no doubt.'

Golvan nodded. 'Aye, only one possessed would have flung themselves to such a death.'

'What of the matter now?' asked Arthur.

'We will wait for the fire to run its course and the building to fall cold, then the men of Zennor will take down the walls stone by stone,' replied Blyth. 'We shall not allow its ruin to linger above us.'

The old man nodded.

The priest began along the path and passed the other men, heading out of the gate. 'There is naught else to be done here, for the time being at least.'

Benedict and Arthur followed, Jago glancing at the hint of the body that he could discern and then hurrying after them. Golvan paused by the wall. Sighing, he shook his head, unable to comprehend what would drive someone to end their life in such a terrible way.

Blyth and the others faded into the mist as they moved along the eastern boundary of the garden and began down the grassland beyond. Golvan watched for a while as he continued to settle his stomach and then pushed off from the wall, following after them.

Gerens shifted as cramp brought pain to his legs. The end of the sword tapped against the stones.

Golvan stopped at the gate, his brow furrowing. He looked over to the far wall.

'Have they gone?' whispered Thomas.

Gerens looked back at him and held his finger to his lips. He listened intently, heart hammering against the anvil of his ribcage. He adjusted his grip on the sword and moved towards the corner of the wall a couple of yards before him.

Golvan took a step back into the garden and stared at the wet stones, gaze passing along the length of the wall as he sought any sign of disturbance.

'Will you be returning with us?' came Blyth's question.

Gerens fell still.

Golvan glanced over his shoulder, the figures of the other men only weak shadows in the mist. Looking to the wall one final time, he set off after them, glad to be away from the ill-fated cottage and the corpse it contained.

Gerens listened, hearing the diminishing sound of the farmer's passage. He moved to the corner and carefully peered beyond, seeing Golvan vanishing into the mizzle. Settling back against the wall, he released his grip on the hilt and flexed his fingers before wiping perspiration from his forehead with the back of his hand.

'They are leaving,' he whispered to Thomas, relief apparent in his expression.

'What now?'

'We wait,' replied the smith. 'If we leave too soon we risk discovery for the mist carries sound with ease.'

Thomas stared at Gerens as he forced voice to the question he hardly dare ask. 'Was the man real?'

Gerens turned to him, already having anticipated the enquiry. 'What man?' he asked, hoping his eyes held firm the deception.

'There was a man in your company.'

The smith shook his head. 'There was no other.'

Thomas searched his eyes, but found no trace of a lie. 'Golvan spoke as though he saw a body within the flames.'

'I heard no such words,' said Gerens with certainty, hoping that he would be convinced.

Thomas studied the smith and then nodded to himself.

''Tis time we made good our escape.' Gerens moved from the cover of the wall, remaining low.

'Will you not return to the village?' asked Thomas, unaware of the fate that had befallen him.

343

'I will take you away from here and return later,' he replied, not wishing to reveal his banishment nor the location of his new life. 'Come, we must go,' he said, leading the way south along the hillside.

Thomas glanced back at the ruins of his home. 'Fare ye well,' he said softly, his heart heavy as the burning cottage receded like a dream into the arms of the mist.

They passed through the grassland and moved onto the southern slopes of Trewey Hill, following the vague path down to the vale where Bersaba's hut rested. As it came into sight, Thomas' steps faltered as he spied its reality for the first time.

'Is that truly the home of Bersaba?' he asked, coming to a stop and staring sadly at the stone wall sheltering the oak and growth of shrubs.

Gerens halted and glanced over to the remains before looking back. He was about to respond when he saw Thomas' expression change to one of dismay.

Returning his gaze to the circular wall, he found that a figure had risen into sight. A woman with long dark hair stood inside the ruin, her features indistinct in the mizzle.

Thomas stared and shook his head. 'Why will you not leave me in peace?' he called to the woman.

Gerens glanced over his shoulder. 'You know this woman?'

There was a moment of stillness and then Thomas slowly turned to the smith with a look of awe. 'You see her?' he asked in a breathless whisper.

The smith nodded. 'Aye.'

'She is real?'

Gerens gave another nod of confirmation.

Thomas looked to her in wonder. 'Rosita,' he said, her name filled with need.

She moved through the opening that marked what had once been the entrance to the hut and made her way to him. Thomas walked to meet her, his back hunched against the pain of the burns.

They flung their arms about each other in blessed reunion. Holding Rosita tightly, Thomas began to weep with the relief of discovering their time together had not merely been trick of his mind. He wished never to find release from her embrace, never to be parted from her again.

'Thomas,' she whispered, staring into his eyes as tears spilled down her pale cheeks.

'Rosita,' he responded, his heart aching with need.

'Come, we should make good our escape,' said Gerens.

Thomas glanced over his shoulder. 'This is Rosita. She is not of these parts,' he stated.

Gerens nodded. 'I am Gerens the smith,' he introduced, his words confirming her reality.

Thomas took her hand, savouring the solidity of the contact. 'We must go,' he said softly, beginning to lead her away from the hut.

Gerens made for the path through the bracken. Thomas and Rosita followed, the walking stick he had made for her padding upon the ground with a regular rhythm.

Thomas glanced back at the misty hill lying to the north as they entered the ferns, wishing he could glimpse Ocean Mist one last time. He sighed and then turned to Rosita, finding her smiling at him, eyes still glistening with tears of relief and joy.

'You are all that I need,' he whispered, giving her hand an affectionate squeeze as they passed into the paleness.

Epilogue

The mist thinned as they descended the hill behind the coastal settlement of Penzance. The sweeping arc of the bay set out before them was bathed in sunshine, the mizzle at their backs as it lay heavy upon the last stretch of land reaching into the ocean.

Rosita let out a cry of excitement, startling Thomas and Gerens. They turned to her as she sat between them and found that she was pointing at Carrack Looz En Cooz, which rested in the embrace of sparkling waters in the middle distance. The cart's passengers took in the panorama of the southern coastline, noting the priory buildings at the Mount's summit and a march of trees sheltered in the lea of its landward side.

Rosita took hold of Thomas' arm and spoke to him in her native tongue, the words tripping over themselves as she pointed at St Michael's Mount once again.

'I think she wishes for us to go there,' stated Thomas. 'Would you be willing to take us?'

Gerens looked over and nodded. 'Aye, and then I shall take my leave.'

'So be it,' he agreed as Myrtle took them down the hill.

The cart moaned as it rocked, wheels sinking into the mud of the track. Thomas winced and inhaled sharply as he bumped his back against the wood of the seat, the burns flaring with pain.

Rosita looked at him with curious concern. He angled his back towards her and carefully lifted the bottom of his shirt, revealing the injuries which had been inflicted upon him.

She gasped, covering her mouth in horror as she stared at the blistered and raw skin. Reaching out, she stroked the healthy skin about the burns and spoke again in her alien language, the words filled with empathy and care.

Thomas let the shirt fall back into place, feeling the wool brush against the wounds. She raised her hand to his cheek, stroking it with the backs of her fingers. He smiled and leant forward, the two of them briefly kissing before settling into each other and taking in the view. The gentle sea breeze wafted against their cheeks and carried the fading chill of winter, Thomas drawing as much warmth as he could from Rosita's closeness and wishing he was wearing his long leather coat.

The cart passed onto a tract of flat land between the undulating hills. They followed the track as it wound behind a small settlement which was merely a few fisherman's cottages. Mackerel were skewered onto a frame above one of the fire holes in the thatched roofs as they were smoked in readiness for eating, Thomas' mouth watering in response to the sight.

The track took them further inland as it skirted a saltwater marsh. They looked across its rippling expanse, the dark figure of a moorhen passing between whispering reed stalks to the left.

The land rose gently away from the marsh as they moved south-east. The settlement of Marghas Byghan came into view as it faced the Mount, resting between the slope of a hill and the sea. Another track branched off to the north and Gerens pulled on the reins, bringing Myrtle to a halt.

'I will leave you here,' he said. ''Tis not far to Carrack Looz En Cooz. The tide is receding and you only need walk across the sands.' The smith nodded to the right.

Thomas glanced over. 'You have my lifelong gratitude for what you have done for me,' he said as he turned back to the smith and held out his hand.

Gerens reached in front of Rosita and the two men grasped each other's wrists. 'I hope you will find a new place to call home.'

Thomas nodded and then climbed down, the cart tipping slightly with his movements. Rosita looked to the smith and smiled, leaning forward and giving him a kiss on the cheek.

'Gracias,' she said in parting, jumping down to stand beside Thomas amidst the dune grass at the trackside.

Gerens gathered up the reins and gave them a flick, guiding Myrtle to take the wagon along the track leading north. 'Fare ye well,' he called over his shoulder, raising his hand in parting and hoping Carrow would ne'er realise the truth of his murderous actions before the burning cottage.

'May your journey be a safe one,' responded Thomas as both he and Rosita waved in return.

They stood side by side and watched as the cart moved away with slow inevitability. Rosita took hold of Thomas' hand and he turned to find she was smiling brightly.

She began to lead him towards the shore. They moved through the dunes, the high grasses brushing against their legs. Rising to the top of the sands, they were brought to a halt by the sight that greeted them. They stared at their majestic destination, the Mount rising high in the bay and the sun glinting on the waters receding down the curved beach before them.

* * *

Thomas walked into the priory gardens situated on the south-eastern slopes of the Mount. He paused as the gate shut behind him and looked out over the beds neatly arranged beneath his vantage point, a few of the resident monks kneeling beside them as they tended the plants. Trees were regularly spaced along the wall at the bottom of the gardens and he presumed they helped protect them from high winds. A small orchard rested in the far corner, its trees barren and waiting for the onset of spring.

He turned to the right, looking along the wall at the top of the gardens as it sloped upwards. His eyes widened as he spied a huge figure sitting upon a bench, the rising rocks of the Mount his backdrop.

'The giant,' whispered Thomas, noting the creature's protruding brow. There was an air of calm about him as he sat motionless and wrapped in a long dark coat.

His feet forced into motion by his intrigue and wish for rest, Thomas walked alongside the wall. Nervousness caused

349

his stomach to flutter and his palms to become clammy as he drew ever nearer the bulk of the creature and noticed the sneer upon his face.

Thomas's steps faltered and he wondered whether he should turn back. Narrowing his eyes, he studied the giant's face and realised that the apparent expression was caused by a deep scar in the creature's top lip.

He came to a stop before the vacant side of the bench and battled his nerves. 'May I,' he said with a tremor in his voice as he indicated the empty space, noting the word 'friend' carved into the backrest.

The giant slowly nodded without turning from the view of the ocean.

Thomas seated himself, the timbers of the bench creaking their greeting. He carefully rested his back against it, the burns causing him to grimace temporarily. Looking to the vista afforded by the elevation of the seat, he could feel the presence of the creature beside him and was able to see its gathered darkness in the periphery of his vision, though he felt no threat.

He took a deep breath and relaxed, feeling weary after the ordeal he had been through that day and glad for the respite. There was something about the giant that encouraged peace and contemplation.

Thomas thought about their arrival upon Carrack Looz En Cooz and of the meeting with Arranz, who had recognised him from his visit to Zennor late the previous year. It had become apparent that Rosita had been a maid aboard a Spanish ship carrying pilgrims to the Mount. It had been caught in a storm and passed many miles west of its intended destination, sailing around Land's End in the turbulent swell and running aground on rocks off the north Cornish coast.

He sighed. Rosita had been taken to see the captain of a ship at anchor in the bay in order to arrange passage home. It seemed their time together may be coming to an end and the sadness which accompanied this prospect weighed heavy in the pit of his stomach and tightened his heart.

Sighing again, Thomas tried to clear his mind. His eyelids slowly fell, time passing in the wash of the tide and call of gulls as he drifted into slumber.

'Thomas?'

His eyes opened to the sound of Rosita's voice and he discovered her standing before the bench. Arranz accompanied her with and a man dressed in a shirt similar to the one she had made for him, though fashioned of deep red linen. Thomas turned to find that the giant was no longer beside him. He wondered if the creature could have been an illusion and decided not to ask about its presence for fear of revealing his malady of imaginings.

'Fortune favours you,' said Arranz as he stood to the left. 'Rosita has been granted passage back to Spain on the San Valentin, which sails on the evening tide.'

Thomas shivered, the gardens now in the shadow of the high rocks as the sun sank into the west. He smiled thinly at the mention of the ship's name, recalling the red hue of the full moon. It had only been the previous night, but felt as though it were a memory from another lifetime after all that had happened since, and in a way he supposed it was.

Rosita said a few words in her native tongue to the man beside her in the red shirt and then smiled at Thomas.

'She has arranged for your passage on the ship also and asks if you will take the journey with her,' said the man in a heavily accented voice.

Thomas looked at Rosita in surprise. She nodded her encouragement, expression hopeful.

'Come,' she said, holding her hand out to him.

Thomas stared at it a moment, recalling the promise ne'er to go to sea that had been made to his mother upon her deathbed. 'For love,' he said in the hope that her spirit would hear his words.

He took hold of Rosita's hand and stood, smiling at her. They embraced and shared a kiss before turning to Arranz.

'There is a rowing boat waiting to take you both to the ship,' he stated. 'It readies for sail and if the winds be fair you should reach Donostia in five or six days.'

351

'Donostia?' asked Thomas as Arranz began to lead them down towards the gate to the gardens.

'It is also known as San Sebastian on account of the monastery dedicated to the saint that is located there,' replied Arranz over his shoulder. 'It is on the northern coast of Spain and so your journey will not be as long as it may have been. Some from the south of that country are at sea for weeks in order to make their pilgrimage to Carrack Looz En Cooz.'

They arrived at the gate and Arranz exited, the translator following. Thomas glanced back along the wall as he and Rosita left the gardens, his gaze briefly settling on the bench as they made their way out.

* * *

Gerens went up the ladder with a small mallet in his right hand and a sprig of oak in the other. Placing the stem beside a nail which he had already driven partway into the wood, he then beat the nail's head over until the sprig was held firmly in place.

Nodding to himself, he then made his way back down the straining rungs and stepped to the mud before the door of the new forge. He moved to stand by Nonna, taking her hand as he turned to the trio of green oak leaves, Daveth standing on the far side of his mother.

'We ask that you watch over us, Dor Dama, so that our time here may be fruitful and the beat of my hammer remains steady and true,' he said. 'May we partake of your bounty and may your grace and goodness keep us from harm.'

'Blessed be,' said Nonna with a nod.

They briefly stood in silence.

'I should return and prepare supper,' she stated.

'I will be in shortly, my love,' replied Gerens with a smile.

Nonna gave his hand a squeeze before releasing it and turning to the cottage set back to their left. She made her way over, Daveth following behind, his attendance of the brief blessing having been a subject of contention.

Gerens watched them enter and then looked up at the leaves once more, the last rays of the sun edging their vibrant colour with soft gold. He thought of all that had transpired, of

352

his forced departure from Zennor and Nonna's wish to accompany him, of Jowen's passing, of the arrival of Manow who was Zethar and of the events which had unfolded during his brief return to the west.

He shook his head and sighed. The image of Thomas and Rosita at the side of the track as he began his homeward journey came to mind and he hoped that they fared well.

'May you be forever green,' he said before making his way across the muddied grass to the cottage.

* * *

The rigging creaked and the sails billowed as gulls followed in the wake of the ship. Thomas stood at the bow with his arms about Rosita, cradling her stomach as she leant into him and rested her head against his cheek. They were approaching their destination, the sky above a vivid blue and feathers of soft purple cloud colouring the southern horizon above the peaks of distant hills.

He looked to the coastline, his gaze no longer haunted by the ghosts of his past as he imagined the babe growing within her. A wooded mount rose from the waters before a curved bay of pale sands and Thomas was gladdened by its presence. Here, at the end of the voyage, was an echo of Carrack Looz En Cooz from which they had set off.

They passed beside the mount, its rocky cliffs towering to the right. A hill rested to the left, the settlement of Donostia gathered at its southern foot and connected to the mainland by a spit of sand. The captain barked orders and the sails were gathered in by the crew as the ship readied to weigh anchor in the shelter of the bay.

Rosita turned in his arms and looked up at his face with a soft smile. Thomas moved his lips to hers and they kissed beneath the warming sun, wrapped in the gentle wash of waves and caressed by the breeze.

'I am home,' he whispered as he stood within the embrace and looked into her eyes.

Afterward

Song of the Sea took eight weeks to write, the longest it has ever taken me to complete a work of fiction and four times as long as most of my novels, including *Where Seagulls Fly*. It also involved far more research than any other novel to date, hardly a day going by when I didn't need to look up at least one piece of information. These facts ranged from the clothing of the era to the construction of wattle and daub buildings, from traditional Cornish names to the correct collective noun for seagulls.

As with *Where Seagulls Fly*, the story contains a personal element which is relevant to my life. In this case it is an existence at the periphery of society and the feelings of loneliness that can accompany it, along with the wish to find someone with which a profound connection is shared.

My own peripheral existence is due to living a very different lifestyle to the majority of people in the western world and beyond. It is somewhat isolated and makes me more of an observer than a participant when it comes to 'normal' everyday life. Though it is quite a unique position which I would not wish to change, it does give rise to intense feelings of loneliness and longing from time to time.

This book also seeks to blur the boundaries between good and evil to a degree. This is because they are not absolutes, but are actually matters of perspective and context.

Included below are some Cornish to English and Spanish to English translations. These have been given for words and phrases that were either not explained within the novel or require a little further explanation. In addition to these is a short list of facts related to the story which I think you will find of interest.

I hope you enjoyed *Song of the Sea* and that its melody stays with you for a long time to come.

Cornish to English Translations:
1. Dor Dama: 'Earth Mother,' also known as the Earth Goddess, a figure common to many native belief systems around the world that are in harmony with nature.
2. Carrack Looz En Cooz: 'Grey rock in the woods,' which is the Cornish name for St Michael's Mount.
3. Kernow: 'Cornwall'
4. Tas: 'Father'
5. Mamm: 'Mother'
6. Tewal-Tan: 'Dark-Fire'
7. Drei: 'Bring'
8. Synsi: 'Hold'

Spanish to English Translations:
1. Te adoro: 'I adore you'
2. Yo de largo para el hogar: 'I long for home'
3. La tormenta: 'The storm'
4. Los brazos arriba: 'Arms up'
5. Te quiero: 'I want you'
6. Te amo: 'I love you,' but in a more profound way than its literal translation. It would only be spoken to the love of your life or soul mate.
7. Voy a tallar ahora: 'I will carve now' (the 'h' in ahora is not pronounced)
8. Vamos a bailar: 'Let's dance'
9. Mirar la luna: 'Look at the moon'

Selected Factual Elements Relating to *Song of the Sea*:
1. A hut circle can be found to the south of Trewey Hill, where Bersaba's abode is located in the novel.
2. The use of the word 'bitch' in a derogatory sense may seem modern, but the first time it was employed as such in the written word can be dated back to 1330 and it is likely that it was used verbally for many years prior to that date. It was initially used as an insult in regards a woman's promiscuity and sensual nature by way of reference to the behaviour of a female dog in heat, something that befits Golvan's aspersions in regards Nonna and Gerens.
3. New Year's Eve in 1290 did in fact fall on a Sunday.

4. The town of Lostwithiel was the capital of Cornwall at the time the story is set. It was made the capital in around 1280 by Edmund, Earl of Cornwall.

5. In 1290 King Edward issued the Edict of Expulsion, which expelled all Jews from England. It wasn't until 1657 that they were permitted to return by Oliver Cromwell.

6. There was a full lunar eclipse on Wednesday 14th February 1291. Such eclipses can cause the phenomenon known as 'blood moons.'

7. Cornwall was a stronghold of Pagan religious beliefs in the Middle Ages. These essentially involve the reverence and personification of the natural world and to this day Paganism still has a significant following in the area. Many people confuse Paganism with Satanism, though they are completely different. This is possibly due to both employing the pentangle symbol, which is a five pointed star also known as a pentagram and was once used by Christians to represent the five wounds of Christ.

8. Punishments for poaching in the Middle Ages were very severe, from losing a hand to being sewn into a deer skin and hunted by dogs.

9. The Latin spoken by Father Blyth during the exorcism is the 'Vade retro satana,' which means 'Go Back, Satan' or 'Step Back Satan.' This is the Benedictine formula used during Catholic exorcisms in medieval times and its translation is as follows: 'Let the Holy Cross be my light. Let not the dragon be my guide. Step back Satan. Never tempt me with vain things. What you offer me is evil. You drink the poison yourself.'

10. During the 12th to the 14th Centuries Catholic pilgrimages became increasingly popular throughout Europe, particularly along routes which linked sites related to Saint Michael. This, along with its strong bonds with Mont Saint-Michel on the north coast of France, meant that St. Michael's Mount was a popular location for pilgrims.

11. Marghas Byghan is the earliest recorded name for the town now known as Marazion (Maraz-eye-on) which looks out over St. Michael's Mount. The name means 'Little Market' and the relationship between Marghas Byghan and Marazion is clear phonetically. Many believe the town's name was Marghas Yow, which means 'Thursday Market.' Such a market was granted to the monks upon the Mount in

1070, but the settlement pre-dates this and therefore could not have been named after it.

12. The widespread use of French in England after the Norman Conquest gave the English word 'you' the same association as the French 'vous.' The use of the word 'you' and its derivative 'your' began to take hold in the 12th C and became prevalent during the 14th. At the time *Song of the Sea* is set 'you' would have been increasingly employed in speech. Younger generations are more likely to adopt linguistic changes and so the younger characters use the word, whereas the older characters of Bersaba, Jacob and Conwenna Trewey, Lacy Lugg and Manow/Zethar Carrow continue to use the more archaic ye, thee, thou and thy. However, there is also some purposeful mingling of the old and new, especially in relation to the speech of Jago and Father Blyth, as such would have occurred during this time of change in the English language.

If you enjoyed *Song of the Sea* then try *Where Seagulls Fly (2013 Edition)*, *The Hanging Tree* or the contemporary fairy tale set on the Isles of Scilly called *The Magical Isles Trilogy*. All are by Edwin Page and available in paperback and Kindle formats.

Look out for his forthcoming historical novel set in western Cornwall. Entitled *The Shepherd of St Just*, it is due for release in 2016.

59992927R00202

Made in the USA
Charleston, SC
18 August 2016